UPRISING

UPRISING

THE SUSPENSE THRILLER
by Randy Boyd

WEST BEACH BOOKS

UPRISING is a West Beach Book

West Beach Books
PO Box 68406
Indianapolis, IN 46268
www.westbeachbooks.com

This novel is strictly and entirely a work of fiction. All references to real people, events, establishments, organizations, or locales are purely and solely intended to give the novel a sense of reality and authenticity. All other names, characters, incidents, organizations, or locales are strictly the product of the author's imagination, as are those fictionalized events and incidents that involve real persons and entities. Of the fictional characters, any resemblance to actual persons, living or dead, is entirely and purely coincidental.

Designed by Alan Bell

"I Don't Want To Bring Your Gods Down"
Words and Music by Terence Trent D'Arby
© 1989 MONASTERYO MUSIC
All Rights for the USA and Canada Controlled and Administered by
    EMI VIRGIN SONGS, INC.
All Rights Reserved   International Copyright Secured   Used by Permission

Publisher's Cataloging-in-Publication
(Provided by Quality Books, Inc.)

Boyd, Randy.
        Uprising / by Randy Boyd. — 1st ed.
        p. cm.
        Preassigned LCCN: 98-96304
        ISBN: 0-9665333-7-2
        1. Afro-American gay men—Fiction. 2. Gay men—
Fiction. 3. Assassination—Fiction. 4. Los Angeles
(Calif.)-Fiction. I. Title.
PS3552.O8817U77   1998   813'.54
                              QBI98-845

First Paperback Edition: September 1998

10   9   8   7   6   5   4   3   2

*For Mom,
Emerson and Rick,
and Kathy*

Acknowledgements

FIRST TO THOSE who have helped make this particular segment of my lifelong, personal uprising possible: To my mom, my biggest supporter: thank you for every ounce of love you give me. To my sister, Angelia: thanks for keeping at it, Big Sis. To the rest of my family: peace and love. To my second family, the Mancias, from the tallest to the smallest: *muchas gracias*. To Kat: you'll always be part of my heart and soul. Plus, more thanks: To my posse that was with me during the homestretch of this book, Philly, Billy and Henry. The Ale, baby! Pacers and Cavs represent! To Jake, for the luxury suite at the United Center and a whole lot more. To Rob Held, for the tons of tickets to one of the most special places on earth to me, Market Square Arena. May it rest in peace soon. Also, much thanks to Ben Barrett, Mike Doyle, Valentine Birds, Lysette Cardona, Eugene Rogolsky, Mitch Goldman, JoAnn Hickey, Warren Reingold, Neal Miller, Jerry Zamarin, John Preston, Darryl Pilcher, David Kalmansohn, Rondo Mieczkowski, Harton, Sandra, Darren and Louise. And to the rest of my friends who send good thoughts my way everyday: much love and thank you.

Now to those who helped directly with *Uprising*, the suspense thriller by Randy Boyd: Deep, never-ending gratitude to Eric Wilson, Sundiata Alaye, Richard Labonté, Alan Bell and Joshua De Mers. All of you were right *there* when I needed you most. You are all truly angels who have helped me soar. Thanks to Julia Ryan and Emile Easton for watching my back. Thanks to Phil Shiban for being Phil Shiban. Thanks to the Federal Bureau of Investigation for being real and cool. Plus, sincerest thanks to Robert Gaylord, E. Lynn Harris, Karen Dale Wolman, Luis Franco, DC and Zach. You have all contributed to the fruition of a dream.

UPRISING

You and me,
we belong together
like guilt and religion.

—*Terence Trent D'Arby*

ONE

H E HURRIED the last couple of feet to the pay phone, stride deliberate and heavy, eyes glancing both ways down the dark deserted street to make sure he was alone. Grabbing the receiver and dialing subconsciously, he repeated in his mind the words he prayed to hear on the other end of the line: You tested negative, sir.

The clinic picked up; it was a woman's voice, soft and professional. In the spare split second available, he imagined her saying it: You tested negative, sir. "Calling for my results," he sputtered out, too nervous to worry about altering his voice. He gave her his code number; she put him on hold. I'm happy to say you tested negative, sir, his brain chanted. The mantra that had gotten him through the last week.

He turned to peer up at the lights on Santa Monica Boulevard in the distance: a warm gust of wind came along and smacked him in the face, slightly ruffling the fake bushy eyebrows and fake gray-tinted beard that helped turn him into an old man. In a mild panic, he reinforced his disguise, straightening the eyebrows and beard and the nappy-haired wig under his green fisherman's hat, pushing the wire-rimmed glasses up on his nose, making sure the small latex beer belly was secure underneath his faded blue workman's shirt and yellow golf jacket. He then used the reflection in the glass encasing surrounding the phone to check his face and the makeup that gave him crow's feet and raisin-like skin on his cheeks and brow. He looked like somebody's old black high school janitor if anybody bothered to notice.

Maybe I shouldn't have gotten tested this way, he thought. Maybe I should have gone to a doctor of the rich and famous who could keep his mouth shut. Maybe I should have never come down to West Hollywood dressed like this. A thousand—make that a million maybes—

The line clicked. When the woman finally spoke, he only heard one word:

"...positive..."

Eyes shut, total blackness, the line went silent, the world went dead. Total blackness and death. That's all he felt. That and the rest of the world finding out, somehow, some way, someday.

The receiver fell and began swinging like a twisted pendulum, the woman's faint voice crying out to the night from within. For a moment, he stood there, eyes unfocused, lips trembling, mind disoriented. Then he began walking, too dazed to affect the limp that usually went along with the old-man getup. He thrust his hands into his pockets, grabbing at the envelope with the wad of cash in the right pocket and the blank check in the left. Complete thoughts were hard to come by. It was enough of a battle putting one foot in front of the other. He moved down the darkened sidewalk, thinking of everything and nothing, but mostly the headlines.

OTHELLO'S DEADLY SECRET: STAR IS GAY AND HAS VIRUS, The Enquirer would trumpet. Time, which years ago ran a cover story proclaiming him POP'S NEWEST ICON, would ask some sensational question like: BIGGEST AIDS VICTIM YET? And Rolling Stone—which only last year said that "along with Michael Jackson, Madonna and The Artist, Othello is one of those rare musical visionaries who thrives on transcending the decades"—they would say something like: "An AIDS-related casualty sure to have 10,000 times the impact of the deaths of Queen front man Freddy Mercury or gangsta rapper Eazy-E."

A car horn assailed him, stopping him in his tracks. He discovered he was about to walk into an intersection and hopped back onto the curb just as a black Hummer made a sharp angry turn past him. Only then did he realize he had wandered up to Santa Monica Boulevard in the heart of West Hollywood, the neon signs and endless stream of cars all adding to the chaos in his mind.

A drink. He needed a drink. He hadn't had a sip of alcohol in years, part of the way he made sure the lean body underneath the senior citizen's outfit remained tight and worth millions. But now he craved alcohol, owed it to his nerves. How else was he going to get through the next minute?

He stumbled into the first bar he saw, a dimly-lit, narrow corridor with green walls and dark wood. From the bodybuilder bartender in a tight white T-shirt, he ordered a shot of JD, then another, then a beer to chase away the fire in his throat. Once finished, he stole glances at the half dozen men scattered about the bar: the trio of young Latinos practicing dance moves near the restroom in the back, two slender white boys playing pool, the bartender wiping the bar. Did any of them have it? Or was it more like which ones? Help me, he fantasized pleading to them, as if he'd just been mugged out on the street.

To perpetuate the fantasy, he turned away from the bar and faced the room, desperately wishing he could say something to each and every one of them. He even opened his mouth, daring himself to speak. Then his eyes caught the video screen on the wall above the Latino boys. On it, he saw a younger version of himself. His first single, he realized, "Fun In the Sun" from the early '80s when he was in his late-teens. Sporting an Afro and a red headband, he was bopping around a Universal Studios downtown city block, wielding his electric guitar and galvanizing hundreds of people into a street party. A piece of fluff in retrospect, but it reached number two in *Billboard* and started it all.

The video only made life worse at that moment. Hastily, he reached into his pocket for the muscleman's tip and threw a five on the bar, realizing in the next second a big wad of the cash from the envelope in his baggy workman's khakis had fallen on the floor in the process. A couple thousand, mostly in hundreds, must have been lying there, exposed. In a panic, he eyed the others. They had all seen it and were looking at him with suspicion, awe, curiosity. Abruptly, almost apologetically, he knelt down and began cramming the cash into his jacket pockets, not bothering to organize it. When he was finished, all eyes were still on him as he rose up. Momentarily, there was a stalemate—Othello with his stuffed jacket, the Latinos no longer dancing, the pool players no longer cueing their sticks, the bartender ever-so-slightly leaning over the bar. Othello paused, trying unsuccessfully not to look at them. Then, he did the only thing he could have done: escaped through the front entrance.

Santa Monica seemed busier than before, full of even more clamor as he landed in the middle of the sidewalk and made an effort to distance himself from the bar while still walking like an old man with aging bones. Dozens of boys hurried toward him, then past him, their voices loud and carefree. From the street, cars blared music. Up and down the sidewalk, men and women passed out flyers promoting boycotts, street patrols, dance clubs. Everyone seemed to have such a vibrant purpose except him. A block from the bar, he stopped and turned in all directions, signs he'd never noticed before overloading his senses: a poster in a bank window announcing an AIDS benefit, T-shirts in a storefront declaring I'M NOT GAY BUT MY BOYFRIEND IS, hot oiled pecs on video boxes stacked in a pyramid in the porno store window, a billboard featuring two men lying stomach-down on a beach, an ad for gay vacations.

That last one caught him off guard more than the others.

Gay vacations? They actually have gay vacations? The thought provoked another realization: he had never walked down Santa Monica as himself, only as the old man. A nauseous wave sank in his stomach. Was it the JD or the revelations invading his life? He began walking again to keep from collapsing, this time feeling even more lost amidst the bustle of openly gay life around him.

"NOW FOR THE DOOZY of the night," Travis Little Horse announced from the podium as he moved his thick mane of jet black hair over his shoulder and out of the way. "Assemblyman Weeks and his latest anti-gay, anti-AIDS, anti-*life* bill."

A muffled collection of moans and groans came from the thirty or so men and women seated in the folding chairs in front of the podium, their reaction echoing off the rafters of the boarded-up leather bar that now served as the headquarters for ACTNOW.

"Like it or not, folks," he added in defense of the meeting's agenda, "Weeks is our next target, right after Mercy Hospital."

In a corner in the back of the room, still looking like an old black janitor, Othello sat in a daze, slumped against the brick wall to his right. At least he made it here, he figured, considering the hell his life had become in the last hour.

"Arnold Weeks needs to have a flaming fist shoved up his ass." Next to the podium now was the one with dyed red hair who went by the name Freedom and had seemingly every orifice on his body pierced. He and Travis had started ACTNOW after deciding Queer Nation and ACT UP weren't militant enough in their activism. "Hog-tie him," he went on, "grease up a couple dozen arms and reach for his fucking tonsils." To this, he received a mild round of laughter and applause that was half appreciative, half nervous. Some of ACTNOW didn't know how to take Freedom, who was known behind his back as The Zealot, a title he accidentally found out about and claimed with pride.

"The bill will never get through anyway," said a heavyset black man in his forties. "I say we forget this two-bit politician from Simi Valley and focus on the gay bashing right here in our own backyard."

"I say we focus on the military," said a woman with a blonde mohawk, prompting several groans in anticipation of the weekly debate that went nowhere. Even though ACTNOW wanted to be more militant, there was widespread disagreement on exactly how militant and where the group should focus its energy.

"California Assemblyman Arnold Weeks is a puppet of the most vile man in America." Freedom popped a cassette into the TV/VCR combo on top of the bar behind the podium and cranked up the volume. "Listen to this and tell me if you think we're wasting our time going after the rednecks. This is the latest direct from the Senate floor in DC."

On the thirteen-inch screen appeared Jimmy Herman, the senior

US Senator from South Carolina. He was a bald, heavyset man well into his sixties with thick round glasses, chipmunk cheeks and razor thin lips. "If gays wanna kill themselves," he said with a thick Southern drawl, "let 'em, but we must stop funding their perverted disease with decent people's tax dollars. Let them get on with eliminating themselves from the face of God's green earth. That's fine with me, the Lord Almighty *and* the decent citizens of America."

Wadded-up paper and empty soda cans were sent hurling toward the screen, accompanied by boos and hisses.

"Your two-bit politicians hold this man up as a role model." Freedom paused the tape. "Are we gonna stand by and let them get away with this crap?"

The discussion continued for another half hour before Travis quelled the debate the way he usually did, by saying they'd take up Weeks, Herman and the rest of the bigots once again next week.

"Maybe we should change our name to Act Like Wussies," Freedom said as a last jab as the meeting adjourned.

Othello remained seated and watched the other members filing out. ACTNOW had some of everything, white boys with nose rings, butch dykes with their bike helmets in tow, black folk in African dashikis, Latinos, Asians and a lot of people who wore their AIDS diagnoses on their sleeves. It was their audacity that led Othello to the meetings six months ago, when he first decided that, if Michael Jackson could lurk around Disneyland dressed up like a freak, Othello could venture down to West Hollywood and just walk among his people disguised as a harmless old man. It started with the bars, bookstores and coffeehouses, and he never said much to anyone for fear of being found out. It was enough for the most part just to be among them. Besides, he was never sure what he was looking for—love, sex, connection, nothing, anything. Then, one day, he stumbled upon an ACTNOW meeting just about to start. Now, he only went to the meetings, never the bars, bookstores or coffeehouses.

After most of the room had cleared, Othello stood up, steadied his legs and approached Travis, who was near the podium wrapping up a conversation with two older, bearded men. In sharp contrast to Freedom's fiery hair, multiple piercings and pale, sinewy body, Travis

Little Horse was like a California redwood. He had broad shoulders and a tapered waist on his six-foot-four Navajo frame. He had to be late thirties, a few years older than Othello, and was known around LA's activist circles for his brains as well as his brawn. If only he didn't have a lover, Othello had thought to himself on more than one occasion.

Travis turned to find the old black man waiting quietly and immediately extended his hand. "Joe, how are you tonight?"

"Been better, been worse," Othello murmured in his scratchy old man's voice, exchanging a handshake with his worn, wrinkled hand that in reality was a skin-tight, caramel-colored glove with tattered fingernails and fingerprints that didn't match his own. He felt a pang of guilt that Travis only knew him as Joe, but there was no other way.

"Shall we?" Sensing the old man's distraction, Travis indicated the small room ten feet away. Othello nodded and allowed Travis to lead the way to what used to be the deejay's booth. "This is good timing," Travis said once the door was closed behind them. "We've got a lot of battles ahead of us. We're going to need to bail a lot of brothers and sisters out of jail. That is, of course, if we can agree on what and what not to do. I'm sorry we had to bore you with the usual dissension."

Othello mumbled absently, then removed the white envelope from his pants pocket and the rest of the money from his golf jacket. Handing the bundles to Travis, his geriatric hands were shaking, not from the exchange, for he was used to that, but from the woman at the clinic's voice still ringing in his brain.

"Bless both of you, Joe." Travis guessed thousands. At least five, maybe even ten. "Make it to the membership rally in the park tomorrow? Maybe you'd both like to come."

"That's a question, Mr. Little Horse." Othello turned toward the window. "You know the deal. No questions."

"I just thought—"

"I'm just her friend, who's been her gardener forever. She sends me down to do this because she knows I like men. She's older than dirt, got more money than she knows what to do with, and she wants us little fairy boys—her term, not mine—to have something to fight with." He turned to face Travis. "On two conditions I seem to have to remind you of every time we do this."

"No questions and it's all anonymous," Travis said apologetically.

Othello rotated back toward the window, thinking: and the studios are worried I can't act.

"And you'd better believe we appreciate it," said Travis. "Still, I can't help but think *you'd* get something out of being there, even if you stayed in the background."

Othello stared out the booth, swallowing hard and breathing even harder. A handful of men and women were piling up the folding chairs, openly gay men and women, living and fighting every day in the trenches. "I'd like to go," he whispered. He felt the urge to reveal himself to Travis right then and there and ask him about the virus that was inside both of them: what it meant, what it felt like, what the hell a newly diagnosed person was supposed to do now. "I'd give almost anything," he paused, almost sounding won-over, "but it can't be done." Without looking back, he flung the door open and made his escape, getting only a few steps before stopping, desperate to recant and do more than hand over a few thousand dollars he wouldn't miss.

But he couldn't. He was Othello.

The sweat from the wig stinging his eyes, he fumbled in his pocket for the blank check, written on one of the dummy corporations set up for the restaurant, intended for one of the monsters otherwise known as his thankless siblings. It was still blank because Othello couldn't remember which monster needed how much. Check in hand, he startled when Travis came up from behind to ask if he was all right. "Yes," he lied, then indicated Freedom who was at the bar, ejecting the videotape. "Can I have that cassette? The old lady will appreciate seeing it. And a pen. I need a pen."

Without another word Travis retrieved the video from Freedom and a pen from his own shirt pocket.

"I want you to take this check," Othello told him. "The old lady gave me permission to use it if I thought the group was worthy." Using the cassette as a writing surface, he made the check payable to ACT-NOW and scribbled in the amount. Then he signed it with a signature that was simply an elaborate version of the letter H. "You do what you have to do to fight for all of us," he said, grabbing Travis's forearm and forcing the check into his hand. Through glassy eyes, he gave Travis one final nod, then walked away, leaving the leader of ACTNOW and his organization $20,000 richer.

IN THE RUSTED tan Impala he used for his secret junkets, Othello swerved his way through the Hollywood Hills with all four windows rolled down and a ferocious spring wind swirling around him. Even though he knew the hills well, he was going much too fast for the curves, which came upon him every few feet and caused the Impala to veer wide and smack against the brush bordering the dark narrow road. Only a few minutes removed from the ACTNOW meeting, his body was still trembling from the events of the last few hours, his mind still caught between disbelief and devastation. On the radio, a deejay's baritone voice crackled: "Here it is, the new number one song, the second single from his *One Nation* album, Othello with 'Go For Love.' I cannot wait for the upcoming tour—"

He could only make it through the revved-up drum intro before he punched the first dial button he could reach; but on this new station, the syncopated dance melody fading away was just as familiar. "Former number one song for you on the Power Station," the female deejay chimed. "That was the title track from Othello's *One Nation* CD. Man, that album is *still* on top of the charts after debuting there nine weeks ago. It's number one on both the soul and pop—"

This time he turned the radio off. It always seemed to happen that way: no airplay for hours, then they'd all do something by him. Sometimes they went in cycles and played his older stuff for days at a time. Usually he sat through every single play he stumbled upon, videos on TV included—hell, he never tired of his own masterpieces. But racing through the hills, the only thing he could focus on was the image of one virus-filled cell, planted there years ago by Unknown, swimming around the channels of his body, hungry to attack, destroy and humiliate.

The Impala fishtailed and skidded to an abrupt stop parallel to an unmarked wrought-iron gate that was flanked by purposely nondescript shrubbery. The private entrance. With the opener in the glove compartment, he opened the gate, and after righting the Impala, drove slowly up the long winding driveway, trying to catch his breath and remove the fake eyebrows, beard, wig and gloves.

Of the many properties he owned, only this one felt like home. The Big House, he called it. It was a two-story, Mediterranean-style villa, bathed in white with eight bedrooms and two guest cottages, built on two separate lots merged into one, giving him a safe buffer from the world outside.

After the Impala was tucked away in the eight-car garage, Othello staggered into the foyer feeling as though he'd just stepped off an all-day amusement park ride that hadn't been amusing. Minus the fake hair, latex and most of the makeup, he shuffled his way to the winding staircase, staring straight ahead but aware of the presence of some of the house staff in his immediate periphery—two, perhaps three of them.

"Is Sweeney here?" he mumbled. A woman's voice answered, but he failed to register her response as he climbed the stairs.

Once in the master bedroom, he threw the videotape from the meeting onto the nearest white marble nightstand, unintentionally knocking over a digital clock and the flashlight kept there in the event of an earthquake. He then plopped down at the foot of the bed and stared straight ahead at the empty six-foot-high fireplace which was taller than him by a couple of inches.

So this is how I'm gonna die, he thought.

He began to replay all the orgies he had organized in the early '80s—naked boys in naked rooms that were bare except for what was essential for all-night sexfests: mats, mattresses, slings, booths, glory holes, nooks and crannies in darkened mazes. The designs varied, but never the intent and never two rules: check your attitude at the door and everyone wears a black leather hood. Total anonymity. That was the only way Warner Brothers' rising star could have his cock and eat it, too.

And so Sweeney—his manager, the only person in the world he trusted, the only person who knew it wasn't the girls he was singing about—good ol' Sweeney would recruit the boys from the bars, the colleges, the gyms, the pornos. And they came by the dozens in those days, to the Temple, Othello's private name for the specially designed underground hideaway in a small house at the base of the Hollywood Hills, bought expressly for those occasions. They came all right: black, white, red, brown and yellow, most of them young like Othello. And because he loved them the most, he gave Sweeney a thousand dollar bonus for each buffed-out blond boy he reeled in. But no matter their skin color, they all fucked, sucked, licked and swallowed like there was no tomorrow, for it was the tail-end of the golden years and they didn't know they were fucking, sucking, licking and swallowing death. They had no idea.

Othello felt alive on those nights, tasting and caressing flesh for the pure hedonistic sake of tasting and caressing flesh, then moving on to another human being, then another, then another, then another, losing himself, finding his sexuality, all while a black leather hood made him one of the boys.

Of course, it hadn't been entirely fulfilling. The next day, he would always feel alone and empty, only part of his soul satiated, the other part screaming for companionship and love, something he'd craved since adolescence. But with each album and single and video, he became bigger and bigger until the prospect of ever being gay without a mask became a pipe dream. By the mid '80s, the plague was full blown and the orgies had ceased. Since then, he'd only had one-on-one encounters—still arranged by Sweeney—with a handful of bodybuilder hustlers who catered to the elite and discreet. But recently, even those furtive sessions had stopped, coinciding with his increasing fear of what may have invaded his bloodstream back in the good ol' days.

So this is how I'm gonna die, he wanted to utter aloud. Instead, he eased himself back onto the bed and tried to find solace in the latest platoon of drugs that were extending life and minimizing discomfort for many of the people he saw at the ACTNOW meetings. It didn't work. Hoping for distraction, he picked up the remote he found under his thigh and pointed it toward the forty-six-inch television screen in the corner to the right of the fireplace. Seventy-two channels later, zilch. He grabbed the ACTNOW videotape and made his way toward the VCR on top of the TV.

Thirty-two years of life in the closet, he thought, putting in the tape. I've sucked a ton of cocks and never held hands with a man. I've listened to a shit-load of fag jokes in the studio, danced around bitches I couldn't care less about, pretending "baby, baby, I can't live without you," and now I could die from AIDS without ever saying "I love you" to another man.

He sank back down on the bed and the Southern drawl of South Carolina Senator Jimmy Herman took over the room: "Homosexuality is the scourge of the American Dream from which we can trace most of society's evils." His thick round glasses were steaming up, his chipmunk cheeks flush with anger. "They do not belong in the military, nor our schools, nor in decent American neighborhoods near decent American families." He was beating his fist on the podium in front of him. "If gays wanna kill themselves, let 'em, but we must stop funding their perverted disease with decent people's tax dollars. Let them get on with eliminating themselves from the face of God's green earth. That's fine with me, the Lord Almighty *and* the decent citizens of America."

Othello killed the VCR and sat paralyzed for a second. Then quickly he rewound the tape just a bit.

"...get on with eliminating themselves from the face of God's green earth."

This time he paused it.

"You slimy motherfucking bastard."

He heaved the remote at the screen, but failed to break the glass.

"Bastards. You're all bastards."

His tone was full of disgust and astonishment, as if it had taken him this long to fully realize the ignorant and hateful nature of the world. Yes, people were that stupid and vengeful, it all seemed to be saying.

"This...."

He tried to speak, let the anger come out verbally, but no words came to him so he bolted up, grabbed the poker next to the fireplace, and like Ken Griffey, Jr., whacking one out of the park, he yelled, "Bastards!" and swung at the mantle, sending glass statuettes, bronze trophies, miniature gold records and four Grammies flying into pieces. Then, he went for the stereo system between the fireplace and television, smashing its glass case until all that remained were shards on the floor. Next, he began hacking at the stereo system itself. "Bastards!" He had to yell something with each blow. "Fucking bastards don't!—won't!—fucking bastards—!"

Once the stereo was mutilated, he turned to the mirror that was as big as a picture window on the wall on the other side of his bed. First, he threw the poker at it, then picked up the mangled pieces of stereo and hurled them into the image of his bedroom, each one cracking up the mirror until it resembled a distorted puzzle. He then grabbed another poker from the fireplace and headed for the hallway that was almost as long as the entire house. There he was met by two of his live-in staff, his Asian house manager and the Mexican maid, both of them looking helpless and afraid. "Away from me!" was all he could yell, and not bothering to see whether or not they obeyed, he proceeded to destroy anything he came across: two ancient vases from one of the Japan tours, a small statue of a naked Greek boy, the old wooden benches from the Renaissance, the ornate lamps from Italy. At the far end of the hallway, he toppled over the armoire from Paris, sending dozens of glass vases crashing down, and swatted at the gaping ficus plants and attacked the French impressionist paintings on the wall. When he ran out of objects, he began whacking at the walls themselves, saying "Bastards!" over and over until he realized both staffers were still watching him, their eyes ripe with confusion.

"Get outta here!" He hurried back into the bedroom.

Jimmy Herman was still on pause. He thought of striking the screen with the poker but suddenly had a better idea. He raced out of the bedroom, through the now empty hall, down the stairs and out the front door, not stopping until he reached the guard's booth at the end of the main driveway.

"Gimme your gun," he ordered the red-headed young guard, who hesitated.

"If there's a problem, sir—"

"There's no problem I can't take care of myself. Now give it to me."

The next-to-last thing the guard wanted to do was give Othello the gun. The last thing he wanted to do was get fired.

Nine millimeter in hand, Othello made his way back to the house. "I'll show you indecent, you fucking slimeball." When he reached the bedroom, he pointed the gun toward the senator's head. He'd never fired a gun in his life, wasn't even sure if he'd ever held one, but all he could think of was killing the man who epitomized the hate and prejudice that was killing him. Jaws tightly clinched, he cocked the trigger. His hand started shaking, making the gun's aim unsteady. He thought of the giant screen he was about to shatter and doubt began to undermine his conviction. What the hell was he doing? Mad enough to shoot a TV? Crazy enough to fire a gun? At a TV?

He thought of all the glass shattering and the mess. Then, he thought about the mess his life had suddenly become, faster than overnight. He imagined the one virus-filled cell swimming around the channels of his body, and in reality, he knew it was more than one cell, more like an army of cells, marching, attacking, destroying.

He realized he had brought the gun down and quickly raised it back up, eyeing Jimmy Herman's head on the other side of the barrel. But in a matter of seconds, his vision blurred and his eyes became flooded with tears. He dropped the gun and fell to his knees, weeping uncontrollably, as if the true meaning of the woman at the clinic's words finally struck home. Slumping over, he let out all the frustration and fear, sobbing, while in the background, the tape unpaused itself and began to play, Senator Herman's words once again filling the bedroom.

"...fine with me, the Lord Almighty *and* the decent citizens of America...."

WHEN THE MORNING sun flooded through the skylight above the second story hallway, the long corridor resembled a battlefield the morning after a battle. Broken remnants of the previous night's rampage were scattered about, the white walls scarred with violent black streaks. Under the cascade of sunlight, Yoli, the Mexican maid, and Giles, the young Asian house manager, quietly chipped away at the clean-up job, an all-day task at best.

In the bedroom, the door slightly ajar, Othello sat obsessively alert on the edge of the bed, poring over the newspaper clippings and videotapes that ACTNOW had given Joe The Gardener from time to time to show the little old lady what they were up against. On the big screen, Pat Robertson was saying abstinence was the best cure for AIDS. In the clipping he was reading, a conservative radio talk show host was calling AIDS babies the innocent victims. Othello noted the gist of each one's message, then hastily moved on, fast-forwarding the video while flipping through the newspapers until Doris, his thirty-five year-old plump black secretary, walked in.

"Did you get it?" he asked right away.

"The men are still working on it," she said in her husky voice. "What did you do to that poor machine last night?" The ACTNOW tape was stuck in the VCR and Doris and two repairmen were in the kitchen downstairs trying to extract it.

"I must have hit it along with everything else." Othello gestured to the wreckage in the room. "But I swear, it was still working last night, afterwards."

"Uh-huh," she said skeptically, then backed out of the room.

"Doris, I must have that tape," he said as a last command, his eyes fixed on the television and a new VCR. When he was alone again, he took another bite of the toast that was his breakfast and ran a hand over his hair, which was still short from his last video. Since waking just after dawn on the floor between the bed and the big screen, he'd change into a pair of brown silk pajamas and washed the old man's makeup from his face; but he'd yet to leave the bedroom and remained unshowered and unshaven.

With morning, sanity had returned somewhat. At least now he was able to digest the fact that, although he was positive, the bruise on his right forearm that had ignited the panic in the first place was already vanishing and he was positively asymptomatic. He also knew he'd have to have his blood monitored and maybe look into smuggling the latest drugs into the Big House; but this morning wasn't about labwork and lesions. This morning was about taking note of every piece of anti-gay rhetoric he could get his hands on.

There was a knock on the door, followed by footsteps entering the room. Without looking up, Othello knew it was Sweeney. He also knew that even though it was only 7:00 a.m., his manager would look immaculate: suit by Armani, horned-rimmed glasses by Calvin Klein, persona by Log Cabin Republicans.

"Just remember: *you* work for *me*," Othello said defensively.

"You been hanging with some heavy metal boys behind my back?" Sweeney tried for humor as he walked around the room and surveyed the damage, keeping his urge to panic in check. He knew Othello wasn't a wild child who went around trashing places for sport and counted on finding out what happened, but in time.

"An overwhelming number of teen suicides are gay-related, Sweeney, can you believe it?"

"You've got to get dressed, O. We've got a meeting in less than an hour."

"I'm not going to any meeting."

"It's the one you wanted with MTV about their contest proposal."

"Forget MTV," Othello said absently, gesturing to the sea of clippings. "These people think we're vermin."

Sweeney came over to the bed and bent over, talking in a low voice. "O, don't you think Doris might see you looking at all this?"

"The subject interests me. I wear my red ribbon come Grammy time."

"True." Sweeney knew there was no point in arguing. No one ever talked Othello Hardaway into or out of anything. "But do this later. This meeting—"

"You don't understand." Othello turned to him, realizing for the first time his manager and only true friend was truly worried. Right then Othello wanted to confide in the only person who knew he was gay and the only gay person Othello could talk to without a disguise. He started to speak, then choked back the words.

"What is it, O?" asked Sweeney, their faces inches apart. "If you can't talk to me about it, who can ya?"

The first time Sweeney said that was years ago in the elevator at Warner's. Othello had just signed his first contract and was heading home when he ran into this preppie Irishman with reddish brown hair also going down. As Othello went on about his big break, they began to recognize each other from the cruise restroom at the San

Bernadino junior college they both once attended. At first Othello was terrified, to think he'd finally signed a recording deal and someone in the business had seen him the one and only time he'd tricked in a t-room. But Sweeney must have noticed the scared look in his eyes for he had said, "I'm not a tattletale. If you can't talk to me about it, who can ya?" Two hours later, after lunch, they were friends. Eight months later, Sweeney was Othello's manager.

"What gives, pal?" Sweeney pleaded now.

Othello choked back the urge to cry again. He trusted Sweeney more than anyone, but Sweeney was also conservative, so much so that Othello kept him in the dark about the ACTNOW part of his West Hollywood junkets. Still, he desperately needed to reach out. "I," Othello began, "Sweeney, what would you say—"

"Got it," suddenly came from the doorway. It was Doris with the Herman footage, breaking the mood for sharing secrets. Othello leaped up and seized the tape.

"Sweeney. You tell everybody who was going to be at that meeting," he paused, "the contest has potential, and, oh, I don't give a...just please," —his spirits lifted, he shooed them away, waving off Sweeney's protests— "both of you, out. Doris, tip the men big."

Door closed, all alone, he inserted the videotape and sat on the corner of the bed directly in front of the screen. Immediately the senator and his drawl popped on:

"Homosexuality is the scourge of the American Dream from which we can trace most of society's evils. They do not belong in the military, nor our schools nor in decent American neighborhoods near decent American families."

With the remote, he put the senator on pause and stood up. It was all he needed to hear to know that last night's rage was not the rage of a man going insane. His anger now was even more volcanic, unclouded by the disorientation that possessed him hours ago. His body was on fire with hate. Hate just as fierce as that which had been directed at him his whole life. It was all crystal clear now. Not even thirty-two years of being in the closet or the safe buttress of money and celebrity could hide the bitter reality: politicians legislated against them, bashers stalked the streets and preyed on fags, and no one except those in a small circle cared one bit about the dying.

The gun from last night lay halfway underneath the bed. Deliberately, he picked it up. Steadily, he raised his arm. And as sure as anything he'd ever done, he pulled the trigger and watched the frozen frame of Jimmy Herman, senior senator from South Carolina, shatter into a thousand pieces of exploding glass.

TWO

THE PHONES were ringing off the hook in the large rectangular office atop Hollinquest Towers, fighting to be heard over the chaos of several meetings taking place simultaneously. Twenty of Hollinquest, Inc.'s top-ranking executives were scattered about the room. Some were on the big leather couch next to the floor-length window overlooking the Manhattan skyline. Others were around the glass-top desk opposite the main double doors. Still more were near the bank of twelve TV screens broadcasting twelve different channels to the right of the desk. In the middle of it all, at the glass-top desk, sat Jasper Hollinquest, taking phone calls in rapid-fire succession, examining and signing documents being shoved his way, and struggling with Albert, his six-foot-eight, two-hundred-seventy-pound, muscle-bound hairdresser who was styling Jasper's hair for the press conference.

"Keep moving, Mr. H., and you'll end up looking like Liza on a bad hair day," Albert threatened with his baritone voice. Jasper ignored him, leaning over the desk to grab a spreadsheet while keeping an ear cocked to the underlings surrounding him.

"Sir, the Palace does not own the parking structure next to it," explained one of the legal eagles, a square-jawed Harvard boy.

"Sir, now we have word they may want to re-examine the casino revenue figures," said the lone black executive, a tall, slender preppie in his thirties.

"Five minutes, Jasper," said Hopper, the bald chief financial officer. "Maybe we ought to postpone this."

"Nonsense," said Jasper. "The place is mine." He picked up the red phone. "Winnie, still there? Tell our pal Abdul he can keep his private suite with all the bells and whistles." He covered the mouthpiece and said to Hopper: "That way he can still impress his little teenage mistress." He then spoke into the phone: "Got it, Winnie? Two minutes. I'm not hanging up." He tossed the receiver to the square-jawed Harvard boy.

"Too many danglers, Jasper." Browning, the white-haired second-in-command, approached the desk. "We can't do this. In five minutes?"

"Three now," said Jasper. "But mark my words: in *two* minutes, Tl e Palace in Atlantic City will be ours. Or should I say mine?"

"It's that little Arab boy's till he decides to quit stalling," Browning warned, but Jasper merely grinned and buzzed his secretary.

"Lisa, is Shelly Hammel in the media room yet?"

"I'll check, sir," said an efficient young voice.

"Only my best reporter can cover me," Jasper said to no one in particular, smiling confidently as he surveyed the roomful of suits hammering out the details of the acquisition of one of the boardwalk's highest profile casinos.

Jasper didn't need the place. He truly did have enough in life, if that notion was at all possible. And no matter what else he acquired, CNC, the Cable News Corporation, would still be his top priority and true pride and joy. Where it had once struggled to cover dog shows and begged for local feeds, it was now a major player in the world, dispensing news internationally twenty-four powerful hours a day and raking in twice as much as his other six cable networks combined. The Palace would be a sidelight, something to add to his arsenal of hotels and skyscrapers along the Eastern seaboard. A new toy in reality. Blame it on the mid-life crisis. He was in the dusk of his forties, and although the media still made a fuss over his full head of healthy brown hair and fraternity boy looks, *he* was starting to pay more attention to the crow's feet around his eyes, his slightly hefty build that only seemed to want to get heftier and the crook in his nose, broken in his youth, which he swore was becoming more and more noticeable these days.

"Jasper, we've got to cancel," Browning said, but the Harvard boy raised the red phone and mumbled to Jasper:

"Sir, Mr. Winterfeld."

Jasper waved Albert off his hair and grabbed the phone. "Talk to me, Winnie." The room grew still, anticipating disaster and fallout firings. Jasper listened intently, his face offering nothing. Then, after thirty agonizing seconds, he tossed the phone back at the Harvard boy. "Deal," he announced, receiving a relieved round of cheers and applause.

BY DESIGN, the media room was small so that no matter how many reporters showed up, the place would appear crowded. Not that Jasper or Hollinquest, Inc. needed any help getting the world's attention. From tabloid TV to the *Wall Street Journal*, the eyes of media loved to focus on Jasper Hollinquest. Today was no exception. Over forty reporters filled a space designed for twenty, bombarding Jasper with question after question on his latest acquisition: "How will this affect your day-to-day running of CNC?" "Do you plan to renovate?" "Is Las Vegas next?" "Is it true you were advised to wait to buy the Palace until after your divorce settlement?"

Like a man who thrives in the spotlight, Jasper stood in front of the company logo and behind a podium, fielding each volley as if he'd done it in his sleep a thousand times. "I'm still top dog at CNC and plan to stay that way." "By the time we're finished, the Palace will no longer be the *second* largest resort hotel in Atlantic City." "Vegas? No plans at this time, but tell those boys not to go to sleep out there." "If you want to know about my divorce, ask the folks at *Inside Story*. They seem to get the scoop before I do."

To that, he received an appreciative round of laughter. Jasper and Mandy Hollinquest had been regulars on tabloid TV since filing for divorce six months ago.

He answered their questions for another twenty minutes until

Browning, as scheduled, approached the podium and whispered in his ear.

"Duty calls," Jasper then said. "Thanks for coming and see you at the Palace."

The questions kept flying, but with Browning, Hopper and a gang of suits flanking him, he escaped through his private exit and made his way down the hall to the helipad.

"Before you take off," Hopper said as they walked, "we got our paws on something you're going to want to see."

"Messenger it to me at the beach house."

"No," Hopper said. "Now. In your office."

Jasper halted and eyed his friend of fifteen years, knowing only one thing could be so urgent. Seconds later, Jasper, Hopper and Browning were storming through the double doors of Jasper's office.

"No calls, Lisa," Jasper told the intercom. Hopper turned on the middle screen of the bank of televisions and inserted a tape in the VCR built into the adjacent wall. "How bad is it?" Jasper asked anxiously, refusing to sit.

As an answer, Hopper pressed play. Onto the screen popped Mandy Hollinquest, a face all of America knew since the former secretary married the CEO three years ago. This time she was on *American Diary,* giving an interview from the terrace of the Central Park West penthouse she'd been staying in since going public with the divorce. She was wearing half the amount of makeup that was normally caked on her rather large face, her thick blonde lion's mane almost golden against a sun-drenched backdrop of lush green tropical plants. "At first, it really was paradise," she informed the unseen reporter. "I told my mother just before she died: 'Don't worry; your Cinderella has married the prince.' Unfortunately," she paused to hold in her tears, "paradise was just one big fat illusion. He monitored my shopping trips, my luncheon dates, who I worked out with. He was more obsessed with me than his companies."

Hopper paused the tape. "Need to hear more?"

"When does this air?" Browning asked.

"Prime time tonight," said Hopper.

Jasper paused in reflection. Browning and Hopper waited. A grin wiped across Jasper's face. "The gold digger done good," he declared, prompting relieved smiles from his two most trusted colleagues.

Two minutes later, he was saying good-bye to them on the helipad, commending them on a job well done, then running under the swirling blades to the copter with the letters JH on the side.

"To the beach house, Bobby," Jasper said as he climbed aboard and dropped into the seat behind the pilot. The copter took off immediately and Jasper settled back and let out a long contemplative sigh. To think he ever loved her. To think he ever thought he was more hetero than homo. He thought about their $300,000 wedding at his ranch in Virginia and how he had really tried to make it work in those first few months. But give up boys for a whole lifetime? He knew better now. And so did Mandy, and thank goodness she was willing to bail out of this his way. For a price.

With one last glance at the top of Hollinquest Towers, he went over the press conference and Mandy's performance. Both had gone well, he decided. His acquisition would get more publicity and the world would have more fodder to assume he was straight. Browning had been right on with the suggestion to have them play as a double bill for the couch potatoes of America tonight.

"Know something, Bobby?" Jasper said to his pilot. "I'm pretty damned brilliant."

When Bobby didn't answer, Jasper looked toward the cockpit for the first time and discovered that Bob Varney, his pilot of seven years, had been replaced by a hulking figure with dark anonymous glasses and linebacker shoulders.

"Who the hell are you?"

No answer.

"Where's Bob Varney? Where's Old Bob?"

The hulking figure remained silent.

"Hey, who are you? You hear me?"

The pilot swung around and stabbed Jasper's thigh with a syringe. Before Jasper could react, he was unconscious.

"HERE WE GO," Coach Dugan yelled across the court. "Last-second, full-court drill, one more time."

To a man, every one of the Chicago Bulls moaned while getting into position "one more time" for the twelfth time.

"I think the old man forgot we swept Detroit in the regular season," Deon Anthony mumbled to Piper Adams, the pint-sized point guard.

"I think he forgot we're defending champs," Piper said. The Bulls hadn't played a real game in a few days while waiting for the playoffs to start, and Al Dugan, Chicago's salty old coach, was putting them through the kind of workouts usually reserved for pre-season training camp.

"Check this out," Deon whispered to Piper with a mischievous grin.

Coach Dugan's whistle echoed off the over 23,000 empty seats in the United Center. Carl Boatwright, the seven-foot Aussie, inbounded the ball to Piper, who spun around the defender, dribbled once and heaved a long pass to Deon who was at half-court. "Anthony, the three-point line!" Coach Dugan yelled. Barely suppressing his smile, Deon caught the ball nowhere near where he was supposed to be, then casually threw up a skyhook from half-court that hit nothing but net.

"Bulls win," he declared, flinging his arms in the air and receiving a muffled round of laughter from his teammates. From the far sideline, Coach Dugan stared his star player down until the court fell silent again.

"Last-second, full-court drill, one more time," Dugan said.

"Come on, Coach," said Deon. "Them the only words you know?"

"What else would you like me to say, Deon?"

"How about: That's it for today, men?" Deon walked to within ten feet of Dugan, then stopped. The other Bulls stayed even farther back, forming a jagged circle around the two. The entire basketball universe knew this was Deon Anthony's team. The six-foot-six guard with dark chocolate skin, hard sinewy muscles and a smooth, shaved head had no peers in the game. But this time, Coach Dugan tried to hold his ground and be more than a mere traffic controller who shuffled the other players in and out in ways that best complemented The D.A., as the media called him.

"Every regular season game against the Pistons was decided by three points or less," Dugan said.

"Not the one I scored sixty-two in," Deon cracked, receiving a stone-faced glare in return. "Seriously, Coach, we need a rest. You're too intense. Shutting the press out today, this early in the playoffs? I'm speaking for all of us."

Al Dugan wasn't sure whether or not to believe that last part. Sure, they respected his all-world talent, but Deon didn't always speak for the team. Without taking his eyes off The D.A., Coach Dugan announced: "Anybody who wants to stay can do so on a volunteer basis. The rest of you, practice is over."

Several basketballs dropped to the ground, a few chuckles float-ed through the arena, and every single Chicago Bull headed for the locker room. Chalk up another victory for the league's leading scorer, highest paid player and biggest product endorser.

In the shower stalls in the locker room, Deon soaped his torso while making a point to seem oblivious to the presence of human flesh parading past. But Doaky Dawkins, the big black center, saun-tered by, meaning trouble. Doaky wasn't his type—no one on the team was his type—but he could never get over the size of Doaky's dick, which was the longest and thickest Deon had seen in all his years of practically living in locker rooms. As Doaky walked by, Deon had to use super-human strength to avoid looking. He couldn't afford to stir up the rumors around playoff time, rumors that first started among his high school teammates in Calhoun Falls, South Carolina, then festered for four years in the athletic department at the University of South Carolina and subsequently followed him around the pros the last eight years, rumors that he was a fag and had a thing for little black sissyboys.

It was true, and perhaps because he'd never married to cover it up, a good number of people on the inside of the sports world knew about him. But as long as he didn't openly admit it and was seen dat-ing women every now and then, the rumors remained just that, and no one ever went public or said much to his face.

After showering and changing, Deon made his way to the play-ers' parking lot, stepping outside the arena in Chicago's inner city and bristling at the crispness of a cool but sunny April morning. Most of the other team personnel had already left and he was glad to be alone heading to his black Range Rover in a lonely corner of the lot.

He had just bought the car not more than a month ago, so it shocked him when each time he turned the key, the engine hissed and wheezed but refused to turnover. Finally, he got out and lifted the hood, just as a yellow cab idled up next to him.

"Trouble, Mr. Anthony?" The driver was a heavyset, unshaven man in his forties, his voice gruff and country.

"I know I got gas in it," Deon said, still looking under the hood.

"Why don't you let me give you a ride? No charge. You don't know how excited my daughter Emily would be to hear I had the world's greatest basketball player in my cab."

"No charge, huh?" Deon said, picturing Charlie, his baby, taking the car out and messing it up like he did everything mechanical. Briefly, he wondered if Charlie had taken the Range Rover out dressed as a boy or a girl; but before he could give it further consideration, Piper Adams, the pint-sized point guard, drove up in his red vintage Mustang convertible.

"Need a lift?"

"Looking that way," Deon said, still poking around the engine even though he knew nothing about cars.

"Hop in, man," Piper said. "Have the dealer come get that piece of junk."

"Mr. Anthony," the cabby hastily interjected, "it'd be a thrill for me and my Emily." Inside the cab, he felt around on the seat next to his thigh, making sure the syringe was well-hidden underneath a gray towel.

"Come on, Deon," said Piper. "Ain't got all day. Got me an inter-view with sweet Lola Rogers from BET."

Giving up on the Range Rover, Deon slammed down the hood and regarded his two options.

"Jump in," Piper said, cranking up Tupac on the stereo.

Not in the mood for Hyper Piper, as his teammates called him, Deon opted for the cab. "You don't want to keep sweet Lola waiting," he said as he locked up the Range Rover.

"Later." Piper sped off and the cab driver breathed a sigh of relief, tucking the syringe farther under the towel as Deon rounded the cab and jumped in the back seat.

"Devonshire View Towers off Lake Shore," Deon said. "Know it?"

"Don't worry about a thing."

They rode in silence through the urban streets of Chicago until, a few blocks away from the United Center, Deon noticed something wrong.

"Devonshire View is north. Where you going?"

"You're absolutely right, Mr. Anthony." Through the rear view mirror, he eyed Deon. "I guess I'm so excited and all, can't wait to tell my wife Emily."

Deon mumbled something that sounded like nothing and stared out the window. Half a minute later, his attention turned back to the cabby.

"I thought you said Emily was your daughter."

The cab pulled to a stop. They were on a deserted street, the buildings lining it vacated and boarded up. The cabby paused, then turned to Deon, who was still waiting for an answer.

"My wife and daughter, they both have the same name," he said with a smile. Deon offered no response. "Matter of fact, before we go any farther, would you mind giving me your autograph for them?"

With a suspicious nod, Deon said "sure," already making plans to have the guy drop him off back at the United Center.

The cabby turned back toward the front to retrieve a pen and paper. "It'll make their day," he said, then swung back around to Deon, reaching at him with his right hand and jamming a pencil in Deon's thigh. At first, Deon thought it was an accident. Then he realized the pencil was a needle. Then he was out cold.

JASPER HOLLINQUEST sat alone in the long rectangular room, fingers tapping incessantly on the big mahogany conference table. Surrounding him and the table were two empty chairs, stark white walls and not much else. A six-foot-high fireplace stood at the far end of the room. At the other end, his end, a metal door was bolted shut.

There were no windows, and since he'd been stripped of his watch, he had no idea of the time of day. His brown suit felt tight and wrinkled. He'd been wearing it since the helicopter, however long ago that was.

He'd been in the room maybe half an hour and was about to get up and stretch his legs when the door unbolted and in stumbled a tall black man in red sweats, his eyes blindfolded, his hands restrained behind his back. He was being prodded into the room by two rather large men, the same type of thugs that had escorted Jasper here. "I'm telling you, don't get rough with me, man," said the black man. "I ain't taking no more shit."

Paying no attention to his threats, the thugs worked silently to remove the rope around his wrists, then the blindfold. When the black man could see again, he squinted, his eyes adjusting to the white of the room. He then saw Jasper sitting on the other side of the table and recognized the famous tycoon just as the famous tycoon recognized the famous basketball player. "What now?" Deon asked angrily, but before Jasper could say anything, the metal door slammed shut behind Deon, leaving them alone. "What the hell is this, man?" Deon pleaded. "Why am I here? Where are we?"

"Wish I could tell you," Jasper said calmly. "We met once before, at the Garden during that grueling seven game series with the Knicks a few years back."

"We said two words, hi and bye. What's this all about?"

"You just wake up in a bed in an otherwise empty room, then get led down some stairs to this?" Jasper asked, tracing circles on the table.

Deon came toward him. "I don't care who you are; this is kidnapping."

"Just hold your horses, Deon." Jasper stood up. "Anthony." He was taken aback to find himself dwarfed by the basketball giant who was now a foot away. "You're damned right this is kidnapping, but I was kidnapped, too. So don't come after me."

Deon stared him down, trying to discern whether to trust him or beat the hell out of him. Then, as if his personality suddenly changed, his face softened and he sat on the conference table. "Then who's after us? What do they want? Or is it how much?"

"I'm in the dark just like you." Relieved he was still in one piece,

Jasper walked around the room, searching but not finding any clues. "You get some kind of injection that knocked you out cold?"

"By some strange-ass cab driver."

"I was in my helicopter. Somebody switched pilots."

Deon blew a sarcastic breath. "They probably fucked with my car this morning. If it's still morning."

"'No harm will come to you,' they said when I woke up feeling like I had the worst hangover of my life. 'You're going to a meeting—'"

"'—you'll be glad you did.'"

"Exactly," said Jasper. "And did they tell you the bit about messages being delivered to cover your whereabouts."

"Till tonight, when they promised I'd be back home. Safely." Deon stood up. "But why, man, why? The two of us, why?"

Jasper remained silent. He knew Deon Anthony was gay, not only from the buzz in the sports department at CNC, but years ago, one of the pretty boys Jasper kept at his homes across the world knew of a black boy who claimed to have been with Deon. But Jasper wasn't about to open up and suggest he shared the athlete's penchant for men.

Deon turned away. He was sure a media man like Jasper had heard the fag rumors about him. But could that have anything to do with whatever brought them here? No way was he gonna come clean and bring up the possibility. "Man, this place gives me the creeps. Like I'm underground or something." His eyes wandered to the high-beamed ceiling. "What the...."

Jasper looked at Deon and understood the shock, having gone through it himself earlier. On the ceiling were little stark white sculptures, a sea of naked bodies wrapped around each other in different poses, each body intertwined with another in some sort of chaotic, ritualistic orgy.

"They're all men," Jasper informed him. "I can't decide if they're in ecstasy or agony or both."

"Like some sort of cathedral," Deon said, still in disbelief.

"More like a temple, wouldn't you say?" observed a man's tenor voice from the far end of the room.

Deon and Jasper turned to find the fireplace revolving. It was disappearing into the wall as one just like it appeared in its place, only this one was holding a short black man standing where a fire would normally rage. He was dressed in a black leather jump suit and as the fireplace came to a halt, Jasper and Deon both recognized the face that was as synonymous with superstar as Michael Jackson or Madonna.

"Sort of like what Michelangelo would have created if he'd been allowed to truly bear his soul," he added.

Othello stepped off the hearth and felt an instant rush of nostalgia for a room he hadn't visited in years. "Gentlemen, please have a seat," he pronounced. "I trust formal introductions aren't necessary."

"Just what in the devil's name is this all about?" Jasper looked ready to come after him.

"Please, I'll explain every—"

"You must be some kind of loony," Jasper said. "Kidnapping is—"

"I'll explain everything if you promise to be a good boy and have a seat." Othello glanced at Deon, who seemed to be truly stunned to be in Othello's presence. "Like you were told, you're not going to get hurt. This is a meeting and I guarantee you'll be glad you came. Besides, we're not going to get anything done and get out of here if we all don't settle down and get acquainted." He remained focused on Deon, hoping to get "the brutha" to comply so Jasper would feel outnumbered and follow suit. Deon eyed Othello, then Jasper, then begrudgingly took a seat at the table. "Thank you," Othello said. "*Monsieur* Hollinquest?"

"Get on with it," Jasper commanded, refusing to sit.

"I trust you were treated well." Othello began strolling around the room, regarding the ceiling wistfully.

"Look, man," Deon said edgily. "I got a game—"

"Which you'll be back in time for."

"Like Jasper said, this is kidnapping."

"Once you hear me out, you'll realize there was no other way for the three of us to meet without letting the world—or at least our families or staff or whoever—know. This way, it's our little secret."

Jasper scoffed. "What about your thugs who shot us up with— what the hell was that?"

"The drug was harmless, just a convenient way to make your

journey here stress-free. And those aren't my thugs. I borrowed them. Call it the collection of a favor from some people I don't want to get in bed with ever again." He shuddered thinking of singing at Johnny No Legs' teenage daughter's birthday party in Vegas years ago, when he had two hits under his belt and was grateful to be wanted by anybody.

"I owe you big for making my butterfly's day," the wheelchair-bound, baby-faced mobster had told him afterwards. "Ever need a favor, you name it."

Finally, Othello collected.

"Don't worry about them," he told Jasper and Deon, "the thugs, I mean. They think you were brought here for a surprise party. Even they have no clue what's about to take place in this little bunker in LA—"

"LA!" shouted Deon.

"You kidnapped us to the freaking West Coast?" said Jasper.

"I got a playoff game tomorrow!" Deon said. "And golf today. I don't miss my golf game for nothing."

"You'll be back tonight on my special red eye," Othello promised. "Without the benefit of drugs. Gentlemen, please—"

"Man, you're more messed up than Bobby Brown," said Deon.

"Why don't you just tell us the reason you committed this felony," said Jasper.

"Forgive me for not being more centered," said Othello. "This room holds some pretty sacred memories for me, memories I'll never be able to re-create no matter how long I live. I called it—call it—The Temple, and I couldn't begin to count how many boys I sucked, fucked and got fucked by in here, all back in the old days, of course."

Jasper shifted nervously. Deon, who had been staring at the table, looked up in shock.

"It was marvelous. You should have been there. In fact, maybe you were, hell, I don't know. What I do know is those were the only times I felt alive as a gay man."

Silence invaded the Temple, all three of them taking turns eyeing one another, daring the other two to speak.

Finally Deon asked: "Why you telling us this?"

"So you can open up, too," said Othello. "So we can all open up and not be afraid to admit to each other we like to suck dick."

"Look, sucka, don't come accusing...."

"If you think you can get one cent...."

Deon leaped up and both he and Jasper started to protest, their fiery words mixing together, forming one violent threat. Standing near the head of the table, Othello blanched, then quickly collected himself and moved toward Jasper's side of the table. Hollinquest was only an inch taller than Othello, Deon a whole stratosphere.

"Oh, puh-lease, gentlemen," Othello cried when he was a foot away from Jasper's red face. "What do you take me for? You think I haven't done my homework? Deon, everybody but the public knows about you. And Jasper." Othello let out a small laugh and looked toward the ceiling. "In this room, a mess of years ago, I overheard one of the boys saying he was thinking about going to Bora Bora to spend a month with you in your house there. Guys, guys, we're all practicing homos, okay? Get over it."

"I've had people hurt for doing a lot less to me," warned Jasper.

"That's the whole point of this," Othello said sharply. "Look, both of you. I'm not here to do you wrong. Please, hear me out."

They said nothing. Othello took that as a green light and went over to the fireplace and pushed a button under the mantle. From the ceiling over the opposite wall, a large television screen descended. To the right, on the wall behind Jasper, a huge map of the United States came down. From underneath protruded a desk full of phones, faxes and computers.

"Please, have a seat." Othello said, receiving the desired effect of stunning them. Both men sat down. "My brothers, I give you our link to gay America: big screen TV with satellite hook-up and closed-circuit capabilities, the latest computer technologies. And a map." Othello walked over to the giant Rand McNally, standing in front of Texas. "A map to chart the war."

Jasper shook his head. "I'm beginning to see Jacko isn't the only wacko."

"What war you talking 'bout?" asked Deon.

"The one being waged in this country every day. Between the

three of us, we're worth over a billion dollars—"

"You ain't touching my money," said Deon.

"Oh, we really don't need that so much," said Othello. "I'm just trying to point out the magnitude of power the three of us hold in our hot little hands." He cradled his palms together as if he could feel the talisman of salvation within them. Jasper started to speak, but Othello cut him off. "This is not about blackmail, Hollinquest. I'm talking about setting our people free." He walked around the table, speaking to his soul as much as the other two men. "All over America, gays are already at war and what are we doing about it? People are dying of AIDS left and right and everyone talks as if it's all over and there's a cure. Scores of teenagers and grown men are beating up gays like it was sport, killing them even. Politicians and religious leaders are encouraging laws that are eating away at our souls. We've got to fight. It's already war; we just need to decide whether or not we're gonna be in it. Or are we going to sit by in our closeted castles and let our brothers and sisters continue to die?"

Othello stopped, part of him unsteady, the other part amazed at the feeling of clarity possessing his mind. In the few days since testing positive, he was beginning to feel more and more like himself—no, better than himself.

"Why'd you kidnap us to tell us this?" asked Jasper.

"Would you have come any other way, especially without telling anybody?" His question was met with silence. "I hope we can get over how we were brought together and focus on why." He regarded his two guests who both seemed lost in reflection. Would either one of them go for it? Was either one of them single and attracted to him? Yes, he needed them for the war, but he also needed a helluva lot more than that. "What matters, gentlemen, is that we're here, together, and this is our chance to do something right by the world."

"I do plenty of charity work," said Deon.

"Telling kids to stay off drugs and hit the books," said Othello. "But do you ever tell those kids that you also happen to be gay?"

"Ain't nobody's business."

"It's your business when some of those same kids commit suicide because they feel evil for wanting to take a big dick up the ass."

"You can't tell me how to live my life," yelled Deon.

"I'm not trying to!" Othello shook his fists out of frustration. He took a few deep breaths. The room grew still. "Look, I'm not saying come out. Hell, I'd rather cut off my right arm than do that." His voice quivered at the mere thought of going public, especially now that he had the virus. "I'm just saying: there are gays out there fighting and dying every day, and the three of us, with our big bad powerful selves, we could make such a difference. We could make *the* difference. We could run the war."

"Why us?" asked Jasper.

"*Because,*" Othello said impatiently, "because between each of us, we have all it takes."

"To what?"

"To let the whole world know not to fuck with gays anymore. To do whatever we want to do." To put a hole the size of a melon in Jimmy Herman's head, he wanted to add; but that would have been getting way ahead of himself and he wasn't sure if they were ready for his ultimate goal. He wasn't even sure if *he* was ready for his ultimate goal. "For example, Jasper, you've got the power of the press right at your fingertips. CNC decides what's on America's conscience as much as anybody. It's your toy. Even without coming out, you alone can make gay rights an issue as big as anything."

"Hmmmph," Jasper mumbled skeptically. "And just what do *you* have to offer to this war? Our pop star turned political genius."

"I can be the link to the foot soldiers in the streets. The group ACTNOW, I trust you've heard of them."

"Yeah, yeah, sure," said Jasper.

"I haven't," said Deon, causing Jasper and Othello to regard each other, then Deon. "Don't look at me like that," said Deon. "Guys is just who I go to bed with. It's got nothing to do with who or what I am. I ain't never been in no gay bar or been around a whole group of gay people or wanted to live a gay life or nothing like that. It's just who I go to bed with."

Othello glanced at Jasper, who also seemed leery of the star athlete's stance. "We could debate that one all night," Othello said, "but ACTNOW, Deon, is a gay activist group. Action Coalition To Unleash

National Organized Warfare. Of course the 'u' is silent, so to speak, more of a jab toward ACT UP whom they splintered off from. Anyway, think of them as modern day minutemen, if you remember history."

"And you've got this so-called link to them?" asked Jasper.

"To the top," said Othello. "I already give them a ton of money on the sly. They're good men. And women. They're fighting for all of us. They don't quit and they believe in violence if it comes to it, just like those rebels called Colonists a couple of hundred years ago. But they need resources, money, coverage, access to places and things."

"What about me?" asked Deon. "Why'd you drag me into this?"

"Because, my friend." Othello stood over him. "You have the inside track to Senator Evil himself."

"Jimmy Herman?" Jasper asked, to which Othello nodded.

"I barely know the guy," said Deon.

"Yes, but you do know him." Othello's voice changed to that of a Southern belle's. "You're both down-home, South Carolina boys, go to the same charity events back home. Why, he was one of yo' biggest fans in college, weren't he, that man?"

"Man, get outta here."

"It's true." Othello went back to his own voice. "And that, Mr. D.A., is crucial. That man has done more harm to gay rights than everyone else combined. We need you, Deon, as a connection to the senator, his inside moves, his plans, neat little things we'll need to know about him and the rest of his posse."

"I never see the old bugger," said Deon. "This is crazy."

"Not as crazy as the lengths we all go through to hide our personal lives."

Abruptly Jasper stood up. "I don't need to hear this. I make up my own rules."

"Some rules," said Othello. "We can't even love who the hell we want in the light of day. You feel like a total human being? Well, I don't and I'm gonna do something about it." He paused, his tone softening. "Your frustration can't be that far off from mine: all the money in the world, people to wipe your ass if you tell them to, but then again, politicians, religious freaks, hatemongers and everybody who's got an opinion has more of an influence on gay rights than we do. Shit, guys, doesn't it make you angry enough to just wanna, *wanna*...take charge of all the madness? Well, we can do it, fellas, us, the three of us, like nobody can. Come on, men, whaddaya say?"

He fell silent and waited. Both Jasper and Deon looked away, deep in their own thoughts. Othello knew he had gotten to them, but how much?

Deon was the first to move, rising up and pacing back and forth on his side of the room. Except for his gigantic black and red Nikes squishing against the cement floor, the Temple felt dead. Then, on his seventh trip up and down the entire length of the table, he stopped and glared at Othello, who was only two feet away.

Got 'em, Othello cooed to himself, suppressing a smile. Deon stepped toward him. Othello readied his right hand to shake. Deon also raised his right hand, but suddenly it formed a fist, a fist which Othello saw speeding toward the center of his face.

This time, it was the pop star who was out cold.

THREE

THE BEDROOM was pitch black, the air stale with the musky scent of sex and sweat from the night before. In the bed, tangled up in the sheets, was a young brunette, out cold until the phone on the far nightstand came alive and jolted the whole room awake. She startled but tried to remain asleep, counting on the man whose condo and phone it was to kill the noise. But the ringing persisted, not even rescued by an answering machine. "Get it already," she moaned, covering her head with a pillow. When she didn't feel stirring on the other half of the bed, she investigated with her arm, which was met only by the flatness of the mattress. Her head popped up; he wasn't even there. Exasperated, she tugged at the curtain over the bed, letting in a sliver of daylight, then reached for the phone herself, mumbling hello and blanching at the indecipherable squawking of some bitchy female on the other end of the line.

In the adjacent living room, Raider Kincaide was huffing and puffing his way through his usual morning ritual of forty-five minutes on the rowing machine. Only wearing a pair of beat-up white sneakers and some old gray sweats from his Dartmouth days, he was rocking back and forth furiously, sweat flying off his thick blond hair and smooth upper body, drenching the apparatus below. Ever since he was eighteen, he'd been six-two, one ninety, his body ripe with athleticism. But now, at twenty-nine, he had to work harder to keep that same toned physique, the physique that helped make him a three-time all-Ivy-Leaguer in lacrosse in his heyday.

He was almost done with the machine, ready for the one hundred pushups, when the girl in the bedroom poked her sleepy head into the living room and asked:

"Do you have a wife?"

"Ex-wife, why?"

"The phone," she groaned and disappeared. Reluctantly, Raider leaped up and followed her, picking up the cordless as the girl plopped back into bed and laughing to himself at the thought of wearing her out last night.

"Adele?" He held the receiver away from his ear and braced himself for the onslaught from the other end. After a pause he said: "What do you need to know for? Her name is Sheila."

"*Cheryl,*" came from the bed.

Raider didn't bother to correct himself. Instead, he listened impatiently at his ex-wife's harassment, offering a "yeah, uh-huh" every few seconds as she rambled on about needing more child support and whether or not he was going to pick up his son after school like he was supposed to for a long overdue visit. All the while, Raider couldn't help thinking of a stupid twenty-one year-old kid who married his girlfriend of seven months just because she was pregnant and he was Catholic. It was a marriage that disintegrated in two years, around the same time he dropped out of law school.

After two minutes of her nagging, he was ready to hang up on her but was saved by call waiting. "Oh, there it is," he said expectantly. "That call from the office, that—that critical case, gotta go...yes, I know...yes, I'll get the kid, gotta go...bye...yes, bye. *Jesus Christ,*" he said once he clicked her off. There was no critical case at the office—hell, she thought he was a part time paralegal and personal trainer anyway—but coincidentally, on the other line, was his boss George Dockweiller's secretary.

"Dock wants you in a-sap," she said after his hello. A-sap was her way of saying ASAP. "Got a UC assignment I'm guessing."

"Money," Raider said. It was his word for awesome. "I'm on my way." He hung up, wondering what kind of undercover job Dockweiller had in mind.

"Who's Sheila?" Cheryl asked from the bed. "Last week's?"

"More like night before last," he mumbled to himself, grabbing the white towel draped on the headboard and heading for the shower.

An hour later, he was roaring through DC on one of his Harleys, past the Jefferson Memorial, past Capitol Hill and the Washington Monument, then past his personal favorite when it came to the town's tourist traps, Ford's Theater where Lincoln was shot. Soon after, he was at FBI headquarters in the J. Edgar Hoover Building on the northwest side of Washington, strolling nonchalantly through the maze of outer office cubicles. When he reached Dockweiller's office, he knocked but entered without waiting for an answer—he was one of only a handful of people who possessed that privilege. Dock was standing up, his tall lanky frame facing the window behind his desk. "Word has it you didn't leave Sally's alone last night," he said, surveying the dome of the Capitol in the distance.

Raider grabbed the chair in front of the desk. "Sir, in the five years I've been with the bureau, have you ever known me to leave Sally's Bar and Grill alone?"

Dockweiller let out a hearty laugh. Raider loved fueling his boss's imagination when it came to Raider's sexual exploits, especially since Dockweiller had been married for thirty years and his own legendary tales all came from the sixties.

"I will say she was a wild one," Raider added. Dockweiller turned around and regarded him curiously, as if sizing him up for some task. Awkwardly, Raider stared back at Dockweiller's sunken, weathered face, trying but failing to read the man they called Dock Eastwood back when he was the bureau's top undercover agent.

"Raider, tell me," he said, slowly circumnavigating the office. "You ever hear of a group called ACTNOW?"

"Don't think so." Raider shrugged. "Wait—I have heard of an ACT UP, a bunch of radical gays."

"These guys are worse. They make ACT UP look like pansies—

well, I guess they're all pansies." Dockweiller paused to chuckle at his own joke.

"What are they so worked up about?"

"What else? Gay rights, AIDS, anything left of left. They torched a priest's car in San Diego. In Sacramento, they once planted a fake bomb in a politician's home. Damn near killed the fool with a heart attack."

"To think gay guys would have the guts."

"Oh, yes. The fairies mean business. For some time we've known ACTNOW has been getting an influx of cash for bail money, lawyers and general terrorism from an anonymous wealthy source. Now we think that source may have slipped up. Last week, the group deposited into its bank account a $20,000 check from something called HFR."

"And?"

"We did some of our 'creative' research and found out HFR stands for Hardaway Family of Riverside and it's tied to a place called Papa Daddy's, an ethnic burger joint on the outskirts of LA, near Riverside. Papa Daddy's is owned by Othello Hardaway, better known as just Othello."

Raider had been sitting there casually, following along quite unassumingly. It took a beat or two for him to put it all together.

"*Othello?*" he gasped, turning around to Dockweiller, who was behind him. "Wait a minute: you're telling me Othello is *gay?*"

"That part we've known for years," said Dockweiller.

"*The* Othello?" Raider asked, wondering how could his boss could be so calm about this. "I would have never thought—I mean, a guy like him—he can have any girl he wants." Raider pictured Othello as he'd seen him in videos, a smooth-skinned, studly black man with sex coming out of his pores, a small but ripped body, killer abs, deep mischievous eyes, dances like he's fucking, always has the hottest chicks in his videos. Of course, he never touched them much. But Othello a fag? "My kid loves him," Raider said aloud. "I just bought him his latest album for...." he trailed off, still digesting it.

"Lots of stars are gay," said Dockweiller. "We still got lists, you know."

"Who?" Raider said too eagerly. Dockweiller thought about it, then started to speak just as the phone rang. As his boss sat down at his desk and took the call, Raider imagined in his mind a new version of Othello, a man who liked to take it up the ass. Or give it. And probably suck dick, too. He couldn't understand why in the world any guy would want to do that to another guy, even all the religious stuff aside; and for a fraction of a second, for the sake of argument, he *almost* allowed himself to visualize opening his mouth, going down, encompassing another man's—

But then he thought of the time in college, junior year, when he beat the crap out of another student who followed him from the library to his moped in the parking lot one night. "Hey, stud, wanna fuck a sissy?" the guy had said. The faggot ended up spending two days in the hospital, and because some bitch happened along and summoned campus security, Raider spent the night in jail, only to be released the next morning when his lacrosse buddies "persuaded" the faggot not to press charges.

When Dockweiller hung up the phone, Raider was dying to ask about the other names on the department's gay list. But when his boss failed to bring up the subject again, he quelled his curiosity so as not to appear too eager to talk about it.

"I'll cut to the chase, Kincaide," said Dockweiller. "We need someone to infiltrate this ACTNOW, ascertain how dangerous they intend to be, and most of all, we want to know how involved Othello is in their operation." Dockweiller leaned back in his chair. "Of course, this means two things: going to Los Angeles where they're holed up and becoming an insider, as if you were one of them. Gay."

"Why me?" was the first thing out of Raider. "You know I'm not gay, sir."

"Of course not, Kincaide. You're like the kind of son I would have wanted if my wife hadn't had five daughters."

"What, then you're saying I act gay?" Raider was almost out of his seat.

"Far from it. I knew you'd—"

"Why not just go straight to Othello himself?" Raider asked, trying to lift the burden suddenly dropped in his lap.

Dockweiller laughed. "And while we're at it, maybe he'll do an interview with *20/20* on why he's pumping teenage America's hard-earned dough into a group of radical gay *feygelehs*."

"But why me?" Raider bolted up and walked to the window. "What about McKenzie or...or Goose? He's always prancing around imitating 'em anyway."

"You don't have to be a limp wrist to be gay, Raider." Dockweiller indicated a thick file on his desk. "Othello's got a thing for blonds, big muscly blonds. And let's face it: they don't come much more big, muscly and blond than you."

"Why don't they get someone from the LA bureau?"

"Harbinger, my old buddy there—he called me and asked for you. Guess I've been talking you up to him so much over the years, bragging about you. He thought you'd be ideal for this, said any man who could bust the Martelli cocaine connection could take out these guys in their sleep."

Raider glared out the window. "None of the Martelli gang tried to hit on me."

"No, they just cut their enemies into a thousand tiny pieces. But you nailed their butts. And you busted those militia sickos who were targeting Atlanta. You're the best, Kincaide. That's why I'm asking you. And you know that's all I'm doing. I can't make you do this. It's your decision, company policy."

Like a petulant son, Raider's stare remained fixed on the world outside. "If I say yes, what's my cover? Flamingo dancer? Hairdresser? Figure skater?"

"Don't worry, we won't give you a whole gay background to remember. You'll still be Raider Kincaide, hetero Dartmouth lacrosse legend. We think Othello will go for the jock bit. Plus, if he's smart enough to have you checked out, you'll be legit. Only fictional thing will be: instead of joining the FBI after quitting law school, you puddled around your real life hometown, Nantucket, working at your father's motel. That's where you lived until you moved to West Hollywood to come out and be what you always knew you were, gay." Dockweiller rose up and stood a foot away from Raider's back. "This is the kind of assignment I would have killed for in my time."

"You became a legend nailing hard-nosed Mafia types, not radical gays torching priests' cars."

"You know I wouldn't ask you if I didn't believe in you a hundred percent and know that someday you're going to be just as much a legend around here as I am."

Raider stared out the window as if the only way out were to jump. But it *was* up to him. No agent could be forced to do undercover work. He rested his head on the window pane, breathed a shallow sigh and closed his eyes, shutting out the world outside for as long as he could.

"Think about it, Kincaide," Dockweiller finally said. "You can inform me of your decision first thing tomorrow morning."

BRIAN, JR., BURST through the front door first, barely waiting for Raider to turn the key. "Careful now," Raider said laughingly, but his son ignored him and ran for the couch, diving on it and making the sound of an exploding bomb. Raider smiled. His boy was just like him at eight, whitish blond hair that would darken eventually and full of enough energy for six boys.

"We've secured the living room, Dad, I mean, Sergeant."

"Sergeant? Boy, never let your ol' man be anything less than a five-star general."

"I'm the general," Brian protested.

"Just for tonight then," Raider said as he checked the mail. "Why don't you put your overnight bag in your bedroom and call your mother, General."

When his son was out of sight, Raider ducked into his own bedroom and retrieved the plastic shopping bag on the dresser, fishing from it the unopened CD. Othello. *One Nation.* A present for Brian to make up for not seeing him for a month. Trying to buy the kid's love, he realized, but whatever worked. This morning's meeting in Dock's office still fresh in his mind, Raider tore open the package and placed the disk in the CD player on the dresser, making sure to keep the sound low. The first thing he heard was a sustained organ note, eventually accompanied by Othello speaking somberly:

You've got one life.
We've got one world.
I've got one wish,
and that's for one nation.

When Raider bought music, which wasn't regularly, it was usually that of the old rock bands from his college days. But now, as the organ note gave way to a dance beat, he found himself listening to Othello like never before, becoming engrossed in music that took on a new but as yet undefined meaning. So caught up was Raider that he didn't notice his son had entered the bedroom until they were inches apart.

"Daddy, is this mine? For me? Huh, Dad?" Brian had picked up the CD case and was beside himself.

"Gimme that, son." Raider swiped the case.

"But, Daddy, you got this for me, right?"

Raider knew he'd been nabbed. Othello's songs were all Brian had been singing since the album came out. "Sure," Raider stammered, killing the music.

"Then why can't I have it?" Simple enough question.

"Uh," Raider murmured painfully, then knelt beside his son, searching his innocent blue eyes. To have his own boy listening to Othello? Now that he knew what he knew? "Son, uh...." He tried to come up with an explanation a kid would understand, but after some rather long agonizing moments, he failed. He wasn't even sure if *he* understood why his son shouldn't listen to a gay guy's music. No parental group had come down on the album for sexual content as far as he knew. His boy was standing patiently, waiting for an answer. "Son," he finally said, "just let me listen to it first, to make sure it's okay for children. And if it is, you'll get it later."

The disappointment is his son's face would eventually wear off, Raider reasoned, and maybe by then he'd be more interested in the latest space-powered, teenage karate heroes or those Goosebump people, whoever they were.

"QUIET, EVERYONE, please!" Travis Little Horse shouted over the uproar, and the thirty men and women gathered for the ACTNOW meeting slowly if not begrudgingly began to settle down. "Meeting's dragging, folks. We voted on this an hour ago. We will continue to have ten people harass Assemblymen Weeks wherever he goes, but we will *not* stake out his teenage daughter as Freedom suggested." Travis shot a disappointed look to Freedom who was also at the podium, his flaming red hair all over the place after the heated debate. "True, we are not in this for public relations," Travis added, "but little Becky Weeks has not done one thing to hurt us."

There was a general murmur of approval from the other members, including Othello, who was in the back of the room, dressed as the old man Joe with his geriatric makeup, fake eyebrows, beard and wig, wire-rimmed glasses, latex beer belly, green fisherman's hat, worn khaki pants and yellow golf jacket over his blue workman's shirt. Up front, Freedom tossed his head back defiantly, the long dangling earring in his right ear shimmering in the bar's overhead lighting.

"These people need to suffer," he said.

"Weeks will get his," Travis said, "but not his daughter and not tonight. I think we've had enough for one day." Most of the members groaned in agreement. "We'll take up the mayor controversy next meeting. Anybody with suggestions can see me before you go— wait—wait," he called out as everyone began to disperse, "a couple of announcements, especially about the protest at the hospital Saturday...."

Raider Kincaide stepped into the boarded-up bar to find the ACTNOW meeting apparently ending. An Indian-looking man with long black hair was speed-reading through some sort of list and half the people in the room were standing up, poised to leave once the list was finished. Raider knew he'd be late, especially after stopping at a 7-Eleven for a six pack of Bud Light and downing half of it in the back alley as a shot to his nerves. From just inside the door, he surveyed the place, digesting the fact that he was now standing in a room full of gay people. Radical gay people at that.

After the last announcement, Othello rose up, gingerly as an old man might, and cut a clear path to Travis, who was swarmed as usual at meeting's end by a handful of other members. Standing just outside their loosely formed circle, Othello found himself next to a black-haired man he recognized from the porno movies of the mid-to-late '80s. The man was in his late thirties now, with a goatee, his body more trim than muscular as it had been during his video days. At the meetings, they called him Georgio; but in the movies, he had gone by a name Othello couldn't remember. Standing three feet apart, they made eye contact and smiled. Wanting to avoid scrutiny, Othello averted his eyes, wandering if Georgio had caught the virus working in all those movies, thus providing his motivation for being here. And if that were true, he wondered if Georgio regretted taking all those dozens of dicks of the porno stars up his ass.

"That Freedom's something else," Georgio suddenly said to him, to which Othello nodded but remained mute. "But I see his point. Hell, I'll try anything."

This time, Othello barely heard him. His attention had been commandeered by the sight of a tall blond man looking a bit lost near the door. He was a big boy, Othello noted right away, his body made hard by sport more than a gym. His jeans fit him well, his white T-shirt even better. He seemed close to Othello's age, but his smooth tanned skin made him appear younger while his full head of hair, which was slightly tousled, added an air of ruggedness to him. He stood there not talking to anyone, eyes darting around the room nervously. There was something about him—something Othello couldn't quite put his finger on—that set him apart from the men streaming past him out the door. Othello looked at Travis, who was still occupied, and knew he had a choice: wait patiently for Travis to finish or wander in the vicinity of the blond guy. What Othello would do once he reached him, he didn't know. What he did know was that he had never seen anyone quite like this at ACTNOW and he had to have a closer look.

Instead of making a beeline for him, Othello headed toward the door like a curve ball gone mad, arcing wide around the perimeter of the room, periodically glancing the blond guy's way to check for eye contact, of which there was none. When he reached the entryway, he found himself behind the man and browsed the table full of literature, his attention more focused on the hulking figure whose broad shoulders and expansive back were but a few feet away. Othello had never said more than two words to anyone at the meetings other than Travis, but knew he'd never be able to live with himself if he walked away without trying to make contact.

He took the four steps necessary to lodge himself in the man's periphery. It worked. The man glanced at Othello, but then just as unassumingly, glanced away, his eyes more interested in scanning the room. Of course, Othello thought sourly. Not attracted to an old black geezer. It was a look, or nonlook, Othello was used to seeing during his secret junkets, a look that said his kind didn't warrant consideration on the attraction scale. The rebuke didn't work this time. Othello stepped a little closer so there was no denying his intent to socialize. They stood shoulder to shoulder, facing the room. "Ending early tonight," he said in his scratchy senior citizen's voice. "A big brouhaha tapped everybody out."

The blond guy glanced at Othello ever so briefly and nodded in acknowledgment.

An excruciating lull followed.

"Your first time here?" Othello finally asked.

"Uh, yeah," the man said after having to think about it.

"What made you decide to come?" Othello wondered if the man had also just tested positive and decided to become politically active. Talk about having something in common.

"Me? I just, well, I don't know, wanted to check it out." Abruptly, Raider did a double take and took a good look at the old black man, it just now occurring to him the guy might be trying to hit on him. He took a step back and flashed a hesitant half-smile, thinking: this old man can't be gay. "Tell me something," he said. "You work here?" He suppressed adding: you clean up or something?

"Nobody works here. The bar hasn't been open in years."

"So what brings you here?" It came out unintentionally accusatory.

"Like everybody else," Othello stammered.

"You mean, you're," Raider paused, his legs dancing in place, "you're one of us?"

"What's the matter, never seen an elderly black gay man before?"

Outwardly, Othello's tone was defensive. Inwardly, he began to panic. Was something wrong with his disguise? Was his face coming apart? Did this guy know something?

"No, it's not that," Raider began apologetically. "Well, sort of. It's just that I didn't know what to expect here." Backpedal, he told himself, not the right first impression. "I mean, I know ACTNOW is militant and I thought that meant—"

"No old fogies?"

Raider laughed sheepishly. "I'm sorry. I just got here a few days ago from Nantucket, never been to California. Guess I'm seeing all kinds of new things out here. But I like it. Don't get me wrong."

"Yes, well, out here gays come in all kinds of configurations." Othello began gently feeling his face to make sure it was intact.

"That's why I'm here," Raider said purposefully, folding his arms over his chest.

The tone of this last statement struck Othello as strange. He didn't quite know how it was meant or how he should take it. Curiously, he eyed the blond man while some instinct in the distant reaches of his mind urged him to slowly back away. But he couldn't just leave, especially now that they were actually conversing. To deflect the momentary bout of anxiety, he looked away and caught a glimpse of Travis, who was across the room, putting on his leather jacket as if to leave. "Could you hold on one tiny second?" he quickly asked. "I've got to talk to Travis before he goes. I'll be right back."

"Well, I'd better be—"

"Don't go away, all right? Promise?" Flashing wide sensitive eyes, Othello held out until he received a reluctant nod, then headed straight for Travis, catching him just as he was walking away from the podium.

"Joe," Travis said when he saw the old man.

"We need to talk." Hastily, Othello led the way to the deejay's booth and waited until Travis closed the door before removing two manila envelopes from his pants pockets. "Here's five grand. Bail money. Plus, there's good news."

"I don't know what could be more good than this." Travis eagerly took the cash.

"How about an end to the group's indecision about how radical to get?"

"That and the money? Sounds too good to be true."

"Boss lady has an idea." As an old man might, he let out a series of hacking coughs, then paused to catch his breath while trying to decide how much to reveal about the possibility of new allies in the war.

When Othello came to on the Temple floor after being knocked out, Hollinquest and Anthony were standing over him with vengeful smiles. "We should do this more often," Jasper had said. "If nothing else than to see the world's greatest basketball hero punch the daylights out of the world's most delusional rock star."

"Give me another shot at this," Othello had asked, remaining on the floor and feeling his face for blood, relieved when he hadn't found any.

"Why should we?" Jasper had asked.

"Because I've got all of our best interests at heart," Othello had said. After an hour of pleading, he'd finally gotten Jasper to agree to a second meeting, this time without Mafia thugs and needles. Then, only after making Othello grovel some more and receiving an approving nod from Hollinquest, Deon had consented to join them. Still, neither would-be accomplice was remotely close to enlisting.

"The old dame," Othello said now to Travis, "she's trying to convince some of her rich old widow friends to contribute to the cause, said they've all lost too many gay friends to AIDS."

"Who are these goddesses?"

"That you'll never know. But we might be in for some major resources, the kind needed to do some of the more out-there things you and Freedom talk about. But they need you to show them what you can do. Forget the people in the group who don't want to escalate. Find out who wants to follow you to the next level, team up with them and give these ladies something to see, say at the hospital rally or with Arnold Weeks."

Show me who's ready for bloodshed, Othello concluded to himself.

Travis glanced down at the envelopes of cash and let out a laugh that bordered on sinister. "Joe, my friend, tell these little old ladies: it's showtime."

Raider had moved over to the literature table and was feigning interest in the various flyers. In reality though, he was sizing up the few ACTNOW members who were left. Two feminine-acting men were sweeping the floor. Two butch-looking women were moving a podium. Nothing too noteworthy was going on, except, at the opposite end of the room, inside a small glass booth, the old black guy was talking to the man he called Travis, the Indian who had read the final announcements. Even though they had privacy, they seemed to be speaking in hushed tones. Then the old black guy forked over two manila envelopes and the Indian's face became animated with appreciation.

"Hey," Raider said to the body in his periphery. "Who's that guy Travis is talking to?"

"Travis? Where?" a man's thin voice responded.

Raider took his eyes off the exchange in the booth to discover the man he had spoken to was unlike anything he'd ever encountered in person. He was as tall as Raider, but skinnier than skinny, with fire-engine red hair and rings coming out of his ears, nose, upper lip and both eyebrows. Around his neck were pearls like Raider's Aunt Geraldine used to wear and his white tank top said: AIDS, BABY.

"Th—the booth," Raider stammered.

"Oh. That man? He's some old Geritol-type who shows up sometimes." Freedom gave Raider a once-over, his right eyebrow lifting approvingly. "Just between us girls, he comes here bearing gifts from some rich old fag hag."

"Fag hag?" Raider was confused.

"Uh-huh," he said teasingly, trying to impress Raider with his knowledge. But Raider didn't know what a fag hag was and didn't want to let on.

"Is the fag hag black or white?"

Freedom shrugged. "White, I assume, some old Hollywood has-been we think."

"And what's Travis do again? I forget; I'm new."

"He thinks he's the leader, but I'm the real balls behind this outfit. My name's Freedom. What do they call you besides a brick shit-house?" Freedom's hand reached for Raider's pecs, immediately caus-ing Raider to flinch and step back just in time to avoid being touched. For an instant, they both froze, like animals of different species in the jungle, eyeing each other for the first time, unsure of the other's prowess.

"Geez," Freedom finally said. "No need to cop a 'tude. Take it as a compliment, whydontcha?" With that, he picked up a stack of flyers, hugged them to his chest and walked off in a huff, leaving Raider shaken by the thought of losing his cool and ready to get the hell out of here to regroup.

Othello came out of the deejay's booth just in time to see the back of the blond man turning for the door, on the verge of vanishing into the night. "Wait," he mumbled reflexively to himself, then cast caution aside and hurried over to him, reaching him at the threshold. "Not so fast."

Raider halted and swung around, wondering, What now? But it was just the old man, not the freak, and for that he was grateful.

"Leaving without saying good-bye?" Othello asked. A feeble line, but it was all he could think of.

"Meeting's over," Raider said in a friendly tone.

Othello cleared his throat, paused, then said nervously: "There's a great coffeehouse down the block. We could go. I could tell you all about ACTNOW."

Raider laughed. "I'm sure you could."

"I'll even throw in a tour of West Hollywood if you want. A spe-cial one for people fresh off the boat from Nantucket."

"I don't think that's such a good—"

"And you can tell me all the Nantucket jokes you know."

Raider let out an all out guffaw, for being hit on by two guys already and for the old man's persistence. But since he had taken this job—and since the old man had something to do with Travis—maybe it wouldn't be such a bad idea to befriend the guy while not doing anything to make him think he could fondle Raider like the weirdo flamer. "Look, I do have to go," he began politely, then indicated a yel-low flyer on the table. "See you at the hospital rally on Saturday?"

Othello brightened, then just as quickly fell sullen. "Can't make it," he said. It wasn't even the issue of being unmasked. Saturday was the second meeting with Jasper Hollinquest and Deon Anthony.

"Well, I'm sure I'll see you around." Raider turned to leave, having had more than enough for his first foray into the gay world.

"You'll be going to all the rallies from now on?" Othello asked.

"Looks that way," Raider sighed, leaning out the door.

"Wait," said Othello. "Your name."

"Raider."

"Raider, I'm...Joe."

Raider nodded, paused a beat, then said, "See you around, Joe," before finally making his exit. For a moment, Othello stood in shock from the swiftly moving current of events. Then, something inside told him that Raider wasn't the type of person who'd come to an ACTNOW function. And what that meant to Othello at that instant was that Raider would probably never come back, even though he said he would, which meant that Othello might never see Raider again.

Quickly, Othello bolted out the door. Santa Monica Boulevard was alive with cars on the street and bodies on the sidewalk. Frantically looking in both directions, he saw no build that resembled Raider's. Then, with a second look to his left, he caught a glimpse of a broad-shouldered man slipping from the crowd and ducking into the darkness of a side street. Time stopped; fear swelled in his stomach. He was at a crossroads, he knew: follow and pursue or perhaps regret it for the rest of his life.

To keep in character, he limped to the corner. When he reached the side street, he saw that the disappearing body had indeed been Raider, but he was already half a block away and in quite a hurry. The street was empty and residential. Othello shed the old man gait and sprint-walked down the sidewalk, unsure whether to call out Raider's name or be ready to duck behind a parked car if he turned around. But Raider was moving much too fast to care about what was behind him, and when he was near the end of the block, he darted into an alleyway on the right.

Othello ran to the alley only to find it empty. He went down it anyway, determined not to let this man walk in and out of his life in the span of a few short breaths. Halfway down the alley, next to a

Spanish style house, there was an opening to the left, a driveway extending to the front of the property. Othello charged down it. When he reached the point where the driveway met the street, he ducked behind a parked car. Across the street, Raider was heading up the stairs to a large modern apartment building. In a matter of seconds, he slipped a key into the double-glass doors and was gone.

Othello stood up but stayed behind the car, knowing this was as far as he should go tonight. He was out of breath from the chase, but also relieved to find out that Raider, Last Name Unknown, formerly of Nantucket, Mass., lived in an apartment on Havenhurst Drive in the heart of West Hollywood. Because even with just these few facts, Othello could have his manager Sweeney check up on this man, this, oh, so wonderful, gorgeous man.

FOUR

On the thirty-five-inch monitor suspended from the ceiling, dozens of gays and lesbians jammed the grassy knoll separating Mercy Hospital from an adjacent thoroughfare, their anger channeled into one rancorous chant: "Mercy has no mercy! Mercy has no mercy!"

"Gentlemen," Othello began, circling Jasper and Deon, who were both seated around the mahogany conference table, "I give you Mercy Hospital, the sick bay in East LA with the absolute worst reputation in all of Southern California for caring for AIDS patients. They have doctors who don't give a damn, or worse, don't know enough about the disease. They have health care workers who still freak out at the sight of PWAs. And, as icing on the cake, they have Justin Piatkowski, Mercy's top administrator who is also a former member of the arch-conservative John Birch Society." He brightened at what he saw next on the monitor. "Oh, this is good."

Hours ago, at daybreak, before the meeting at the Temple, twenty of ACTNOW's most hard-core soldiers had chained themselves inside ten of the hospital's empty rooms, vowing to stay there until Piatkowski resigned. Now, the LAPD was carrying them out by their limbs and hoisting them into a black and white police bus. The sight sent the ralliers into a frenzy, forcing the remaining cops to form a wall sequestering the protesters on the knoll to prevent them from interfering with the arrests.

"The ones going to jail have the most balls." Othello moved closer to the screen for a better look. "Our Green Berets. Our Navy SEALS. Our Dirty Dozen types." He paused to take note of each ACTNOW soldier being carried through the hospital's glass doors. Some of them were whisked away too fast to recognize. Others were twisting and turning in defiance and he couldn't see their faces. He did, however, notice Georgio, the former porno star, and Travis, who had a mischievous smile on his face. And, of course, there was Freedom, shouting obscenities and struggling with the two officers holding him. Othello also saw the two butch lesbians who always held hands at the meetings, both of them with plump bodies and short hair, and the guy who was always talking about setting fire to right wing buildings. He was black, slightly heavyset and wore dreadlocks.

"How we getting this on TV?" asked Deon. He was slouched down in his chair as if he were a bored high school student.

"Closed circuit satellite," Othello said, scanning the screen. "But rest assured: the camera crew has no idea who they're beaming this back to."

Jasper shifted uneasily. "How do you know they're not going to find out?"

"They won't."

"How do you know they won't?"

"Because I know." Othello turned from the monitor. "The crew thinks it's shooting footage for a possible gay cable venture. Believe me, Sweeney is meticulous." To get things done, Othello had decided to open up to his manager about his ties to ACTNOW and his meetings at the resurrected Temple. Predictably, the preppie Irishman blew a gasket, but when he realized Othello would do this with or without him, he agreed to comply, to help ensure Othello's safety if nothing else. "Trust me," Othello told Jasper and Deon. "Everything we do will be so diverted and deflected, it couldn't possibly be traced back to us. No one will break us if we don't let them."

"Most of them look like they got AIDS." Deon winced at the screen "All skinny and shit. I can't be thinking about that kind of stuff right now. The playoffs is the most intense time of the year for me."

Othello walked toward Deon. "Would you feel the same way about 'the playoffs' if your life was on the line like some of these people?"

"Hey, man, I'm negative, man, so don't even try that."

Othello turned away. It wasn't any easier dealing with these two the second time around. And now, Deon had to trumpet the fact that he wasn't damaged goods. Of course, he was negative, Othello thought, and probably Jasper, too, which is perhaps why they didn't share his will to fight.

"As intriguing as all this sounds," Jasper had said at the end of the first Temple meeting, "no way am I committing to something like this under these circumstances, being drugged and kidnapped and not knowing where the hell I am." And Deon had agreed with him. It was then that Othello suggested they meet again and negotiated the terms: no injections or kidnappings next time and all three men would decide the date. As an act of faith, Othello had offered to pay for their transportation and expenses, but both Jasper and Deon declined. He did finally convince them the Temple would be the safest place to meet. But short of that, the only other thing Hollinquest and Anthony agreed to was hearing him out.

Othello stood with his back to his two still-unwilling accomplices, trying hard to find the strength to be patient. "Deon, you're from a poor background. What if you never made it big and couldn't afford top notch health care and weren't lucky enough to be negative?"

Deon tried to come up with an answer, but Othello didn't wait for it.

"And, Jasper, you've been rich forever—"

"I made myself what I am," said Jasper.

"True, but you were born well-off to boot. But what about that boy who was thinking about living with you on Bora Bora, the one I overheard talking in this very room years ago?"

"What about him?"

"Were you ever with him?"

"How the hell should I know?" He shot a smile to Deon. "Been with so many boys in so many places."

Deon laughed. Othello went on: "Which is probably why you're in that awful mess with Mandy right now."

"It is awful, isn't it?" Jasper paused, then said with a grin: "Which is just how I and America like it."

Othello and Deon looked at one another, then back to Jasper.

"It's all an act?" said Othello.

A smirk wiped across Jasper's face.

"Man, that beats me dating Mariah and Tyra," Deon said and he and Jasper laughed. Othello couldn't share their amusement. All he could think of was all the energy they all spent living lies.

"Anyway," he said. "What about all those boys? And their friends? Have any of them just wasted away while there was nothing they could do? Or got fired from a job for being a fag? Or gotten the living shit kicked out of them for coming out of a gay bar at the wrong time? Or maybe one of them shot his brains out because he couldn't cope with being an evil queer anymore."

Jasper bowed his head in retreat. Deon stared straight up at the naked bodies intertwined on the sculptured ceiling.

"You still haven't given us one serious detail," said Jasper.

"We could start by making sure the people in the trenches have enough resources to fight the everyday fight. There are countless groups out there struggling for the rights the three of us don't have the guts to come out and fight for, but they're all underfunded. They need ammunition, supplies, cash. Cash that we won't miss."

"What kind of groups you talking about?" asked Deon.

"Any kind of gay group doing something positive—hell, take your pick. We'll figure that out as we go along." Othello paused, tight-lipped and steely. "Gentlemen, we have the power to create an all-out uprising, emotional, spiritual, political and physical, one that lets the world know once and for all: don't fuck with queers. Give us our rights or face some serious-ass consequences. Treat us with respect or we'll blow your fucking heads off."

"You speaking literally?" asked Jasper.

"That's something else we can figure out as we go along. With the kind of power we three can generate, the possibilities are limitless, from private funding of groups to using ACTNOW for guerrilla warfare."

"You'll never catch me exposing myself to them," said Jasper.

"You don't have to." Othello flashed a smile. "We already have a liaison: the person I go to the meetings disguised as."

Both Deon and Jasper paused to take it in.

"Just what kind of disguise is this?" Jasper asked.

Othello shook his head. "Not until you join forces."

Deon eyed Jasper and said to Othello: "You're not kidding about this."

"Is Jimmy Herman kidding when he says we should be stripped of our citizenship?" Out of the corner of his eye, Othello saw the image on the monitor change and glanced at it. This new shot was of several dozen protesters chanting inches away from a row of statuesque policemen. The cops were in riot gear complete with helmets with clear shields over their faces. Othello eyed the screen unassumingly, then was stunned to realize the muscular blond in the middle of the protesters, the one who loomed bigger and taller than most of the men and women surrounding him, was Raider. His Raider, Still Last Name Unknown, for Sweeney had yet to receive any information on him.

Momentarily Hollinquest and Anthony ceased to exist. Othello became absorbed in the sight he'd been hoping to see all morning, inwardly breathing a great sigh of relief to discover his instincts had been wrong about Raider not being the type to attend an ACTNOW function. He looked so valiant and adorable, punctuating his chanting with his fist in the air. His face was a bit vacant after all those hours of protest, but there he was all the same, in the trenches, a new warrior, only a few days removed from the shores of Nantucket. At that instant, Othello desperately wanted to be out on that grassy knoll, yelling and raising his fist right alongside him, joined together in the fight.

"I've got to go now," he heard himself say, then looked to Jasper and Deon, noting their confused reactions. "Something very pressing."

"What the hell...." Jasper said.

"Can you wait here?" asked Othello.

"I got a charter back to Chicago in one hour," said Deon.

"Wait for what?" asked Jasper.

"Well, have you made a decision anyway?" asked Othello.

"Absolutely not," said Jasper.

"Just like that?" said Deon.

Othello bit his upper lip, contemplating. "In that case, meeting adjourned." Hastily, he began collecting the files scattered on the table. "You need more time; take more time. It's a big decision, I understand. Deon, you need to get back for the start of the Detroit series anyway. Good luck. Really." He hurried to the fireplace. "Jasper, hopefully you can see your way to getting this protest on CNC. And how about an hour-long special on the state of gay rights?" Too frantic to wait for a response, Othello hastily tapped at the buttons under the mantle to retract the monitor, desk and map of America. "We'll be in touch through Sweeney. Until we meet again..." He raced to the door, opened it and stopped, searching for the right words. "Uh...bye," he said and was gone, leaving behind two flabbergasted guests.

Like a character in a movie trying to be two places at once as two different people, Othello embarked on a mad dash, first up the winding, wrought-iron stairwell, then through a series of dark narrow hallways leading to the garage of the house. Once there, he flung open the trunk to the old Impala, his inconspicuous car, and ripped away the blanket covering his incognito wardrobe.

Quickly, he rummaged through all the clothes that were there in case he were in public and needed to look plain or blend in. Carelessly, he tossed aside faded jeans, oversized shirts, baseball caps, makeup kits, several pairs of sunglasses, casting them over his shoulder like a lovestruck teenage girl in a panic trying to decide on an outfit while her date waited downstairs, getting to know her parents. After some rather anxious moments, he found what he was searching for, the senior citizen get-up. Wasting no time, he left the rest of his emergency wardrobe on the floor, gathered the old man's bundle in his arms, hopped in the car, opened the garage door and sped off, burning rubber in the process.

RAIDER SAT ALONE atop the peak of the grassy knoll facing Mercy Hospital, determined not to leave until he'd had one significant lead

in the case. It was late afternoon now and he was one of only six protesters left. The other five, four men and one woman, were at the bottom of the knoll, critiquing their effort, while Raider sat dejectedly,
contemplating his own performance and not feeling too good about
it. In the last five hours, he'd barely said a word to anyone except for
what was absolutely necessary. "Fine and you?" "Some water? Sure." "A
sign? You bet!" Not exactly the kind of topflight methods they teach
you at Quantico to gain people's confidence and learn their secrets.
But maybe it was enough for now that he was here, becoming a familiar face and getting used to the idea of pretending to be one of them.
Passing himself off as a dope dealer or money launderer was a piece
of cake, but a fudge-packer—as his father called it—that took some
work. He pondered the idea of taking it up the butt for a second, but
it seemed too painful so he changed the channel in his mind.

All day long, he had been astonished at how angry and vengeful
gays could be. They were really pissed off, he realized from the
moment he arrived as the police were carrying several of them away
for causing a ruckus inside the hospital. Remembering other scenes of
radical gays on the evening news—scenes he never paused to consider before—he wondered when they had turned into such a vocal,
aggressive bunch.

They did, however, welcome him without question. At the same
time, it was unsettling to realize that the women looked right through
him, not the least bit interested in him as a sexual animal, something
he'd *never* experienced before while around a bunch of honeys. On
the other hand, the guys gave him more looks than he knew what to
do with. But, he told himself: better than them *not* looking. Thinking
about it now, he had to laugh at this whole ass-backwards world he'd
gotten himself into.

The double-length city bus with the accordion link slowly crept
away from the corner, unblocking Othello's view of Mercy Hospital
across the street. He was dressed as the old man and still full of adrenaline from the hectic journey to East LA, a journey that saw him weav-
ing through traffic like a madman and almost getting into an accident
twice. But upon seeing the hospital, his heart sank. Only a few listless
bodies remained; the protest had all but disappeared. When the stop-

light changed, he crossed the street in a daze, like someone who knew they'd already missed the plane but wanted to go to the gate anyway. He stepped onto the sidewalk and surveyed the knoll. Much to his astonishment, Raider was one of the handful of soldiers remaining, sitting on the grass twenty yards away, alone in his thoughts. Othello walked toward him, taking the fact that Raider was still there as a signal from the gods that they should keep getting to know one another.

"A trooper to the end, I see," he said in his old man's voice when he found himself directly behind Raider's broad back. Raider turned unassuredly, then saw who it was and jumped to his feet.

"Joe." Raider sounded pleased to see him. "Thought you couldn't make it."

"I couldn't. The dame I garden for let me off a little early. I just got here."

"Then you missed all the excitement." Raider was speaking to him in that louder, plain-speaking tone used for children and the elderly.

"But I'm glad I caught you. How'd you like protesting? I don't know if you ever did it back in Nantucket."

"This was definitely my first time." Raider shook his head pensively. "It wasn't half bad either. I can see why everybody's pissed off at the hospital. Honestly."

"Wish I could have been here with you, your first time and all. It would have been my first protest, too."

"Yeah," Raider said vacantly, then added: "Well, I'm starving, Joe."

Othello was trying to summon the courage to suggest they grab a bite together when he heard:

"You hungry at all?"

For a moment, Othello was speechless, then thanked the gods once again for this unexpected sign. After he accepted, Raider suggested the hot dog stand in the small park on the other side of the hospital. Othello heartily agreed, asking himself: what could be more romantic?

Casually, they strolled around the sun-drenched grounds, Raider giving Othello his version of the day's protest and Othello drinking in every word as if he were hearing about it for the first time. Then, at the slice of grass that served as a modest park, they bought sodas and hot dogs—Othello two, Raider four—then commandeered one of the concrete picnic tables under a nearby palm tree, Raider sitting on top of the table with his feet on the concrete bench and Othello straddling that same bench facing Raider.

"Tell me, Raider," Othello began once they were settled in. "You have a lover?"

Raider had just chomped down on half of his first dog. Taken aback, he turned to Othello, cheeks stuffed but motionless. After a beat, he gulped down the squishy mass of bread and meat, then choked out: "Nope."

"Is there anyone special?"

"Not really." To make the job easier, he had decided to answer questions about his love and sex life as if the girls were guys. But now, he wasn't so sure telling Joe he was single was such a good idea. "I'm actually taking a break from the dating game these days," he added. "I just got burned by a bitch of a guy, Adam, and I don't need anymore liars or one-nighters or dating period."

"Me, too," Othello chimed to avoid seeming too eager. "Dating. Who needs it?" He took a bite of his dog, a bit dejected, then asked: "So why'd you move to LA?"

Othello sat spellbound—with Raider's muscular thighs in a pair of faded blue jeans at eye level—and listened as ACTNOW's newest recruit talked wistfully of his life, how he grew tired of working in his father's motel and came out West to be a personal trainer, how he graduated from Dartmouth but didn't want to spend the rest of his life in a business suit, which is why he dropped out of law school a few years back.

"Did you play sports at Dartmouth?" Othello asked.

"Lacrosse," Raider declared proudly, already done with three of his hot dogs. "I was leading scorer two years running. And I'm still first on the school's all-time list."

Othello imagined Raider charging down the field, carrying that little ball in the netting attached to that long stick, dodging around clumsy oafs from places like Princeton and Cornell, heaving the ball

past some wobbly-legged goalie. Score another one for the Dartmouth Big Green.

"I bet you were unstoppable," he said baitingly.

"Well, yeah," Raider demurred, "I was money."

"Money?"

"Yeah, you know: good," Raider explained, then proceeded to
replay seemingly every highlight of his three years as an all-Ivy
Leaguer—with Othello not minding one bit.

"Is that where you got the name Raider?" he asked when he could
get a word in. "I'm assuming it's a nickname."

"Yeah, but it started when I was a little kid and used to love the
Oakland Raiders, the *first* time they were the Oakland Raiders. I had
a Raiders everything: ski hat, jacket, bed spread, rain parka, those little statues with the bobbing heads. My dad used to call me Little
Raider. Then, when I was in college, I was notorious for leading panty
raids." He laughed nostalgically, not noticing the uneasy reaction in
Othello's face. "One night, I told one of my buddies about my nickname as a kid and every time we went on panty raids after that, they
called me Panty-Raider. Eventually, that's all anybody called me, then
it evolved to just Raider."

"So you dated girls at Dartmouth?"

Raider's heart and chest collided in panic. He'd been so busy
rambling on about himself, he'd forgotten he wasn't supposed to be
the panty-raiding type. "All the guys did," he said hesitantly, taking a
swig of soda to collect himself. "I just went along."

"Yeah," Othello said, thinking of his videos. "I think we've all just
gone along in some way or another at some point,"

"I was confused and tried to convince myself I was straight. I
even got married, which was the stupidest thing I've ever done."
Inwardly, Raider chuckled. This was true, straight or gay. "The only
good to come out of it was my son, who's eight now. She's got custody.
It's a messy couple of years I'd rather not talk about, but anyway, that's
how I got my name."

"Little Raider, huh? Well, Little Raider's not so little anymore."
Othello reached for Raider's thigh, grabbing it, rustling it firmly.

Raider smiled uneasily. He was relieved he hadn't blown his

cover a split second ago and knew he mustn't cause any more suspicion by reacting negatively to the old man's fondling. To appear gay,
he had to let it happen to a certain extent. He'd seen how affectionate
they were with each other today at the rally, everybody kissing each
other on the lips so casually. He felt Joe's raisin-skin hand on his
thigh, but the old man's grip was like that of one of his gym buddies,
short and to the point with no excessive roaming or lingering. When
he realized this, he decided it was okay. Hell, he was almost ready to
admit it was sort of flattering. "My real name's Brian," he said modestly as Joe removed his hand.

"Brian what?"

"Kincaide." Raider eyed him doubtfully. "Are you really gay, Joe?"

Othello's fake right eyebrow ruffled upward. "Why do you ask
that?"

"You just don't seem...something about you."

"Why else would I be here?" Is he on to me? Othello wondered.
But nothing in Raider's eyes said "celebrity." A look the real Othello
knew all too well.

Raider remembered the flamer from the meeting, Freedom, who
claimed Joe was sent to ACTNOW by some fag hag. Could Othello be
the fag hag? But what the hell was a fag hag? He decided to try something. "Boy, there was a pretty interesting looking fag hag here today.
You know who I mean?"

"Fag hag? That's not very politically correct, is it?"

"Huh?"

"Fag hag?" Othello repeated, as if his point were obvious.

Raider averted his eyes, hoping for divine inspiration. There was
none. "Well, do you know who I mean?" he asked again.

"What does she look like?" Othello asked, giving up on the les-
son.

She, Raider noted. Fag hags are she's. Of course: hag. "She was just
loud, that's all. Thought she might have been the one you work for."

Othello tried to hold his alarm in check, taking longer to chew in
order to stall. "What do you know about the lady I work for?"

"Just that she's a fag hag and she donates money to the group
through you." Raider noted the nervous dance in Joe's eyes.

"And how did you come about this information?"

"Freedom told me. At that meeting where you and I met."

Othello tried to laugh it off. "You can't believe everything The Zealot tells you, everybody knows that. He probably told you he runs things, too."

"Yeah," Raider admitted sheepishly, suspecting that even if Freedom were stretching the truth, ol' Joe was hiding something.

"The woman I work for couldn't care less about what I do with ACTNOW." Othello took another bite of hot dog and averted his gaze to a young black woman in the distance. She was picnicking on the grass with her wheelchair-bound daughter. "Anyway," he began, trying to deflect attention away from himself. "What kind of guys do you like, Raider?"

"All kinds really." His motto with girls: it's all pink on the inside. Then, he saw a way to let the old man down easy. "No offense, Joe, but usually I like 'em around my own age, give or take a few."

Deliberately, Othello took sip of soda, then asked: "How about black guys?"

"Black guys?" He'd always wanted to be with a black chick. "Sure. Black guys are studs." He had an idea. "Hell, give me some guy like Deion Sanders or Denzel Washington any day. That smooth black skin. Or who I really have the hots for is Othello."

"Othello?" His head raised, his eyes widened, his heart stopped.

"Sure," said Raider. "That's one black man I'd love to personally train, if you know what I mean." Unassumingly, he took a long gulp of his soda while Othello tried to catch his breath and keep from shouting something, anything.

This must be what it feels like to be destitute and suddenly win the lottery, he thought. Too good to be true. But it was true and right then and there he could have leaped up and touched the sky while screaming like they used to do at Riverside Baptist, back when he was Li'l O. In the images racing through his mind, he envisioned revealing himself at once to his first, only and last boyfriend and telling him about Hollinquest and Anthony, his funding of ACTNOW and his plans to escalate the movement. He also saw Raider moving into the Big House, becoming the subject of his every love song, being promoted to second-in-command in the war, being there for him when—*if*—he got sick.

But Othello also knew he was getting light-years ahead of himself. He still didn't know if they were compatible—as if that mattered—and how the virus would fit into their equation. There was also the background check still in the works; and as Othello sat there, trembling at his luck, a small sliver of his brain was able to remember that despite the fact that he was falling, hook, line and sinker for this man, if Raider Kincaide wasn't who he said he was, a lot more was at stake than a shattered heart.

But this had to happen. This was going to happen. *They* were going to happen.

"You know, Raider," he began teasingly, "people tell me I look a bit like Othello."

Raider scoffed so hard the soda he was gulping down backed up in his nose.

"Really," Othello said. "I can be just as sexy and romantic and fun and you-name-it as him, honest."

"I told you, Joe, I'm only attracted to guys my age. I'm flattered and all, but—"

"Raider, I can't tell you how much I enjoy your company," Othello said eagerly, his voice ripe with possibility.

"Me, too, Joe." Raider stuffed the last half of his last hot dog in his mouth, balled up the wrapping and shot it into the waste basket five feet away. "Two," he said with a fist in the air, then added: "You're all right."

"Oh, I'm gonna make you see I'm more than all right." Othello rose up and sat next to Raider on the top of the bench.

Raider held his hands in front of him, clearly meaning back off. "Now hold on, my man, Joe."

"My man, Joe, oh, I like the sound of that."

"Now, Joe, don't go ruining—"

"Can't we go somewhere, somewhere private? You won't regret it, guaranteed."

"Listen." Raider scooted away. "We can be friends, okay, nothing more."

Othello let out a little laugh.

"Now I'm serious, old man." Raider's tone darkened, catching Othello by surprise.

"I'm sorry, Raider. It's just that you don't understand."

"Understand what?" Raider snapped back, thinking: I understand perfectly what you want.

Othello glanced around the park. In addition to the mother and child, two young nurses were on a cig break next to the hospital's side entrance. And the Armenian hot dog vendor was still there, not more than fifteen yards away. It was insane to even contemplate removing the gardener getup in such a public place.

"I gotta be going, Joe." Raider stood up. "No hard feelings, okay?"

Othello mumbled an okay that was inaudible.

"Later," Raider said and left without waiting for a response. Othello called out to him three times, the third plea drawing the attention of the nurses and black mother. Opting for caution, Othello fell silent as Raider crossed the park, his athletic physique becoming smaller and smaller. Othello thought better than to make matters worse by going after him. There had been something very unsettling about the paranoid look in Raider's eyes. And even though it hurt to watch him disappear, Othello stayed on the bench until the all-Ivy Leaguer was through a cluster of trees and out of sight.

When he was gone, Othello headed for the Impala, but not before stopping at a phone booth on the street corner opposite the hospital. "Sweeney," he said once he got an answer. "Did Jasper and Deon get out of the Temple okay? Good. And how about the report from back East? It is? Give it to me." He listened carefully as Sweeney rattled off a plethora of information about Raider, then after ten minutes, hung up the phone.

His last name really was Kincaide, first name truly Brian. And Nantucket, the Dartmouth lacrosse team, the marriage and the kid— it all checked out. He was who he said he was. Now, all Othello had to do was show the man from Nantucket Old Man Joe's true identity.

FIVE

GAME ONE of the Bulls-Pistons series was the kind of game where Deon Anthony found himself in The Zone, that place on the court where everything he did was unconscious, every move he made instinctively right, nearly every shot he threw up hitting nothing but net. From the opening tip, he took control of the game, kissing a three-point bomb off the glass to give the Bulls a 3-0 lead. In the second quarter, he sent the 24,000 United Center faithful to its feet with a breakaway slam dunk that made it 36-17, Bulls. Early in the third quarter, he floated high above the rim and gently tipped in one of Piper Adams's patented alley-oop passes for a 75-39 advantage. In the fourth quarter, The D.A. stole the ball at half-court and drove down the lane past four Detroit players, finishing it off with a reverse jam in which he changed directions in midair three times before slamming it home, making the score 98-58. His last shot before Coach Dugan spelled him for the night was an off-balance jumper from the baseline where he didn't even see the basket. But you don't have to see the basket when you're Deon Anthony and you're in The Zone. The shot rattled in and Deon finished with fifty-six points. His supporting cast then finished off the Pistons 132-76, and the Bulls took a 1-0 lead in the best-of-five, first-round series.

After the rout, the hallway leading to the locker room was jammed with VIPs important enough to get past security. Moving steadily, Deon waded his way through the sea of heads below him, accepting accolades but more focused on showering, getting through the press conference and resting up for game two. But when he saw who was standing just outside the locker room door, his hopes for a peaceful post game were shattered.

"Deon, ol' boy!" It was Big Daddy Callahan, all six-foot-eight, three hundred pounds of him, his frizzy white hair covered by the white straw cowboy hat that never left his head. "Boy, I tell ya," he bellowed when Deon reached him. "You played one perfect game of ball out there. Reminds me of the old days when you were a Gamecock. How are ya, ol' buddy?"

"Fine, Big D." Deon felt his knees give way as he tried to recover from the shock of seeing the University of South Carolina's biggest booster in the Windy City. Like an embarrassed relative, he led Big Daddy a few feet away from the locker room to minimize the scene the old geezer was about to make.

"Told you last summer at the golf tourney I'd get up here to see you play one of these years," said Big Daddy. "You're playing great as ever, boy."

Big Daddy called all the black players at South Carolina "boy" and the white guys "young man." Back when Deon was a freshman, the coaches told him to laugh it off. You didn't cross Big Daddy Callahan. He was the biggest man in Columbia, literally and figuratively. He was also the reason most of the athletes worth anything came to USC. Having Big Daddy on your side meant you got things the regular student body only dreamt about and you also got out of any trouble you found yourself in, as long as the press didn't get there first. These days, Deon only saw Big Daddy at alumni functions and at the annual charity golf tournament the tobacco baron co-sponsored with Jimmy Herman.

"Not a good time, Big Daddy. The press is waiting. League rules say I gotta talk to them." Deon turned away, but Big Daddy stepped with him.

"You get my telegram, D.A., wishing you good luck?"

"Sure, thanks, see ya down home."

"And how 'bout Senator Herman's? You get his?"

"Probably." Deon feigned uncertainty. If Big Daddy Callahan was the Gamecocks' biggest fan, Jimmy Herman was a close runner-up. They were also the best of friends and like Siamese twins when it came to worshipping Deon. They would also sooner join the Nazi party before they believed the rumors about him.

"Say, how's your golf game?" asked Big Daddy. "Jimmy and I can't wait to have you back at the tournament this year. You will be there, won't you?"

"Most likely." Deon shrugged. It was for charity, hell, and he never turned down a game of golf.

"Say, I was wondering...."

Here it comes, thought Deon, all too familiar with the voice of someone who wanted something from him.

"Any chance you might get some other athletes to come with you? Say Larry Bird or Brett Favre? Or maybe the white kid on your team from Utah, Kersey Stevens? We figure we need another athlete and we have you to represent the black—excuse me—Afro-American community."

Deon shook his head and glanced at the Lovabull cheerleaders streaming into their dressing room farther down the hall. If it weren't for the little black kids who benefited, Callahan could shove his tournament up his fat white ass.

"Gotta go, Big Daddy," he said, walking to the locker room door and opening it halfway. "Playoff time. That's all that's on my mind."

"But, Deon, boy—"

"Let me tell you something, Big Daddy." He looked him squarely in the eye. "If you want me or Kersey or anybody else in the athletic world at your golf tournament ever again, you'll erase the word 'boy' from the microchip in your brain, you hear me? If I *ever* have a black Gamecock recruit *ever* tell me you or any other alumni called them boy, I'm like this with SC." He ran his finger across his throat as if to slash it, and with that, he flung the locker room door open and left Big Daddy standing there alone, his purpose for visiting Chicago unfulfilled.

HOME, ESPECIALLY AFTER a game, was a peaceful oasis for Deon. From the moment he walked in the door, his muscles began to relax. And by the time he was out of his pinstripe suit, into some well-worn Hanes sweats and plopped down on the couch in the den, dozing to ESPN's *SportsCenter,* the aches and pains of another night on the court were becoming but a memory.

Few souls penetrated his penthouse on the north side of Chicago. Both Deon's parents were dead, Mom minutes after she gave birth to her only daughter, who was stillborn, and Dad a week after his only son signed his first multi-million dollar contract with the Bulls. Save a few distant aunts, uncles and cousins who were experts at calling him collect and giving him a sob story, he was familyless. Except for his baby.

"Here you go, sugar." Charlie sauntered out of the kitchen carrying a large frosty mug, his green silk kimono flapping in the breeze created by his gait, which was all hips and ass. "A strawberry protein smoothie, just like you like it."

"Ah, yes, with a victory." Deon planted a long kiss on his Charlie's ass as Charlie sat the mug on the glass coffee table.

"Don't be falling asleep to these highlights now," Charlie warned with his soft but husky voice as he sat down. "You know what I need tonight."

"A *slaaaaam dunk,*" Deon said. Charlie daintily covered his mouth with his hand and made a face as if he were shocked by such crassness.

Although he was by no means muscular or stocky, Charlie wasn't nearly as small as Deon's last and only other lover. At five-ten, Charlie would have towered over Jerome, but just like J-Boy, Charlie was dark skinned, rail thin, ultra smooth and a bit feminine. Actually, quite a bit feminine. Charlie could act sissified with the best of them, only with Charlie it wasn't acting. It was a way of life. It was also a way of life for Charlie to sometimes become Charlene.

That was what got him kicked out of his house in the projects of

Chicago when he was fifteen. That was also how Deon first saw him eight years ago, when basketball's newest millionaire came to town to meet and greet the city. After the festivities, Deon slipped out of his hotel room, hopped in his rented Mercedes and cruised down Madison near the stadium—long before the city cleaned up the neighborhood and ran the hookers elsewhere. That night, on a dark corner a few blocks down from where he was about to become one of the biggest sports legends of all time, The D.A. saw what he immediately recognized to be the boy and girl of his dreams peddling his wares. They spent the weekend in Deon's hotel and began living together when Deon moved to Chicago a few months later. Cinderella and Julia Roberts had nothing on Charlie/Charlene Dubois.

J-Boy, Deon's last lover, hadn't been so lucky. Jerome died in the early days of the plague, back when Deon was only a college all-American and didn't have enough money to help with J-Boy's medical bills. That was one thing that was going to be different when Charlie got sick. If Charlie got sick.

"Isn't that what they call traveling?" Charlie asked now, pointing to the TV and a highlight from the Knicks-Magic game.

"Nooooo," Deon said laughingly.

"Well, what's traveling then? Oh, never mind," he said with a flip of his wrist. "I'll never understand this or any other game you sweaty grown men play."

"That's 'cause you don't want to." Deon leaned over and kissed his neck just as the phone rang. Charlie was the closer of the two and lunged for the cordless on the coffee table, then handed it to the owner of the house.

"Deon Anthony," said the voice on the other end. "It's Jasper."

"How'd you get my number?"

"CNC has everybody's number." There was a pause while Jasper waited for a laugh, which wasn't forthcoming. "Anyway, just calling to wish you good luck in the playoffs, nothing more."

"You sure?" asked Deon.

"Absolutely. Tell me: you think you're going to go all the way this year?"

"Why should this year be any different?" Deon said jokingly and waited for Jasper's laughter, which wasn't forthcoming.

"No." Jasper paused. "I want to know if you really and truly think you're going to go all the way this year. All the way."

Suddenly Deon realized Jasper wasn't talking about the playoffs, but the Temple and Othello. "I don't know," he stammered, feeling Charlie's eyes resting on him. "I can't say. Because I don't know."

"Well, good luck, anyway. Of course, I'm rooting for the Knicks."

"Think you'll go all way?"

"Unsure, very unsure." There was a long pause as both of them waited for something more from the other end of the line. "Well, good luck."

"You, too," said Deon.

Jasper hung up the phone and settled back in the plush leather chair in the smoking room of his penthouse atop Hollinquest Towers, once again feeling relaxation envelop his feet as Bruce gently massaged them while sitting on the carpet.

"I didn't know you knew him, but I guess I should have figured," Bruce said, more consumed in his task than his comment.

"Just calling him to schmooze," Jasper said, arching his head back and closing his eyes.

"Think Senator Herman will fall for it?" Bruce asked absently. Taken aback, Jasper slowly reared his head to glare at Bruce, but all he saw was a thick mass of dirty blond hair falling downward.

"Fall for what?" Jasper asked cautiously.

The seriousness of Jasper's voice caused Bruce to look up and shrug. "I assumed you might be trying to get Deon Anthony to use his influence with Herman because Herman is head of the Senate Foreign Relations Committee. You know, from one good ol' Carolina boy to another, approve of Ambassador-elect Middleton, help my friend Jasper with his cash cow."

Jasper eyed Bruce suspiciously, studying his unassuming baby face, a face that would earn him the label pretty boy long past twenty-five. Then, after a prolonged pause, a Cheshire cat grin wiped across Jasper's face.

"Don't ever let them say I didn't hire you for your brains," said Jasper, prompting Bruce to smile as he continued his foot massage.

The kid's all right, Jasper thought, remembering that unathletic but toned eighteen-year-old who came to spend a month with him at his Maui ranch.

Back then, Bruce was just one of several young men he kept around the world, no more or less special than the boys in Martinique, Mykinos or the villa in Cannes. But Bruce had ambition. He was on his way to the University of Missouri for journalism and wasn't afraid to talk politics and business with Jasper. "I'm gonna be the male Barbara Walters," he kept telling Jasper in between moonlit romps in the Pacific surf. Now, seven years later, he was Jasper's most steady boy and a fledging reporter for CNC, a job he received only because he was truly qualified.

"So you think it will work?" Bruce asked, moving behind his boss and massaging his shoulders. "Does The D.A. have that much influence?"

Jasper sighed. "It's a long shot. I don't expect anything from it."

Bruce only understood part of the link. In truth, Jasper didn't need Deon to talk to Jimmy Herman. What he needed was for Herman to stop holding up the president's ambassadorial appointments in an effort to promote the senator's ultra-Christian, right-wing agenda. Months ago, Herman had vowed that, unless the White House and Capitol Hill passed tougher abortion laws and drastically decreased AIDS funding, the long-time chair of the Senate Foreign Relations Committee would block all appointments by grinding committee business to a halt. Thirty ambassadorial nominees were still awaiting confirmation and Herman wasn't budging. Fifteen percent of the country's embassies were without ambassadors.

There was one country in particular that Jasper cared about: Belize and its dozens of miles of tropical beaches owned by Hollinquest, Inc. The current regime in the fledging Central American paradise was fighting his development plans, which stood to make Jasper billions. Which is why his old pal Arnie Middleton was soon to be Ambassador Middleton. As soon as Herman stopped playing games with the Senate Foreign Relations Committee.

"Maybe I can do a story and publicize Herman's tactics," offered Bruce.

"I'll keep that in mind." Jasper closed his eyes and wondered how far Othello intended to go with this gay uprising. More importantly, he wondered if he should dare involve himself in it.

Feeling a sudden shot of restlessness, he rose up and went over to the floor-length window, staring at the millions of lights glittering in the Manhattan night. He knew the skyline well, the tourist traps, his own hotels, his rivals' buildings where he loved to imagine bleary-eyed executives staying up half the night trying to figure how to keep up with Hollinquest, Incorporated. And no matter how many times he stood at that window and surveyed the city he'd spent his entire life in, his gaze always seemed to roam toward the woodsy cruise haven in Central Park known as the Ramble. In his college days at Columbia, he was a regular there, sometimes looking to receive a midnight blowjob, sometimes eager for the scent of another man's cock, sometimes fucking, standing up, of course, pants around the ankles. And only at night, too, in the darkest recesses of the park. Darkest and most dangerous, but that's how he had to play it.

Those days seemed like a lifetime ago, before he owned a single piece of property, before the Cable News Corporation, before he was more than just one of New York's scions, running around the city with all the other rich kids, spending the money his family had made from the shipping business. A lifetime ago, indeed, but no matter what, those nights at the park would always be with him, for better and for worse.

He fingered the crook in his nose and glared at the black hole that was Central Park by night, remembering what very well may have been the worst period in his life. Then, in an effort to banish the memories flooding toward his conscious, he turned away from the window, vowing to someday break his addiction to dwelling on the past.

THICK BLACK SMOKE shot out of the exhaust pipes of the four white twenty-foot-long moving trucks lined up in pairs at the end of the alley, their engines revving, their steady roar breaking the silence of an otherwise quiet, overcast Sunday afternoon in suburbia. At the other end of the alley, four more trucks were positioned in the same way, and in between sat two maroon minivans. Scattered among all the vehicles were a dozen ACTNOW members, conferring with each other on last-minute details, checking maps and distributing the black hoods they were each about to don to go with their black outfits.

Near the middle of the alley, Othello huddled in the back doorway of a warehouse, pretending to scratch his fake beard but in reality checking it for the tenth time in as many minutes to make sure it was properly secured. Being here in Simi Valley—a right wing haven forty miles north of LA—was the biggest gamble he'd ever taken dressed as the old man Joe. But this was a must. For several reasons.

Pushing up the prescriptionless glasses on his nose, he glanced both ways down the alley, searching but not finding what he was looking for. The other ACTNOW members knew he was there, but were too caught up in the operation to care, reminding him of those Navy commercials where military personnel ran around the deck of a large carrier, preparing to launch some hi-tech aircraft.

Since it was one of the reasons he was there, the main reason supposedly, he made a mental note of who had enough fire in them to be a part of this escalation of the war. Of course, Travis and Freedom were there, along with Georgio, the former porno star, and the dyke couple who looked like twins with their matching short hair and plump bodies. At the last meeting, Othello had overheard them being called Liz and Beth. Beth was older, forty-something to Liz's thirty-something. He didn't know the names of the other members there, so to remember them, he gave them each a moniker based on a characteristic of theirs. The bearded white man in his thirties who always came to the meetings in overalls became Overalls; the young black woman who often dressed in African regalia was Afro. The heavyset black guy with dreadlocks who constantly talked about burning things became Rasta, and the short, bald man in his fifties who was always full of fiery rhetoric was now dubbed Sparkplug. The young queeny Asian in the short black cutoffs he decided to call Miss Saigon, and the butch fellow in his forties with the huge bushy mustache and cockney accent became English. The white preppie man who often showed up to the meetings still wearing his business suit was, what else? Business Suit.

But there was one person missing. Othello surveyed the alley again, then made his way over to Travis who was with Georgio, placing cardboard over the license plates of the vans. "Have you seen him?" Othello asked in his scratchy old man's voice.

"We're all accounted for," Travis said without looking up.

"Not Raider."

Travis looked around hastily. "He was at the strategy meetings, but it's all right. We'll still have enough people. Liz and Beth were going to ride together, but Beth will just take his place."

"Did he say he would be here?"

"No time, Joe." He held Othello by the shoulders. "Now, make sure you stay back and way out of harm's way. No one will be able to help if you get into trouble." Without waiting for a response, Travis took off for the far end of the alley.

Dejected, Othello retreated from Georgio and the vans, searching for Raider and replaying in his mind the meeting with Travis at ACTNOW's headquarters a week ago.

"The hospital thing was good," Othello had told him. "The old lady was impressed." He then handed Travis another $7,000. "But she wants to see something more radical. She says take this money, find out who's willing to go beyond Mercy and show her more."

"How about showing her how we can screw up the Assemblyman Weeks fund-raiser?" Travis had said, and when the leader of ACTNOW told Othello about the plan, Othello decided to watch in person from afar to judge for himself the best candidates for putting a bullet into Jimmy Herman's head. He also told Travis about the new member of the group who showed promise, Raider Kincaide, and admonished him to recruit Raider for Simi Valley.

But Raider was a no-show and Othello could kick himself for checking the impulse to simply show up at Raider's apartment and reveal his true identity, an impulse he'd had hourly for the last week. But the rational side of this brain had told him to hold out, test Raider in the rebel department. Now, as Othello stood alone in the alley, he was beginning to deeply regret ever having a rational side of his brain.

"People, let's roll!" Travis shouted as he ran down the alley toward the vans. The plan was simple enough. Eight trucks. Seven en-

trances to the Hacienda Hotel, site of the Re-elect Arnold Weeks Dinner. Two trucks block the main entrance; the other six cover the other
doors. Each driver was to lodge his or her truck at the designated
entrance, then run like hell to the getaway vans waiting at either end
of the hotel. On the back of each truck was a sign that said: WARNING:
BOMB ON BOARD. By the time the bomb squad discovered this to be
untrue and the trucks were removed, it would be too late for breaded
chicken for the disciples of Assemblyman Weeks.

All the drivers got in their vehicles and pulled their hoods over
their heads. Travis, standing on the running board of his van, waved
them away. The trucks took off in both directions. Travis then
plopped down in the van and gave Joe a thumbs up and a smile.
Trying to hide his disappointment, Othello gave him a military salute
in return, but was interrupted when he noticed someone racing down
the alley toward them. It was Raider, Othello realized, his heart coming back to life. The man from Nantucket was truly a rebel after all.
He was twenty feet away now, flagging down Travis and Othello, filling Othello's head with visions of the Dartmouth lacrosse legend in
his heyday, his thick legs churning down the field, his sweat-soaked
jersey pressed against his steely chest, the sides flapping in the wind
flying past him as he charged through hapless competitors, face
straining with both ecstasy and agony, all-Ivy League glory just seconds away.

But in this case, Othello and Travis were just seconds away, and
Raider, a few years removed from his all-Ivy League days, reached
them slightly winded.

"Got lost," he said, trying to catch his breath. In reality, he'd gone
down to San Diego last night, desperate for a break from West
Hollywood and wanting to get laid. Mission accomplished, with some
blonde he met in a bar near the beach, but the traffic back to
Fairyland had been hell.

"We're covered," Travis said from the van. "You stay with Joe,
make sure he's all right. Glad you made it anyway." Then Travis, seeing the last of the trucks disappear, took off, leaving Othello and
Raider alone in the alley.

"Thank God you made it," Othello said, the smile on his face showing his relief. Still out of breath, Raider put his hands on his hips and flashed his own toothy grin that said: here we go again with this guy.

The street to the north of the alley was desolate, the mostly industrial buildings lining the two-lane road all closed for the weekend. Unlike the trucks, which were taking a circuitous route, Othello and Raider headed straight for the hotel a few blocks away.

"You really had me worried," Othello said as they walked, "but I'm glad to see you want to do this."

"No way was I gonna pass this up," Raider said, remembering how Travis had taken him aside at the last meeting and told him about this little shindig for some local politician. "Anything to bust their asses," Raider had said to Little Horse, jumping at the chance to gain his confidence.

"I'm also hoping we can..." Othello racked his brain for the right words: "well, get started on a better foot as far as getting to know each other—that is, so I can show you I'm not just some old pervert lusting after your body."

"Yeah?" Raider said, sounding unconvinced. "Then why did we need to go somewhere more private than that park?"

"For our friendship...." Othello paused.

"Yeah...and...."

"And...." Othello stopped. To say more than friendship meant risking Raider becoming angry as he had at Mercy. And so Othello fell silent, which only served as further incrimination. As if he'd scored a point in some game, Raider flashed a knowing grin.

"Let's just do our part for gay rights today, Joe, okay?" Raider said, then turned the corner onto a street that was full of more life than the previous, a street more commercial than industrial with small one-story storefronts and a steady stream of traffic flowing in both directions. When Othello had caught up to him, Raider asked: "So why aren't you in there today, driving and stopping the bigots yourself?"

"My reflexes aren't what they used to be. But I had to at least see it."

Bullshit, Raider said to himself laughingly. One thing had

become instinctively clear: ol' man Joe was no innocent bystander in all this. He had to be more than that to be a one-man cheering section for these wannabe terrorists today. Maybe even Joe's rich old fag hag was in on this with Othello. Maybe Joe was reporting back to both.

"Something I don't understand, Joe," he said. "I know we wanna mess with this fund-raiser and all, but why not just phone in a bomb threat to the hotel?"

"Bomb threats aren't going to get you on *American Diary* or even in our own gay papers anymore." said Othello. "We gotta be big. Even bigger than this."

"This Weeks guy anyway—is he that bad? We don't hear much about him back in Nantucket."

"Arnold Weeks is a canker sore on California politics. Once he showed porno tapes of guys into scat in the assembly to show how disgusting and perverted gays are. Another time, he tried to make it a felony for people with HIV to have sex. With anyone. Safe or unsafe."

"What's wrong with that?"

Othello stopped and froze, and after a few more steps, Raider noticed and also stopped, then turned to him.

"What's wrong with making a law saying HIV positive people can't have sex?" Othello asked in disbelief. "How about the right to privacy? How about the fact that an HIV person can have just as much sex as anyone else, only he or she should practice safe sex *as we all should.*"

"Okay, okay, don't get so riled up—"

"I am not riled up! I'm just shocked at your...what kind of things go on back there on that fantasy island you're from?"

"All I know is, the thought of getting AIDS scares the crap outta me. That's the single most thing I think about when I think about—not that I think about...." Raider checked himself, too many things going on in his head all at once. "I mean, aren't you terrified of getting AIDS?"

For a moment, the only sound between them was the passing traffic. Othello turned to the storefront next to him, a closed cleaners. His boyfriend was slipping away before he even got a chance to reveal himself. And Raider hadn't come to ACTNOW because he was positive and needed to fight for his life; that much was evident now.

"Who isn't terrified?" Othello turned to Raider. "But if you only play safe, you won't get it. Period. Everything Arnold Weeks does comes from hate. And ignorance. Why can't you and I have safe sex— that is, assuming we would both want to and say you or I were positive?

"I don't know." Raider shrugged and stuffed his hands into his pockets. A bus roared by, causing him to pause and turn toward the street. "Sometimes I wish all the people with AIDS were forced to get some kind of tattoo, a little one, say right where your crotch meets your waistline. That way, when you strip down for sex, you see that and you know for sure who has it."

And Othello would have one of those little scarlet tattoos and Raider would run away from him faster than he ever ran on the playing fields of Dartmouth.

Othello remained silent. How could a fellow gay man be so insensitive? How could life be so cruel? To dangle a dreamy god in front of his face, inject said god with lust for Othello's true identity, then rip him away with poison and fear. Wasn't anything ever plain and easy? "We better step it up," he mumbled, bent on avoiding further debate. They began walking again, this time a little faster, and Othello tried to reassure himself that all this Nantucket boy needed was a good dose of safe sex education, then sex, unbridled, sweaty and passionate. How could they not fall in love then?

The Hacienda Hotel was on Meridian Boulevard, a busy four-lane, divided thoroughfare that cut an east-west path through the heart of the Simi Valley business district. At eight stories, the hotel was the largest building for several blocks and sat back off the street, completely surrounded by parking lots. The front of the hotel was bustling now. Cadillacs, Chevy Blazers and Jeep Cherokees pulled up to the valet parking attendants. Excited middle-aged couples were getting out in formal wear. In the lot between the hotel and the street, still more couples were parking for themselves and heading toward the gala, ready to honor their symbol of traditional family values at $250 a head. Six hundred guests were expected. Several dozen were already gathered around the front of the hotel.

When Othello and Raider reached the T intersection where

Meridian met the driveway that led to hotel, Othello halted abruptly. "This is as close as I can get," he said with trepidation as he stood directly across the street from the hotel. "I shouldn't even be this close."

He mumbled this last bit to himself, but Raider heard him anyway and eyed Joe for a moment as the old man sat down at the adjacent bus stop. "Damn, wish I was in there," Raider said, looking at the hotel, making sure Joe heard him.

"If we play our cards right, maybe we'll both have our day. Together."

Raider looked at him unassuredly, but before there was time for further reaction, a diesel-powered rumble permeated the air, causing them both to turn toward the road.

The eight trucks rolled past them, their occupants sporting black leather hoods. Sparkplug, the short bald man in his fifties, was in the lead truck, followed by Rasta, the black man, Afro, the black woman, Liz, Georgio, Overalls, Beth, and Freedom. The vans were already in place on either side of the hotel, Travis and Miss Saigon in one, English and Business Suit in the other.

Othello stood up. The trucks were coming from the west and needed to make a left turn to enter the hotel's driveway. The light was green with an arrow. Three cars in front of the trucks made the turn, followed by Sparkplug, Rasta and Afro. The light turned yellow. Speeding up a bit, Liz and Georgio made it through. Too quickly, the light turned red. Two cars in the oncoming lane took off as soon as they got the green light; but because Overalls, Beth and Freedom had to keep up with the others, they all made the turn anyway. The cars had to slam on the brakes, almost smashing into the trucks driven by Beth and Freedom. The screeching caused the banquet-goers in the parking lots to take notice of the street, then the sight of eight white trucks caravanning toward the hotel.

"Ready or not," Othello murmured, moving toward the edge of the sidewalk.

When they came within fifty feet of the hotel, the first four trucks—piloted by Sparkplug, Rasta, Afro and Liz—broke off and headed for the four back and side entrances. The last four trucks—

driven by Georgio, Overalls, Beth and Freedom—turned to the right and headed straight for the front of the hotel.

"Time to kick some conservative butt," said Raider.

Georgio and Overalls were going about forty when they reached the valet parking area directly in front of the hotel, looking as if they were about to smash into the line of cars waiting to valet park. Several of the parking staff and guests dove out of the way. Then Georgio steered onto the sidewalk and slammed on the brakes, leaving the grill of his truck inches away from the six glass doors that made up the main entrance. Overalls did the same, coming to a stop next to Georgio and forming a V with their two trucks underneath the hotel's concrete canopy.

"Pay dirt!" declared Othello.

With similar precision, the scenario was repeated around the building, at the single-door entrance on the far side of the hotel, at two entrances in the back, including a service entrance, and another side entrance to the hotel bar. Out front, Beth was coming to a stop in front of the hotel restaurant entrance to the left of the main entrance while Overalls and Georgio jumped out of their trucks and took off running—Overalls to the left, Georgio to the right—as the crowd looked on with confusion.

"Faster," Othello said, then turned his attention to Freedom's truck, which was seconds away from a single set of double doors twenty feet to the right of the main entrance.

Freedom Clark decided a week ago he wasn't just going to park his truck and run off like a wuss. As he headed toward the entrance, he sped up, then gave the wheel a hard jerk to the left before jamming on the brakes with both feet. The truck fishtailed 180 degrees as it hurdled toward the building. Freedom then threw his entire weight on the brake, rising out of his seat as he did, his hands still choking the wheel, his face locked in a grimace. The back of the truck collided with the set of double glass doors, finally coming to rest five feet inside the hotel amidst shattered glass and tangled metal.

"A perfect ten from the Romanian judge!" Freedom cried out.

He's practiced that, Othello thought to himself, not sure if he was horrified or proud.

With a triumphant yelp, Freedom jumped out of the truck. "Take that, bigots!" he shouted at the crowd of shocked guests twenty feet away. "Down with fascism! Down with fascism!" he repeated over and over, getting louder and louder each time. The crowd began to congregate near the valet parking drop-off and most were beginning to understand that they were under siege.

"What is he doing?" Othello tried to get a better look but was too far away. Traffic was brisk, but he had about fifteen feet before the next car passed him. Hastily, he limped across the street, barely beating a convertible sports car speeding past. Immediately, Raider darted across and joined him. Not wanting to press his luck, Othello stopped on the median strip, which was three feet wide, and watched from there as Freedom seemed to inch closer and closer toward the crowd, taunting them with his fists until Georgio, who was running by on his way to the getaway van, grabbed Freedom by the neck of his black tu tleneck and tried to drag him to the van thirty yards away.

"Get in the goddamn car, Freedom," Othello said, then looked around to see how the others were doing. In the van to the left of the hotel—powered by Travis and Miss Saigon—Afro, Liz and Overalls were jumping in one after another. In the van on the right, English was holding the door open as Rasta and Sparkplug dove in while Business Suit sat anxiously behind the wheel, foot ready to pounce on the accelerator.

"Get your bloody asses in here!" English yelled to Freedom and Georgio.

"The van'll take off without 'em," said Raider. "That was the deal."

"If everyone would just do as planned, this would be over with," Othello said, the fear for his own safety growing by the minute.

"They're gonna leave us!" Georgio told Freedom as he struggled with him. "Where's your head?"

"Fuck you!" Freedom said to Georgio, then repeated it to the crowd, then flipped them off and turned toward the van, his tirade apparently over.

"Go home, you pervert!" suddenly came from a tall thin man who stood above most of the crowd.

Astonished, Freedom swung back around, took one good look at the man, recognized him, then exploded, telling the crowd how some-day he was going to blow every last one of their fucking heads off and trying to yank off his hood which was getting in the way of his anger. When Georgio saw this, he made a valiant effort to restrain Freedom, pulling him toward the van by his belt and repeatedly knocking Freedom's arms away from his hood, which was halfway off now.

The man in the crowd seemed to relish Freedom's reaction and began hurling insults back, prompting some of the others in the crowd to do the same, some of them even throwing cans and bits of trash at Freedom and Georgio.

"This isn't supposed to be happening," Othello pleaded, not expecting this much trouble when he decided to be part of this day.

The van to the right—the one that Freedom and Georgio should have been in by now—started moving forward steadily, then made a sharp U-turn and headed toward the back exit as planned. The sound of burning rubber prompted Georgio to give up on Freedom and make a run for the van. Then, when he realized he was about to be stranded, Freedom flipped one last bird toward the crowd and took off. Forty yards later, the van slowed down just enough for both men to jump inside, then sped off to catch up with the other van, which was already halfway down the street that bordered the back of the hotel.

Othello breathed a sigh of relief and leaned against the light pole on the median strip, but his respite was short-lived.

"That girl," Raider said, pointing to the left side of the hotel.

On the ground, next to the truck lodged in the entrance to the hotel restaurant, was Beth, the older of the lesbian couple. She was sit-ting upright, holding onto her ankle and rocking back and forth. Three of the valet parking attendants were standing over her, and now that The Freedom Show was over, many of the banquet-goers joined them, forming a curious and uneasy circle around her.

"Raider, we've got to help her," said Othello.

"You know the rules," Raider said. "Anyone who gets caught gets caught, and as long they don't implicate ACTNOW, we'll bail 'em out."

The crowd was getting larger and larger, some of them gesturing angrily toward Beth.

"After what Freedom did, they'll lynch her," said Othello. "She doesn't deserve that. Plus, your showing up late split up her and her lover."

Just then, a tall man waded through the crowd and up to Beth. He stood head and shoulders above the others. Othello realize he was the man who had taunted Freedom. To get a better view, he stepped on the base of the light post. The man was talking to Beth, then the group. Then he turned back to Beth and snatched her leather hood off, holding it up to the crowd and spitting out what appeared to be heated words of condemnation. When he turned toward the direction of the street, Othello realized who the man was.

"That's Arnold Weeks doing that!" he said, his voice ripe with terror.

Raider took a good look at Joe, saw that this was as good a chance as any to score points with ACTNOW and took off across the street, dashing through traffic and racing toward the angry mob, leaving Othello alone on the island, helpless to do anything but stand and watch.

"This lady," —Arnold Weeks turned a scornful eye to Beth—"*if* you can call her that, is the antithesis of American family values! She and her immoral cronies are the kind of indecent filth I seek to protect our children from." The crowd, which now numbered at least fifty, murmured in agreement, their choruses swelling until Raider reached them and yelled:

"Everybody step back!" He then proceeded to make his way through the human barricade. "Security," he said, flashing the inside of his wallet too quickly for anybody to notice what was truly inside. "There'll be no more violence on top of what's already happened. Back up. The law is on its way." When he reached Beth, he knelt down and asked: "Can you walk?"

"If it's out of here, I can," she promised. Raider helped her up, then acted as her crutch and began leading her through the crowd.

"Sick dyke," said a man's voice.

"Pervert!" said a female's tearful voice.

"Disperse I said!" Raider paused to glare at the crowd, which stared back unassuredly. Decisively, he began walking again with Beth in tow.

"Where are you taking her?" came from Arnold Weeks as the crowd began to part, letting Raider and Beth through.

"I'm holding her across the street until the police get here so none of you does anything you'll regret later on."

"I want her right here for the media to see," said Weeks.

"So a riot can start?" Raider kept walking. "Is that what you want, innocent people—your people—getting hurt, going to jail?" To that, the politician had no response save clenching the hood in his fist and gritting his teeth. Then, just when Raider and Beth were about to clear the crowd, a young black man came running up to them, clad in what looked like a black hotel security blazer.

"You don't work for us," he informed Raider. "Let me see some ID."

"I can run if I have to," Beth whispered too loudly under her breath.

"He's no security," Arnold Weeks decided. "He's one of them queers!"

Raider swung around to Weeks, instinctively ready to kick his ass, but then he noticed the suddenly suspicious faces of the white suburbanites in front of him.

"You're a faggot, aren't you, boy?" Weeks asked, realizing he was getting to Raider. Still clutching onto Beth, Raider scanned the crowd, sensing the changing tide. Then, before he could think of what to do next, a red-headed, freckled-faced teenage boy spoke out from the vicinity of Beth's truck:

"A bomb." With a surreal calmness, he pointed to the sign on the back. "There's a bomb on this here truck."

All hell broke loose in every direction. The air was filled with shrieking and screaming. The crowd took off, away from the trucks, the direction for most being toward the street, which provided the farthest distance from the impending explosions. Raider grabbed Beth's hand and made a break for it, losing himself in the panic-stricken crowd but still hearing cries of "get 'em!" and "don't let them get away!"

Othello, who was stranded on the median strip, was unable to hear what had transpired. He had no idea why Raider, a hobbling Beth, the valet parking attendants and seemingly the entire throng of right-wingers were stampeding straight toward him. His first split-second reaction was that it had something to do with them all finding out his true identity. Then he realized that was beyond illogical. But they were still coming. He turned to run back across the street, momentarily forgetting that he was in the middle of it. He stepped off the median strip to find a pick-up truck speeding toward him. With a nanosecond to spare, the truck swerved to avoid him but sideswiped a compact car in the next lane, sending both vehicles careening toward the sidewalk. The compact met a telephone pole, the truck a row of newspaper boxes just ahead of that. Stunned, Othello jumped back onto the median strip.

Surrounded by the mob, Raider and Beth raced for the street, unsure of who was after them and who was merely trying to escape being blown to bits. Once out of the hotel driveway, the crowd ignored the light and spilled out onto the intersection, adding to the confusion caused by the accident. Oncoming cars began breaking left and right to avoid hitting masses of bodies, causing fender benders and more chaos.

As the crowd began to reach the middle of the intersection, Othello was at a loss for what to do. Then he saw Raider and Beth coming and decided to hold out for them. "Get me out of here," he pleaded when they reached him. Raider grabbed him by his jacket and herded him and Beth toward the other side of the street. To get across as quickly as possible, they split up to weave through the maze of traffic, which was at a standstill now with dozens of drivers out of their cars, looking around or attending to the crash victims. When they reached the sidewalk, Raider yelled for them to break right. Othello followed but lost sight of Beth.

"Raider!" Othello shouted as they ran. "Where's Beth?"

Raider stopped and quickly scanned the sidewalk, noticing that the people running their way were more concerned with their own safety rather than Raider or Joe. In the distance, near the newspaper stands, he spotted Beth, taking off on a motorcycle that was parked next to a smashed-up truck. As Raider saw her, so did the poor sap who owned the bike, a long-haired hippie in a fringed jacket. Must have been helping out with the accident and abandoned his Yamaha.

Now, he was chasing it down the street and losing the race.

"She's covered." Raider pointed her out to Joe, making a quick mental note to admire her guts and laugh about the poor sap later. "C'mon," he then said, wanting to save the old man from getting caught in all this.

Before they could take another step, the sound of sirens pierced the air, momentarily paralyzing them until Othello saw Arnold Weeks crossing the street thirty feet away, looking like a man on a mission.

"What are we waiting for?" Othello took off, sprinting down the block as fast as he could. "Weeks is back there," he said when Raider caught up with him a few seconds later. Raider glanced back to see the assemblyman running their way along with the black security guard who had tried to bust him. They were about a block away, but with all the banquet-goers and onlookers on the sidewalk, Raider wasn't sure if he and Joe had been spotted. They ran anyway, past restaurants and office buildings, faster than most of the people around them. They came to a corner, ducked around it and stopped. After a couple of deep breaths, Raider peeked out. Weeks and the guard had slowed down but hadn't given up.

"Still on our trail," Raider said, and he and Othello took off down the block. It was a short one. At the next intersection, they broke left and were now running down another long boulevard parallel to the scene of the crime. Darkened mom-and-pop businesses lined this avenue, which was like a ghost town compared to the chaos one street over. Raider saw that as bad. Weeks and the guard would spot them immediately. The block was long, too, no easy outlets in sight.

"Our best way. out is up," he decided, stopping and pointing to the roof above a check cashing store which was closed. "I'll climb up, then pull you up."

Othello nodded, as if he had a choice. Raider, star athlete that he used to be, scaled the building in no time: right foot on the window ledge of the check cashing store, left foot up higher between a crack in the brick wall. Then, because the check cashing store had a large sign over it that stood in his way, he pulled himself up over the awning hanging over the pet store next door, then onto the roof. "Hurry," he then ordered Othello.

Othello glanced each way down the sidewalk, took a deep breath for courage, then began the same steps Raider had taken: right foot on the window ledge, left foot up higher between a crack in the brick wall. Then he heaved himself up on the awning, amazed at how easy it was. But just as he stood up, ready to step from the awning to the roof, the tattered fabric gave way, ripping and sending Othello straight down as if he had fallen through a trap door. Raider, who had his back turned, plotting their next move, swung around when he heard Othello's yelp, simultaneously extending his hand and diving for Othello's wrist. He caught it as he landed stomach down on the roof, which left Othello hanging in midair, the ground a few feet below him.

"Hold on—Joe—!" Raider grunted.

Othello's body twisted side-to-side in midair. When he twisted to the right, he saw Weeks and the guard at the intersection half a block away. They were flagging down a police car with their backs to Othello. "Over—there—!" he cried through a strained voice.

"Don't—let—go—!" Raider used every ounce of muscle in his right bicep to lift Othello inch by grueling inch until Othello was able to get a foot on top of the awning's railing. Othello then hurled himself over the edge of the roof, unintentionally collapsing on top of Raider in a sooty cloud of dust. They lay there, catching their breath in the missionary position, Othello noting how hard and massive Raider's body felt underneath his own and Raider realizing he'd never felt more awkward in his entire life.

The moment only lasted a few beats. Hastily, Othello rolled off Raider, and lying on his stomach, sneaked a peek at the street below. Weeks, the guard and the police car were coming down the street, their motions telling Othello they were trying to figure out which way to go.

"Joe, over here," Raider whispered urgently from the opposite edge of the roof. A fire ladder provided an easy escape down the back of the building. Once on the ground, they ran three blocks down the alleyway, then carved their way though a series of residential streets before ending up on a deserted dead-end road behind a physical plant. Out of danger, they came to a stop, keeling over and gasping for air.

"I can't tell you how much you saved my life," Othello said, leaning against a tall cement wall and grabbing his chest.

Still out of breath, Raider held himself up by clutching onto a chain-link fence ten yards across from the old man. Then, opportunity knocked. "Oh, I think there's a lot you can tell me, Mr. Joe The Gardener."

"What do you mean?" Othello asked.

"I mean I want to know who the hell you are."

Othello felt his eyes widen, praying they wouldn't betray him.

"You claim to be this old man, but you sure as hell run like a young buck."

Othello tried to collect himself. "When you're scared you'll run like the world's fastest athlete."

"Not when you're pushing whatever age you claim to be pushing."

"I'm not claiming anything. I was scared. I ran."

"I'm not buying it, Joe!"

"We don't even know if Beth is okay, let alone everybody else, and you're questioning my running?"

Raider moved toward the old man, backing him up. "I put my life on the line out there today and for what? For who? Who are you? Why are you in this? You could be some kind of cop or traitor or FBI type, trying to send me and the rest of ACTNOW up the river. Why should I trust you? Why should anybody in ACTNOW? Who the hell are you, *Joe?*"

Othello felt his heels hit the cement wall. "Let's go somewhere and discuss—"

"I'm not taking another step, here or anywhere else, until you quit lying to me. Now, I really like you, Joe, but it's beginning to piss me off that I don't even know who I'm dealing with."

"I'll tell you who you're dealing with if we could just go somewhere—"

"Nowhere, Joe, until you cough up some answers."

Othello took a long, nervous breath.

"Okay. Okay. I've been wanting to do this since the night I met you." Slowly, he removed the wire-rimmed glasses. Then the fisherman's hat. Then the nappy-haired wig, letting them all fall to the ground. "And what you did over there shows me how much guts you have." Gently, he peeled away the bushy eyebrows. "And now I'm gonna have some guts." With both hands, he rolled down the gray-tinted beard until it was all the way off. And he stood there, feeling naked and vulnerable, eyes searching Raider's for some kind of sign.

Raider had suspected Joe of some kind of deceit; but this—this was the furthest thing from Raider's mind, the last thing he expected. And now, he wasn't sure which was more unbelievable, the realization that he was standing a breath away from one of the most famous human beings in the entire world, or the fact that he had hit pay dirt in his infiltration of ACTNOW. Either way, both sensations left him shocked beyond belief, as shocked as he was when he found out Othello was gay in the first place.

SIX

THE RUSTED, TAN Impala came to a stop in front of the private entrance to the Big House. Night had fallen on the Hollywood Hills, the full moon casting a somber glow on the chaparral-filled slopes, the city lights below shimmering like millions of tiny electric stars. Waiting for the gate to open, Othello eyed the rear view mirror and tried to get a good look at Raider, whose face was lost in the reflections draping the windshield of his idling black Jeep. Othello still wasn't sure how to define Raider's reaction to seeing the real man behind the old man in Simi Valley well over an hour ago.

"Aren't you going to say anything?" Othello had asked, still backed up against the wall, their faces inches apart.

"If I knew what to say I wouldn't be standing here like a zombie," Raider had said.

"This is a good thing for you?"

"Why should it be bad?"

"You can't tell a soul."

"Count on it."

"Not even ACTNOW knows about this. They think I'm just Joe."

"Oh, you're far from being just...a Joe."

They had both been consumed by nerves, speaking too fast, as if neither one could afford to pause and think. On a nearby street, a siren screamed by, followed by even more in the distance. "Had enough of Simi Valley for one day?" Othello had asked. It was then that they agreed to retreat to his fortress in the hills.

The drive back gave Othello a chance to listen to the news radio accounts of the fiasco. No one was seriously injured, no one arrested. No group had claimed responsibility for the siege, but authorities suspected any number of gay rights extremists. The cops had already linked the trucks to a rental company, but false IDs were used by the two white males renting the vehicles. Disguises may have also been worn by the two males. Police, however, were looking for a white woman who was unmasked at the scene and a blond man who some say helped her escape. There were also conflicting reports that an elderly black man was seen with them, but so far, police couldn't confirm this. Meanwhile, Assemblyman Arnold Weeks called the act cowardly and said the fund-raiser was postponed, not canceled.

When the gate finished opening, the Impala rolled up the driveway. Othello turned the radio off and tried to sort out the day's events. The good news was there were at least a dozen ACTNOW soldiers who might be willing to wage his kind of war. The overshadowing bad news was the way this particular battle played itself out, with Freedom's crazed and dangerous actions, Beth's stumble and Othello's brush with being exposed. On top of that, he wasn't even sure the whole truck idea had been a good one. Was that the best they could do? he thought, tapping on the wheel. What's it gonna take to kick some real ass?

He pulled to a stop in front of the house, his attention shifting from Simi Valley to the unsettling fact that he was about to let another human being—even if it was Raider Kincaide—into the dark, private world of his cavernous closet. Still in the old man's clothes, makeup and beer belly but without the glasses, fake hair and hands, he crawled out of the car, truly feeling the soreness of an old man, and motioned for Raider to park beside him. A few seconds later, they stood a few yards apart in the stillness of the night, as if they were two strangers coming face-to-face for the very first time. Raider still had that wide-eyed look on his face, encompassing shock, fear and awe.

"Inside," Othello said, indicating the house and leading the way without waiting for Raider to follow.

The first image Othello encountered upon entering the foyer was a disheveled Sweeney, looking like a frightened parent waiting for his child to get home after a rock concert at which there had been a riot. Instantly, Othello felt guilty for not calling to reassure his manager he was unharmed, but, well, nothing was going right today. They both started to speak, till the fear in Sweeney's eyes turned to confusion when Raider entered the picture by stepping through the door.

"We're fine," Othello offered, surprised by the "we."

But Sweeney had all kinds of panic bottled up and had to diffuse some of it. "Othello, my God, the news—"

"It's okay, Sweeney, I'm all right, physically anyway."

"Did anybody...." Sweeney stopped, eyes dancing between Othello and this stranger.

"Nobody saw me," said Othello. "As *me* anyway. Except...Raider, this is my longtime right-hand man, Sweeney. Sweeney, this is the one and only man from Nantucket."

When the two had exchanged enough awkward mumbles, Othello excused himself from Raider and led Sweeney into the hallway, waiting until they were out of earshot before starting in:

"We've got a lot of work to do. I need to get in touch with Travis Little Horse. Get me a number. And I caused an accident today. See if there's a way we can find out who the parties are and send them some anonymous cash, somehow, some way." Othello started down the hall, then, having forgotten the most important task, swung back around. "Oh, and Sweeney, get me a meeting with Hollinquest and Deon Anthony pronto. In fact, faster than pronto. In fact, I don't want to bother waiting for them to get out to LA. I'll go East. As soon as the plane can get out of here." He turned away, but Sweeney grabbed him by the arm.

"Now, O, *you* listen to *me*," he commanded in a tone usually reserved for carrying out his boss's orders to other people. "I'm worried about you. All this guerrilla activist business? Do you realize what you risked out there today?"

The mere suggestion sent a chill down Othello's spine.

"And what about your career?" Sweeney added.

"I can't think about those things right now."

"You can't think about the next single? And video? And tour dates? What about your *real* life, O?"

Othello paused, wishing he could tell Sweeney about the virus and make his manager understand his new priorities. Maybe Sweeney could even find him a doctor, something Othello knew was necessary even though he was feeling fine. But now wasn't the time for confessions. The time might never come.

"This *is* my real life now," he said, then started back down the hallway.

"And what about this guy?" Sweeney whispered harshly, prompting Othello to turn around.

"Sweeney," he began, barely suppressing an impish grin. "You are a lot of things to me and I'd hate to try to make it through a week without you; but one thing you are not is my mother." 'Nuff said, meeting adjourned, Othello pushed on.

In the foyer, Raider was staring at the skylight, seemingly for lack of anything better to do. "Is that your...boyfriend?" he asked upon seeing Othello.

"There is no boyfriend, Raider." Othello let out a mild laugh. "Sweeney is my go-to man, my manager who manages my life."

"What did you mean, 'the one and only man from Nantucket?'"

"I had Sweeney check you out. I hope you don't mind."

"What did you find out? That I'm the big bad wolf?"

"Just that you are who you say you are, a Dartmouth man from Massachusetts with an ex-wife and a kid. Only they live in DC now, right? Tell me you're not upset."

"I'm not upset," Raider said guardedly. "I've got nothing to hide."

"I have to take precautions." Looking up at the skylight, Othello let out an exhausted sigh. "People like Arnold Weeks and Jimmy Herman would kill to find out what I'm doing."

"Jimmy Herman? The senator?"

Othello lowered his head and muted the thought. "I'm tired and sweaty and I need to clean my face and get out of these geriatric clothes. How about a shower? Separate, of course."

"No thanks." Raider shifted uneasily.

"You're welcome to it. I might even have a change of—"

"Really, that's okay, really."

After an awkward pause, Othello asked: "Mind if I change?"

"It's your house."

"You'll wait?"

"I've got nowhere to go."

With that settled, Othello led him to the den off the hallway, encouraged Raider to help himself to the bar and took leave of his man from Nantucket, hoping that when he returned, they would no longer sound like a couple of bumbling junior high kids on their first date.

Once he was alone, Raider surveyed the humongous room filled with dark wood and leather and estimated "the den," as Othello had called it, to be larger than his entire condo back in DC. In the center of the room alone were four brown sofas, all framing a large coffee table the size of Delaware. The walls were lined with enough bookshelves to start a small library, except for the wall to the right, which resembled an electronics store. Opposite the doorway were floor-length glass panels, giving the whole room a backdrop of the moonlit night. Back in Nantucket, Raider's family owned and lived in the back of a seaside motel. The only way he went to Dartmouth was by working security around Hanover for four years every night after practice. Until now, the closest he'd ever come to a house this luxurious was when his ex-wife used to watch *Dynasty*.

He circled the room and fantasized calling his boy Brian, waking him up in what would be the middle of the night back home: "Guess what, Sleepyhead? I'm smack-dab in the middle of Othello's mansion. That's right, son, *the* Othello." *The* Homo, he suddenly thought, then dropped the idea, instead imagining phoning his boss Dock Eastwood: "Sir, not only have I made contact with Othello, I'm standing in his den at this very moment."

Laughing to himself, Raider continued around the room, knowing better than to snoop lest he be caught by some surveillance camera or servant. It was enough for now to be this far behind enemy lines, face-to-face with the reason Dock assigned him to the job. He walked over to the wall unit containing every home entertainment gadget ever conceived of in Japan and noticed a videotape lodged halfway in the VCR. No harm in checking it out, he decided after looking around to make sure he was still alone. He pushed the tape all the way in, pressed play and turned on the adjacent television set.

Othello appeared on the screen, looking at least ten years younger—late teens maybe—with a small Afro and baby-soft cheeks. It was his first video ever, Raider realized, for "Fun in the Sun," the upbeat dance tune. He was playing a guitar on a city street, singing and dancing with a cast of hundreds dressed in glitter and spandex. Raider smiled nostalgically, having seen the video a million times in his own youth.

The clip only lasted a few seconds, followed by more short pieces of footage of Othello through the years. After "Fun in the Sun," he was standing in an office, surrounded by men in suits, accepting a huge gold-plated record in a frame. "First album, first gold," said the silver-haired man next to him as a dozen camera bulbs flashed in their faces. Then came fuzzy black and white shots of a father and son fishing off a dock and Raider recognized the video for "Call Me Daddy," the huge ballad from his second album. Raider's ex, Adele, had bought that song for him when Brian was born.

Next, Othello was at the American Music Awards, clutching a trophy and blowing a kiss to the camera, which sent a throng of teenage girls in the balcony into a frenzy. Then he was at the Grammies, performing another ballad, "Love Me Today," with a choir backing him up. Next, at those same Grammies, he was backstage, cradling six awards in his arms. Then came a rapid succession of aerial shots of outdoor stadiums: the Orange Bowl in Miami, Sun Devil Stadium in Tempe, Arizona, Giants Stadium in New Jersey, 3Com Park in San Francisco. They were all packed to the rafters for Othello. The camera cut to him on stage in San Francisco. He was with twelve female dancers, gyrating through "Preacher's Daughter" from his third album, the album that sold like gangbusters and vaulted him to the same stratosphere of music's biggest superstars.

Next came photos of magazine covers: *Time,* half a dozen *Rolling Stones,* a couple of *Peoples* and *Vanity Fairs.* Then there was footage of him going to movie premieres and award shows with some of fashion's hottest models, followed by a seemingly endless stream of more gold and platinum record ceremonies. Then came some of the many Othello videos that had become part of pop culture, reminding Raider of the anticipation and buzz surrounding each new release.

When "Time to Work" came on, Raider couldn't help grinning. It was Othello's lone rap song and had always been one of Raider's favorite videos. All it consisted of was one long, unedited shot of Othello dancing up a storm on a smoky nightclub stage. He was dressed in a white tank top and faded blue jeans, showing off his best moves, grinding until he was dripping with sweat, not even bothering with the usual lip sync. MTV had a field day with "Time to Work." Raider himself used to watch every play he caught, envying the way black guys could dance, like it was sex to them.

"If the world only knew," Raider said, shaking his head.

"We're working on a compilation package for Christmas."

It echoed from across the room, startling Raider. It was Othello, standing at the doorway. He was wearing a pair of loose-fitting brown silk pajama bottoms, the top still draped over one arm.

"Christmas," Raider repeated, not knowing what else to say.

"Yeah, you know, a greatest hits thing with a video retrospective, together in a box set." Othello entered the room.

"Sorry, I didn't mean to assume I could look—"

"Please, it's nothing the whole world hasn't already seen."

They were separated by the brown leather couches and Raider stood in awe to see for the first time the real Othello, scrubbed and clean and not hidden in poor man's clothing. He was only now slipping on the pajama top, affording Raider a prolonged glimpse at his perfectly round hairless pecs, ripped abs and tiny torso. Raider wasn't looking because he *wanted* Othello, he reassured himself. He was simply studying the world famous star the way anybody would. Nothing wrong with that.

"Did you want to watch more of this?" asked Othello.

"Whatever you want to do, I mean, only if you want to."

"What I'd like to do is relax out on the terrace while Sweeney fixes us something to eat, and try, if possible, to forget this day ever happened."

Raider agreed. Othello led him though the set of double doors onto the patio that stretched across the entire length of the house and bordered a steep, black hole of a canyon below. To the left was an Olympic-sized pool along with a Jacuzzi, to the right, a handful of patio tables and chairs. And in front of them, Southern California by night.

"Un-fucking-believable," Raider said when he saw the view, making his way to the terrace's edge which was lined with shrubbery.

Othello said nothing, momentarily preferring to stay behind and inhale the sight of his Nantucket man taking it all in. When he did join Raider, he stood right next to him, too close Othello realized too late, as close as good friends or lovers. The sudden intimacy proved awkward, forcing Othello to stammer:

"You can have a seat if you want."

Raider took him up on it, claiming the stone bench to his right. Othello promptly claimed the bench to his left, unwittingly putting more distance between them than he had wanted as they both searched for something to say.

"It was some day out there, huh?" Raider finally uttered.

"Yeah, yeah, quite a day!" was all Othello could think of.

More silence. Everything seemed different now that they were Raider and Othello and not Raider and the old man, as if words, thought and all social order had been sapped from their brains. Othello would glance over at Raider, or vice versa, their eyes would inadvertently meet, then, with nothing to say, they would both smile and turn back toward the night.

"Great view," Raider said eventually, bobbing his head up and down like an idiot, he was sure.

"Thanks," Othello said, sounding as if he were taking credit.

Why is it so different talking to him now that he isn't old Joe, Raider asked himself scornfully. In reality, he had a zillion questions he was dying to ask, not only about Othello's association with ACT-NOW, but about his life in general. And here was Raider's big chance and all he could think of was how relatively small the guy seemed in person.

"So I guess you were shocked to see it was me," said Othello.

"Shocked isn't the word," Raider said laughingly, loosening up a bit.

"It's not, huh?" Othello said, matching Raider's over-enthused tone. "I really wanted to tell you the minute you said you had the hots—you were attracted to me—Othello me, that is—outside the hospital."

"I told you that. Right," Raider remembered. Hanged by his own noose. The momentum of their conversation vanished and silence returned. After a few seconds, Raider came up with an opener he was proud of: "Saw that new Mariah Carey video the other day. It was money."

"Wrong!" Othello said, his voice resembling a game show buzzer.

"Of course, it's not as good as Whitney Houston's last—"

"Wrong!"

Undaunted, Raider tried again. "Then again, Paula Abdul has a new one."

"Which looks like a Juicy Fruit commercial."

"What about the latest Boys II Men?"

"Boring."

"The last one from Seal?"

"Not bad, but not...great."

"I give up," Raider said. "Let me guess: the only one making good music videos is...you."

"Of course not." Othello stood up. "There must be *one* other person *somewhere*."

They both broke into laughter.

"But really," Othello said. "Those people are all fine, but most of them are boring to look at. A video has got to be different from everyone else's, put the artist up on a pedestal, take the audience somewhere they've never been, create a world all its own filled with sex, power, guts and images people wanna talk about."

"Mariah doesn't do that?"

"By bopping around like a little girl with the same hairdo video after video? I don't think so. Artists like me—or Michael Jackson or Madonna and Janet, too—we have a vision of what we want our image and music and persona to be. And it's gotta be different and better than your Paula Abduls. I don't just bop along to somebody else's songs and do what some record company big wig tells me to do. I'm in on everything. Everything. It's much more than making catchy little songs that go in one ear and out the other. It's a whole attitude, a statement, a vision."

"So what's yours then? I don't mean to sound dumb—"

"I'm a true artist. I write and read music, can play my own instruments and truly sing. Plus, I've got attitude and dramatics and dancing and sexuality like nobody. Why don't you know, Raider Kincaide," he snapped his fingers and spun around once, "I'm the baddest mutha around!" He delivered it with a knowing smirk, achieving the desired effect of making Raider laugh. "And I can sing whatever kind of song I want and perform for all kinds of people— black, white, straight, gay, rock, country western—hell, I got folks in Nashville calling all the time wanting to cover 'I'll Never Be In Your Man's Shoes.' And I also do rock. Hell, 'Fun In the Sun' was basically a rock song with funk."

"I never thought about it, but you're kinda right."

"My music's all inclusive. It says: Let's get funky, let's party, let's get serious. Let's make hot, raw, passionate love. Let's talk about relationships, what people do to each other, what we're doing to the world. Let's come together, don't matter if you're black, white, straight...." he broke off, turning toward the lights to the east that made up Hollywood. "'Course, it's all kind of stilted, the sexuality part anyway. Except for a few ambiguous Prince-type lyrics, I've played it pretty damned straight. But I do have a vision, even if I have been holding some of it back."

"The gay part."

"I guess that's what I have ACTNOW for these days."

"What all do you do for them? If you don't mind my asking."

Othello threw a sideways glance toward Raider. "Right now, I just go to the meetings and give them a little cash." Then he turned to face him. "But what would you say if I told you I want to do a helluva lot more?"

"I'd say we could use all the help we can get. How much more?"

"How much more do you think ACTNOW should do?"

"Depends." Raider stood up, nonchalantly taking in the view. "How far do they wanna go?"

"How far do *you* want to go, Raider Kincaide?"

"I'm still new at all this, you know, but I want whatever it takes for us to get equal rights."

"Whatever it takes," Othello repeated, looking Raider squarely in the eye. "On that, we think exactly alike."

Raider sat down and tried not appear too eager to learn Othello's secrets. "But why go as Joe? Why not just funnel the cash through someone else?"

"I go to listen, not so much to the meeting mumbo-jumbo, but to the guys talking about their boyfriends, their lousy jobs, roommate problems."

"Why would you want to hear about all that?"

"Because I wouldn't otherwise. It's lonely up here in the Big House, Raider. I know that must sound like the most tired line a famous person could ever say, but I am alone. I'm lonely. I've never been the type to have many friends and I either get bored or uptight around the straight people I come in contact with. Sweeney, who's usually too busy working for me, is the only gay friend I have." He sat down on the same bench as Raider. "That is, I hope, until now."

Raider had been absorbed in Othello's intimate revelations. He turned to the pop star and smiled. "Looks like the day wasn't so bad after all."

Flushed with emotion, Othello looked away to the lights below, hoping to hide his giddiness. "I'm so glad you came to ACTNOW," he said. "You'll be like me, watch. The more injustices you become aware of, the more anger you'll feel. Sometimes I sit in those meetings all disguised up, listening to them debating, and I want to just scream: To hell with all that, this is what we should do."

"Which is what?"

Othello turned to him with a grave expression. "Total warfare. Until we force the straight world to understand not to mess with us."

Thinking of his eight year-old boy, Raider grew nervous at the idea. As if the world didn't have enough problems. And no gay man was going to *force* him to do anything. "Sometimes I wonder if terrorist acts are such a good idea, Othello." Felt weird, calling him Othello for the first time. "The world's already changed a whole lot. People are a lot more tolerant now, aren't they?"

"When was the last time a straight person did something for you?"

"I'll have to get back to you on that one."

"I'm sorry. I shouldn't be so hard on you. I have to remember you're still a rookie activist."

Raider chuckled. "You make it sound like a TV show."

"*Raider Kincaide, Rookie Activist,* this fall on Fox," Othello bellowed in an announcer's voice. "I can see it now." They shared an easy laugh, then Othello added: "And I'd be sure to watch it each and every week."

Raider bowed his head to the terrace to conceal the smile involuntarily stretching across his face. "So tell me, Othello," he said, purposely diverting the spotlight off himself. "Is Othello your real name? Or is it something like Arvid Sprugglemeyer?"

"Yes, that's my name: Arvid Sprugglemeyer. How'd you guess?" They both laughed. "No, I was born Othello Hardaway in Riverside, California, in nineteen sixty-something or other."

"Nah, really?"

"Yes, really," Othello said, savoring the lilt in Raider's voice. "Momma gave all of us the most bizarre names in the history of history. I have brothers named Ramses, Apollo and Hamlet, two sisters named Cleopatra and Medusa. It was awful, the crap we used to take in school."

"So do Medusa and the gang know you're gay?"

"They're in the dark," Othello said regretfully. "I only see them on holidays. Or for business meetings. I set them all up in one thing or another, restaurants, auto parts store. But we were never close. Or should I say I was never close to them?"

"Growing up, I never got along with my family either."

"They know you're gay?"

Raider scoffed. "My dad would kill me if he thought for a New York minute I was a fudge-packer—that's what he calls it, not me."

"Families," moaned Othello.

"You got that right." Raider chuckled. It wasn't so bad after all, talking to a famous star like Othello. For a couple of seconds here and there, Raider could even forget the guy was gay. Then again, most of the time, this glaring fact stood out and Raider could see nothing else. It was during those moments that he wanted to ask certain questions he'd never asked of anyone.

When did you first know you were gay? Why are you gay? Do you like to be the man or the woman? Have you even been with a woman? Maybe you should try it.

But Raider kept his trap shut on such matters, fearing his ignorance might blow his cover. Instead, he thought about Simi Valley and found himself laughing inwardly, but apparently not inwardly enough.

"What?" Othello promptly asked.

"Nothing—but I know I'm not going to get away with just saying that, am I?"

"Absolutely not. Tell me."

"I was just thinking about our escape today."

"What about it?"

"You..." Raider started laughing again, "don't take offense, but you...kinda run funny."

"Funny?"

"Yeah, I don't know, like a chicken or something."

"*A chicken?*" Othello leaped up. "What do you mean a chicken?"

"Just what I said: a chicken. The way you were flapping your elbows and kinda running bow-legged like." Raider stood up and mimicked Othello to illustrate his point.

"I do not run like that, Raider Kincaide of Nantucket Island," Othello protested with an ear-to-ear grin. "I was probably trying to stay in my old man form—"

"Nope. I ain't buying that, Othello Hardaway of Riverside, California." Raider sat back down. "You were scared shitless and you were running for your life."

"Well, maybe I was, but you were, too, scared shitless, that is."

"Nah," Raider said, all smug. "That's called adrenaline, pure and simple."

"Yeah, right. Well, if I run like a chicken, you took off like a crazed, I don't know, wild boar or some other safari animal."

"Hey, I got us out of there, didn't I?"

"Yes, you did." Othello dropped his playful protest. "And for that, I'll be eternally grateful." With a genuine smile, he gazed into Raider's eyes, noticing the man from Nantucket's cheeks turning a pale shade of red. The moment just a bit too honest, they both turned away and each let out a shy chortle, followed by silence, this time minus the awkwardness.

"What would the world think," Raider arched his head toward the moon, "if it knew Othello danced like a sex machine but ran like a chicken?"

"What would the world think if it knew Othello was a practicing homo?" Othello said somberly.

"I'm still having a hard time with it myself, to be honest."

Othello nodded to the city lights below. "At least once a day, I wish the whole world knew which gender I was really singing about. I wish I could make my videos with gay men like me, making love or just living life. I wish I could be a bigger gay rights activist than Madonna, only openly gay and proud as hell. I'd tell the public: This is what I am, take it or leave it. And I'd do it all through my music. I'd be butch sometimes and other times, I'd be as queeny as they come. I'd be masculine *and* feminine like I really am inside."

"You don't want to do that," warned Raider.

"Why not?"

"That's why people have such a hard time accepting gays now. The ones that act all girlish give it a bad name. Or some of the ones in ACTNOW, with all the nose rings and colored hair or chaps with no butts—"

"Raider," Othello began bitterly, "the world is going to have to accept *all* of us, not just the straight acting mainstream middle class types. Whether you're a drag queen or a macho ex-college athlete, we're all fighting for the same thing: the right to be ourselves."

"Fine then," Raider said sourly. "Come out and fight for all of them. You've got enough money and power."

"I wish I could just snap my fingers, call a press conference, and do just that."

55

"What's stopping you?" Raider asked, his tone still irascible.

The mere idea made Othello so nervous his breath froze in his lungs. "The same thing that keeps a lot of people in the closet: fear. Only I got so much to fear I tremble just thinking about it. And now, after today, the police might be looking for someone of Joe's description."

Othello was shaking so much, if he were a girl, Raider would have gotten up and held onto him to calm him down. "I'm sorry, Othello. I didn't mean to upset you. And anyway, nobody in Simi Valley is going to trace a vague description of an old black man back to you. On the radio, they said some witnesses thought he was just trying to get away from the chaos like everybody else. Things were way too hectic for the police to have anything to go on." The theory didn't seem to help. Othello remained silent. "Maybe we should talk about something else," Raider offered. "Better still, maybe I should just leave."

"Don't do that." Othello quickly banished the panic attack and rejoined Raider on the bench. "Why don't we give the politics a rest. Besides, Sweeney is cooking up some of his special turkey burgers for us and I'm sure it won't be much longer. In the meantime, we could take a swim—the pool's heated."

"Forgot to pack my suit," Raider said as an out.

"I don't think anyone's going to arrest you up here for going in your skivvies, or even skinny dipping, if you'd like."

"I—I don't think so."

"Then how about the Jacuzzi? After the day we had—"

"Othello, no." Raider put a firm hand up between them.

"I could put on some music, this whole terrace is equipped with—"

Raider let out a terse breath. "You're just like the old man. Lecherous."

"I don't mean to be presumptuous. I'm not even suggesting we hop into bed tonight—"

"Good—"

"It's just that—I'm not sure how this is going to come out, but— what I mean is—I like you, Raider. Very much. And I'd like to get to know you. And I'm not sure how you feel now that you know who I am, but you did say you were attracted to Othello when you thought you were talking to an old man. So I was hoping we could, I don't know...." he broke off, unable to find the words.

Raider smiled, part nervous, part flattered, part trapped. Just his luck he had to go and say Othello was hot. But also just his luck he and Othello were hitting if off so well. "The thing is, Othello, we just met and all, truly met—the real you and me—and I don't know either. I mean—I—I...."

"You don't want to have sex right off the bat?"

Raider paused, thinking: that could work. "Yes, that's it exactly."

"You're looking for a lover?"

Pause again. "Well, eventually." Then he quickly added: "But also the old-fashioned way. I like to get to know a person real well. *Real* real well. I mean, *really* well."

Othello's face brightened. "Me, too, Raider; that's exactly what I want. I've had it with sport nookie. I've had it with being lonely, too. Especially...." He stopped himself. Yes, the virus might present itself as a major issue between them, but there just had to be a way. "Especially since I'm not getting any younger. The point is, Raider Kincaide of Nantucket Island, I like you a whole lot and if you like me, maybe we can see where that takes us."

Raider clasped his hands in front of him, grateful he'd staved off Othello's advances, at least for tonight. "Sounds like a plan," he said affably, and they shared a relaxed, easy smile, Raider feeling less threatened, Othello feeling more hopeful.

"This sure has been a day of highs and lows," Othello said. "Now, if I can just turn the lows into something good."

"How?"

The frustration of the day coming back to him, Othello didn't answer.

"How you gonna do that?" Raider prodded.

Othello's face lit up with an idea. "Come back East with me and find out," he said baitingly. "You need to lay low with ACTNOW after today anyway."

Raider tried to fake a smile but only half succeeded. "You don't give up do you?"

"Do you want me to?"

Raider thought about that one for a second. Othello giving up meant shutting Raider out, which meant not getting to the bottom of Othello's involvement in ACTNOW. "I guess not."

Othello smiled hopefully. "Does that mean I can put you down for a trip back East, courtesy of Othello Hardaway Airlines?" Waiting for an answer, Othello held onto his lower lip with his upper teeth, his eyes wide and eager, like a child whose Christmas wish was finally within reach.

SEVEN

THE ROYAL SUITE was as silent as a morgue in the dead of night. The one-way mirrored window muted the sound of fortunes being won and lost in the casino below. With his back to the window and the gambleholics—anyone still at the crap tables at 3:00 a.m. had to be a gambleholic—Jasper Hollinquest guzzled down another scotch and soda and imagined putting his entire empire on the line in a single game of black jack. This meeting was just as risky, he figured, but at least it was on his own turf, The Palace Hotel and Casino, his latest conquest and the perfect place for secrets to be kept secret.

The front door opened. Deon Anthony stood in the frame, his head barely making it. "Everybody here yet?" he asked in a gruff voice, sounding as if he'd been dragged to Atlantic City against his will. Knowing that by "everybody," Deon meant Othello, Jasper shook his head and walked to the wet bar on the wall opposite the door.

"You made up your mind yet?" Jasper asked rather nonchalantly.

"Hell no," Deon said, full of disgust or confusion or both.

In the private underground garage of the hotel, Othello slammed the door of the green Lexus and began a determined walk across the concrete. From the passenger side, Raider emerged and matched him stride for stride.

"Calm and steady," Othello told himself, feeling more nervousness than he thought his body possessed as he marched toward the double-glass doors marked: PRIVATE GUESTS ONLY.

"You sure I can't go in there with you?" Raider asked. "You look like you could used a big dose of moral support and that is what I'm here for."

"I'm meeting these people to *save* the revolution, not blow it to bits by bringing in a surprise guest. No offense, but this ain't *The Jerry Springer Show*."

"Yeah, but I can tell—"

"I should have left you on the jet."

"I couldn't let you come here alone. You're walking into some kind of fire; I can see that much in your eyes. Whoever 'these people' are, they're not your friends, and you need a friend right now."

They reached the entrance. Before going through, Othello stopped and turned to Raider. "Your support means a lot. And as soon as I win this round, life will be a lot easier for you, me, ACTNOW and everybody. And I'll tell you more then, promise."

Raider started to speak, but Othello opened one of the doors and stepped into a small lobby, barely acknowledging the guard behind the security desk before spotting the three elevator doors beyond him. "Which one to Suite 656, or does it matter?"

The guard was a heavyset white man in his thirties. He stood up abruptly, his hand inching toward the gun at his hip. "Only Mr. Othello is allowed beyond this point."

Taken aback, Othello and Raider eyed each other. "Fine," Othello said, still looking at Raider. The guard then went to the middle elevator and inserted a key in the adjacent slot.

"Is this safe?" Raider whispered to Othello.

"Hope so. Wait here with Biggie Small II. I should be back by...I don't know. If I'm not back by...dawn..." he swallowed hard, "help." He would have traded half his fortune for a kiss for good luck, but thought better than to ask, especially with the guard there. Instead, he made a solo trek to the elevator, turning and staring at Raider until the doors closed, separating them.

With Othello gone, the lobby grew even smaller for Raider.

Except for the gold velvet walls, the elevators doors and the guard, there wasn't much else in the room. 656, Raider repeated to himself a couple of times.

"We meet again." Othello said when he opened the door to the Royal Suite. As if he owned the place, he made a beeline for the window overlooking the casino and drew the tall navy curtains closed.

"No one can see in here either way," Jasper said as he sat atop the solid oak desk near the center of the room.

Othello completed the task anyway. "I do hope the third time's going to be a charm."

"Depends." From a large couch on the opposite side of the room, Deon was consumed in a miniature game of craps on the coffee table. "You gonna run out of here in the middle of the meeting again?"

In the lobby to the private entrance, Raider looked at the guard with an expression that said he was bored and uncomfortable, not to mention powerless. Enjoying the ego trip, a wicked grin wiped across the guard's face every time they made eye contact. After enough of this—one minute's worth—Raider excused himself and disappeared into the parking garage.

"Don't let my ending that meeting early belie my seriousness about all this," said Othello. "There was something I had to do and you two weren't ready to make up your minds anyway."

Deon shot a glance to Jasper, who returned his sullen expression. They've talked on their own, before today, Othello decided.

Unlike before, a small regiment of blue-suited guards were now scattered about the parking garage, six of them, Secret Service wannabes with stoic faces. Who the hell is Othello meeting? Raider asked himself. The guards took note of him immediately, as if they were expecting him. With them watching his every move, he put on a humble act, milling around the garage, musing at the expensive cars until he saw a door marked: PUBLIC CASINO. He ambled his way toward the door, smiling at the blue suits on either side. "Good a time as any to win my fortune," he said, full of deference. When they offered no reaction, he slipped past them, and once through the door, he hustled his way through a series of corridors which eventually led to a junction where the main lobby met the casino. Having no intention of gambling, he headed for the public elevators, then pushed the button for the sixth floor.

Jasper stood up, thought about another drink, but decided against it. "You've still been pretty scarce on details."

"As I said before," Othello began, "a lot of groups need money. Hospices, legal defense funds, youth organizations, AIDS services, crime watch groups, hot lines."

"Even if I wanted to give them some of my hard earned money," Deon was still playing craps, "and I'm not saying I want to—how would we do it?"

"That would be the easy part," said Jasper. "We set up a trust fund, filter in the money anonymously and groups apply for grants."

"And it never has to be traced back to us," said Othello.

"But I'm not suggesting this is the answer," warned Jasper.

"Then what the hell are you suggesting, Jasper?" Othello asked.

The sixth floor from the public elevators was full of carbon copy doors echoing down twin hallways going in either direction. Noting the room numbers, Raider took the corridor to the east, the direction of the private lobby. Halfway down the hall, he heard the elevator bell ring out, prompting him to hurry past a bend in the hallway and duck into an alcove where the soda and ice machines stood. Peeking out, he saw two of the blue suits getting off the elevator—were they onto him? They stood for a moment, listening in their ear pieces, then split up to check out the floor. The next door down from Raider was unmarked, a utility room perhaps, credit card-type slot for the lock. With the bend in the hallway as his only cover, Raider moved to the door. From his wallet, he retrieved a magnetic card and inserted it into the lock.

"Start your gay revolution." Jasper went for another drink after all. "Hell, there's a few politicians I'd like to see on the ropes for my own purposes. But why not start it without me? And know that you'll have my full moral support. Honest."

Deon laughed and rolled the dice again. Sensing he was losing them, Othello drew a breath. "Tell me something: how do you two deal with your anger?"

"I got no anger," Deon insisted.

It wasn't a utility closet, more like some sort of mini-boiler room.

With a pen-sized flashlight, Raider checked it out until he heard the door, which he'd left slightly ajar, begin to creak. Quickly, he ducked behind it just as it opened, remaining frozen as the blue suit flipped on the light and gave the room a once over from the doorway. Finding nothing, the man left, returning the room to darkness and shutting the door. In those few seconds of light, Raider had seen all he needed to see: an air-conditioning duct high on the wall.

"No anger?" Othello said to Deon from the center of the room. "Then why are you so pissed off at me?"

"Because you kidnapped me and dragged me to LA, dipping into my private life."

"What if the whole world knew about your private life?" Othello moved closer. "Think you'd still be on the cover of all those sports magazines?"

Deon stood up. "What, you gonna out me now?"

"That's not the point of this, goddamnit!"

"Gentlemen, please," Jasper said, not knowing what to do if these two black men started fighting in his suite.

Standing on top of a boiler, Raider used his pocketknife to unscrew the vent to the air conditioning duct. Then, with not much room to spare, he crawled through the frosty metal tunnel, heading due east, counting the number of ceiling-high wall vents he passed.

The Royal Suite was calmer now, even if the tension was still thick. On one side, Deon stood over the couch and the miniature crap game, his posture rigid and noncompliant. Across the room, Othello leaned against the big screen television, arms folded, one hand rubbing his head, anticipating a headache. From his desk in the center, Jasper eyed Othello and said: "Rock Star isn't going to out anyone. He knows I can use the power of the press to destroy every last fiber of him."

"You also have the power to expose the bigots as assholes," said Othello. "And make people understand what groups like ACTNOW are fighting for."

"Just what the hell is ACTNOW fighting for?" asked Deon.

"Us."

"They're not going to help me get past the Knicks once we put away Detroit tomorrow."

"No," Othello said, "but they just might make you feel better about being a closeted faggot."

The last vent had been to an empty but lavish bedroom. The next one had to be part of the same suite according to Raider's calculations. He slithered toward it, then heard what sounded like Othello's voice:

"...do the things us rich and famous don't have the guts to do."

That's my boy all right, Raider decided with a touch of cockiness. The only view he got was of a wall and some navy curtains, so he eased back a bit—making sure he couldn't be seen—and cocked an ear toward the room.

"And you want this war televised on CNC?" asked Jasper. "Official channel of gay rage."

"If your network makes it an issue, the rest will have to follow."

"He's got you on that one," said Deon.

CNC, Raider thought. Jasper Hollinquest just bought this hotel. And owned CNC. White voice, proper speech, private suite. That rich guy, a fag? What about the babe he's married to?

"So you two do it," Deon said, his tone brightening. "I'll just be the world's greatest basketball player, and maybe a hundred years after I die, everybody can discover that I was gay. That'll be my contribution to all this."

Othello moved to the center of the room. "Meanwhile, how many boys who look up to you will bash a fag? Besides, you're an important link—"

Who was the other voice, Raider wondered. Sounded like a home-boy, said something about playing ball. He strained to get a view, but could only see a sliver of a very tall black man's back.

"—to Herman," Jasper said, finishing Othello's thought. "What do you want with him?"

"His head on a platter would be acceptable," Othello said, then retreated just a bit. "He sets the tone for all the hatemongers. He needs to be dealt with. And I'd hate to see him cost you another couple billion."

Jasper eyed him knowingly, surprised but impressed Othello had done his homework.

"What you two talking about?" asked Deon.

"Your buddy Senator Evil stands in the way of Jasper's conquest of the Belize coast." Othello kept his eyes on Hollinquest.

"How do you plan to deal with him?" asked Jasper.

"You're the expert on that," Othello said. "Or are the rumors about your nefarious dealings just a lot of smoke?"

Jasper looked him square in the eye. "I could have both you and Senator Evil erased before the next telecast of *CNC: The World Today.*"

Othello's expression was just as steely as the billionaire businessman's. "I just might call your bluff on one of those accounts,"

Deon started for the door. "Man, this shit is crazy. I got no time for this."

"Just hear me out." Othello tried to grab his arm as he stormed past, but Deon jerked himself free and kept going. "Deon," Othello pleaded. "Jasper?"

"Don't look at me."

"You're right, Deon, this is crazy," Othello said. Deon grabbed the door knob, but didn't turn it. "And I'll get out of both your lives for good if that's what you want. *If* you just give yourselves one minute to hear me out."

Impossible, thought Raider, so flabbergasted he almost said it aloud. The Deon Anthony? Gay? The D.A.? The all-time, all-star, all-scoring, all-dunking, all-world, greatest ever? Say it isn't so, can't be, not in this lifetime, not in this universe!

Deon held his ground at the door. Othello didn't wait for the pendulum to swing the other way: "Just listen to this. If you want to leave then, so be it." He reached inside the brown bomber jacket he was wearing and pulled out several papers, then began reading without looking up:

"March 2nd of this year: a gay man in Cincinnati gives a ride home to a fellow student at night school. When the gay man admits his sexuality, the fellow student beats him, smashes his head against a tree and robs him. The attacker tells the victim, 'Now you know what I think of fags.'

"March 4th: a gay student at Florida State University reports getting threatening phone calls and messages slipped under his dorm room door, saying things like, 'Watch your step, cocksucker' and 'All homos must die.' Three days after filing the report, the student, a freshman, commits suicide by jumping off one of the school's buildings.

"Same day, March 4th, a gay bookstore in Lancaster, Pennsylvania, is bombed for the third time. The night watchman hired to protect the place, a straight man, is killed. The day before, the KKK held a parade in protest of the city's nondiscrimination ordinance.

"March 9th: a drag queen in Denver, Colorado, who is also a prostitute, is beaten severely by three men who tell him, 'Next time, we slit your faggot throat.' The victim, who required reconstructive facial surgery, did not file a report because, after a previous assault, the police refused to take a statement and arrested him for soliciting."

"That's enough," Deon said, his voice quivering.

"March 16th: at a gay beach in East Hampton, New York, four pick-up trucks full of teenagers pull into the parking lot and block the exits. Over fifteen males armed with bats and crowbars jump out and shout to beach-goers, 'We're gonna kick some queer ass.' Before anyone is attacked, police arrive and allow the teenagers to leave unarrested, unpunished."

"I heard about that," Jasper said softly.

"March 17th," Othello went on, "a disabled gay man in San Diego reports being harassed for months by neighbors who shout 'fucking pervert' at him and threaten to burn down his house. Someone shot and killed both his dogs and the neighbors have thrown eggs and firecrackers at his house. His landlord is also trying to evict him without just cause. The man weighs a hundred and twelve pounds and is dying of AIDS."

"Shit, man," Deon mumbled.

"March 18: a lesbian on the street in Chicago is harassed by two men who spit at her and tell her, 'You look like a man, take it like a man.' The victim runs into a store; the attackers follow and grab her by the throat. When the victim finally frees herself and runs behind the counter, the store owner refuses to call the police because she is a dyke. Same day: a gay man in Manhattan reports a series of phone calls from his lover's family who threaten to kill him if he visits his dying lover in the hospital. Same day," his eyes were beginning to water, the pages beginning to blur, "a gay bar owner in Seattle is found outside his bar in the morning, strangled by an electrical cord. A baseball bat is also found inserted in his blood-soaked anus—"

"We get the point, Othello," Jasper said soberly.

"Not if you don't join the revolution." Othello's eyes remained fixed on the pages in front of him. Deon's head was buried in the door, his hand no longer on the knob. Jasper had set his drink down and was staring out the window into the darkness.

Raider lay lifelessly in the duct, the chill of the cold air starting to get to him. He was reminded of Dartmouth and the night he beat the shit out of that guy who came on to him. For the first time ever, the incident was suddenly disturbing to him. But that was different, he told himself, not sure how or why.

"All these things happened in the last thirty-some days," said Othello. "I didn't even get through all the list. And every thirty days, more violence just like this keeps happening over and over and over. Even if you aren't in the trenches of the war, surely you know someone affected by this kind of hate."

"*I'm* affected by this kind of hate," Deon said defensively, his voice thick with tears he was determined to choke back. Tears for J-Boy—his lover before Charlie—and how he had to die in such an inhumane way, alone and broke, exiled from the University of South Carolina graduation ceremony even though he'd spent three years of his life cheerleading his heart out for them. Exiled from Deon, who was too worried about his rep to see his dying lover.

"Those stats," Jasper began.

"Documented," said Othello. "If you want proof—"

"I don't need proof," Jasper said. The only proof of the wrath of the homophobe he needed was the crook in his nose, a permanent gift from the Puerto Ricans who terrorized the Ramble in Central Park during his years at Columbia. And yet he kept going back, because he hungered for male flesh and that was his only outlet. The PRs beat him half a dozen more times after that, once puncturing his lung and putting him in the hospital for two weeks. "Othello's right, Deon. Hate is very much alive and well in the real world."

"Maybe I've gone about this the wrong way. Forcing you to come to the Temple. But I never imagined you'd be so resistant—"

"How would you feel if one of us had kidnapped you?" asked Jasper.

Othello paused. "I guess none of us is used to others telling us what we can and cannot do."

"Not since I was about fourteen," said Deon.

"But can't you see my heart is in the right place?" Othello moved toward Jasper. "And since you're used to having things your way, doesn't all this piss you off? Don't you just...just wanna *bust* some heads sometimes?"

"That's what you want to do, isn't it?" Jasper said. "The money and CNC, that's all fine and good, but what you really want is to bust some heads, and I mean literally."

"I don't know," he said, purposely downplaying the strength of his conviction so as not to scare them off. The first priority was getting these two on board and giving them a taste of the power they could all possess. "Part of me says, 'Hell yes, bust heads.' Part of me says, 'Be civilized.' But one thing I'm sure of: the more I become involved with ACTNOW, the more I admire their will to fight."

"What are they capable of?" asked Deon, joining Jasper at the oak desk.

"I'm still trying to figure that one out."

"They involved in that Simi Valley mess?" asked Jasper.

Othello bit his lip teasingly. "Do we have a revolution or not?"

"If we do this," said Jasper, "we vote on every single thing and I mean *everything*. And majority rules."

"Agreed."

"Wait a minute," cried Deon. "If we do what? What are we talking here, ACTNOW or setting up this trust?"

"First we make a commitment to band together," Othello said, "and at least do the trust. Then, if we want to do more, say with ACT-NOW or anybody, we figure it out and vote on it as we go."

"I would want to give money to every single minority hospice in this whole damned country," said Deon. "*If* we do this."

"Give me something hard to do." Othello eyed Deon, then Jasper. "So are we in or are we in?"

Jasper ran his hands over his face as if to wash away some deeply-hidden pain. "Maybe this is our one chance to do something."

"Each of us," Othello said, "with one vote, running the revolution from the Temple, like three wise men."

Jasper laughed skeptically. "You can't stop being dramatic for one half of one second, can you?"

"Call it my calling," Othello said impishly.

So that was it, Raider thought with a sneer: Othello wanted to be the headliner in the ACTNOW terrorist act with some pretty big named co-stars by his side.

Jasper and Deon searched each other for last minute objections. Receiving none, they both turned back to Othello.

"In." Jasper extended his hand to shake, but Othello turned to Deon, who sighed a big sigh, thought about it one last time, then also extended his hand and said:

"Ditto."

Othello grabbed both hands reaching out toward him and raised them in solidarity. "Then we've got ourselves a kick-ass revolution."

They each broke into laughter that was part nervous, part triumphant, keeping it up until Deon withdrew his hand and glanced at his watch. "But we're going to have to fire the first shot later. I've got the Detroit Pistons to deal with in a matter of hours."

"Okay, okay," Othello said excitedly, "but how can you think of basketball at a time like this?"

In a panic, Raider realized he had to get the hell out of there and back to the garage before Othello got there first and missed him. He reared himself up by the elbows, held his breath and began slithering backwards.

"The trust fund thing will be a snap," said Jasper. "I can get started on that tomorrow."

"We have to meet around my playoff schedule," said Deon.

"Ah, you won't get past the Knicks anyway," Jasper chided and the two of them traded barbs about the potential next-round match-up. As they did, Othello regarded his partners and wondered if they thought he was off his rocker based on his actions of the past few weeks.

The last words Raider heard had to do with the Knicks and the

Bulls. When he was far enough away to make noise, he picked up the pace, burrowing his way backwards through the duct.

"One more thing," Othello began, nervous but urged on by an undefined force within. "So you'll understand why I've been a little crazed: the week we all met, I found out I'm positive."

The other two men were too shocked to speak. Was it the intimacy of the admission or the fact that this was news that would rock the world?

"I'm fine right now," he said, hoping to discourage morbid thoughts. "I'm telling you because, well, now you know how much closer to the trenches I feel."

Still nothing from Jasper or Deon. Both of them were seemingly waiting for the other to come up with the right thing to say.

"Anyway," Othello said, writing the script for them. "It doesn't have to be a death sentence. And right now, I'm healthy."

"Yeah," Deon finally uttered. "You can be fine for years."

"Right," Jasper chorused.

"Exactly," chimed Othello.

With elbows, knees, hands and feet, Raider tore through the duct, the sweat cascading down his forehead despite the tundra-like air.

Even with the awkwardness, Othello felt a peculiar sense of relief letting this secret out of its cage to two other human beings. As an up-note, he added: "And I want to use those years realizing my potential as a gay man, speaking of which, I know you have to run and be Mr. Sports Legend, Deon, but can't we work out some of the details of trust fund before we go?"

Like a paratrooper returning to earth, Raider dropped down in the pitch black mini-boiler room in a not-so-smooth tuck and roll. Then, using his flashlight, he found the main light switch, flipped it on and began replacing the vent.

"So many logistics," said Jasper.

"The main thing is to kick in some cash to get the ball rolling," said Othello. "Whatever your conscience tells you. Me, I want to start off with, say, half a mil."

His partners regarded him, impressed and surprised. Then they eyed each other.

"I'll match you," said Jasper.

Deon rolled his tongue around his cheek, his gaze traveling from Jasper to Othello.

"Same."

With the vent replaced, Raider peeked out into the hallway, and seeing the coast was clear, crept outside. Three steps later, two blue suits appeared out of nowhere at either end of the hallway, heading straight for him. The security cameras had won this round of hide-and-seek.

"Partners at last," Othello said in relief. "Life is gonna get good."

"At first, we'll have to find the groups ourselves," said Jasper. "Then CNC can do a piece, something like: the new ways nonprofit gay groups are seeking money in hard fund-raising times. We show our fund and the word will be out. And I have just the reporter to do it, my number one boy, Bruce." It came out sounding giddy, as if it were a blossoming romance or the first time Jasper had verbalized it to human ears. The latter was true, but Jasper was glad he said it. If Othello was going to admit to having the virus, he could be open about having a steady.

"Bruce Jones?" Othello exclaimed. "Jasper Hollinquest, you sly dog."

"He's a damned good reporter," Jasper said in his defense, relishing the amused shock on the other two men's faces.

With hard faces and a couple of pieces hidden in holsters no doubt, the two blue suits closed in on Raider, looking as if they were taking no prisoners. Think, he commanded himself. You're smarter than these mugs.

"How about you, Deon?" Othello asked. "Anyone special in your world?"

"Charlie. Eight years," he said with a proud smile. "Yourself?"

"Working on it." Othello flashed a smug grin and the three of them looked at each other and snickered, dizzy with the idea that they were trading secrets *The Enquirer* would kill to possess....

"Mind telling us what you're doing coming out of there?" the older, taller blue suit asked Raider. Both men were within arms reach, handcuff or striking distance. Raider pointed to the door behind him, mumbling inaudibly.

6646622574

To seal their alliance, Othello, Jasper and Deon all shook hands, the atmosphere between them not entirely perfect, but a far cry from their previous meetings and that was good enough for now for Othello. For added safety, they agreed to leave separately, and because of his game, Deon left first.

"We could detain you for trespassing, rock star friend or not," said the junior partner.

Raider let out an exasperated sigh. "Relax, boys. I'm sure," he said like a Valley Girl. He then launched into a series of feminine gestures: hands on hips, flipping of the wrists, a mawkish facial expression. "I had to find a place to take care of...of...you know." He shrugged one shoulder, all girlish, and nudged the senior partner in the arm. "With all you big boys down in that garage, a fella's bound to get a little excited." He fanned his face and added a lisp for good measure.

"You still haven't answered our question," said the confused junior partner.

Raider folded his arms and pursed his lips in frustration. "You want me to spell it out for you? Tell you I went in there to whack off? To beat my meat? To pull my pud? To shoot a big wad of jism dreaming about all you mens in uniform?"

"Sir, please." The senior partner reacted as nervously as Raider might have a few weeks ago.

"Well, there you have it," Raider cried, sensing victory and reveling in it. "You can go in there and see all the jizz for yourself. Right back over—"

"Sweet Jesus," the junior partner wailed.

"Oh, yes, girlfriends," Raider said. "I shoot big loads, big, big, *big* loads. Loads that end droughts and famine, especially when I'm thinking about hunky hunks like you and you, the two of you, you two."

The senior partner was too disgusted to look at him. "Just get the hell out of here."

"Fine, if you're going to have that kind of a bitchy attitude." Slipping out from under them, Raider placed his hands on his hips and began a seductive strut down the hall, like Bacall or Bergman from some '40s movie. Waiting for the elevator, he leered back at them several times with disdainful eyes. Then, just before disappearing into the elevator car, he ran his hand through his hair and gave them one last sassy flip of his head. When the doors were closed behind him, he doubled over in hysterics.

Jasper was staying the night in the Palace, so Othello was the next to leave the Royal Suite. High on success, he walked swiftly to the private elevator, eager to celebrate with his man from Nantucket.

Raider's elevator made a stop on the third floor to let on an overweight couple straight out of Podunk, killing the levity of his ruse and restoring the panic to get to the garage first.

Othello tapped his foot impatiently as he descended the private tower, hoping Raider hadn't been too bored but fully confident he could make it up to his lacrosse legend.

Raider almost mowed over the couple from Podunk when the elevator reached the ground floor. Then, he had to make a furious sprint through what seemed like miles of endless corridors, retracing his path back to the garage....

Othello's elevator opened onto the private lobby. Only the guard was there, no sign of Raider. Flinging open the double glass doors to the garage, Othello fully expected to find Raider standing next to the Lexus. But the only people visible were three men in blue suits, huddled together in a far-off corner. Certain that Raider was in the car, he crossed the lot to the Lexus. It was empty. A thought invaded his mind. He heard himself gasp. Jasper Hollinquest had done something with Raider; it was all a trick. He turned around and headed for the private lobby, his fury accelerating with each step. Then, just as he was about to open the doors to the lobby, Raider appeared out of the darkness to the left, so swiftly and abruptly he almost crashed into—

"Othello—" Raider gasped, panting for air.

"Good God" was all Othello could utter.

"There you are!" Raider sounded relieved.

"Where were you?" Othello asked, his voice edgy due to his fright.

Raider bent over, hands gripping at his pants. After a few more breaths, he stood erect and glanced around the garage. "You were gone so long," he said in a hushed tone. "I got worried."

"You went looking for me?" The dread in Othello's eyes turned to enchantment.

"Uh-huh," Raider stammered modestly. Forgiving and forgetting was that easy when you were a golden boy. The smile wiping across Othello's face had "my hero" written all over it.

"Let's get out of this place," said the pop star.

"What about the meeting? Did we get what we came for? You had me scared to death."

"Put it this way," Othello said, glancing around. "You and I have got some celebrating to do in the form of moonlight dancing."

With that, Othello headed for the Lexus, full of more hope than he'd ever known in his personal life. For the briefest of seconds, Raider lingered behind, wondering what in the hell Othello had in mind now. Then, he too made his way toward the Lexus, thinking of the boys back at the bureau and how they were gonna flip their lids with envy when they found out what ol' Panty-Raider Kincaide had uncovered in the gay underworld.

EIGHT

"I REFUSE TO TAKE another step unless you tell me right now where you're taking me," Raider demanded, the amused tone of his voice betraying his threat.

"Just make sure you keep those beautiful blue eyes of yours shut." Othello dragged his willing captive by the hand in the pitch black night.

"I smell fish," Raider said, trying to keep up with Othello's eager pace. "And the sea. I know the sea."

"Eyes closed," warned Othello.

"And this is some kind of pier. You making me walk the plank?"

"No peeking. I'm watching you."

"I don't think I can keep 'em closed much longer," Raider teased.

"Hold it right here." Othello let go of him and walked farther down the dock. "Are you in suspense?"

"Like I'm at a Hitchcock movie—now can I look?"

Othello tried to calm the butterflies in his stomach. "Simon says yes."

Raider opened his eyes and saw hundreds of boats bobbing in a sleepy marina. Directly behind them was the blackness of the Atlantic at 5:00 a.m.

"Well?" Othello said, full of anticipation, receiving a bewildered look in return. For lack of a better idea, he began singing as a way of explaining:

> The love boat
> now will be making a special run,
> to celebrate
> saving the re-vo-lu-ti-on.

Raider's mood did a U-turn, from playful to concerned. "But...."

"At this time of night—or morning—when we'll have the ocean all to ourselves." To alleviate his nervousness, Othello raced ahead to the small yacht five slips down. "And this is *The Girlfriend*. Of course, it still says *The Lady Kate* on the side, but it won't for long. I think *The Girlfriend* is a much better name, don't you?"

"You own this?" Raider moved trance-like toward the boat.

"I do now," Othello said. Just then, a weary-faced Sweeney emerged from below deck. He was sporting a double-breasted navy jacket and a white captain's hat. "Admiral Sweeney, you remember the man from Nantucket."

"How could I forget?" Sweeney muttered as he stepped onto the dock.

"Shall we cast off then?" asked Othello, clearly the only one having a good time so far. Looking at Raider, he extended his arm toward the yacht as if to say "lead the way." Raider hesitated, trying to figure out what other options he had other than going on a romantic cruise with a love-starved homosexual pop star. Deciding there were none, he shrugged and boarded Othello's love boat. Othello, beaming an even brighter smile than before, turned to follow but was halted by his manager's firm grip.

"One second, buster," Sweeney began, his stare like a laser through his wire-rimmed glasses. "Do not forget that this is in exchange for giving me one whole day for music business and music business alone."

"You have my word," Othello said in a hushed, embarrassed tone, and that ignited a brief but furious dueling gripe session with both of

them talking and neither one hearing the other until Othello finished
with: "Now's not the time, all right?"

Sweeney then shut up, folded his arms and stared at the sky.

"Now," Othello muttered, chagrined smile covering gritted teeth.
"All aboard."

The Atlantic was awash with blue-tinted moonlight, the white-
caps acting like tiny speed bumps as *The Girlfriend* raced out to sea.
From the engine room, a pouting Sweeney piloted the controls, following instructions to "be invisible" while navigating the boat to a
safe, romantic distance from the Jersey shore. On the upper deck, near
the bow, Othello and Raider stood huddled together without actually
touching, bracing themselves against a herculean wind that only
seemed to grow colder with each nautical mile. Then, when the lights
of Atlantic City were mere pinpricks in the backdrop, *The Girlfriend*
came to a stop and began bobbing effortlessly in the night.

"What more could we ask for?" asked Othello, thankful the air
was a bit warmer now that the wind was no longer attacking them.
"We've got total privacy, a damn near full moon, the fresh sea air, plus,
the revolution just got a much needed shot in the arm."

"This celebration and all," Raider said, watching Sweeney head
for the cabin below. "You knew you'd win these people over, didn't
you?"

The only response Othello offered was a laugh that was somewhere between modest and cocky.

"'Fess up," Raider prodded, envious and fascinated at the same
time.

Pensively, Othello gazed at the lights on the boardwalk in the distance. "I've yet to meet a person whose will is stronger than mine."

Raider's face stiffened. He turned away from Othello and stared
northward. "So what's next?" he asked, more serious now.

"Full speed ahead. The revolution's about to shift into high gear.
But first...." He indicated Sweeney, who was reemerging from the
cabin with a bucket of champagne and two long-stemmed glasses.
Like an automaton in a bad mood, Sweeney placed them in the middle of a coil of rope on the deck near the cabin, then flashed a disin-
genuous smile and disappeared down below. "Jealous," Othello

snapped after him, then turned back to Raider. "A toast." When they each had a glass, he went on: "To full speed ahead. In more ways than one." Othello chugged his drink; Raider faked a sip.

"So what exactly does full speed ahead mean?" asked Raider. "With the revolution, that is."

"Must we talk about it here, tonight? I'm in the mood for—" *love* was what he wanted to say "—getting to know each other more."

"But it's your job to educate me. I wanna feel your fire." Raider's voice was full of passion, his eyes eager like a student's.

"The war is about to escalate on many different levels," Othello began as he busied himself with a refill. "From helping the little people survive the daily onslaught of homophobia to," he paused, finished pouring, then contemplated the motion of the bubbles in his glass, "to bringing down the biggest bigots who serve as role models for the ignorant. Jimmy Herman to name just one."

"Talk about your assholes," Raider said full of disgust, faking another sip.

"The other week, I got so mad at him, I assassinated him on my big screen TV." Othello took a swig of champagne, then added with a sullen voice: "Not a bad idea, wouldn't you say?" He scanned Raider's eyes for any kind of reaction, but the man from Nantucket only offered a "hmmmph" and turned toward the sea, most likely dismissing the incident as the temper tantrum of someone who could afford a thousand TVs. "Anyway, there's still a lot to be worked out, but tonight we got some very important backers."

"And they are?" Raider asked eagerly, testing Othello's honesty.

Othello set his glass inside the coil of rope and gazed up the coast, squinting and mulling over the ramifications of putting Jasper and Deon at risk. Most likely Raider Kincaide, Rookie Activist, wasn't ready for the whole truth. *Maybe* when he confessed his undying love for Othello they could talk of financial moguls, basketball legends and assassination plots.

"Othello," Raider said with a lilt in his voice, "you said you'd tell me what's going on if I came back East with you."

"And I told you: we got more backers. I don't want to jinx things just yet. These people are still new at this, just like you." His tone brightened. "And to think, you were going to save me tonight if things got ugly. My big stud in shining armor." Standing side by side, Othello put his arm around Raider's shoulders.

"Well, I don't know what I would have done," Raider said with a modest grin, thinking: I knew this was coming, bet he couldn't wait for an excuse to get his paws on me.

"With these biceps of steel?" With his other hand Othello cupped Raider's arm. "I'm sure you would have come up with something worthy of Indiana Jones."

Raider laughed with mock skepticism. "You think so?"

"I know so. With your athletic prowess?"

"My playing days are long gone." This time he took a real sip of champagne, partly in hopes of loosening Othello's grasp on his upper body. "But you still think I look like an athlete?"

"Are you kidding? With pecs like these." Othello's hand landed in the middle of Raider's chest. "And legs like small tree trunks?"

"What do you mean, *small?*" said Raider.

"Small compared to a California redwood," Othello corrected himself, "but quite large compared to the average man. And you're far from average."

"You think?" Raider asked baitingly, a doubtful glint struggling to break through the smile plastered on his face.

In an effort to get closer, Othello moved in front of Raider until less than a foot separated them. "Yes, I do. And I also think you're fishing for compliments, Raider Kincaide, you know you're a man's man."

Raider scoffed, and in a sudden desire for breathing room, retreated from Othello and leaned over the railing, focusing on the champagne glass rotating in his hands. "I was not fishing for compliments," he said defensively.

"Yes, you were," teased Othello.

"No, I wasn't."

"Yes, you were."

"I said I wasn't. Now drop it."

Taken aback by the edginess in Raider's voice, Othello decided not to pursue it. "Doesn't matter," he said, leaning over the railing next to Raider and gazing out to sea. "I'm too ecstatic to argue. I'm so happy I could cruise around the world. Or maybe up to Nantucket. Let's do it. Seriously. We could head up to Nantucket. You could show me your hometown and all your old haunts."

"Nantucket?" Raider dismissed the idea with a terse breath, as if it were the most ridiculous notion of the night. "I haven't been back to that place in years," he said scoldingly.

Deliberately, Othello stood up straight, a grave expression creeping over his face as he eyed Raider, who was staring unassumingly at the Atlantic.

Years? But you said you just moved to LA from Nantucket.

Time stopped for Othello. An instinctive nerve told him to question this contradiction right away, but the shock held him back. Raider hadn't tried to correct himself either, his slip apparently too subconscious for him to notice. In the dead silence, a new reality sank in, as resounding as a death knell in Othello's mind: Raider had lied. Raider was lying. Raider was capable of lying to him.

Othello averted his stare to the darkness of the horizon, the sight of the man he wanted to be the love of his life too ripe with confusion and pain. He wasn't even sure how long the silence lasted, but it was Raider who broke it.

"You know, recently I went out and bought *One Nation*," he said, leaving out the part about buying it for his son and refusing to give it to him after he found out Othello was a homo. "Then I listened to every song for any hidden gay messages."

"And?" Othello said vacantly.

"I don't know." Raider chuckled. His tone was one of amusement, fully oblivious to having just severed a heart.

"The album is a flop as far as I'm concerned," Othello said. What was Raider trying to pull? he asked himself. Was it just an innocent white lie? Or was it bigger than that, as in Raider was after Othello's money or trying to out him to the tabloids? Or could it have something to do with the clandestine endeavors that were suddenly consuming Othello's life? In short, who the hell was this guy named Raider Kincaide?

"A flop?" said Raider. "It's been number one for weeks."

"Creatively a flop. I was trying for some kind of 'we're all one people' concept, but I failed to mention the most important people of all: queers."

"What do you suppose would happen if you did come out?" Raider asked, assuming talk of the album was the source of Othello's somber mood.

Othello shrugged, struggling to stay with the conversation, debating whether or not to proceed with the night's plans even though his dreams were in the process of being run through a paper shredder. "Maybe people would do what you did, buy my albums to look for hidden messages, try to reinterpret every little thing I ever did."

"The controversy alone might sell zillions," mused Raider.

Othello sighed a defeated sigh. "This wasn't supposed to be a night for business."

"Then let's talk about the revolution—"

"No," Othello said flatly, poised with newfound determination. "No more talk period." If his dream man was not to be, at least Othello was going to know how it felt to be in his arms one time. He turned to Raider in full command of the few feet of deck between. "We—or at least I—came out here for some moonlight dancing."

He relieved Raider of his champagne glass and nestled it inside the coil of rope. Then he walked over to the door of the lower deck cabin and gave it three steady knocks. From a small speaker stationed on the upper deck above the engine room came the crackling sound of a sultry saxophone backed by the slow rhythms of a syncopated drum beat. Othello flashed a confident, mischievous grin, then stripped off his brown bomber's jacket, revealing a tight black turtleneck which matched his black jeans.

"That's 'Succulent,'" Raider said guardedly, recognizing the steamy romantic ballad from *One Nation*.

"Correct for fifty points and a trip to the bonus round."

With one arm extended above him, he spun around twice—a patented Othello transition on stage—then began gliding his hands over and around his face as if to frame it. From his face, his fingers slid down over the rest of his body, sensuously tracing the contours of his chest, stomach and finally, his ass. From there, he began swaying his hips in time to the song's long jazzy intro, moving his arms as if he were sculpting the air, his body flowing to some inner rhythm. It was a performance for himself as much as his audience of one, proof to both of them that Othello was a sexual force to be dealt with. On the opposite side of the deck, Raider looked on, clinging to the railing behind him, caught between trepidation and curiosity, especially as Othello began singing along with the song while looking directly into his eyes.

> Strawberries can be so sweet.
> And honey, oh, can be quite a treat.
> But, baby, I bet nothing in this world can beat
> the taste of a little bit of you
> mixed in with a little bit of me....

Still singing, Othello sauntered across the deck until he was inches away from Raider, not touching him but teasingly simulating caressing his hair, shoulders and torso. With an uneasy smile and bugged-out eyes, Raider played along, not dancing but not diving into the ocean either.

> Succulent
> is what you are to me.
> Can't you see, sugar,
> this is our every fantasy....

Gently, Othello took hold of Raider's arms, extending them, dancing with them, forgoing singing along with the CD in favor of some playful eye contact. "Succulent" was in full tilt now, its smooth, silky melody meshing seductively with the hypnotic rocking of the Atlantic. And Othello, on the CD, was wailing about how tasty it could be if two bodies gave in to their deepest dreams. To accentuate his point, he wrapped Raider's arms around his waist and placed his own arms around Raider's back, becoming engulfed for the first time in the natural smell of his lacrosse legend's flesh and hair, gradually lapsing from a performer performing into an ordinary soul who craved the feeling of being caught up in a loving embrace.

As if he were a talk show host reluctantly agreeing to be a trooper and participate in some sort of stunt on his show, Raider went along with this dance. As long as Othello didn't try anything more, he reasoned. Felt weird as all hell though, dancing with another guy. *A gay guy at that.* But stay cool, he demanded of himself. Think of the glory that awaits once you bust up the gay Goodfellas. Besides, how many chicks—and guys—the world over would kill to be in your shoes right now, having Othello crooning over them, lusting after them, dancing with them. This last thought produced an inner chuckle and he was able to lighten up a bit, even firm up his grip on his male dance partner.

Othello felt Raider's arms clinging to him tighter and a fresh burst of adrenaline raced through his body. He snuggled closer to Raider, his chin nestled comfortably in Raider's shoulder, his lips a breath away from that tanned neck and the moist golden locks tickling it. "No other song on earth makes me feel this sexy," he murmured as their bodies slowly rotated around the axis of each other. As deflated as his heart was by The Lie, as suspicious as his mind had now become, it was impossible to dismiss the pull toward the man dancing in his arms on a yacht in the middle of the moonlit ocean. And Othello realized right then and there he wanted Raider just as much if not more than before. His nose brushed across the strands of blond hair falling down Raider's neck, and with his fingers, he reached up and twirled them. Then, he kissed Raider's neck, ever so lightly, reveling in the faint taste of sweat that could have just as easily come from the playing fields of Dartmouth.

"Othello, we shouldn't," came from Raider in a barely audible drone. "We're gonna take it really slow, remember?"

"I don't want all of you tonight," Othello whispered, his tongue purposely brushing against the inside of Raider's ear. "Just a little bit."

Raider arched his head toward the moon in an effort to free his ear. "I don't feel so comfortable with your manager here."

"Sweeney won't bother us." He kissed Raider's large Adam's apple. "I ordered him to go to sleep."

"Still." Raider tried to peacefully untangle himself from Othello's arms, but Othello was just as resilient, not letting go of Raider, not letting Raider go.

"We're allegedly celebrating, remember?" said Othello.

"Can't we allegedly celebrate without this?"

"Not when there's enough chemistry between us to blow up a science lab." With one arm struggling to remain around Raider, Othello used his free hand to cup Raider's chin, intent on planting a kiss smack dab on his—

"Enough already, all right?"

Abruptly, Raider tore away to the opposite side of the deck and lunged for the railing, looking for a moment as if he were about to leap. Instead, he grabbed on as if for dear life and glared at the dark moody waters below.

"Sorry, I'm sorry," Othello said, horrified and guilt-ridden. "I didn't—I'm sorry—"

"It's all right, okay, cool." Raider insisted hastily, fighting for equilibrium and sanity. As he began to regain a portion of both, he realized no gay man in his right mind who'd already admitted to having a thing for Othello would have overreacted like that, and now, he had to do some swift backpedaling or else this case was as good as dead. "Look, I have a confession." He turned to Othello, who was frozen in the middle of the deck, a stupefied look on his face. "This is all very flattering, really, but I have to tell you the truth. I'm not very experienced when it comes to gay sex."

"Not very experienced?" Othello felt another lie coming. He walked over to the speaker through which "Succulent" was still humming and disconnected it. "Just exactly how not very experienced are you?"

Raider bowed his head to the deck. "I'm not very experienced at all," he said rather sheepishly, then quickly came back with: "but I do know that I...that I like...that I want to, you know—"

"No, I don't know, Raider, why don't you tell me?"

"Look, I don't want you to get mad at me—"

"What am I supposed to do? You told me you once had a lover, Adam, and that you've had your share of sport nookie—"

"Well, I lied, okay? Sort of."

"That's an understatement, wouldn't you say?"

Raider exhaled nervously. "Adam was my wife, Adele, who you already know about, and most of my sex in the past was with women. Not all, mind you," he added quickly. "I told you different because I know some militant gays look down on guys for being bisexual. You know that's true. I heard it myself at the meetings. This whole group of guys was bad-mouthing that actor Duke Whatley for being bi. And I didn't know if you would look down on me for having had more women than men in the past, even though I know all's I want now is men. I'm still trying to come out and feel comfortable with all this, you know. The last thing I wanted you to do was reject me for being bi because I think you're a nice guy. And I kinda like you. So I lied."

Othello threw his head back and let out a long breath, his hard-boiled stance crumbling involuntarily. Raider picked up on this and took it as a cue to drive home the "poor li'l stud" act.

"Is that what you're gonna do now," he asked like a crestfallen boy in need of reassurance, "reject me?"

"You probably overheard some people at ACTNOW bad-mouthing Duke Whatley because he's claiming straight, not owning up to even being bi. Most gays, militant or otherwise, don't have a problem with bisexuals."

"But what about you?"

"I couldn't care less about that. I'm just upset that you lied."

"Well, can you forgive me now that you know why?" Raider said, creasing his brow and kicking the charm into overdrive. "I just wanted you to like me."

Othello massaged his temples for relief. "Not quite the night I planned." He looked up at the stars. "Any more surprises?"

"None," Raider proclaimed, confident he was well on his way back into Othello's good graces. "Promise."

"So what else have you lied to me about? We might as well get it all out on the table right now."

Raider was surprised by the question. "Well, nothing," he said, staring into Othello's eyes ever so briefly before letting out a terse breath and turning toward the sea, the matter all wrapped up in a neat little bundle in his mind.

Othello stood there as rigid as a statue, the question of honesty far from resolved. Then he decided it was time to tell Sweeney to take *The Girlfriend* back to the Jersey shore. He was no longer in the mood for moonlight dancing.

NINE

KANSAS CITY, MISSOURI: Sisters Unite Bookshop has security cameras installed to combat the recent rash of vandalism to the lesbian and feminist bookstore. In the past year, vandals have written anti-gay obscenities on the storefront dozens of times, thrown dildoes through the front windows, and twice broken in and looted the cash register. Now, thanks to the Triangle Fund, cameras will catch any and all vandals in the act.

Washington, DC: Serve and Protect, a crime watch group formed to fight gay bashing near gay establishments, receives a substantial influx of cash to aid in their operation. Now, the group is equipped with walkie talkies, cellular phones, video cameras and minivans to help combat the area's gay-related hate crimes.

Miami, Florida: Rainbow House, a non-profit home for gay and lesbian teenagers, is awarded a grant for much-needed repairs and improvements to the old Spanish-style mansion that houses up to twelve teens abandoned by their families. The money will go toward fixing the plumbing, new furniture and adding six computers to the house library. A scholarship fund is also set up to allow each member of Rainbow House to attend college upon emancipation from the group home.

Indianapolis, Indiana: Hoosiers With Heart, the city's largest AIDS service organization, is given enough money to move into a brand new facility. Their old building was owned by the Catholic church, which fought them on many sex-related issues and prevented them from conducting safe sex seminars and distributing condoms on the facility's premises.

Houston, Texas: Beacon Hospice for persons with AIDS finally opens after three years of financial struggles and legal battles, thanks to a grant from the Triangle Fund.

Boise, Idaho: The Rainbow Task Force, the city's main gay and lesbian organization, is awarded enough money to hire lawyers to fight an unlawful eviction prompted by anti-gay factions within the community.

"GENTLEMEN," OTHELLO announced, eyeing the US map on the wall of the Temple and sticking a red pushpin into Boise, Idaho, "the Triangle Fund is a winner. It's sweeping the nation and rising up the charts faster than one of my hits."

Jasper and Deon laughed, but Othello could tell they were both brimming with pride and satisfaction. As planned.

"We need to help out a whole lot more black folk," Deon said as he sat at the conference table, poring over the reports.

"I'm for the crime watch gangs myself," said Jasper. He was leaning against the console underneath the map, scrolling the computer monitor. "Here's twelve more that could use some assistance. Definite yes vote for me."

"And six more groups are forming across the country." Othello turned away from the dozens of red pushpins scattered across the states. "Just think: we, the Three Wisemen, are inspiring a whole nation of gays without stepping one foot out of our miserable little closets." In the next beat, his grin disappeared. The part about miserable little closets sounded more like an accidental admission than the joke he had intended. He stared at his feet, speechless, embarrassed.

"Wait until my boy Bruce does his piece on the Fund." Jasper sat down at the conference table, trying his best to ignore Othello's comment. "They'll start coming to us instead of us having to seek them out."

The admission also made Deon uncomfortable, but no way was he gonna touch that one. "Next on the list is this initiative in Maine. Some kind of measure to ban any mention of gays in discrimination laws."

"That's an easy one," said Jasper.

"Twenty grand gonna be enough?" Deon looked across the table to Jasper, the money expert.

"That's what they're asking for, that's what they get."

"Cool," Deon said, then looked to Othello.

"Unanimous," Othello mumbled from behind Jasper.

"Next up," said Jasper, "a gay nudist colony in Michigan. They're claiming one of those militia groups is trying to run them out of the county."

"Nudists?" said Deon. "How do we know they aren't trying to rip us off?"

"Nobody rips us off," Jasper promised with a cold glare.

"Still," said Deon. Unlike Jasper, whose men were running the Fund, and Othello, who had his manager checking the books, Deon was flying solo on this venture. He had no accountants or lawyers he could open up to about his latest investment, a fact that made him the most gun-shy when it came to approving grants.

"Rock Star, what do you know about these nudies?" Jasper turned around to find that Othello had moved to the end of the table and was facing the revolving fireplace. "Rock Star?" he repeated.

Othello startled and turned back to his partners.

"The Michigan nudists," said Jasper. "Deon's unsure; break the tie."

Othello shrugged, his mind only partially in the room. "Beats the hell out of me." His partners blanched. It was the first time Othello had ever been noncommittal in a vote. "Well, it's been a long day," he offered as an excuse. It was past midnight in Los Angeles, the late start of the meeting due to game two of the Bulls-Knicks series earlier in the afternoon in Chicago. Deon and the Bulls won easily, 112-99, to take a 2-0 lead in the best-of-seven series. But Jasper and Deon didn't seem to buy Othello's excuse. "Juice, soda, anything, anyone?" Othello asked, trying to deflect attention away from himself. When they shook their heads, he made his way to the buffet table on the wall opposite the US map, already forgetting what their question had been.

In the two weeks since Atlantic City, life had been one dizzy roller-coaster ride for Othello, between getting the Fund up and running, trying to find an AIDS doctor but not knowing where to turn, listening with apprehension then relief to reports that said the cops were no closer to identifying the culprits from Simi Valley, and most of all, Raider, the man from Nantucket who hadn't been to Nantucket in years. So far, Othello had avoided seeing him since The Lie, using music business as an excuse, which was pure fabrication because, much to Sweeney's discontent, he'd been neglecting *One Nation* as per usual since testing positive. Now, this morning, Raider had called with an offer to come over and cook dinner sometime. How could Othello say no, wanting so desperately to have Raider in his life? But how could he say yes, knowing how much was at stake?

Mineral water in hand, he rejoined his partners, sitting for the first time since they arrived. Foregoing the head of the table, he sat on Deon's side.

"I move we hold off on the nudists," said Jasper. "Investigate."

"This is all fine," said Othello, "but the radical factions need a boost, too, Queer Nation, ACT UP, and my personal favorite, ACT-NOW." Earlier tonight, Othello had dressed as Joe and attended his first ACTNOW meeting since Simi Valley. The group was in complete disarray. Those not part of the Weeks debacle offered various and often polar-opposite opinions about the anonymous terrorists, while in the secret meeting conducted afterwards by Travis and the other members who participated in Simi Valley, there was just as much disharmony and disagreement about what they had done and what to do next.

"Those groups would give the Fund a bad name," said Jasper. "I can see now the Christian news networks linking all our charity work with tattooed, pierced radicals urinating on the steps of the capitol."

"So what," argued Othello, remembering the heavily censored shots of ACTNOW doing just that over a year ago. "This isn't about public relations."

"It's not for the Fund," Jasper declared, "end of story."

"I agree," Deon said. "Although I was at the White House the same day they did that, you know, right after we won the championship. Some aid runs in with a Southern accent: 'Gays are pissing on the Capitol! Gays are pissing on the Capitol!' I 'bout died busting a gut."

Deon and Jasper laughed and reminisced about that day, which was Othello's cue to tell them they were right: supporting radical activist groups wasn't for the more pristine Triangle Fund, and that was why they should escalate the war on a separate front by secretly getting behind the more hard-core rebels, ACTNOW in particular. Instead, he veered off course. "Let's just keep on trucking down the list," he mumbled, not fighting the fight he had planned, and most troubling of all, not understanding why.

CORVALLIS, OREGON: Free Oregon receives a Triangle Fund grant to fight a proposed city ordinance that would prohibit the teaching of positive gay images in schools.

Santa Monica, California: Inroads, an acclaimed performance arts center predominantly used by gay and lesbian artists, is awarded a grant to replace the one revoked by the National Endowment for the Arts. The NEA had partially funded the theater space for the past five years, but recently succumbed to conservative congressmen who attacked the theater for its "immoral" content. Now, government funding will no longer be necessary.

Chicago, Illinois; Cleveland, Ohio; Detroit, Michigan; East St. Louis, Illinois; Camden, New Jersey: AIDS hospices and services organizations located in urban neighborhoods in each of these cities are given substantial grants to provide improved services to its mostly minority clientele.

"BROWNING, HOPPER, in," Jasper commanded from behind his desk. "Everybody else out. Jump!"

Eight Armani-suited executives scurried out of Jasper's Manhattan office. When they were gone, he smiled at his two most trusted colleagues standing on either side of his chair—the white-haired Browning and the bald Hopper—and aimed a large remote control toward the bank of televisions on the opposite wall, turning all twelve of them on his toy, CNC, and his boy, Bruce Jones, who was standing on bustling Madison Avenue, thin blond hair blowing in the wind, looking like the recent Missouri School of Journalism graduate that he was.

"At a time when charitable contributions are otherwise becoming more and more scarce," he began, "some gays and lesbians have found a new source of support and are calling it a welcomed ray of hope."

"Give it to us," Jasper said with a proud grin.

"The Triangle Fund has been in place only a few weeks and has already given out over twenty-five grants." The report cut to footage inside the Fund's office in a New York brownstone. Half a dozen gay men and women were answering phones, working on computers, conferring on reports, all looking quite business-like. "AIDS organizations and political activist groups are chief among the applicants so far, but fund spokesman Harold Bookman" —cut to a shot of Harold, the black man in his forties Jasper had chosen to run things— "says the Triangle Fund will consider any and all requests for grants from the gay and lesbian community."

On the big black sofa in his den, a comfortable smile wiped across Deon Anthony's face as he watched Jasper's lover's report. This is a good thing, he concluded, extending the remote to turn up the volume, but not too much lest he wake Charlie, who was sound asleep against his left shoulder. Damn, he said to himself with amazement. I'm finally doing something for my gay side. 'Bout time.

"CUT, PRINT, CHANGE wardrobe," barked the director, a hefty blonde woman who couldn't have been more than twenty-five. Consciously, Othello didn't hear her. It took the rumblings of the cast and crew surrounding him to bring him back into the present. Then, once he realized he had a few moments of freedom, he rose up from the stool he'd been ensconced on for the past few twenty minutes, untangled himself from the two black supermodels bookending him and stormed through the stark set that consisted of nothing more than the stool in front of a neon version of the American flag.

Just outside the soundstage was his trailer. When he reached it, he flung the door open, then slammed it shut just as furiously, his actions immediately followed by Sweeney flinging the door open again and joining him inside.

"That went well," Sweeney began, then quickly corrected himself. "What am I saying? That sucked. O, could you act like you actually know the models are there? Try to have something called *chemistry* with them? I really want you to think about having this Sharon woman direct your next video—"

"There's not going to be any next video." Othello jerked off the leather jacket that resembled an American flag and slammed it on top of the TV set, knocking over a beverage tray full of sodas in the process. "Rock the fucking vote," he said, referring to the public service announcement they'd been shooting all afternoon for MTV. "Why should I tell young America to get off their asses and vote when we've got uptight assholes like Jimmy Herman around for decades? I should be telling them to rock the fucking offices, storm 'em and...." He snatched a clock off the desk and threw it down the corridor of the trailer. It smashed against the wall.

Sweeney remained silent until he was sure Othello was done. "What you're doing with the Triangle Fund is admirable and more than enough."

Othello scoffed.

"What more can you do?" pleaded Sweeney.

With both hands, Othello rubbed his head, which was shaved bald for the shoot. He didn't answer Sweeney. The Log Cabin Republican wouldn't understand. He'd loved and been loved by the same man for years. No nasty virus inside the gay Ozzie and Harriet, Othello was willing to bet. As much as he truly loved his manager....

He remained silent.

"Better let you change for the next shot," Sweeney said. "And there will be a next video. And soon."

Othello rolled his eyes toward the ceiling, waiting until he heard the door shut to breathe again.

What more can you do?

There was a rap song by some brutha whose name escaped him. How did it go? If I could just kill a man. If I wanted to kill a man. I would kill a man. Something along those lines, but definitely resolute about the rapper's ability to snuff out the life of somebody who stood in his way.

Maybe I should do a song like that, he thought. A song of protest instead of getting more tangled up with Jasper and Deon, instead of Joe becoming linked to Simi Valley and eventually exposed, instead of having my life ripped to shreds by a man claiming to be attracted to me but unwilling to hold me and dance in the moonlight. A song of protest instead of trying to find somebody to put a bullet in Senator Evil's brain.

Good God, can I really end the life of another human being just like that? Even one as vile and despicable as the fat-ass senator from South Carolina?

He tried to wander around the small confines of the trailer, but felt trapped, so he sat on the coffee table, the image of Jimmy Herman being felled by a bullet resonating in his mind like no other time since the night he found out he was positive.

The life dropped out of his stomach. His palms began to sweat. Was he shaking?

If I could kill a man? Would I kill a man?

What made perfect sense before—start an uprising with the assassination of Jimmy Herman—seemed so utterly senseless all of a sudden. Was it the fact that his plan was in motion, albeit seemingly slow motion? Or was it Raider's lie, big or small, that only reinforced the mind-numbing fact that deceit and slip-ups by anyone—Jasper, Deon, Travis, Raider, Sweeney, himself, *anyone*—could someday lead to Othello being caught and exposed to the world, his whole life, his sexuality, the virus and his crazy scheme to kill a politician fodder for a thousand nights of tabloid and network TV, a plot that would rank right up there with O.J.?

"What the hell am I doing?"

He tried to stand but couldn't.

Maybe a song of protest would be better, he told himself, partially trying to lighten the mood. But in the next second, he squashed the idea and rather scoldingly: Yeah, right, while I'm telling the world "baby, baby I want yo' pussy, can't live without that pussy, lots and lots of pussy, oh, how I live for pussy," I'll tell them I got the urge to kill a man who stands in the way of faggots' rights. The reason? Oh, by the way, America, and Southeast Asia, where I made fifteen million alone on my last album and tour, I'm a big fucking homo myself. La dee da.

Killing a man in secret was a helluva lot easier than that. Wasn't it?

At the Big House that night, in his bedroom, which had been repaired to look as good as new, he replayed the videotape of Jimmy Herman's venom, listening over and over to hours of anti-gay sludge whose vile and logic was mind-boggling.

Then, at about 3:00 a.m., he firmly decided: yes, he could have a bastard like Herman snuffed out, and with Othello's smarts and determination and vision, he could get away with it. And this *was* the best way to breathe new life into the revolution and his own gay soul. It was acceptable. It was necessary. With Jimmy Herman, it was downright justified.

THE ALLEYWAY WAS dark and almost empty. Halfway down, a tall Latino man stood behind an old station wagon. The white man who had been facing him only moments before was now on his knees and out of sight, presumably sucking away. At the other end, a lone heavyset man lurked desperately in a doorway, hands in pockets, waiting for more prey. It was a slow night. Midweek. One of the reasons this was a good place to meet.

"Forget about Simi Valley," the old man Joe told Travis. They were standing shoulder to shoulder behind a dumpster. "The old lady is back in the game and more pissed off than ever."

"Do tell," Travis said. "What about the help she spoke of?"

"Slow right now, just like the cruising around here." Joe glanced around to make sure they still had privacy. If any men saw Travis, they might be drawn to that long black hair and sequoia-like figure in jeans, but no one was gonna touch ol' beer-bellied Joe with a ten foot anything. "Her friends *will* come around, she assures me. The old lady has a way of making people come around."

"The more the merrier," said Travis.

"How many are still with us from Level 2—that's what I call the Simi Valley faction."

"Good name for it. Me and Freedom, of course, and six others. Beth, who got left behind—she's out. So's her lover. They both freaked. So did two others. But eight of us are ready for more. And we threatened to cut Freedom's balls off if he ever pulls another stunt like that again."

"Eight is plenty. Tell them to be ready. At a moment's notice. Time to work."

The smile on Travis's face said he couldn't agree more.

"I CAN'T SEE THE Fund aiding them, no." Jasper circled the oak desk in the middle of the Royal Suite, passing Deon who was pacing in the opposite direction.

"What they're doing is just as legit as your crime watch groups," said Othello. He was also pacing the floor, as they'd all been for the last few minutes. "Or your black hospices, Deon."

"How we gonna control people like that?" Deon argued. He was the reason they were meeting at the Palace in Atlantic City. The Bulls had just polished off the Knicks at Madison Square Garden to take a commanding 3-1 lead in their series. "We give them money, next thing you know they've used it to, I don't know, burn something."

"You might have ties to ACTNOW," said Jasper, "but you can't convince us that you can control groups like Queer Nation and Gay Rage."

Othello paused. "Okay, then. How about just my gang, ACT-NOW? ACTNOW we can control."

"Even so," said Jasper. "The Triangle Fund isn't for them."

"You're right," said Othello. "I now see the error of my thinking. If we funnel money to them, it's got to be cash on the sly, no publicity, no CNC pieces. Just private backing through their leader, Travis Little Horse, like I was doing on my own before the Three Wisemen."

"You trust him that much?" Jasper stopped pacing and stood across the desk from Othello.

"How?" Deon stood next to Jasper.

"The disguise I once mentioned." He put on his scratchy voice. "Just call me Old Man Joe, a gardener for a rich old widow." He told them about the fool-proof disguise and the envelopes of cash he doled out to Travis to be used how the old lady wanted. "So far he hasn't given me the slightest reason to think he'd put a knife in my back."

Jasper moved closer to Othello, as if to further scrutinize him. "There was an old black man seen running from that deal in Simi Valley."

Othello sighed. "I didn't mean to get that intimate with the hands-on operation, but yes, it was me. And was it ACTNOW? Yes and no. It was more like an offshoot comprised of people willing to go a step further than the rest of the group. I call them Level 2."

"You believe in taking chances don't you," Jasper said warily.

"The old man has been officially dropped as a suspect," said Othello. "There's no link."

Taking it all in, Deon sat down at the desk.

"I could still give them cash on my own," Othello said, "but I want this to be a group effort. United we stand, et cetera et cetera."

"The blond fellow who helped the woman," Jasper said, trying to remember the CNC report on the incident. "Who was he?"

"Just a guy." Othello averted his eyes to the floor. "One of the soldiers."

"What do they want to do next?" Jasper asked, his tone full of curiosity, amazement or both. "This Level 2, or would it be 3 now?"

"What would you have them do?" asked Othello. "Any hatemongers piss you off lately?"

Deon, who had been quiet for a while, put his long legs on the desk and thought about Charlie, who had to run for his life last week. He'd been shopping near Michigan Avenue, not even dressed as Charlene, but he must have been swishing up a storm like he always did when he was on a shopping trip. Turning up a side street, he found himself being chased by four, maybe five guys who started calling him names and saying they were gonna rape his ass with a crowbar. He got

away only after dropping most of the bags he was carrying and running into a restaurant. He came home crying and terrified, reminded
of his days and nights on the street.

"Maybe we can help them somewhat," Deon suddenly heard
himself say, but decided against telling them about his lover's ordeal.
"On the sly through this Joe—but maybe not."

"We can vote on their acts just like the Fund," said Othello.
"Think of them as our personal strong arm."

"This shit is pretty dangerous," Deon said.

"So is being a faggot in the good ol' U. S. of A."

Othello walked over to the window overlooking the casino, giving Deon time to think about his boyfriend's little run for his life in
Chicago. He made a mental note to praise Travis and his buddies for
a job well done, especially seeing as how they carried out the orders
blindly. Travis had said Charlie was scared shitless, tossed his loot and
pissed in his pants. Poor kid. Anything for the cause though.
Terrorizing one Charlie might save a hundred Charlies from the real
deal. This was war. In war, there had to be sacrifices. He turned back
to his partners. "So, Wisemen, do we evolve into even more powerful
mutha fuckas or not?"

"By doing what?" asked Jasper. "Get specific."

Othello paused, then made his way to the desk where he
retrieved a folder and handed both Jasper and Deon a series of newspaper clippings. "In a small Kentucky town, three weeks ago, a thirty-
six year-old gay man named Jeffrey Glenn was arrested for lewd con-
duct in a cruisy park. Mr. Glenn had AIDS and was on his last legs.
Now, I don't know if he was cruising or not, but according to another friend who was with him, when Glenn told the police he had AIDS
and wasn't there for sex, the cops roughed him up quite a bit, calling
him everything from a fruitcake to an infected faggot and smacking
him with their batons every time he tried to plead his case. Three
hours later, Jeffrey Glenn was found dead in an isolated jail cell.
Official word is he hanged himself, but the coroner's report says he
had four broken ribs and internal bleeding."

"Must have been black, too," said Deon.

"In this case, being a queer with AIDS was enough."

"Says here one inmate heard him crying for help for hours," said Jasper. "But the officers—the same two that arresting him also were supposed to guard him at the station—refused to give Glenn medical attention because he was bleeding and they didn't want to go near him."

Othello shook his head. "The friend he was with alleges he heard the cops say they were gonna finish Glenn off at the jail."

"So the friend is the key witness," said Jasper.

"Yeah, yeah," Othello said, "and internal affairs is doing their investigation, but we all know what that'll lead to. Plus, the friend won't get involved, says he's tired of fighting the system and he's dying, too." Othello paused to let the whole thing sink into their collective conscience. "The people left over from Level 2—they want to go to Kentucky and pay the two arresting cops a visit."

"What kind of a visit?" Jasper asked. Othello told them. Both Jasper and Deon fell silent, digesting the plan. Waiting for an answer, Othello sat down on the couch underneath the casino window. Several minutes passed without a word, no one making eye contact, each Wiseman locked in his own private reflection.

Finally, Deon was the first to speak.

"Do it," he uttered, thinking of all the creeps who ever chased Charlie, not to mention J-Boy, his first lover who was just as effeminate and probably got harassed just as much.

Othello checked the triumphant yelp swelling in his chest and turned to his other partner. "Hollinquest?"

Jasper rubbed his chin. "Give her a shot."

"Gentlemen," Othello began, not bothering to conceal his grin, "next time we're in the Temple, please remind me to nail one of those red pins into the bluegrass hills of Kentucky."

JACK GATO—TALL, burly, mid-forties with a black bushy mustache and dark Russian features—entered his ranch-style home in Elliotville, Kentucky, thoroughly exhausted from a ten-hour shift upholding the law. It was 8:00 p.m. and the whole house was dark. His wife Sally and ten year-old daughter Megan were apparently out. Odd, he thought.

They hadn't called down to the station to tell him they wouldn't be home tonight. He pondered this rare aberration in the family routine as he grabbed the mail off the television set just inside the front door and absently reached for the adjacent floor lamp.

Jack Gato never turned on the light. The next thing he knew, chunks of his body were being crushed with massive force, his back, his gut, his groin, his cheek, his other cheek, his skull. Baseball bats...thugs...three of them...maybe four...with no faces...dark faces...dark masks...stockings...no black leather....

It all happened too fast. He was unconscious in fifteen seconds flat, a limp entanglement of flesh showered in blood. A small white piece of paper floated down toward the floor, slow and graceful like a lazy snowflake, landing in front of his body, which was lying in the fetal position. Don't fuck with queers, the snowflake read.

TOOLEY SIMS, a thirty-six year-old red-headed country boy who'd never been out of the state of Kentucky, knocked on the back door of Harlan's Barber Shop, calling out Harlan's name several times. It was way past closing time, which was sundown, but ol' Harlan had cut Tooley's hair since Tooley was a toddler, and Tooley had a date with LouAnn Hubbard tonight, so Harlan had agreed to meet him at the shop after supper.

Having come right over as soon as he got off duty, Tooley was running a bit early. The shop was still dark and empty. Tooley lumbered his tall, spidery body back toward his black pickup truck parked in the alley, ready to prop up his feet on the dash and catch a few Z's 'cause Lord knows LouAnn Hubbard could wear out half the force before she got tired.

He was just about to open the door and hop in the cab when two men came out of nowhere from the right. At first, he thought they were niggers, but then he realized the blackness he was seeing wasn't skin, but dark gloves and clothes and hoods. Instinct told Tooley right away they were after him on the count of what he'd done to that fag in jail.

"Freeze!" He whipped out his gun, but they kept coming, baseball bats pounding in their hands. He shot the faggot on the right, a direct hit to the chest. Both would-be attackers stopped. The wounded one staggered a step before hunching over and falling to the ground. Tooley lowered his gun, staring and gasping at his work. Then, he realized he should order the other guy to get down on the ground. But it was too late. The back of Tooley's skull came crashing into his eyes. The last thing he saw was the wounded man leaping up, his body unblemished, as if he'd hadn't been hit at all. As if he'd been wearing a bulletproof vest, Tooley realized as his gun fell from his hand and clunked on the pavement. He felt his body twist and turn violently, giving way to blow after blow by two more hooded men behind him.

He remained conscious through the whole thing, but his mind was nowhere near coherent. When the blows ceased, he was on the ground, his lower body rolled halfway underneath his truck, rivers of blood coating his face. The eye pressed into the concrete was partially open, and with it, he was able to make out a blurry cloud of white as close as his eyelash, as thin and flat as a small piece of paper. Or an oversized snowflake.

"CHECK THIS OUT, baby," Charlie said from the other side of the bed, indicating the newspaper he was reading. "Front page, too—"

"Shh," Deon said as he propped himself up against the head-board, more intent on watching himself on ESPN's *The NBA Today.* "You should be looking at me," he told Charlie, pointing to the television at the foot of the bed.

"The D.A. was cranking on all cylinders at the United Center tonight," said the announcer's voice over a shot of Deon driving between two Knicks for a slam dunk. "Forty-six points, a whopping nine rebounds—"

"What does he mean, *whopping?*" asked Deon. "Like I don't rebound. That sonofa—"

"But, honey," Charlie said, "some queers did a number—"

"Boy, hold on," said Deon, increasing the volume via the remote.

"...but it took this clutch three-pointer late in the fourth by Anthony to send the Knicks packing and the Bulls into the next round against either Charlotte or Boston," said the announcer over the replay of Deon's bomb from the top of the three-point arch with twenty seconds left. New York never recovered; the Bulls were on to round three.

"Listen, Deon," Charlie insisted. "These Kentucky cops got a bloodbath, literally, by some angry queens wearing leather hoods."

Deon muted the television and listened intently as Charlie read aloud the entire article, his husky voice full of dramatics, especially during the descriptions of the cops injuries.

"What do you think about all this?" Deon asked when Charlie was finished.

"Shit, I love it! Every Mark Furman, Jr., in this country needs to have some sense beaten into him. *Bap. Bap. Bap.*" He jerked his shoulders side to side as if taken the blows himself. "Why, what do you think?"

Deon smiled a knowing, cocky smile. "Charlie, my girl, have I got news for you."

JASPER WAS IN THE study of his Manhattan penthouse when he heard the news. He was at his rolltop desk, working his way through a stack of spreadsheets, when CNC's Bobbie Baretta, the female anchor with the blonde helmet, caught his attention on the small television on the bar next to the desk:

"Two Kentucky police officers are in critical condition tonight after being brutally attacked late last night."

"Jasper, look," said Bruce, glancing up from the *Newsweek* he was reading on the chaise lounge in the far corner. They fell silent listening to the report. Details were sketchy. Only one of the cops could even talk and no witnesses could be found. When the report was over, a smile found its way to Jasper's face.

"Monsters," Bruce suddenly said, catching Jasper off guard.

Jasper turned to him, sizing him up like never before. "Indeed," he then said, and once again, returned to his spreadsheets.

"'DON'T EXPLETIVE WITH queers,' the notes both warned," said the white-haired anchorman from the CNC Headline Network, Jasper's other news channel.

"Oh, go ahead and say it, damn it!" Othello shouted to the small white television on the wall in a corner of the Big House kitchen. "Don't *fuck* with queers, Blanche, darling; it's don't *fuck* with queers!" He laughed at himself, clearly enjoying today's top story. "They show the cops being carted away in pools of blood, but they can't say the word fuck on TV. I like that word. Fuck. Fuck. Fuck."

"Now this is the only thing I know how to cook, but I cook it well," Raider said as he stirred a steaming twelve-quart pot on the kitchen's center island. "Back in college, half the lacrosse team survived on this in hard times."

"Hard times for a bunch of Dartmouth boys?" Othello said incredulously. He was leaning against the island, his back to Raider.

Raider glanced up curiously, noting but casting aside the edge in Othello's voice. "You think our pals from ACTNOW made a little excursion to Kentucky?"

"How should I know?" Othello moved toward the TV and turned it off. "I've lost touch with ACTNOW since Simi Valley," he said, thankful Raider hadn't been at the lone meeting he attended a week ago.

"Oh, I know you well enough to know you've been in touch with good ol' Travis Little Horse, if nothing else."

"What makes you think you know me at all, Raider?"

Mystified, Raider stopped stirring the pot and returned Othello's serious gaze. "We talk," he shrugged. "We're getting to know each other, aren't we?"

Silence from Othello.

"Besides." Raider added some spices to the sauté pan. "I happen to think it definitely could have been ACTNOW, the Simi Valley chapter anyway."

No answer.

"And I bet it was all the brainchild of Othello Hardaway," Raider said, going for a romantic and playful tone. "How else did you know fuck was the censored word just now?"

Othello scoffed. "What else could it be? Don't dance with queers? Don't eat with them? It had to be fuck. Fuck with a queer, get fucked."

Raider looked up, trying but failing to read Othello's face.

"I'll go set the dining room table," Othello said tersely, grabbing the silverware off the island and escaping the kitchen for the adjacent dining room, a small intimate room done in beechwood with a view of the LA basin below.

It killed him to have this kind of tension with the man he wanted to be The One, but the fact remained: Raider was lying about his life and was not to be fully trusted. He wasn't just an ex-jock who'd spent most of his life in rustic New England hamlets. That much made sense now and jibed with a feeling smoldering within Othello since the day they met. There was definitely more to Raider Kincaide, instinct told Othello. The time between Raider's boyhood on Nantucket Island and his arrival at the ACTNOW meeting in West Hollywood had been full of something that made him world-weary and city-wise beyond what a lifetime in a sleepy resort town—save four years in the Ivy League—would have afforded. Othello even had the impulse to have Sweeney recheck Raider's background, but ultimately nixed the idea out of fear of inviting any more trouble into paradise, or killing paradise all together.

But, in truth, there was no paradise since Atlantic City, only frustration and desire that refused to go away, which only made matters worse because Othello knew that loving a dishonest Raider could not only break his heart, but also destroy the uprising. And even with all the doubt and danger, Othello still possessed the impulse to fit this square peg into the round hole of his life. Raider just had to be on the up and up and fall completely and irrevocably in love with him, he convinced himself a dozen times a day. And maybe The Lie was a molehill of a lie, one they'd laugh about years down the line, say on their tenth anniversary. Either way, only one option seemed acceptable: keep the man from Nantucket around, test him and still pursue love. Othello wasn't sure he could stop now even if he tried.

"Pasta à la Raider Kincaide," Raider said in an Italian accent, standing at the doorway with a big bowl in hand. In return, he received the first half-smile of the night from Othello.

Midway through dinner, Raider was relieved that despite the setting, dinner wasn't turning into the romantic affair he had feared. True, soft jazz was playing on some unseen speakers and Othello's staff had the night off, but not once did Othello put the moves on him—no small black hand reaching across the table as they sat on either side of one corner, no deep-meaning looks coming from Othello's usually piercing eyes, no Othello playfully trying to feed him or serenading him with "Succulent." Just eating. And small talk. Very small talk. Which, by the end of dinner, led Raider to suspect something was wrong.

"Othello," Raider said with a gruff laugh. "You don't like my cooking? I smell or something tonight?"

"What do you mean?" Othello offered nonchalantly.

"If I didn't know any better—you're kinda distant. Makes me think it's not my imagination and you *have* been avoiding me."

"Avoiding you?"

"Since...really Atlantic City. I thought we were okay about that night, my not wanting to dance and all."

"I'm fine," Othello said with the enthusiasm of a robot. They went back to eating in silence until Raider couldn't stand it anymore.

"So you like my pasta *à la* Raider?"

"Fine."

"I could've put way more garlic in it. Sorry, it's the only thing I know."

"More cooking than I ever done."

End of that train of thought. The silence resumed.

What the hell have I done wrong? Raider wondered to himself. Have I said or done something since Atlantic City? In Atlantic City? He racked his brain but came up with nothing. He'd still been working out, using the rowing machine he charged to the bureau, doing his usual push-ups and sit-ups, even boxing near the beach a few times. Was it possible Othello was no longer attracted to him? No longer impressed with his physique and athleticism?

"Look Othello," he heard himself say, his voice surprisingly nervous. "Talk to me."

"About what?"

"Anything. Your music. The revolution."

"I don't want to talk music or the revolution."

"Why?"

"I just don't."

"But why—"

"I'm afraid—" Othello said abruptly, refusing to make eye contact. "I'm afraid I have to cut the evening short. A meeting, you know, first thing in the morning. That's the business, speaking of the business."

For a moment, Raider sat there reactionless. What is it: you don't like me anymore? he felt like saying, but realized how ridiculous that would sound.

They walked like strangers to the front door of the Big House.

"Good night," was all Othello was going to offer as he opened the door. Then he added: "Let's be in touch. Between my music things."

Otherwise speechless, Raider nodded as he crossed the threshold. Then, after the door was shut, he let out a great big "damn."

Inside, Othello leaned against the door and fought the urge to swing it open and beg Raider to come back inside. Forever. Think with your brain, he pleaded with himself, not your heart, not your soul, and least of all, your dick. But as he stood there listening to the sound of Raider's Jeep speeding down the driveway, he took an exhausted, hollow breath, knowing in the end which of the four would win out.

TEN

"**L**ADIES AND GENTLEMEN," said the female flight attendant's voice, "as we begin our final descent into Louisville International Airport, please make sure your seat belts are fastened and tray tables fully locked and in the upright position...."

From his aisle seat in coach, Bruce Jones tightened his seat belt a little tighter and began counting backwards from one hundred. He wasn't afraid of flying the way he had been as a child, but some rituals were harder to break than others. If nothing else, it helped him to relax, something he figured he needed on this trip.

Counting backwards worked; the plane landed safely. Brimming with confidence, he made his way through the gate and into the terminal, holding tight to his briefcase containing his tape recorder and laptop. His first stop would be the rental car counter, then it was on to Elliotville, a small hick town just outside Bowling Green.

THE BEARDED, MIDDLE-AGED fag peered over the deli counter, the girlish goo-goo eyes he was making magnified by his bifocals. "How was the workout?" he asked demurely, nodding toward Raider's sweat-soaked red tank top.

"Fine. Whatever," grunted Raider. Why did everyone in this freaking neighborhood leer at him? If he hadn't been so hungry after the gym, he would have driven to a store in the normal part of town, instead of Mayfair Market in the very bowels of West Holly*weird*.

"Thick or thin slices?" asked Four Eyes, no doubt just another excuse to lean over and gawk at Raider's crotch straining through a pair of cut-off gray sweats.

"Thick." He refused to lay eyes on the man again. Instead he surveying the crowded aisles to his right, thinking: every single guy in the joint is gay except me.

At the checkout line, he hastily chucked the package of roast beef and six pack of Bud Light on the counter, hoping the Mexican checkout girl would get the hint and hurry up with the young Asian "couple" ahead of him. But any idea of a quick exit disintegrated when into the market walked that flaming fag with the flaming red hair who tried to fondle him at the ACTNOW meeting and made such a mess of things at Simi Valley. This time, he was wearing tight leather shorts that stopped at the crotch, tall black army boots and a silver sequined muscle shirt. And, of course, enough ear, nose and eyebrow rings to disgust every God-fearing mother in America. What was his name? He sure recognized Raider right off, flinging one arm in the air like the world's biggest sissy and heading straight toward him.

"Hey, bupka!" he cried loudly, swishing past the Asians who were on their way out. "Didn't know you shopped at *Gay*fair." With him was a shorter man who thankfully didn't look as wacked out. His hair was normal and brown, his only visible piercings two sizable loops in both ears. "Freedom," the flamer said, commandeering Raider's hand. "And this here's Davy, non-activist." Regrettably, Raider also shook hands with Davy, whose eyes were just as glowing as the deli fag's, prompting Raider to quickly turn back to the checkout girl who had begun ringing him up. "Haven't seen you at the meetings lately," said Freedom.

"Got what I came for," Raider mumbled to himself while handing the Mexican girl a wad of ones.

"Hope you haven't abandoned us like chickenshit Davy here."

"Chicken?" Raider repeated absently, more concerned with bagging his own groceries and grabbing the change.

"Maybe your hair scared him off," joked Davy.

Freedom ignored his friend and started to manhandle Raider's right bicep with both hands. "Fuckin'-A, man. We need this."

"*Hey!*" Raider shouted, snatching his arm back and clenching his fist. Freedom gasped and his buddy jumped back. They were on the verge of a scene, Raider realized, stealing a glance at the checkout girl and the line forming behind him. "Look," he began unsteadily, dropping his arm and trying unsuccessfully to find a friendlier tone. What do you say to a freak like this? "Shit. Talk to you later" was all he could come up with, then he swiped up his groceries and walked away without waiting for a response.

Outdoors, the California sunshine was a welcomed sight. As the market's doors closed behind him, he dumped the roast beef in a trash bin in front of the store and walked hurriedly to his car. Right now, the thought of eating anything handled by a gay guy....

He collapsed in his Jeep, out of breath as if he'd gone through more than the mental gymnastics it took shopping at Mayfair Market. With the plastic bag holding the six pack in his lap, he slumped over until his head was resting on the wheel. "Get the job done and get the hell out of here," he ordered himself.

This was the hardest UC work he'd ever done. Pretending to be a dope dealer who got off peddling crack to junkie mothers was cake compared to pretending to be a fag. He knew at any time he could call it quits, say *adiós* to Othello and Boystown and return home to his Harleys, his son and Sally's Bar and Grill. It was FBI policy. Yet that option never seriously entered his head. Why? he asked himself daily. Simply put, he could smell the glory. Each night, going to bed in that West Hollywood apartment, he envisioned the legendary status sure to be his amongst the boys in the bureau after Panty-Raider Kincaide ferreted out this whole bizarre plot against God and country by three world-famous, in-the-closet homos. Why, he could retire on the book and movie rights alone, not to mention becoming a fabled agent whose name was invoked with reverence by and for all the rookies at Quantico, just like his boss and mentor Dockweiller.

But in the deepest recesses of his mind, Raider also knew there was more to his drive than mere fame and fortune. By becoming submerged in the gay world, he was exploring territory he never thought he'd explore in *twelve* lifetimes. Not that he ever, *ever* wanted to have sex with a guy, but now, at least while he was under for the count, he could let his mind roam a little freer and think about things he previously didn't know how to think about, nor want to think about. Over the last several weeks, certain memories would pop up out of the blue like ghosts, until now hidden in the shadows of his psyche.

On the plane out to LA, he had told himself he never once thought about being with another guy. Now, he had to confess this was untrue, as unnerving as it was to admit. When he was a kid—fifteen, maybe sixteen—he thought about homo-sex more than once, but more in the sense of wondering why one guy would want to be with another guy. To try to figure that one out, he would imagine putting his mouth on one of his buddy's dicks or having that buddy's lips around his own penis. It seemed so weird, he remembered thinking every single time. He also imagined getting cornholed, even stuck his finger up his butt once, when he was seventeen. But it hurt like hell and that's when he knew for sure he'd never be a fag. What a relief, the teenage Raider thought.

There were also other memories that now demanded attention, like all the crazy questions he and his pals used to put to each other in high school. It was always a matter of: if you were forced to choose, which would you rather do? Eat a ninety year-old woman's pussy, or give a buddy a blow job? Have your right arm cut off, or only have sex with guys for the rest of your life? Take a dick in your ass, or in your mouth? Lick a filthy public toilet seat in the restrooms near the beach, or let Philip Larsen, the school fag, suck your dick? Posing these kinds of stupid questions was their favorite past time while hanging out at the shore, drinking beer. And now that Raider thought about it, the questions almost always had to do with homo-sex. If anyone ever sounded as though they would actually *commit* any of the gay acts, everyone else would laugh in disgust and called that person a fag for a couple of minutes. But the homo-sex option was almost always part of the game.

And then there was Lenny, his best friend at Dartmouth, the straightest guy Raider knew other than himself. Together, the two of them terrorized Hanover, New Hampshire, for four years, not missing one hot girl or killer party between them. They hardly kept in touch these days—Lenny had snorted his life away—but back then Raider and Lenster must have screened every straight porno video on the market and they never failed to talk about the male star's "hose-potential" and how they both loved to see the stud jizz in the movies. "We can admit that to each other because we're not fags," Lenny used to say. And when he got drunk, which was often, he also used to say, "Panty-Raider, man, before I die, I'm gonna fuck you in the ass, man, I swear." To that, Raider would laugh, then they'd hit each other, hurl a derogatory name or two and start wrestling or boxing.

To think now that Lenster might have really meant it, that Not-So-Skinny Lenny might have had gay tendencies. For the first time in his life, Raider conceived it as possible. No way did Lenny Jerricho look like a fag, but neither did some of the guys Raider saw walking around West Hollywood. Some of them actually came off like guys he could have played sports with. Did Lenny turn out to be gay? What about the buddies of his youth who used to joke about it so much? Any of them ever try it? Ever want to?

Drudging up all these incidents from the past was unsettling at best, yet Raider couldn't control the mechanism in his brain that rendered these memories insignificant until now. It was this job, he knew, and West Hollywood and Othello pursuing him. And Freedom and ACTNOW and Jasper Hollinquest and Deon Anthony—*Deon Anthony* for Christ's sake; who wasn't gay? Who didn't think about it? One thing was for sure: Raider wanted to bust the case and get the hell out of Boystown before he had to deal with that $64,000 question.

He lifted his head off the steering wheel and started the engine, trying to forget about Freedom and the deli guy as he flicked on the radio. A rock song was playing. Thank God it wasn't Othello. To avoid the prospect of hearing his sultry come-ons, he turned it to an all-news station, hoping to catch some baseball scores. What he heard instead as he pulled away from the parking lot and onto Santa Monica Boulevard was a woman's voice reporting the news:

"...will not say if the beatings in Tallahassee and Bradenton, Florida, three days ago, as well as the one yesterday in a Dallas suburb,

UPRISING 163

are linked to the attacks in Elliotville, Kentucky. However, CBS Radio News has obtained information that similar notes have been left at all four sites, reading: F-word with a queer, get F-word, past tense. So far, no one has been killed, but several victims remain hospitalized."

"Shit," Raider said, feeling like somebody sucker-punched him in the face.

Fuck with a queer, get fucked.

Those were Othello's exact words in the kitchen the other night. Like hell ACTNOW isn't involved, he thought with disgust. And that shrimpy little black motherfucker is in there right along with them.

Eastbound traffic on Santa Monica Boulevard was bumper to bumper. He swung the car around and hung a swift and furious U, cutting off an oncoming city bus and slicing into a small side street heading north toward the Hollywood Hills, home of the rich, famous and, one day very soon, busted.

Snaking his way up the canyons, part of him wanted to do an about-face and head for the LA bureau to set up the wiretapping. Get Othello to brag about the beating, divulge the how, when, where and why and that would be that. Raider would be on his way back to DC for the hero's welcome and the twisted little threesome would be finished. No championship for D.A. and the Bulls this year. *If* Deon Anthony was in on this, and that brought up another problem: were Anthony and Jasper Hollinquest involved? And how much? And who else?

Needing more answers before he could close the case, Raider kept going toward the Big House. Since Atlantic City, Othello had kept his trap shut pretty tightly. Maybe he didn't trust Raider enough. Or maybe there was more to all this than just revenge on some fag-hating good ol' boys. Maybe both.

With a renewed sense of purpose, he powered the Jeep up the last hill and picked up speed on the long plateau overlooking the LA basin, roaring past a handful of tourists taking in the view. At the end of the plateau, a fork in the road wrapped around a chaparral-filled hill. He went right. The road became a winding, narrow street that led to more homes, including Othello's. Feeling psyched now, he charged through the tunnel of tall trees and stucco walls sealing off rich estates, only slowing down on the last curve before the wrought-iron gates of the Big House, the gates of hell, he suddenly thought of them. He was ten yards away from the intercom box when a dilapidated tan car farther down the road caught his eye. It had emerged from what looked like a small wooded area on Othello's side of the street. The Impala, Raider realized, coming from the entrance they had used that night after Simi Valley. It made a right turn, then sped off in the opposite direction.

Old Man Joe was going somewhere.

Raider jerked the wheel to keep from pulling into Othello's property, instead veering into the driveway on the opposite side to avoid being spotted by Othello's cameras and guards. Then, just as swiftly, he put the Jeep in reverse, made a three-point turn and headed in the direction from which he came.

Just before reaching the tourists' plateau again, he stopped abruptly just this side of the chaparral-filled hill. As he did, the Impala sped past from the other prong of the fork in the road that intersected the plateau. Raider had been right: there was only one way out of the small maze of roads near the Big House. As sure as anything, there was Old Man Joe, hunched over humbly, head forward, both hands clutching the wheel, looking to someone in the know like a man on a mission as he passed the view of LA.

Raider waited for the Impala to disappear, then killed the ignition, grabbed his gym bag and hopped out of the Jeep. On the ridge were two sets of tourists fifteen feet apart—a hefty middle-aged couple and a quartet of thirty-somethings. Their cars were abandoned by the road while they marveled at the unending sprawl of Los Angeles below. He ambled toward the first car, a navy Explorer. Unlocked, no keys. The second one, a dark green Grand Am, was ten feet behind it. Unlocked, with keys. Windows down. Just stopped to look at the view. Must not be from LA. Or just plain stupid. In no time, he started the engine, turned the car around and sped off across the plateau, ignoring the panicked middle-aged couple screaming at the back of their disappearing car. Othello would recognize the Jeep, but not Ma and Pa Kettle's rental deal.

Still, he'd have to be careful. He raced through the hills, fast at first, then, when the Impala was in sight, he stayed back just far enough to catch a glimpse of its taillights disappearing around each curve ahead of him. On the straightaways, when he could take his hands off the wheel, he retrieved from his gym bag his sunglasses and the white T-shirt he meant to put on after his workout. He tied the shirt around his head like a bandanna, hiding his blond locks, and put on the sunglasses to mask his eyes. Catching a glimpse of himself in the rear view, he looked like a rocker type or surfer or just plain mad-man, but hopefully one Othello wouldn't be able to recognize.

At the bottom of the hill, there was a long slope that spilled onto the flat streets of Hollywood. At the end of the slope was a stoplight. The Impala was already there, alone, waiting for green. When Raider saw this, he held back a bit, flipped down the sun visor to further cam-ouflage himself and crept toward the Impala, hoping the light would change before they found themselves idling there inches apart. But the light didn't budge and he had no choice but to come right up behind Othello. Anything else would have called even more attention to the Grand Am.

"Turn, you mother," Raider commanded the signal through his teeth. It didn't obey. Scratching his nose to hide more of his face, he saw the old man's—he saw *Othello's*—head arch up toward his rear view mirror, searching. Did he recognize Raider? What the hell would Raider say? Why was he coming down the hill in a Grand Am? What the hell was a T-shirt doing on his head?

Instinctively, Raider felt his hand toot the horn. A split second before, the light had changed and like so many LA drivers, Raider was being an impatient asshole. Othello appeared to fidget, then took off, waving an apologetic hand out the window, apparently too nervous to realize it was one Raider Kincaide.

Following the Impala was child's play, Spy Games 101, the con-gestion of LA only making it easier to blend in with the masses of chrome and steel but still keep track of a vehicle that couldn't get too far away in the maddening traffic. Othello headed south; Raider head-ed south. Through the streets of Hollywood they drove, past double-decker tourists buses and souped-up low riders on the road, and rail-thin rockers dressed in black and hookers dressed in as little as possi-

ble on the sidewalks. Before long, Othello made a left turn and headed east. Raider got stuck at the stoplight, behind two slow-moving
cars, but caught back up with the Impala three blocks later, still staying a cool distance behind. Next, the Impala passed the Chinese
Theater with all the stars' hand- and footprints. A few seconds later,
Raider passed the Chinese Theater. After several more blocks, the
Impala passed Capitol Records, the building that looked like a stack of
records or pancakes, depending on one's interpretation. Soon after,
Raider passed Capitol Records.

Half a mile later, the Impala turned toward the Hollywood sign,
dipping into a residential neighborhood at the foothills and leaving
the traffic behind. With no other cars to cover him, Raider let the light
turn red without making the same left turn. Instead, he checked out
the intersection and fetched his cell phone out of his gym bag.

"Kincaide here," he began once the LA Bureau answered. "I need
you to pick up a black Jeep from Vesper Canyon Road. Hold on to it.
And wash it for me while you're at it. I don't know how you guys live
with this soot and smog day after day. What must your lungs look
like?—oh, and you might need to take care of some pissed-off tourists
who lost their rental car."

He hung up the phone, and made the turn, finding himself on a
quiet but large street lined with palm trees and homes a quarter the
size of the Big House. The Impala was nowhere in sight. He crept
down the road, pretending to be absorbed in the rock song on the
radio, tapping the steering wheel and bobbing his T-shirted head
while surveying the many side streets that shot off this main boulevard.

On the fifth side street, pay dirt. A block down, the back of the
Impala was disappearing into a driveway on the right. A few minutes
later, the Grand Am drove toward the house, then past it. It was a
modest one-story stucco number sitting atop a small hill with stone
steps leading up to the front door. No cars were parked outside. The
Impala was safely tucked away inside the attached garage. All the windows were sealed off with dark curtains. No sign of life inside or out,
although Raider knew all too well that didn't mean there weren't
armed guards around the place, not to mention cameras, dogs or

whatever else a paranoid pop star with a criminal mind might use to protect himself. At the end of the block was a parking space on the opposite side of the street. Deciding it was far enough away, Raider took it, and keeping his sunglasses and headdress on, got out of the car, gym bag in tow.

Before turning onto the boulevard that led to this side street, he had noticed a market on the corner of the main drag. Glad he was still in his tank and shorts from the workout, he jogged the five blocks. It was a small market, mom-and-pop variety, and just as he'd hoped, a couple of bikes were parked outside.

Like a typical Angeleno out for an afternoon ride through the neighborhood, he was soon cruising down the boulevard on a raggedy old mountain bike. Amazing what people will do for you when you flash 'em a federal ID, promise 'em 500 bucks to replace their old bike and tell 'em you'll make sure they'll be on the TV reenactment. He pedaled slowly as he turned onto the street of the house of the Impala, swaying side-to-side as if he had nowhere to go, musing vacantly at the houses passing by. His sunglasses still covered half his face, but now, a bike helmet replaced the T-shirt on his head. Headphones dangled from his ears, leading to a device that resembled a cassette headset and was situated inside his bag swinging from the handlebars.

He didn't even acknowledge the house in question as he passed, riding on the sidewalk on the opposite side of the street, pretending to be consumed by music. Then, just past the house, the bike jerked as if something mechanical had gone wrong. Appearing surprised, he halted, dismounted and took up the body language of someone mystified as he knelt down and checked the gears, spokes, chain, pedal— every inch of his supposedly broken-down bike, never once eyeing the house across the street. With a long line of parked cars between the house and himself, he also used the time to adjust the knobs on the headset inside his gym bag, at first getting interference, then voices:

"...the Dodgers have won eleven and lost four so far in the month of May...." came from somebody's radio.

"...she no home right now. You call back?" came from a man with a Latino accent.

"...the lawn or no allowance...." a woman was saying inside another house.

He peered through the windows of the white BMW beside him and saw a woman in her front window in the house next to the house of the Impala. She was straightening the curtains. Must be Allowance Mom. He tweaked the headset once again.

"...the guy in Dallas might have brain damage," said a white man's voice.

Finally, something worth listening to.

There was another voice:

"The guy in Dallas threw jars of acid on people coming out of gay bars as he drove by. Maybe brain damage will improve his IQ."

The distinctive snarl of Othello, no doubt about it. Next came the white man's voice again:

"All punks who prey on young boys in search of their sexuality in parks need an attitude adjustment in the form of brain damage. Makes me want to meet Travis Little Horse and our foot soldiers and personally thank them face-to-face."

Gotta be Hollinquest.

"If only we Three Wisemen could," said Othello.

Three Wisemen, Raider thought. That's what they call themselves, cocky fools. Must mean Deon's there. Speak up, buddy boy, give your country something to indict you on. Talk to my little tape machine here, you big all-star, defending-NBA-champion faggot.

"Take my word for it." It was Othello again. "Travis tells me these guys are loving it, traveling around in the middle of the night, putting on their little hoods, crushing bones."

"There's a couple of hung-up guys in the NBA I wouldn't mind sending them after, Malone especially. Can you believe a black redneck?"

Thank you, D.A. Slam dunk.

Inside the Temple, Othello circled the conference table, bursting with more pride than he'd ever felt as a gay man while Jasper was sticking pushpins in all the latest battle sites: Elliotville, Dallas, Bradenton, Tallahassee. Since the attack in Kentucky, all three Wisemen had relished the idea of counter-bashing, as Jasper had coined it. The elite force responsible was known as Level 3 and consisted of seven men and one woman from the ACTNOW Simi Valley troop. In Florida, they'd targeted two different trios of gay bashers who were let off scot-free by the courts. In Dallas, they bypassed the judicial system altogether, hunting down the infamous Acid Thrower and sending him on an extended vacation to Parkland Hospital.

"Central Park," said Jasper, pointing to Manhattan on the map. "That's where I want them next. I've got some scores to settle there, even though it won't be the same barbarians who worked me over and broke my nose years ago."

"That's why you like this so much," said Deon, his face hovering over them on the monitor suspended from the ceiling. Due to the playoffs, The D.A. couldn't make it to the Temple in person. He had a date with the Charlotte Hornets in game one of the Eastern Conference finals in a few hours and was using a laptop computer and digital video camera to plug into the meeting from his hotel in Charlotte.

"To counter-bashing." Jasper raised his glass of champagne. "Don't knock it till you've tried it."

They toasted—Jasper and Othello with champagne and Deon with sparkling water.

"Not to break up the party atmosphere," Othello said, "but we do have business."

"I don't know if I can get serious with you in that." Jasper pointed to Othello in the old man getup.

"I always wear it to and from the Temple. This time, I kept it on so you two can see for yourself how I keep the foot soldiers in line."

Outside, the sound started to break up in Raider's headphones, bringing him out of the trance he'd been in listening to the gay Goodfellas. He was sitting on the sidewalk, resting against the tire of the BMW, so engrossed he only now spotted the white-haired old lady in a pink robe in the yard directly in front of him. She was watering her rose bushes, but mostly keeping a suspicious eye on him. To throw her off, he remounted the bike and tried to ride off, then stopped as if there was still a problem. Then, messing with the back tire, he listened once again.

Jasper pointed in the general direction of Dixieland on the map. "Seems as though there's these Marines in South Carolina, two of them, just beat up two queers after accidentally walking into a gay bar."

Othello turned away from Jasper in the room and Deon on the monitor. "Maybe we should move to another part of the country for now."

Jasper eyed him curiously. "Our troops are still in the South aren't they, hiding out, waiting further instruction?"

Deon laughed. "I say we send them after my so-called buddy Big Daddy Callahan, get him to stop pestering me about playoff tickets in Charlotte and that damned golf tournament of his, wants me to get him some white athletes to show up. Fucking racist."

"That's Herman's best good ol' boy, isn't it?" asked Jasper.

"Let's stay out of the Carolinas for now," said Othello.

"What's wrong?" asked Jasper. "You still want a piece of Herman, don't you?"

Othello turned to him. "More than any of these fools we're running around clubbing."

"Well, then." Jasper looked him squarely in the eye. "I'm ready to exchange ideas when you are. He's about to cost me another quarter of a billion in Belize."

"He's also about to open up—get this—" said Deon, "The Jimmy Herman Museum of American Decency."

"Heard about it," said Jasper. "He wants it to be like a freaking presidential library and right wing theme park all rolled into one."

Deon laughed. "Trying like hell to get me to attend the opening as a fellow legend of South Carolina. Already sent a dozen telegrams to the hotel here."

"What we gonna do about that, Rock Star?" asked Jasper.

For a moment, there was silence, Jasper and Othello not taking their eyes off each other.

"This isn't the meeting for Jimmy Herman," Othello said. "D.A. has to get ready to vanquish the Hornets. Jimmy Herman needs our full attention in a full-scale meeting."

"He's right," said Deon. Othello and Jasper didn't take their eyes off each other. "Let's vote on the next counter-bashes so I can go play ball."

Hearing that the meeting was coming to an end, Raider lifted the rear wheel of the bike, spun it around, and declaring it fixed, took off, giving the meddlesome woman who was still watering her lawn a facetious nod as he passed. He ditched the bike on the next block, then returned to the Grand Am and hunkered down in the driver's seat, waiting and replaying just enough of the tape to make sure he had captured the voices of the Three Wisemen in their Temple of Doom:

"This isn't the meeting for Jimmy Herman. D.A. has to get ready to vanquish the Hornets. Jimmy Herman needs our full attention in a full-scale meeting."

"He's right. Let's vote on the next counter-bashes so I can go play ball."

The quality wasn't great, but the words were clear. Certainly enough to be the beginning of the end.

Fifteen minutes later, a long black sedan emerged from the garage of the house, backing out of the driveway, its windows except for the front windshield darker than midnight. Upon reaching the street, it turned toward Raider's rental car, forcing him to slump down and out of sight, but not before he caught a quick glimpse of Sweeney playing chauffeur. "Bye-bye, Jasper Hollinquest, you big homo," he said, figuring them to be on their way to LAX.

It was another ten minutes before the Impala came creeping down the driveway. "Where we going now, general?" Raider asked, refitting the T-shirt on his head as he watched Othello heading off in the opposite direction. When the Impala was at the stop sign at the end of the block, Raider began to follow it, but another car—a white Honda Civic parked a few cars up on Raider's side of the street— pulled out in a hurry in front of him, causing Raider to have to break unexpectedly. The lone occupant of the car made no apologies. He was a white man from what Raider could tell, a man who hadn't been in the car when Raider rode past on his bike, nor had he just gotten in the car. Perhaps he too had been slumped down, waiting?

The Impala had already turned and was heading south on the residential boulevard that led to the main streets of Hollywood. The

Civic reached the stop sign and made the same right turn. A little more cautious now, Raider idled toward the same point and made the same turn.

Like a caravan, they drove down the main thoroughfare at the foot of the Hollywood Hills, westbound. Traffic was just as heavy as before and Raider barely had sight of the Impala. But this time, he didn't need it. Sure as shit, the Civic was following Joe, with bad technique at that, staying too close, always making sure no car separated them, making the lights when the Impala did, even when it meant almost running them. An amateur, Raider deduced, hanging back so he himself wouldn't be spotted.

Through Hollywood they went, retracing the path to the Big House, which Raider took to mean Joe was done for the day. But who was this uninvited third party? And couldn't Othello see he was being followed so poorly?

"Come on, O, you're smarter than this buffoon."

At a chaotic intersection clogged with construction, the Civic lost Othello when an orange-vested worker abruptly held up a stop sign from his post in the middle of the street. Deciding this was as good a time as any to get a good look at the driver, Raider, who'd been in the same lane, sped up a bit and cut in front of a long black limo, pulling up right next to the Civic. At first, Raider pretended not to notice him, instead musing at the lingerie store on the right. Then, slowly bobbing his head to a rock ballad on the radio, he glanced over just in time to see the man turning toward Raider. Their faces froze on each other, the man's stare trying to penetrate Raider's sunglasses. Raider knew the man from somewhere, but with the shot of adrenaline he felt, he couldn't place him right away.

The orange-vested worker lowered his stop sign and began waving them through. The man took off, still very much in a hurry. He was from ACTNOW, Raider realized. The guy in his thirties with a beard who had worn black overalls at Simi Valley. Raider stayed in the adjacent lane but picked up speed, understanding this wasn't good news for Othello.

The canyon road leading to the Big House was a half mile away. Othello pressed the gas pedal to the cranky old machine a little harder now and eyed the rear view mirror to admire the silly grin he knew was splattered across his face. That was when he noticed a Honda Civic bearing down on him awfully fast. That car had been with him for blocks, his brain tried to tell him. Or was he being paranoid? He turned up the canyon road, but then quickly veered off onto a small side street that circled back around to the boulevard at the foothill. You only took this way if you made a mistake and needed to turn around or you were following the car in front of you. The Civic mimicked the Impala's move. This isn't paranoia, Othello decided. Once back on the boulevard, he sped up to forty, darting in and out of the other cars in an effort to distance himself. The Civic didn't let up, cutting the same path as Othello, who tried to get a good look at the driver but couldn't take his eyes off the road for too long.

When Raider saw Othello circle around the canyon road and speed off heading west, he picked up his pursuit, staying on the tail of the Civic. The Impala turned south at the first possible intersection, followed by the Civic five seconds later and the Grand Am five seconds after that. Next, Othello swerved onto Sunset Boulevard, heading west again, away from the glossy high rises and movie billboards toward the sprawling estates of Beverly Hills, going fifty.

His panic increasing by the minute, Othello raced past the Beverly Hills Hotel, the famous fortress that was mostly hidden behind palm trees. The light up ahead was already yellow. He was too far to make it under normal circumstances. He gripped the wheel tighter and floored it, fighting the temptation to close his eyes. The Impala's engine roared like an overworked boiler. The car itself sailed through the air and cascaded back down on the other side of the intersection like a boat rocked by a furious wave, heaving up and down and tossing Othello around like a rag doll. Made it, his senses told him. He looked back only to find the Civic also sailing through the intersection.

Quickly, he put his foot on the brake and jerked the wheel with all his might, making a quick right onto the next side street, a long straightaway lined with mansions and palm trees. The Civic followed. Once again, he floored it and tried to outrun it, but the Impala wasn't built for this and the Civic seemed to be gaining. An alleyway was coming up on the left. He slowed down just enough to make another sharp turn, not anticipating the garbage truck sitting there like a big elephant, temporarily blocking the road.

He had thirty feet to stop. He used twenty-nine and a half.

The Impala fishtailed and came to a screeching halt sideways. The Civic also stopped, still straight, five feet away from blindsiding Othello. Another car, a dark green Grand Am, also stopped, farther back at the beginning of the alley. Othello—his car trapped, his heart racing, his body covered in sweat underneath the old-man getup— shot a glance at his pursuer in the Civic.

The Impala door slammed shut. Othello charged toward him, ignoring the frantic Spanish he heard coming from the vicinity of the garbage truck.

"Joe, it's me, Gus." There was genuine fear in his voice. "You all right?"

"I know who you are," Othello said, relieved when Gus called him Joe, but angry just the same. "What the hell are you trying to do? Why you following me?"

"I'm so sorry. I saw you driving through Hollywood and I want-ed to stop and just say hi. Then you sped off and I figured something might be wrong. I chased you because I was worried you might have had a heart attack while driving."

"What? You saw me where?" Othello asked, his anger not subsid-ing.

"On Franklin," Gus pleaded. "I was coming from Griffith Park and I saw you driving on Franklin near Vine."

"Fuckin' liar," Raider said to himself. He was slumped over in the Grand Am, catching this guy's act with his headphones and listening device. Gus had been on Othello's tail way before Vine.

"You all right, Joe?" Gus asked, full of concern.

"Hell if I am," Othello said, barely able to appreciate the fact that his identity remained a secret. "*You* almost gave me the heart attack. Next time, don't bother. And who's your friend?"

Now it was Raider's turn to panic.

"What friend?" asked Gus. "I'm alone."

"That!" Othello said, pointing to the Grand Am, not satisfied when Gus began stammering for an answer. He turned to see that the garbage truck had moved to the next house and had cleared a path for the caravan, but he wasn't through with his fan club. "You there," he called out to the Grand Am, unable to see the driver who was either hunched down or one short sonofabitch.

Through the headset Raider heard the footsteps and for the life of him didn't know how to get out of this one smoothly, if at all.

"Come out, coward!" Othello shouted, stopping twenty feet from the car. Part of him was scared of risking more than he already had, the other part incensed at the idea that someone was playing games with him. He started toward the Grand Am again, angry, determined.

Raider began to inch his way up, ready to turn on a zillion watts of charm while coming up with a logical explanation. Then he heard sirens closing in.

Othello heard those same sirens and decided whatever was in the Grand Am wasn't as bad as what was heading this way. Hastily, he limped back to the Impala. "Don't ever do this again," he shouted to Gus, then got in his car and took off down the alley.

The Civic did the same, surely not to follow Joe this time, but to also escape the law. But not before Raider had just enough time to sit up and get a good look at the man's license plate.

ELEVEN

THE HOUSE LIGHTS were out in the miniature movie theater that was the Big House screening room. The seven rows of plush oversized seats were vacant save one lone chair in the middle of the front row, occupied by Othello. The movie screen itself was blank; it hadn't been used in months. Instead, directly in front of it, four identical fifty-six-inch television sets equipped with VCRs stood side by side in an arc, looming like four monoliths.

Darting his focus from screen to screen, Othello sat hypnotically as the images flickered in the darkness, filling up the room and reflecting off the red velvet walls. With four rather large remotes in his lap, he resembled a navigator of sorts, clicking to the left, then the right, muting one set, turning another one up, rewinding this scene, pausing that tape. Each screen featured a different Level 3 counter-bashing, caught on tape by Level 3 itself. The footage was shot using night-vision cameras, bathing the violence in ghostly shades of greens, blacks and grays. Crazy, yes, these boulder-sized big screens he ordered up only an hour ago, but in view of the tightrope he was dancing on, made tighter by this afternoon's dangerous chase through town, he felt the need to gawk at these images and confront them face-to-face. To that end, each counter-bashing, which lasted no more than a few minutes, repeated itself over and over on tape.

To the far left, screen one was showing the early moments of the Dallas strike—jagged shots of feet running through an alley. Screen two featured Bradenton, Florida, and a wide shot of a small, two-story apartment building. On screen three, four members of Level 3 were hiding out in their black hoods behind a Tallahassee liquor store, waiting. On Screen four, Othello's personal favorite, a red-headed Kentucky cop was getting out of his truck and heading for the back of a barber shop. Each bashing was moments away from happening when the intercom shattered his concentration.

"Othello, *dahling*." It was Doris, his secretary, who had explicit instructions not to disturb him.

"Go away."

"It's an A-lister. Mr. Kincaide."

More than ever he questioned the wisdom of putting Raider on the list of callers and visitors who had priority status. "On the phone?" he asked.

"In the flesh."

Don't I wish.

He paused the tapes. His nerves were still shot from the Hollywood 500 and he was in no mood for conversation. But this was the first time Raider had ever showed up unannounced and Othello was intrigued.

"Show him to the screening room." He waited a few minutes, then unpaused all four tapes. Before long, the carnage began to mount. On the fourth screen, the one closest to the door, the Kentucky cop fired a shot at Freedom's bullet-proof vest and was about to get his skull crushed. They deserve it, Othello told himself. All of them. On the second screen (Bradenton), a twenty-one year-old blond kid was lying face up on the ground of a parking garage, blood gushing from his face as he fell into unconsciousness while the camcorder hovered over him, recording his misery.

Raider stepped through the doors of the screening room just in time to see a close up of a bloodied face on the screen closest to the door.

"Othello, what the...." He was rendered speechless. His eyes panned the other screens where heads, bones, backs, kneecaps—you name it—were being broken, shattered, crushed, all in night vision. Without words, they watched—Othello knowing he was no longer alone and Raider only remotely aware that he was moving deeper and deeper into the darkened room. By the time the scenes began to repeat themselves, he was standing in the second row of seats, directly over Othello. "So this is what you've been doing instead of spending time with me," he said, void of emotion. "Busting open skulls."

"Yeah, right. " Othello turned his head ever-so-slightly, his eyes still glued to the screens. "Someone from ACTNOW got this from some anonymous source. Maybe from whoever's doing this."

Raider tried to laugh to show his disbelief but was too mesmerized by the bloodbath. "If you're going to lie, you can do better than that." He went for a teasing tone but wasn't sure if he achieved it.

"The folks that did this have submitted these tapes to the networks," Othello said. "To warn all fag-bashers, I suppose."

"They'll be caught." Raider thought of the head honchos at the bureau. And if not caught by him, they'd have his ass.

"They're wearing hoods." Othello shrugged. "Whoever they are."

"What is this 'whoever' business?"

"Like I know these people?"

"Come on, Othello," he said edgily. "Quit playing games with me." He turned toward the back of the room, trying but failing to collect himself. This wasn't supposed to be this hard. Othello was supposed to be head over heels in love by now, too smitten to be discreet. But had Raider's tone been too harsh? He turned back around, worn out from retrieving his Jeep and making it back up the hill to the Big House. "Stop with all this, willya?"

"Stop with all what?"

"Lying, goddamnit."

Othello took his eyes off the screen and shot a glance toward Raider. Feeling too short sitting down, he chucked the remotes onto the next seat, rose up and slowly turned around, shoulders square, posture stiffened, eyes cold. "You seem to have a problem."

"You're shutting me out. You promised to show me the way in all this. Raider Kincaide, Rookie Activist?"

"Promises are sometimes impossible to keep." The wail of the Bradenton kid permeated the room. Othello reached for the remote and killed the sound, then eyed Raider with a piercing glare. "What's all this to you anyway?"

The tension between them seemed impenetrable and something became clear to Raider in the spare second available: Othello was on to him, somehow, some way, to some degree. Was it something Raider had said? The wrong look? Wrong gesture? Whatever the reason, the trust between them had eroded. The sour look in Othello's eyes was unlike any Raider had seen from the pop star. It was Raider's move. Wrong one and his head could end up like the fag bashers.

"What's it to me?" Raider turned to the screens, thought about it, then punched his fist in the air with the gusto of a fratboy calling for another keg. "I'm beginning to love this shit."

"Say what?"

"This is so money. For the first time in my life, I'm starting to feel free about who I really am, deep down inside."

"So you like these bashings?"

"Are you kidding?" Feeling a new shot of adrenaline, he began pacing the aisle, speaking with urgent gestures. "I can't believe you assumed I didn't."

"You didn't say one way or another the other night. Over dinner."

"Well, you didn't ask?"

Othello scoffed. "I didn't think I had to."

Raider took a deep breath and sat on the upright edge of a chair in his row. "I think the reason I didn't say anything is because I didn't want to face something in the past. When I was at Dartmouth, I was involved in a gay bashing."

"You, Mr. All-Ivy Leaguer, Mr. Six-foot-two Mountain of A Man?"

"Well, it wasn't *at* Dartmouth." Yeah, that's it, he thought, making it up as he went along. "I went to another school. In a nearby town. For the night. I heard about guys cruising each other at their library. One night, I got so horny—" no make that lonely, lonely is better "—really more lonely than horny. They didn't know Raider Kincaide from squat there. To make a long story short, a couple guys from their football team—big linemen types—they beat the crap outta me. I didn't want to fight because I thought they'd find out who I was. I was messed up pretty badly, told everybody back at Dartmouth some low-lifes jumped me."

"I'm sorry to hear that."

"But that's why I love this shit." Raider rose up. "The anger from back then is coming out just like I am." He gestured toward the big screens. "I guess I didn't talk about these reverse bashings because it's hard to think about that night."

"Maybe the group that did this can find the punks who jumped you."

"Fat chance. But will you quit talking about some group as if you don't know them? This is what I mean about shutting me out." He remained in his aisle but moved toward Othello. "I know in my heart this is all you. Only you have the guts and the vision, not to mention the brilliance."

Othello turned from him and took a few steps.

"You know, you did promise to let me in on more of all this if I came to Atlantic City," Raider added.

He had to go and bring up Atlantic City, Othello thought with disgust. He turned back to Raider. "I'll say the same thing to you that you said to me in Simi Valley, right after we escaped and when you were all confused about Joe's identity."

"And that is?" Raider asked.

"You could be some kind of cop, or traitor or FBI type, trying to send me and the rest of ACTNOW up the river. Why should ACTNOW trust you? Why should I?"

Check, Raider thought, but far from checkmate.

Raider tried to laugh it off. "Would a guy from the FBI be dating you right now?"

"Dating?" Othello repeated incredulously. "Is that what this is? Is that why you act like a sixteen-year-old virgin on his first date every time you're around me?"

"I told you I'm not that experienced."

"You act like you want to stay that way." Othello began pacing, too hurt and frustrated to look Raider in the eye. "How am I supposed to think anything's going on between us when we don't—can't—and

you want to get to know my world? Don't think for a second I'm
gonna let you in till I'm sure this is going somewhere. This isn't just a
game, Raider. You'd have to be brain-dead not to realize the kinds of
chances I'm taking, even with what little you know about Joe. And you
come in here mad I don't tell you more?" He ended up near the fourth
screen and let out a solitary breath ripe with cynicism.

In the middle of the second row, Raider fell silent, the room's
only noise coming from the tedious hum of the air-conditioner, the
only light from the screens. Raider wiped his brow, which had become
sticky with a light coating ˜of sweat, and staying in his aisle,
approached Othello's back. Then, after steadying his arm, he placed a
hand on Othello's shoulder.

"I appreciate your patience with me," he said softly, hoping
Othello would fill in the rest because he sure as hell didn't know what
else a guy was supposed to say to another guy. But Othello held his
ground and offered nothing. "I know I haven't been the easiest guy to
date. But that is what I consider us doing and it means a lot to me
when you help me out of the closet, even if it means dragging me out
inch-by-inch. It feels so great when you tell me about the injustices
and include me in all your dreams. I mean, you've got guts and I
admire that. Wish I had half." He squeezed Othello's shoulder, keeping his surprise to himself as Othello reached up and placed his own
hand on top.

Not letting go of Raider's hand, Othello turned around, wondering to himself: how is it possible to feel so much for someone you
know so little about? No easy answer came, but truth was, he still had
an avalanche of feelings for Raider, some of them good, some of them
downright frightful. He stared into his Nantucket man's eyes, which
were much softer than before, and when Raider saw a pleasant expression on Othello's face, they shared a modest smile.

"Six months ago..." Othello moved over to Raider's aisle and
grabbed his other hand so he could hold both of them. "...six months
ago, I would have never dreamed that you or ACTNOW would be a
part of my life. But here you are, all of you and...." he trailed off,
swinging their arms sideways, desperately hoping Raider would lean
over and plant a big wet one on his lips. But Raider simply returned a

half smile. "You know I could really use a hug right now," Othello said, not knowing how to ask for a kiss.

Raider arched his head upward as if he expected as much. "Come here," he said commandingly, pulling Othello into him. And just like that, Othello found himself lost in Raider's chest, their arms wrapped tightly around each other, everything about the world safe and right, even if only for a moment.

For Raider, it was a matter of muting the sirens going off in his brain. A small sacrifice, he reasoned, staring at the four massive screens displaying frightening images his government had ordered him to stop.

"After the day I had," said Othello, "this is heaven."

"Tell me all about it," Raider said, oozing sympathy.

"Somebody was after me."

"After you?" Raider said, using shock as an excuse to untangle himself.

"Not *after me* after me, as it turns out," Othello explained, walking directly in front of the big screens, reliving the horror. The version he gave Raider began on the streets of Hollywood, just after Othello had realized he was being followed, and ended with Othello speeding off from the Beverly Hills alley when the sirens closed in. "Turns out, it was just one of the guys from ACTNOW," he said, summing it all up. "Gus. Said he spotted me near Franklin and Vine and chased me halfway to the ocean just to say hi, almost making me crap in my old man dungarees in the process. I guess the third car just turned down the alley at the wrong time and got stuck."

"Gus, Gus," Raider said absently. "Oh, yeah, Gus. What's his last name?"

"Don't know."

"Where were you coming from?"

Othello barely heard him, or at least pretended as much. "Just out," he said absently, shifting restlessly. "If only the Fund were enough," he said to himself.

"The Triangle Fund?" Raider asked. That got Othello's attention; he turned back to Raider.

"You've heard of it?"

"And *you*," Raider suddenly realized, "you're the mastermind behind it."

Othello grinned. "Guilty as charged."

The revelation caught Raider by surprise, as if he hadn't considered the possibility that Othello was also out there doing some good, if you were a gay person at least. So his heart wasn't all stone. Of course, Raider already knew that; he just didn't dwell on it. "There's no end to your talent and vision is there?" he said.

"Guilty on count two."

Raider thought of Gus and his lie about where he first saw Joe. The Honda Civic was registered to a man named Crane Malloy, not Gus, but that was all the LA bureau could tell him until they had time for a full background check.

"Othello," Raider heard himself say, "maybe you should have bodyguards, you know, to avoid people like this Gus guy tracking you down."

"In the real world, I often do, but when I'm Joe...." he fell silent, then came up with another brilliant idea. "Perhaps a big, strong, ex-Ivy League lacrosse hero should be my bodyguard," he said, strands of Whitney wailing filling his head.

"I've got plans of my own." Raider leaned on the seat in front of him with both arms. "To be one of the—what do they call it on CNC?—the counter-bashers."

The idea caught Othello by surprise. He stood between the big screens and Raider, contemplating it, intrigued by it. Another step up for the rookie activist? Another test of Raider's loyalty and intentions? Another risk?

But his thought process was interrupted by Sweeney, who was at the door with a cordless phone.

"O, call from J.H. on his plane, says it's urgent."

Reluctantly, Othello excused himself, guaranteeing a quick return. While he was gone, Raider used the remotes to kill the violence on the televisions, having had enough already. Hold on, America, he said to himself: your streets will be safe again real soon.

Seconds later, Othello burst back into the room alone. "The remote," he ordered Raider, who threw him the one he was still holding. Without breaking stride, Othello caught it, aimed it at the first screen and lodged himself in front of it.

CNC came on, playing the last of the Bradenton footage. The blond kid was writhing on the ground, drowning in his own blood. A man's voice-over accompanied the shot: "This is a prime example of their anti-America, anti-family, anti-justice agenda." It was Jimmy Herman's thick Southern drawl. The video cut to him on camera, finishing his thought from a plush leather armchair: "The people on these tapes are just a step away from being the next Jeffrey Dahmers of this country."

"The people on these tapes are just a step away from beating the living shit out of *you!*" Othello yelled.

"Calm down, O," said Raider. "Maybe we should take a break—"

"No, I wanna put another bullet through the TV!" He walked away, then quickly back swung around. "Why do you think it's so hard for you to come out? They *hate* us. They want to see us eliminated. That's war, and in war there's got to be casualties and my pathetic, lonely life is not going to be the only one."

Othello stopped himself, fearing he'd said too much. He stepped back from Raider, then turned away, the sound of a female reporter filling the void. "I need some fresh air," he decided, then threw open the double doors that led to the terrace overlooking the basin and fled.

Raider remained indoors, not sure if he was to follow or leave the Big House altogether. He turned to the television, which now featured another shot of Senator Herman, Senator Jimmy Herman, brought up at the Temple meeting earlier in the day and at least twice before, the night of Simi Valley and on the yacht off Atlantic City.

The other week I got so mad at him I assassinated him on my big screen TV. Not a bad idea wouldn't you say?

So that was it.

A chilling jolt traveled through his entire body. But this time he kept his cool. Like a good agent. For a few seconds, he even allowed himself to imagine the accolades awaiting him from Dockweiller and the bureau, not to mention Capitol Hill, the White House, Hollywood, the media—hell, the entire secret agent universe. He then made a calm, purposeful journey through the double doors onto the terrace.

The sun was setting and Othello was sitting on one of the backless stone benches that fronted the hedges overlooking the city lights, his arms folded together as if he were chilly, his body rocking back and forth ever-so-slightly.

Soundlessly, Raider approached, then placed his hands on Othello's shoulders and massaged them, firmly but gently. Just a little touching, Raider told himself. The boys at the bureau never have to know. Othello seemed to be responding, too, almost purring like a cat and moving cooperatively with Raider's hands as Raider called up his best sensitive yet deep voice:

"Time to forget all about devils disguised as senators for now."

"That won't be hard to do if you keep this up," moaned Othello.

Raider rubbed him for what seemed like an hour to him, but in reality was probably more like ten minutes. Then, deciding enough was enough, he unhanded Othello's shoulders and straddled the bench.

"You still haven't told me what you think of my becoming a counter-basher?"

"What do you want me to say?" Othello asked, rubbing his own shoulders now.

"Well, if you're not involved, do you think you can introduce me to somebody who knows somebody who knows somebody who's involved?"

"You really wanna do it?"

"So bad I can taste it."

"Then sleep with me."

Every muscle in Raider's face hit the ground as he searched for a way out.

"I'm only kidding," Othello said after a drawn-out beat, but only because of Raider's hesitant reaction.

"Good," Raider said in relief. "That's something that has to be special and happen naturally."

"Agreed." Othello reached up and retrieved a small piece of leaf that had found its way into Raider's hair. "Maybe we do need a break from talk of war. You know you still haven't told me one Nantucket joke."

Raider groaned. Then obliged. "There once was a man from Nantucket, whose dick was so long he could suck it. He said with a grin, as he wiped off his chin, if my ear were a cunt I could fuck it—there, you happy?"

They both broke into laughter.

"And when was the last time you were there?" Othello asked, trying hard to hide the hint of seriousness in his voice.

"Right before I moved here," Raider said absently, then suddenly remembered his words on the boat that night.

Nantucket? I haven't been back to that place in years.

Othello had caught him in a lie and hadn't mentioned anything about it for weeks. But it was still gnawing at the pop icon, which explained so much. Putting ice in his veins, Raider stood up and surveyed the view.

"I think I may have lied to you once and said I hadn't been there in a while."

"You did?" Othello said ever-so-innocently.

"My dad—the one who calls us fudge-packers—he disowned me right before I came out to California. I couldn't go back now if I tried. That's why I told you that, so you wouldn't press the issue of going up there."

"I see."

Raider turned to him. "You're not convinced, are you?"

Othello pursed his lips as if to say, the jury's still out.

"You think I might be some kind of traitor or something," said Raider. "That's why you brought it up tonight. That's what you've been thinking since that night on the boat."

Othello held out, not knowing what to say yet.

"Well, let me ask you something, Othello Hardaway of Riverside, California: would a traitor do this?"

Raider plopped back down on the bench, closed his eyes and dove in, one hand wrapping around the back of Othello's neck while the other arm grabbed his shoulder. At the same time, his lips found Othello's, another man's. A gay man. He was kissing a gay man. Mouth

to mouth. Lip to lip. And why the hell not? He wasn't about to lose the
case to end all cases due to some asinine slip-up about his hometown.
He felt tongue. His brain told him he could bite down; but he didn't.
Couldn't. He went with it. Had to. No choice. Of all the things he ever
allowed himself to imagine doing with a guy—just for the sake of
imagining—kissing was never, ever, not in a thousand years, part of
the picture. But here he was, his tongue dancing with that of a black
gay man. He wasn't even sure if he was breathing. More like gasping
from within. Felt like he was drowning, being sucked under into a
world of darkness, their world. Oh, shit....

Othello kept his eyes open. He wasn't going to miss this, his lacrosse
legend, his strapping blond dream man, holding him with his big manly
paws, his soft, full lips pressing against Othello's soft, full lips with equal
force. Yes, Raider wanted it, Othello reassured himself, and he wanted it
just as much as Othello. With one arm, he held tight to Raider's back.
With the other, he roamed Raider's thick blond mane as if he were God
combing a field of wheat. More than anything, that was what he loved
about white men, the silky strands of flowing hair he could never possess. But tonight, he possessed them, in Raider. In Raider, Othello felt at
that instant, he could possess everything he ever wanted.

"HEY, LITTLE FAGGOT boy," came blazing across the walkie-talkie.
"Faggot boy, come over here."

All five bodies in the van came alive from their various states of
rest, stirring in anticipation.

"Silence," Travis commanded from the driver's seat, turning up
the volume on the walkie-talkie.

"Faggot boy, I'm talking to you," came crackling through.

Directly behind the driver's seat, on one of the crates that served
as chairs, Othello, dressed as the old man Joe, shot a glance to Raider,
who was sitting across from him.

"It's a red Camaro, all right." Trudy was peeking out the back
window of the van. She was the black woman Othello had called Afro
at Simi Valley. "Gotta be them. And there's Gary, ten feet away from
'em."

"Yes!" exclaimed Rainey, the bald man in his fifties Othello had called Sparkplug. "After six nights, the fools had to come back for more."

"Freedom," Travis spoke into the walkie-talkie, "got a fix on the perps?"

"Three of them, just like in the police reports," came from Freedom, who was in the other van. "I could put a bullet through each one of their brains if I had a bazooka."

"Freedom!" scolded Travis.

"Don't worry, I ain't got one. With the shakes, my aim is probably shot to hell anyway."

"Don't let Gary out of your sight," ordered Travis.

"They would have to show up when it's Nervous Nell's turn to be decoy," said Freedom.

Othello's own nerves grew a little more tense, imagining Gary—the short Asian boy he had called Miss Saigon—just around the block on a dimly-lit street, being approached by the thugs who were responsible for five fag bashings in the last two months in Silverlake, an urban neighborhood just east of Hollywood that included a smoldering mix of gays and Latinos. From the police reports, the bashings were always the same: three Latino boys who drove a red Camaro, spoke perfect English and never brandished weapons, pulled up to gay men walking the three blocks between two popular bars, then lured them to the deserted dead end where the vans were now parked for some good old-fashioned fag bashing. So far they hadn't been caught.

"Want some dick?" one of them was heard saying over the walkie-talkie.

"Nellie is going up to the car now," Freedom said.

"You like sucking big thick ones?" the driver said as Gary approached, his legs visibly trembling in his cut off jean shorts.

"I got a thick one for you." Rainey pounded his baseball bat in his hand.

"Driver's pointing toward the dead end," said Freedom. "They're revving the engine."

"Get ready to move," said Travis.

"Be careful," Othello begged of Raider, hoping he'd never regret letting his lacrosse legend talk him into this in the days after the kiss, now over a week ago. Raider nodded once in acknowledgment and began working the night vision video camera, focusing it on the inside of the van and its occupants.

"Not our faces, stupid," Trudy said right before putting on her hood.

"It's not on," said Raider. "Just checking it." Cameraman was all the other members of Level 3 had agreed to let Raider be tonight, as a way of getting his feet wet. Had it not been for Joe's connection to Travis, he wouldn't have even gotten that far. "You be careful yourself," Raider said to Othello, pulling the black leather hood over his blond locks.

"Travis will take care of me." Othello was taking this chance not only to see Raider in action, but also to check out the other eight members of Level 3 in person, to find out who cracked under pressure, who flinched at the sight of blood, and most important of all, who was right for the next and biggest job.

"Still, if I see you in trouble," Raider promised Othello through his hood, getting a smile in return. No one is gonna steal this case, Raider thought: not the LAPD, not Level 3, not some barrio boys out for a little fun.

"Slide on out of here," said Travis.

With their hoods in place, first Trudy, then Rainey, then Raider slithered out the back door and glued themselves to the side of the van that faced away from the street. The other van was closer to the action. From it, three other members of Level 3 emerged: Georgio, the former porno star, Darnell, the black man with dreadlocks Othello had called Rasta, and Gus, the overzealous tailgater in the Honda Civic. Freedom was only a driver tonight because he was feeling ill, the effects of some new medication he assured everyone.

For what happened next, Othello and Travis had a front row seat out of the back window of the van. The Camaro crept into the dead end while Gary followed on foot. The boys then got out, cornered Gary and began pulling down their pants. "You wanna suck some dick?" the middle one said. "On your fucking knees, beg for it."

Gary sank to his knees. The Latinos then zipped up their pants and started hurling insults toward Gary, who was trembling with fear he didn't have to fake. One of the boys spit at him. Another kicked him once in the stomach. Then, in the next second, tan baseball bats went flying toward little brown heads. And guts. And faces. And the rest of their bodies. In no time, all three boys were limp on the ground, next to the Camaro, its motor running and doors wide open. All five members of Level 3 got in shots while Raider captured it all on tape. When the beating was over, the rest of the gang ran to the vans, but Raider stayed behind and took more footage of the boys lapsing into unconsciousness. As if he relished it, Othello thought as Trudy, Rainey and Gary dove into Travis and Othello's van.

Travis started the engine. Freedom's van was already in motion, turning around in the middle of the dead-end ten feet away from Raider. Deciding he had enough footage, Raider ran toward the vans, and seeing that Freedom's was closer, jumped into the back of it as both vans took off, burning rubber down the street.

"Got 'em good," Raider said triumphantly, plopping down on an old tire and brandishing the camera for Georgio, Gus and Darnell who were all removing their hoods, affording Raider a good look at all of them. Especially Gus, *if* that was his name.

Settling onto the crate behind the driver's seat, Othello breathed a sigh of relief that things had gone smoothly. But more than anything, he was dying to learn Raider's reaction to all this. He strained his neck for a view of the other van in the passenger side window, but all he got was a quick glimpse of Freedom veering off down another street and the taillights becoming smaller and smaller. As planned, the getaway vans and their occupants were speeding away from Silverlake in different directions, not to be seen together for the rest of the night.

Money, Raider thought to himself as the vans split up. Time to scope out this half of Level 3 and perform a little Kincaide magic.

TWELVE

THE NOISE IN THE Charlotte Coliseum was deafening. The Bulls had just called their last time-out and 23,000 fans were on their feet, dancing to the most popular song in all of sports, "Rock and Roll Part 2," more commonly known as "The Hey Song" because every crowd in the country knows when to shout "hey!" at the appropriate intervals in the song.

With only 2.2 seconds left in the third overtime and a 110-108 lead, the Charlotte faithful could practically taste what would be the Hornets biggest victory to date, a victory that would give them a 3-2 advantage in the Eastern Conference finals and bring them to within one win of Seattle and the NBA finals, a pinnacle the franchise had yet to reach.

It was well past midnight, the game having been delayed forty-five minutes in the second quarter when Charlotte's big George "Thunder" Hawkins shattered the backboard with a monster dunk. But Hornets fans didn't care. Charlotte was in the midst of its best season ever and The D.A. was having a nightmare of a game, shooting only five for twenty-nine with five fouls and four costly turnovers, the costliest one occurring moments before the time-out, when five-six

Hornet guard Bugsy Webb stripped Deon of the ball and dribbled coast-to-coast for the go-ahead lay-up. Meanwhile, Larry Smith, Charlotte's black-as-coal shooting guard, was unstoppable so far with forty-eight points, most of them when Deon was guarding him. Of all days to have a shitty game, Deon thought more than once during the course of the night.

Through the chaos, the buzzer rang, signaling the end of the time-out. After some coaxing by the officials, both teams broke their huddles and five Hornets and five Bulls took to the floor. Bulls ball out of bounds underneath their own basket.

From the far sideline, Coach Dugan ran his hands through his graying hair and yelled for the Bulls to watch for the double team. Carl Boatwright, the seven-foot Aussie, took the ball from the ref. Immediately Jeff Malone, Charlotte's white seven-footer, charged toward Boatwright, coming to within inches of him. The ref blew the whistle. Delay-of-game warning, Charlotte. A tactical move by the Hornets that was par for the course in this situation. The defense committed it in hopes of getting a glimpse of the kind of play the offense might be running before the ball was actually thrown in.

The players reset. The ref blew the whistle again and began counting to five, the precious number of seconds Boatwright had to inbound the ball. The other Bulls scrambled to break free, especially Deon, who Dugan wanted to have the ball. Even when's he's having an off night, you still go to your scorer in the clutch.

But Boatwright was having trouble getting the ball in and the crowd was screaming for a five-second violation. With under a second to spare, Deon broke free of Larry Smith at a forty-five degree angle to the basket, just inside the three point arc. Boatwright anticipated Deon's move and threw the ball to the spot. Deon got there just in time and caught it. But he wasn't square with the basket. To make matters worse, George "Thunder" Hawkins rushed over for the dou-ble-team, blanketing Deon. Deon dribbled once toward the basket, then pulled up. Hawkins went for the fake and stumbled backwards. But Smith recovered in time to helped out his teammate. Deon stepped back so that he was just outside the three point line and— leaning into Smith to draw a foul, if nothing else—launched a twenty-five-foot, off-balance jumper.

Nothing but net.

The Bulls and their smattering of fans went wild. Deon ran toward the top of the key and leaped in the air, punching his fist toward the rafters in vindication. His teammates then mobbed him as the rest of the arena, players and fans included, sank in disbelief. Final score 111-110. The Bulls were now up 3-2 in the best-of-seven series and on their way back to the Chicago and the friendly confines of the United Center for game six.

As the team plane waited on the tarmac at Charlotte Douglas, a stranger wouldn't have been able to tell if the Bulls had won or lost tonight. By the time they'd showered and dressed, talked to the press, then boarded the bus that took them to the plane, the thrill of victory had all but worn off. It was approaching 3:00 a.m. now and they were in the dusk of a season that was lasting over a hundred games. They couldn't afford to get too high about one win. There was still a lot of basketball to be played before capturing another ring.

Champion Air was the luxury liner of team planes with cute young hostesses serving up gourmet dishes in the buffet compartment, enough music, movies and video games to keep the team distracted on cross-country flights, and plush leather seats big enough for giant bodies spread throughout the plane in four-man booths, giving everyone much needed breathing room. Up front, Coach Dugan was alone, reading a book by one of the Zen masters he followed. In the middle compartment, Piper Adams, the pint-sized point guard, was flirting as usual with the full-figured black waitress behind the buffet table, while Jo Jo Taylor and Marcus Kramer, two smooth-skinned rookies, piled their plates with broiled chicken and mashed potatoes. The third compartment was occupied by two of the assistant coaches—one black, one white, both former players now in their forties—who were busy setting up the VCR to watch the tape of tonight's triple overtime battle. Time to figure out how to stop Larry Smith in game six in Chicago.

In the last compartment, Deon sat alone in a booth of four seats. He was slumped down in his chair, ice pack on the shin he banged against Larry Smith's knee. Holding his gray tweed apple cap over his face, he pretended to be asleep, but was distracted when he heard the voice of a female newscaster coming from the assistant coaches' television on the other side of the partition:

"CNC Overnight has learned there was a beating late last night in Los Angeles— early this morning Eastern time—that police are saying looks very similar to the so-called counter-bashings that have taken place in four other cities."

"Check it out," said a gruff voice from the vicinity of the TV. It was Doaky Dawkins, Deon realized, followed by the female anchor again:

"Now, we want to stress: the footage you see here is from previous beatings, not tonight."

Three players had gathered around the television suspended on the wall in the assistant coaches' compartment. Jamaal Johnston, light-skinned veteran, winced when he saw the night vision shots of a man with long hair taking a baseball bat to the small of his back. "Those fags come into my neighborhood, they get they asses whipped."

Junior Watson, the bald-headed big man with a refrigerator size body, scoffed. "Man, anybody come to your neighborhood, they get they asses whipped."

"Notice they ain't attacked no brothers," said Doaky Dawkins.

"Shiiiiiiit," said Watson, making it sound not only ridiculous but impossible. The three of them broke into a muffled laughter until Watson said, "Shh...D.A.," and nodded to the compartment behind them. Silence ensued, followed by the assistant coaches kicking them out in order to get their work started.

Outwardly, Deon showed no visible reaction except for burying his face deeper into his apple cap and snoring a little to promote the illusion of being asleep. Inwardly, for the duration of the flight, he thought about how many championship rings he had won those guys, guys the media called his supporting cast.

THE INSTANT DEON entered his penthouse on the north side of Chicago, he saw Charlie, sitting in the dark in a chair in the living room where he could see the front door when it opened.

My girl, Deon thought, dropping his garment bag just inside the door.

Charlie rose up and made a beeline for Deon. His tiny frame was all baggy in some of Deon's old Bulls sweats. "Bad day at the office, honey?" he said with his husky voice.

They wrapped themselves around each other without another word, their embrace lasting several minutes and taking them from the foyer to the living room, where Deon sat Charlie on the couch, knelt in front of him and collapsed in his lap in the dark. They stayed that way for twenty minutes, the only sound in the room the muffled sniffles and fragmented breaths coming from Deon.

"You saw how I stunk up the court?" he asked eventually.

"I saw how you showed 'em in the end. I know he's proud of you—same way he is for the counter-bashings and you know it."

"I tried to use him to focus—get in a zone for him—but I couldn't, just like I couldn't do anything for him when he was alive. But I'm gonna be there for you, I swear, I promise. I'll never leave you stranded like that."

"Hush your mouth. I ain't ever coming to that," Charlie assured him, fighting his tears to be the strong one. He knew Deon would have been all torn up even if he hadn't played so poorly. It was the anniversary of J-Boy's death.

"I hate this day," Deon said, "more than any other day in my life."

"I know, baby." Charlie held onto Deon's head and rocked the two of them back and forth, figuring on being there in the living room in that same position well past sunrise.

THE BEDROOM IN THE Manhattan penthouse was dark except for the light flickering from the television set lodged on the wall. On top of the large circular bed, Jasper was fast asleep on his back, still in the day's suit, his reading glasses teetering on the brink of his nose. He had passed out that way an hour ago while going over reports on the millions he was losing on the undeveloped shores of Belize. At the

foot of the bed sat Bruce, naked except for his white briefs, eagerly sizing up the job he had his eye on, male anchor for CNC Overnight.

"Jasper, you gotta see this," he said in a hushed voice when they
broke in with the story of the Los Angeles beating.

In sleep, Jasper was always ready for panic. His eyes popped open
immediately, his throat gurgling with the remnants of his last snore as
he snatched off his reading glasses.

"They did it again," Bruce informed him, "the counter-bashers."

They listened to the phoned-in report from local correspondent
Josh Cameron while the screen showed a map of Los Angeles, indicating Silverlake with a red dot.

"That's five now," Bruce said, his voice full of disgust, "if it's
them, and I'd bet my life it is."

Jasper said nothing. As the report came to an end, Bruce joined
him at the head of the bed, sitting near Jasper's torso with his legs
crossed.

"I was gonna surprise you," he began full of enthusiasm, "but I
can't keep my mouth shut. I'm working on an exposé: just who are
these people and why do they think they can speak for the whole gay
community? What do you think?"

Jasper checked his impulse to sit up. "You run it by Jeevers yet?"

"I want to get some solid facts first."

"So you have nothing now?"

"Just the police reports and two interviews." He saw the shock in
Jasper's face and felt the need to explain. "I took a trip. To Kentucky
to see those two cops from the first bashing. They could barely talk,
their faces were so swollen and distorted. Makes me sick just thinking
about it." He tried to shake off the images and lay on his stomach, per-
pendicular to Jasper, his hands clutched together as if in prayer.
"Jasper, I know I can crack this story. Violence is not the answer to our
problems. As a gay reporter—well, not openly gay, but gay just the
same—I want to get these goons arrested and show positive things
like the Triangle Fund. I just need a sure-fire lead." He had been talking to himself as much as Jasper and suddenly realized Jasper had
been silent for some time. "You don't agree with these terrorists," he
paused, the thought having never occurred to him before, "do you?"

Jasper laughed and patted Bruce's chin as if to say, "silly boy."
"You just keep plugging away at it. I'm sure you'll find your lead."
Eyeing his boss, Bruce thought about it, then smiled, nodding his
head in appreciation of Jasper's support. Jasper yawned and turned
over on his side, away from Bruce, as if to go back to sleep. In reality,
he was wide awake, sleep now the farthest thing from his mind.

HAVENHURST DRIVE, RAIDER thought, glancing up at the street sign as he
made the turn: home of gayboy personal trainer Raider Kincaide. He
burst out laughing, arching his head toward the starry night, and
singing:

If they could see me now,
those block-head friends of mine....

"They'd probably kill me," he decided, still amused. Amazingly,
there was a parking space not far from the apartment building. What
a break, he thought. He pulled into the open spot, jokingly compar-
ing it to the break he received when ACTNOW insisted he be the
videographer for the night's festivities. Fine tuning the parking job, he
glanced at the videotape next to his Dodgers baseball cap on the passenger's seat.
"Thought they'd make the novice earn his bat, huh?"
Earlier tonight, when they met up behind a boarded-up cleaners
in Koreatown, he gladly took possession of the camera. When no one
was looking, he performed a little cosmetic surgery on it, placing tiny
specks of black tape over the red recording light so no one could tell
when he was capturing their mugs. Now he had every last one of them
on videotape, before, during and after the bashing, hoods on and off,
in one van before the beatings, in the other afterwards. He even got
that red-headed flamer to brag about the other bashings.
"Freedom, my man," Raider had said. "Which do you like more,
crushing bones or driving the getaway van?"
"You kidding, man?" Freedom had said between nasty coughs.
"In Florida and Dallas, Freedom Clark was the man. *My* blows were

the blows that sent those rednecks to intensive care."

Thank you and goodnight. It was enough to convict every last one of the members of Level 3. The only one he didn't get a shot of was the real Othello, but he had bigger felonies in mind for the pop star. And switching the tapes had been cake. In the commotion of the getaway, no one even noticed. Now, ACTNOW had a blank tape full of screen noise and would think the rookie fucked up while the real tape would soon join the other evidence in the safe deposit box in a West Hollywood bank.

Raider put on the Dodgers cap, grabbed the tape and hopped out of the Jeep, feeling pretty damned triumphant and wishing he could go out and find himself a nice young filly to keep him and Raider, Jr., company. But the porno videos he charged to the expense account would have to do for the night, just as they had every night for the last several weeks. He couldn't afford to slip-up again, not after the Nantucket fiasco.

Across the street from the apartment building, Othello saw Raider approaching from the opposite direction. He'd been sitting in the Impala for over an hour, not dressed as Joe but as himself with black jeans, white tank top and a faded blue denim jacket. It was after midnight now, the vans having gone their separate ways over two hours ago, and he had to lay eyes on Raider, to see if the rookie activist was closer to being a full-fledged rebel or ready to go AWOL. Except for the two of them, the street seemed empty, so he got out of the car.

Just as he was about to turn into the complex walkway, Raider saw the Impala and knew right away who it belonged to. But he was shocked to see Othello, not Joe, getting out and heading toward him as he quickly slipped the videotape into his back pocket.

"Have you gone insane?" he said in a hushed tone, grabbing Othello by the shoulders. "You're flirting with disaster here!"

"If I spend another minute in that costume I think I'll blow my own head off."

"People walk their dogs around here at all times of the night."

"I needed to see you, to make sure...to see how...are you all right?"

Raider looked both ways down the street, and deciding they were alone, let go of Othello. "More than you know. Here." He removed his baseball cap and placed it on Othello's head. "Disguise your noggin at least."

"Thanks." Othello smiled a bashful smile, as if Raider had just handed over his Dartmouth letterman's jacket. "So you were okay with what you saw tonight?"

"I can't wait for more. But you shouldn't be here. You heard Travis say we don't contact each other for at least a week after tonight."

"That doesn't apply to us." Othello glanced around nervously. "Can we go upstairs. To talk?"

"No," Raider said too quickly. Barbie Walsh, Cherry Grove and a dozen other porno starlets were all over the apartment, showing their wares on glossy video boxes. Not to mention getting upstairs without Othello trying to scope out his butt and spotting the videotape. "My place looks like one of your California quakes hit it."

"Like that matters."

"Here's a better idea: how 'bout a drive? I'm too stoked to sleep anyway."

Othello agreed and Raider indicated the topless Jeep just down the street, letting Othello walk ahead of him. When they reached it, he unlocked the passenger door first, letting Othello climb in while he slipped the tape underneath a dirty towel in the back.

They drove in silence, first south past lonely commercial thoroughfares, then onto the freeway heading west until it segued into the tunnel that spilled onto Pacific Coast Highway going north. Several times Othello began to speak but stopped himself, not wanting to compete with the wind. Raider also remained quiet, hoping Othello would eventually pronounce himself exhausted and ask to be taken back to the Impala. But Othello showed no signs of fatigue, and when they snaked their way through the Malibu portion of PCH—the mountains on one side, the ocean on the other—he yelled to Raider: "There's a clearing coming up. You'll love it."

A mile later, he told Raider to slow down and pull over. Obediently, Raider brought the Jeep to a crawl and crossed the highway, bringing the car to a halt on a large patch of earth jutting out over the ocean. There were no other signs of life around them, just the occasional headlights of a lone vehicle approaching then passing in the darkness behind them, and the moonlit Pacific in front.

"Not bad," Raider said as he killed the engine, truly meaning it. "This your private little place?"

"I've been here before. I thought we could use the peace and quiet, you know, after, well, the sounds of breaking bones."

Raider adjusted his seat to give himself more room. "You regret being there? Or doing it altogether?"

"No, I don't regret it. Do you regret it?"

"I told you I didn't." He looked over at Othello, who seemed far from being at ease. "Let your seat back, relax a little." Feels strange, he thought, telling *Othello* what to do.

Othello did as he was told. The atmosphere in the Jeep began to lighten, both of them taking in the view of the blackness before them and listening to the calming sounds of the ocean's waves.

"This is good," Othello said after a while.

"I have to admit."

"Of course, it'd be better if I did this." Removing the Dodgers cap, Othello leaned over to rest his head on Raider's chest, but bumped it on Raider's chin in the process.

"Whoa!" Raider said, rubbing his face, pretending it hurt more than it did.

"Sorry," Othello offered but snuggled into Raider's chest anyway.

"No problem." Seeing that Othello wasn't going anywhere, Raider took his right arm and raised it as if he were going to put it around Othello. It took a couple of tries, but eventually his brain convinced his arm to complete the task.

"That better?" Othello asked, melting his upper body into Raider's.

Raider mumbled something that passed for a yes.

"I could get used to this," said Othello, "for a very long time."

Raider remained mute.

Othello raised up and looked at him with those piercing brown eyes. "And I could get used to this...." Then, as if it were the most natural thing in the world, he planted a peck of a kiss on Raider's lips.

"Mmm," Raider said as if to mean "yummy." No need to panic, he reasoned. After all, they'd already kissed twice, on the Big House terrace and saying good-bye at the door that same night. A kiss was just a kiss, right Bogey?

"And this...." Othello planted another one, a peck and a half under his chin.

"Mmm."

"And this...." This time it was a lingering kiss on the corner of his mouth.

"Mmm. Mmm."

"And this...." Now the other corner. "And...." Now full frontal lip locking. They were at it again. Forever it seemed. Thank God Othello had full thick lips, the kind he liked on women. But still. And the guy wasn't letting up. The tongue was coming. Oh, fuck, not the tongue. Oh, well. The boys at the bureau never have to know, right?

Othello's right hand roamed over Raider's hair, face and neck; and Raider was startled to realize he had both arms around Othello, one caressing his back, the other gripping his shoulder.

"Whoa," Raider said, unlocking his lips and coming up for air. "The songs don't lie. You are a passionate one, aren't you?"

Othello giggled like a school girl, looking down toward the gearshift he was hovering over.

"You better not break that," said Raider, "else we'll be stuck here all night."

"I wouldn't object," said Othello.

"Let's get out and look at the view." Raider was out the door without waiting for an answer. He went to the front of the Jeep and leaned on the hood five yards in front of the cliff. When Othello joined him, he put his arm around the pop star's shoulders to make up for bolting too fast. Othello responded by putting one arm around Raider's torso.

"You wouldn't happen to have a blanket in the back, would you?" Othello asked with a mischievous grin.

"Just a gas can and some greasy towels, sorry." As if lack of anything to lie on had ever stopped Raider Kincaide before. And he would have to be hornier than usual tonight, with Othello in heat and ready to pounce. If he were ever going to be with a man.... Bet that would seal the deal with Othello, too, wrap this case up in a flash. Hell, he could get 'em now with the audio tape of the Wisemen and video tape of Level 3, but he had zilch on any assassination plot.

He bent down and nibbled on Othello's ear. Damn, I'm crazy, Raider thought. Of all the things I've ever done. Maybe just a blowjob. From one of the biggest names in all of celebritydom. Raider had heard guys were better at it anyway. What he wouldn't give for a quick blowjob right now, here out in the open, screaming when he came like there was no tomorrow. He fronted Othello and grabbed his waist, surprised at how small it was considering Othello's ripped upper body. He kissed Othello some more, then, that being a little too intense, ran his closed mouth over his neck. That was easier. Othello was loving it, too, grinding his pelvis into Raider's, his hands roaming all over Raider's shoulder blades as if he couldn't get enough of all that wide expansive back. One of the most famous stars the world over was off-the-chart horny for him. That was enough to go to any guy's head.

Next thing Raider knew, he had Othello pinned against the hood. On his thigh he could feel Othello's hard-on, pressing through his jeans, aching to get out. Then Raider realized Othello's wasn't the only hard cock. Damn, Raider said to himself, I'm that fucking horny tonight. Just one little quick and wet blowjob, how 'bout it? For the case and because he was on fire tonight. It was Othello or a couple of rounds with Cherry Grove and the videos back at the apartment. Which was it going to be?

"Othello, we gotta stop." Raider scooted off of him, banged his forehead on the hood and took his first sensible breath of the night. "We can't do this. I can't do this." He straightened up and walked toward the ocean. It wasn't worth it. Nothing in the world would make homo-sex worth it—no accolades, no glory, no Hollywood movie based on his life, nothing. Besides, he could bust the case without having to drop his trousers and, yes, he could also wait for Cherry Grove back at his apartment.

Use your fucking brain, Kincaide. Think with the bigger head.

The life momentarily drained out of Othello when Raider let go of him, but he was also relieved, for doing more than kissing and dry humping brought up an infinite number of confusing questions and issues, questions and issues Othello was far from knowing how to handle. And watching Raider brooding at the sea, Othello figured he knew exactly what was going on in his would-be lover's mind.

"Talk to me," said Othello. "It's what I think it is, isn't it? What every dating couple these days has to talk about at some point."

It took a moment for Raider to catch on, but catch on he did. "Sex isn't as easy as drop your pants and away-we-go anymore."

But let's please not talk HIV status, Othello begged the gods above, then said, "True, the carefree days are long gone, but if we never let ourselves not be safe—"

"Safe?" Raider repeated incredulously, speaking from his heart. "What the hell is safe?"

"Well, safe is kissing and what we've done so far."

Seemingly unsatisfied with the answer, Raider picked up a rock and hurled it toward the Pacific. To himself, he thought: reason number 8,075 why to never have sex with a man: disease.

"Safe," said Othello, giving it another try, "safe is learning together what we can and cannot do, then never *ever* putting each other at risk."

"Safe is slowing way the hell down, Othello, pure and simple." He thought about asking Othello if he'd been tested, but figured Othello was as healthy as he looked. Besides, he reasoned, they weren't ever going to do the horizontal mambo anyway. Meantime, until he had enough evidence of an assassination plot, fear of catching AIDS was going to become his newest best friend and foremost excuse for not getting naked with the leader of the Wisemen. "You know, Freedom looked so frail tonight. I'll be damned if I'll end up like that."

"It's good we put the brakes on," Othello conceded. "We're still getting to know each other, I guess, still waiting to make it special and right." He was flustered and didn't know what else to say. Pursuing the issue any more would have surely led to questions about getting tested and he was nowhere near *close* to being close to telling Raider the truth. "So we wait. We slow it down."

"Fine with me," Raider said, picking up another rock and letting it fly in the name of releasing some pent-up energy. "Slow it down. Way down." He made a loud screeching noise as if he were a car trying to come to a dead stop from some astronomical speed.

"I get the picture," Othello said, unamused. "I think we both do."

"Good," said Raider. And that was that.

It was late. The mood for love and/or sex dwindled for both of them. Without having to verbalize it, they both climbed back into the Jeep and headed south, back down the dark twists and turns of Pacific Coast Highway.

THIRTEEN

IT WAS BOUND to happen, Raider mused, standing just inside the doorway of the Spike. From the moment he took the job pretending to be a gayboy, he figured he'd have to someday step foot inside one of their bars. The Spike was a dark and dingy hole in the wall, and since it was still light outside, it took a moment for his eyes to adjust to the place.

The main room was really an oversized corridor, bar on the left, stacked crates on the right, a pool table near the back. And men. Only men. Fifteen or so. What the fuck was the world coming to? A handful of them surrounded the pool table, watching two young dudes setting up a game. Another half dozen lined the bar, figuring out who to take home no doubt. To his relief, he saw what he came for sitting at the far end of the bar. He made his way down the corridor, ignoring the eyes following him and blanching at the industrial-like noise that passed itself off as music.

"Hey, look who's here!" he said when he reached the end of the bar.

"Hey, stud," Gus said. "Cool surprise; grab a stool."

"Thanks." Raider sat down beside him. "Bud Light," he said to the black bartender whose big chest was straining to break out of a thin white tank top.

"This your regular haunt?" asked Gus.

"Actually, my first time here," said Raider. He'd found out this was Gus's hangout from Darnell, the black Rastaman in ACTNOW. Raider had pretended to be romantically interested in the bearded, overall-wearing-speed-chasing liar. It worked. "Kinda glad to see a familiar face," he told Gus now. "And I must say, I'm glad the face is yours."

Gus turned about twelve shades of red.

"Another beer here for my friend here," Raider told the bartender. "And keep 'em coming. For both of us." He smiled at Gus, who seemed taken aback and confused. "I've got nowhere to be," Raider said nonchalantly, "do you?"

"I was gonna hang out all night," said Gus.

"Money," said Raider, getting the grin he wanted from his brand new drinking buddy.

"THE HOMOSEXUAL WAS created by the devil as an act of vengeance against the Lord Almighty, but God uses them as a teaching tool for the rest of humanity, to say: see these people? This is how not to live."

"The most unnatural thing in the world has got to be man lusting after man. All serial killers, gay or straight, have always had tendencies toward this kind of perversion. I bet if you truly investigate your Ted Bundys and that New York killer, Son of Sam, I bet you'll find they too dabbled in unnatural homosexual acts."

"There are people that say AIDS is the cure for homosexuality. Do I believe that? Well, let's just say I don't disbelieve it."

Jasper walked over to the big screen television and turned it and the VCR off. "We don't need to hear any more from the distinguished senior senator."

"Then I take it you both understand how destructive the man is." Othello used his finger to stir his ice water as he sat on the oak desk in the middle of the room. For the last hour, they'd been in the Royal Suite at the Palace Hotel, watching a retrospective on Jimmy Herman's career in the senate.

"Yeah, yeah, old Jimmy boy is vile," said Deon. He was by the window overlooking the casino, his tall frame stretched across the brown leather couch, his gigantic black Nikes on Jasper's coffee table. He hadn't said much all night, yeaing and naying absentmindedly to Triangle Fund business and barely tuning in now as Othello began his pitch. Twelve hours ago, the Bulls lost game six of the conference finals despite forty-two clutch points from The D.A. The series was now heading back to Charlotte for the deciding game and Othello assumed basketball was on Deon's mind. The better to sway him, Othello decided, setting his water down and rising up to walk around the Royal Suite.

"And we're all aware of how much good we've done coming together," he said. "The Triangle Fund has benefited countless brothers and sisters. And once the statistics are available, I'm sure we'll see a reduced rate of hate crimes in some areas due to counter-bashing, especially in the areas where we actually struck."

"Won't solve all our problems," Jasper said. He was leaning against the television, his arms folded skeptically as he waited for Othello to get to the point.

"Nothing ever will. So many fights on so many fronts." Othello was trying to build up steam, telling himself: You've come this far. "As you both know, Jimmy Herman is erecting this museum dedicated to himself and American morals, whatever that means."

"Got me my invitation." From the couch, Deon laughed and rolled over on his side. "The grand opening of the Jimmy Herman Museum of American Decency."

Othello turned to him. "You going?"

"Hell if I know," said Deon. When Jasper and Othello eyed him curiously, he added in his own defense: "He's a big Gamecock supporter. I don't take shit from him or his friends, but the USC connection, that's a loyalty thing, a state thing. You wouldn't understand."

Othello waited until he was back in the middle of the room again and finally said it: "We need to counter-bash Jimmy Herman."

Jasper had just picked up his scotch off the desk and was finishing a swig. "Blow the fucking Nazi museum right out of the ground— empty, of course, so we don't kill the innocent, which, in this case, would amount to the cleaning staff."

"An admirable sentiment," said Othello, "but I'm talking death."

By the look in Jasper's eyes, Othello could tell the tycoon was surprised—no impressed—but before either could get a word in, Deon said:

"That's crazy."

"Think about it," Othello began, not wanting to lose momentum. "A gay man or lesbian, with AIDS possibly, taking matters into his own hands, staring Herman in the face and firing a shot every fag and dyke in this country would want to fire."

Not every fag, Jasper thought, refreshing his drink and picturing Bruce, who had gone to Dallas this morning to investigate the counter-bashing there in his attempt to be the next Dan Rather. "What gay man do you have in mind for the task?" he asked.

"One of the members of Level 3."

"Which one?" asked Deon.

"Not sure yet."

"You wanted this all along, didn't you?" said Jasper.

"I made no bones about my hate for the man and my desire for blood. When we started, I didn't know how far I could go. Now I know."

"This is madness." Deon got up and turned to the casino window. "You're talking life in prison."

"What we've done so far could accomplish that," said Jasper. "More or less."

"We haven't murdered yet," said Deon.

"It won't be traced back to us." Othello moved closer to Deon. "We find one person in Level 3 who is willing to assassinate Herman, provide him or her with the tools and turn 'em loose. Not even the triggerman will know who we are."

"What if they trace the person to Level 3?" asked Jasper.

"At the very worst, they go looking for an old black man. I'll burn the outfit. They still won't have a clue about the Three Wisemen."

"Killing people is playing God," said Deon.

"Jimmy Herman kills people every day," Othello said, "by spitting out hate that people who believe in his ideas use as an excuse to beat up fags, by cutting funding for AIDS, by just being the hateful bastard that he is. There must be thousands of gay men or women out there willing to end his miserable life and would if they could. We're not playing God. We're just conduits of vengeance."

Jasper looked up from his drink. "No one knows about Joe? Other than your manager. And us?"

Othello paused. If he was going to lead the horses to water, he had to be honest with them. "One person."

"Who?" both Jasper and Deon asked.

"My boyfriend."

Jasper eyed him suspiciously. "You said you didn't—"

"We just started being boyfriends." Felt good to say it aloud, even if he wasn't sure it was the right term yet. "He's okay. He's one of the counter-bashers, actually. He wouldn't rat on me."

"You willing to bet your life on that?" Jasper asked.

Othello paused. "He has no clue about you two anyway, even if he did decide to sell me up the river—which he's not going to do." Othello scooped up his ice water from the desk and took a sip, suddenly thankful he'd decided this trip was too important to have Raider along as a distraction.

"My Charlie knows about us," said Deon, to which Jasper and Othello gasped. "He supports me—chill out. He won't tell anybody. We've been together for years. We're tighter than tight. He's my baby-doll."

"Jasper, did you tell Brucie-boy?" asked Othello.

"No, and he'll never know." Jasper went for another drink at the bar. "What's your boyfriend's name?"

"Raider—Brian Kincaide. And don't worry, I had Sweeney check him out before I ever let him into my life."

Deep in thought and seemingly unconvinced, Jasper took a good long swig of scotch.

"Why don't we take this up after the playoffs?" said Deon.

"We can't wait," said Othello. "It's June already. The museum opens at the end of the month with a ceremony that's picture perfect for our uprising's greatest moment. Imagine all those rednecks in their shiny white plantation-owner suits."

"Sounds like a logistical nightmare," said Jasper. "A lot harder than shuffling a few million into a fund or giving some gay boys bats and vans and plane tickets."

"That's where Deon comes in," said Othello. "You know Senator Evil. You can visit the museum beforehand, get the lay of the place so we can plot and plan."

To this, they said nothing. Deon stared at the casino below and Jasper turned away from them. The suite was silent until Othello spoke.

"Remember when we were in this room a while back and you both dismissed the concept of the Three Wisemen as ridiculous. Look where we are now."

More silence.

"Let me ask this," he said. "Is it a matter of valuing Jimmy Herman's life?"

"No," the other two Wisemen said almost simultaneously.

"And Jasper, how about the millions you have tangled up in Belize? You value that? Bet you could recoup your losses a lot faster if your ambassador-elect had the *elect* removed from his name."

"Oh, no." Deon knew exactly what Othello was doing. "This cannot be majority rules. If I don't agree to this and you two go ahead, count me out of the Wisemen period. They'll come after me even if I'm not guilty."

"Then it has to be unanimous," said Jasper. "We agree on that?"

Both Deon and Othello shook their heads.

"It's already unanimous we could give a damn about Jimmy Herman's health," said Othello.

"If we agree to this," said Jasper, "why don't I contact professionals? They'll do a clean job and can't be traced as easily."

"That would be meaningless," said Othello. "We need a gay person, out in the open, sending a message to all the other anti-gay pundits. Who knows, maybe we'll inspire a whole mess of copycats who take care of the rest of the Jimmy Hermans in office, not to mention the homophobic religious leaders."

"I've already heard rumors of other Level 3-type groups in New York and Boston," said Jasper.

"The uprising has already begun, gentlemen," said Othello. "We simply need a spark so powerful and dramatic they *have* to stop what they're doing and take notice."

Deon sat back down on the couch. "Jasper, you seem to know about this kind of stuff. Can we really get away with it?"

Jasper set down his drink and savored the last taste of scotch descending his throat. "With professionals setting up an accident or heart attack or something to that effect, yes. With professionals *assassinating* him? With a well-hated nut like Herman, possibly. Probably. With amateurs? You're asking for a miracle."

"How can they trace us?" asked Othello.

"Depends on how well we cover our tracks."

"Can we trust each other?" asked Deon.

Jasper regarded his partners, first Deon, then Othello. "We already have to do that."

The Three Wisemen eyed each other, each face registering power and vulnerability at the same time. Then Deon picked up his sweat jacket off the sofa and slowly made his way to the door. There, he paused, searching for the right words, rolling his tongue in his cheek, his face more serious than Jasper or Othello had ever seen it.

"I gotta think about this before I put my whole life further into you guys' hands," he said dubiously. And with that, he left the Royal Suite minus one Wiseman.

STEADILY THE MORNING SUN climbed toward its midday peak, shining down brightly on the modest skyline in the distance and bathing the blue-green hills of the golf course with rich golden hues more associated with the coming summer than the fading spring. The course—which was on the outskirts of Charlotte—was deserted except for the party of six bursting into laughter on the tenth hole. Winston Callahan had just sent yet another ball sailing into a magnolia tree far from the fairway—nothing new for the thin man with a permanent six o'clock shadow that made him look older than his forty years. He never took golf or life very seriously. You didn't have to when your father was the biggest man in Columbia, South Carolina.

Also there were Percival Stone, the heavyset, high-powered attorney from Charleston who was never without a cigar and a flask, and Sheriff, a short, feeble-bodied man in his fifties. He had never been associated with the law, nor was that his real name, but for reasons now lost, everybody just called him Sheriff. The last of the South Carolina good ol' boys who had flown up in Percival's plane was Big Daddy Callahan, his six-foot-eight, three-hundred-pound boulder of a body dressed in a white suit with his usual white straw cowboy hat. The lone non-Southerner of the bunch was Kersey Stevens, the blond guard for the Bulls who loved golf almost as much as his teammate, Deon Anthony, the last piece of the puzzle who had arranged the game with a single phone call to Big Daddy.

"Come up and lose some cash," Deon had said to him on the phone. "It's also your chance to ask Kersey to the charity tournament." With or without Big Daddy, Deon would have played a round of golf today as a way of relaxing before tomorrow's game seven against the Hornets; but he wanted to look Callahan in the eye to see if it was possible to tell just how much racist and homophobic blood ran through his veins and the veins of his best friend, Jimmy Herman. The senator was also invited but had been too busy preparing for the museum opening to make the trip.

"Boy, Deon, I sure appreciate you having me and the boys up here," Big Daddy was saying as they watched Percival step up to the tee. "And good ol' Kersey is the perfect choice for the tournament."

Of course, thought Deon. Kersey Stevens had the cleanest reputation in the NBA. The only renegade group he ever joined was the Fellowship of Christian Athletes.

"I knew he was your type," said Deon, getting a confused smile from Big Daddy in return.

With the tenth hole complete, they boarded their carts and drove to the eleventh, a tricky hole in between two small but treacherous lakes. Deon was first up. He sliced his ball into the larger of the lakes to the right of the fairway.

"Hope your game is better than this tomorrow," Sheriff chided, prompting Percival to slap him on the shoulder.

"Bite your tongue," said Percival. His drawl was the thickest. "You know we're rooting for our fellow Southern Hornet boys." He then broke into a whiskey laugh. "Just kidding there, D.A."

Deon shook his head and watched Big Daddy working on Kersey on the other side of the tee. Kersey was resting on the golf cart while Big Daddy hovered over him, waving his hands and looking as if he were using the hard sell to get the two-time NBA all-star to next month's fund-raiser.

"Daddy wants him awful fierce," Winston whispered in Deon's ear.

When the party moved to the fourteenth hole, Deon finally got a chance to get Big Daddy alone.

"How's the senator?" he asked while the others made fun of Winston's swing. "Heard he was in the hospital a while back."

"Two days of testing," said Big Daddy. "Man's getting up there, but he's fine. Still looking forward to seeing you at both the museum opening and golf tournament."

"Speaking of the museum, what's it stand for?"

"Why decency, just like the name says—hey, Winston, son, go ahead and just aim for the trees. Maybe then the ball will make it to the hole."

"So it's not anti—" Deon searched for the word, but only came up with: "minority?"

"Aw, boy—er—son—er—man, it's pro-family. American family —Winston, let me show you how to hit the ball. Excuse me, Deon."

They played on. At the next hole, it was Kersey who made a point to get Deon alone.

"Can you believe that man?" he said, indicating Big Daddy sizing up a putt. "He's ready to sell his soul to get me to that tournament."

"Warned you."

"I told him just because I'm from Utah doesn't mean I'm a red-neck who supports redneck charities."

"Redneck?" Deon repeated, somewhat confused. "It's for inner city kids."

"Told me it was about helping organizations that make sure 'our' people get their fair share of the American pie. You think 'our' means inner city kids with that man?"

Eight years of Deon's life flashed before him, specifically the por-tions spent teeing off at the Jimmy Herman Carolina Gentlemen's Charity Golf Classic. Soon as he got the chance, which was at the next hole, he went up to the co-founder of the tournament.

"Big Daddy, Kersey says you told him the tournament is for white causes."

Big Daddy broke out laughing, and like a chorus, so did the Southern gentlemen behind him.

"That Kersey's a good kidder," said Big Daddy.

"Kersey doesn't tell lies." Deon eyed Kersey, who was teeing off out of earshot.

Big Daddy looked to his chorus for support. "Why, all kinds of folk benefit from the charity foundation. The museum for instance."

"I thought it was for playgrounds for poor kids, homeless families, registering people to vote, AIDS mothers and babies."

"AIDS?" cried Big Daddy. "We got nothing to do with dangerous lifestyle choices."

The whole NBA—not to mention the entire athletic department back at South Carolina—had its suspicions that Deon was a fag. But Big Daddy Callahan and Jimmy Herman refused to believe it and couldn't be convinced if they saw Deon taking it up the butt in a sling hanging from the back room of an Amsterdam leather bar. "Them damn rumors were started by Clemson folks who'll be forever pissed you didn't win *them* the NCAA," Big Daddy used to say.

"So you don't help mothers with AIDS place their kids with loving families?" asked Deon. "Your secretary told me that years ago. You yourself told me...." he broke off.

"Son, don't fret. Those little inner city tykes who worship you get some of the trickle down. You got my word." Big Daddy glanced toward the tee. "You're up, D.A."

In a state of shock, Deon took his turn, slicing the ball for a second time, a rarity for him. He then decided he couldn't stand to be within ten feet of the good ol' boys for another second. He limped away from the tee, grabbing at his right leg. "The knee felt weird on that one," he lied. "Game over for me."

They tried to help, even asked if they could drive him back to the clubhouse, but he waved them off without looking back. "Kersey, you go on and play through," he said, needing solitude. "I'll wait in the car." With that, he took off in one of the golf carts, vowing to never again lay eyes on the likes of Big Daddy Callahan.

For the next thirty minutes, he sat in the rented Ranger Rover in the mostly empty parking lot of the country club, staring straight ahead, trying to think of nothing but game seven. He didn't even hear Kersey approaching until he opened the passenger door and plopped down on the seat next to Deon.

"Some friends of yours I must say, Deon, my man," Kersey said.

"Those aren't my friends," Deon said coldly, keeping his eyes on the hood.

"Glad to hear that. After you left, they had a good old time laughing at the prospect of them helping AIDS victims. I was going to say something, but most of it was out of my circle of conversation."

"What'd they say?"

Kersey paused, as if to edit his thoughts. "Well, one thing I overheard was them badmouthing some male cheerleader from South Carolina. I guess the guy died of AIDS while he was in school."

"Jerome Briscoe?"

"They didn't say his name, but they dogged him pretty good. They actually had the guy kicked out of school right before he could graduate."

Deon went numb, couldn't move a muscle. He'd probably known it all along, just didn't want to admit it. He wanted to close his eyes and shut the world out. He also wanted to be alone. He started the car and left the country club.

When they reached the twelve-story glass tower that was the team hotel, he pulled into the turnaround out front instead of the parking lot.

"You coming up?" asked Kersey.

"Later."

As soon as Kersey was safe on the curb, the Ranger Rover speed off, burning rubber as it swerved back onto the highway. He sped up to sixty-five, then seventy-five, holding tight to the wheel and barely taking his eyes off the road. He stayed that way for most of the next two hours, heading south on Interstate 77, past rolling hills, one-stoplight towns and stretches of just plain nothing. He only stopped twice, once for gas, the other time to relieve himself. The rest of the time, he held to a steady pace of seventy-five, not making a sound, just racing down the highway until North Carolina turned into South. Once inside his home state, he kept going, bypassing the junction for his hometown Calhoun Falls and not going as far as Columbia, site of his alma mater. There was only one place he wanted to see, and that meant veering off the main highway seventy-five miles into his journey and traveling east on secondary roads until he came to a little town called Plainview.

The cemetery was a small one, maybe the size of a basketball court. It was surrounded by swampland and mourners had to climb a steep hill to reach it. Blacks who'd never lived to see the end of segregation were buried there, and because he wouldn't live to see the end of the AIDS crisis, J-Boy had asked his family to make this his final resting place. They had to squeeze in his plot next to a dying oak tree. That was how Deon knew where to find it when J-Boy's family called Deon to say J-Boy was dead and buried. It took Deon five months to get away from basketball to get to his grave back then. Today, more than a decade later, was only the second visit.

He found the oak tree, dying as it had been all those years ago, and the modest headstone that read: JEROME BRISCOE, JR., CHEERLEADER, USC. Once he was above the grave, he sank to his knees and cried for the next hour.

THE CHARLOTTE COLISEUM crowd was delirious, counting down the seconds starting with ten. Bugsy Webb, the five-six dynamo, was dribbling the ball amongst the giants who only halfheartedly attempted to guard him. Chicago was down by twelve and the Hornets were heading to the NBA finals for the first time ever.

When the clock dwindled to four, all ten players on the court stopped moving and waited for the final buzzer. The crowd's frenzy escalated even more. At center court, Deon watched helplessly, hands on hips, eyes glassed over, soul beaten. For only the third time in nine years, the Bulls wouldn't be in the finals, due in part to The D.A.'s worst game ever in the playoffs: seven points, six turnovers, five fouls.

As the clock struck zero, Bugsy Webb threw the ball high in the air. The Charlotte players then dropped their cool act and let loose, dancing, hugging, jumping up and down and goading the fans into even more cheering, cheering that echoed like thunder as Deon and the Bulls made their way to the locker room, away from the celebration.

JASPER WAS STANDING at the window in his office, surveying the Manhattan skyline, when Lisa, his young brunette secretary, delivered the note. It was sealed in an envelope marked CONFIDENTIAL. He waited until she was gone to read it. When he did, his face lit up with a billion-dollar smile.

OTHELLO WAS IN A MEETING with six lawyers and four accountants, a meeting forced on him by Sweeney to deal with some long overdue financial matters. He was at the head of a long conference table in the lawyers' office, taking in their barrage of suggestions, when a cute black male secretary with a huge ass sticking out of his suit pants delivered the note to him. He read it, then, in disbelief, read it a second time. Then he slipped it in the inside pocket of the black suit jacket he was wearing and didn't give a damn about anyone noticing the relieved grin wiping across his face.

The note was unsigned, but he knew who it was from.

"Got some time on my hands." It read. "Anybody else for a yes vote?"

FOURTEEN

JASPER CHECKED AND rechecked the army of knobs and levers on the long console, meticulously scrutinizing every nuance of his plan. In one of the leather chairs to his right, Deon was swiveling side to side, consumed with the sound of smooth jazz piping through a cassette headset. In the back of the room, which resembled a television studio control booth, Othello sighed and contemplated a cup of coffee from the beverage table. He couldn't remember the last time coffee passed his lips, but it was going to be a long day, he figured, crucial but long.

"Go ahead," Jasper said to Deon, nodding toward the console. "Give 'er a whirl."

Removing his headphones, Deon hesitated, then grabbed the flexible metal microphone sticking up in front of him and looked into the one-way mirror on the other side of the console. "So you wanna kill the bum?" he said, changing his voice into that of an old lady's.

"You don't have to sound like your grandmother," Jasper said laughingly. "Speak normal. Your voice will be naturally distorted, somewhere between Darth Vader and Demi Moore." He tinkered with a large black knob. "Here, try it again."

"So you wanna kill the bum Herman, eh?" Deon said, this time hearing his voice, which came out sounding low, muffled and unidentifiable. "Bad as hell," he said like a child learning a new trick.

"All three mikes are set up that way," Jasper informed them. "They'll never know the difference between the Three Wisemen and three little old ladies from Pasadena."

Othello walked over to the console, sized up the controls and the small room on the other side of the one-way mirror. "I must say, *Monsieur* Hollinquest, you've done your job quite well."

Not wanting to involve Sweeney, Othello had consented when Jasper insisted on setting up the day's operation. "I know people," Jasper had informed them in the three-way conference call after Deon's note. "Goons for hire who know how to keep their mouths shut permanently." And so the plan was conceived to grill the members of Level 3 and find out who, if any of them, would be promoted to Level 4, a level consisting of one person and one act, assassinating Jimmy Herman.

Four of nine members from Level 3 were already ruled out: Gary, the Asian, who had barely been able to make it through the counter-bashings without pissing in his pants; Georgio because Jasper objected to the idea of a former porn star pulling the trigger—"Clouds the issue when the tabloids eat him alive," he reasoned; Rainey, formerly known as Sparkplug, because he had quit after the last bashing; and Raider because Othello refused to even consider it. "He's property of me," Othello had said, "not some federal penitentiary."

And so it came down to five candidates: ACTNOW's two co-founders, Travis and Freedom, Gus from the Hollywood 500, and the two blacks, Trudy and Darnell, the ones Othello had called Afro and Rasta. Jasper's rent-a-goons were instructed to bring each candidate to this special room above the Temple. "The old lady wants to meet you," they were informed individually. Then, when they agreed and vowed not to tell a soul, they were to be blindfolded and driven around until they had no idea where they were.

"I think we have our first customer," Jasper said, sitting down in the middle chair and indicating the room beyond the mirror and the flashing red light above the entrance. Jasper flipped a switch on the console, his signal to his men, and Travis Little Horse was led through the door by two escorts in dark suits with dark sunglasses. They guided him to the chair in the middle of the room, then exited, closing the door behind them.

"Welcome," said Jasper, looking to his left at Othello, then to his right to Deon. "You may remove the blindfold."

Travis did so, then rubbed his eyes. "When do I get to meet the goddess who's been so kind to us."

"You're meeting me right now," said Othello, "along with some very important friends of mine." He looked to Jasper and Deon. "This will be the only way you can ever meet me."

"Are you that famous?" asked Travis.

"Never mind that," said Jasper.

"We ask the questions," said Deon.

"This gives you more freedom," said Othello. "The less you know about us, the more we can do for you, and gays everywhere."

The Wisemen paused, waiting for a response. Travis looked around the room. His hands were behind his waist as if they were tied.

"You object?" asked Jasper.

"No, ma'am. I haven't before and I don't now. I need you. We need you."

All three Wisemen eyed each other, the sense of power running through them like currents of electricity.

"Question," said Othello, beginning the interrogation. "Do you enjoy what you're doing?"

It was one of the first questions Othello decided to put to each candidate.

"Immensely," said Travis, "especially when I hear of other groups doing some counter-bashing of their own."

"Fuckin'-A, man," Freedom said when it was his turn, "best thing that's ever happened to this fag boy from Colorado Springs."

"I can't think of anything more worthwhile," said Gus. He looked more nervous than the others and kept glancing around the room and scratching his beard.

"I enjoy it to a point," said Trudy. "I go back and forth on whether violence is the answer. But when I'm in there smacking those little peanut heads, I get off."

"No, I don't enjoy it," said Darnell, his weathered face looking sullen and resigned the whole afternoon. "But what has to be done has to be done. I don't enjoy blowing up buildings either, but I do what I gotta do."

The Wisemen eyed each other pensively after Darnell's answer.

"If there was a Level 4," Deon asked all five candidates, "what would you have them do?"

"Like I said, bomb fucking buildings," said Darnell. "Robertson's TV studio, Lou Sheldon's office, Trent Lott's face."

"I want somebody to die like I'm gonna die any month here," said Freedom, "so I can see them in the afterlife and torture the shit out of them for eternity."

"I see Level 4 continuing with the bashing," said Travis, "but maybe targeting public officials instead of everyday scum."

"Level 4?" said Gus. "Whatever is asked of me, that's my duty."

"Before we do that," said Trudy, "maybe we ought to ask ourselves: is this really working?"

To this Deon covered his microphone and mouthed the words "no way" to his partners. Jasper nodded his head in agreement.

"What if someone dies during one of the counter-bashings?" Jasper asked them. "How would you feel?"

"Evil," said Darnell. "But evil is as evil does."

Gus grew nervous and said: "We shouldn't kill. The Lord doesn't forgive killing."

"I have to get back to you on that one," said Travis.

"How would I feel if a bashee dies?" Freedom shrugged. "Like I've done my job."

As the afternoon wore on, they grew more selective regarding which questions they asked which candidates. The next question Othello only put to Travis, Freedom and Darnell:

"One of my gal pals here thinks somebody ought to put a bullet in Senator Jimmy Herman's head." He followed it with a little laugh just in case he need to explain it away as a joke. "You agree or disagree with her?"

Darnell thought about it for a second, then shook his head in appreciation. "She's all right, got the right idea."

"You got balls, lady," said Freedom. "Why don't you come down to the trenches and fight with us?"

"Death to Herman, hmmm," said Travis. "Yes. Yes."

Othello smiled, secretly hoping Travis would be the one.

"If you could get away with it, would you kill Jimmy Herman?" asked Deon.

"Yes," said Darnell.

"Fuckin'-A," said Freedom.

"Certainly," said Travis.

"If you *couldn't* get away with it," asked Jasper, "but had the chance to be the gay man who killed Jimmy Herman, would you do it?"

"Sure," said Darnell.

"Hell, yes," said Freedom.

"Hell, no," said Travis.

"Why not?" a confused Othello asked Travis.

"I'm better off out of prison," Travis said, "fighting the rest of the homophobes. There's a lot more bigots who need to be brought down besides Herman. He'll never be worth the sum total of my life and what I can do."

Taken aback, all three Wisemen eyed each other, then became lost in their individual reflections in the one-way mirror....

"It's obvious who the assassin should be," Jasper said after the interviews were over and the Three Wisemen had retired to the Temple.

"Freedom," Othello said just as Deon said:

"Darnell."

"Darnell?" Othello repeated incredulously, standing at the opposite end of the conference table. "Hello? He's a bit scary don't you think?"

"The brother doesn't give a damn about himself," argued Deon.

"Neither does Freedom," said Othello. "I know this may sound crass, but when he dies, hopefully any investigation will die with him. And I think it means more if the triggerman has AIDS. I don't know if Darnell has it."

"I'm afraid I'm with Rock Star on this one." Jasper stood in front of the US map, tracing a finger through South Carolina. "The Rastafarian—he looks healthy, manically depressed but healthy. A man in Freedom's position might hold out and not give up any evidence. Hell, he may even commit suicide on the spot if we're lucky."

"You don't mean that," said Othello.

"He's a goner anyway," Jasper shrugged.

"So am I, one of these days—in theory," said Othello. "You want I should just put a bullet to my head, too?"

"Both of you, chill," Deon said. "I see your point, Othello. Besides, I'm not sure I want a brother pulling the trigger anyway. Freedom it is."

"Then we're in agreement," said Jasper, keeping his stare on Othello.

"For better or worse," Othello mumbled.

"Good," said Jasper. "Now, we need to know if Freedom's bite is as good as his bark."

THE BACK DOOR to the old bar was unlocked as promised. Othello, dressed as the old man Joe, glanced both ways down the alley, and seeing no one, took one last deep breath for courage and opened the door. The narrow corridor leading to the bar itself was dark, the only light coming from a lone source in the main room. Carefully making his way past dried-up kegs and stacks of old beer crates, Othello felt his beard to make sure it was on straight and tugged at the Dodgers cap covering his wig. It was Raider's cap, a souvenir from the night on the cliffs of Malibu.

As instructed, the bar was empty except for Freedom, who was sitting quietly at a folding table near the middle of the room. A lone lamp hanging from the rafters directly above bathed him in a dim pool of light. His back was to Othello, and for a moment, Othello watched as Freedom poured a pile of pills from a prescription bottle into the palm of his hands, then popped them into his mouth, threw his head back and downed them with a long swig from a can of Coke.

"Don't worry," he said, not bothering to look around at the old man. "I'm not the suicide type. I ain't got much time left. Why rush it?"

"You're a brave man, Freedom." Othello drew closer but stopped ten feet away, staying behind him.

Freedom turned around, clutching the can to his chest as if it were a prize. "The old dame like my moxie?"

"She likes your desire to end Jimmy Herman's life."

"Does she now?" he seemed genuinely surprised.

"How serious were you?"

Freedom paused. He took another healthy swig of Coke, then blanched as if the aftertaste hadn't been quite what he expected. After that, he coughed several times, his phlegm thick and loud. "The old lady wants to see me do in Jimmy Herman?" he asked skeptically.

"Would you if you could?"

"Answer my question," he demanded. "Is that what she wants?"

Othello stammered. The nerves in his stomach rattled underneath the latex beer belly inside his yellow golf jacket. He walked along the bar, moving to Freedom's front side, dragging his wrinkled hand along the countertop. "She wants to help you fulfill your dream of going out in a blaze of glory, yes."

"No shit." Freedom sat back in the chair, trying to take it all in. "Like a twisted fucking version of the Make-A-Wish Foundation."

"Of course, chances are, you'll be caught."

"I wanna be caught. I wouldn't kill the asshole anonymously. What would be the point?"

"But you can never implicate me or her or anybody."

"I don't even know who the fuck you are."

"I'm somebody who can make your dreams a reality."

For a moment, their eyes locked, as if in that instant, Freedom understood that there was no old lady, only Joe, who wasn't Joe at all, but someone with far more at stake than some faded Hollywood actress.

"Go on," Freedom said, not letting on if he now possessed this truth.

More nervous now, Othello retraced his steps down the bar, back toward Freedom's backside. "She can make it happen. Give you the time, place and means to assassinate Senator Evil, after which you'll be on your own, no help from ACTNOW, Level 3, me or my boss and her friends. After you do it, you'll never see me again. She's not in this to go public in any way, shape or form. She will, however, set up an untraceable, overseas bank account for you with enough to afford a hotshot lawyer and make the rest of your life as bearable as possible, but that's it. End of her involvement."

The bar fell silent. Only the flow of traffic outside permeated the air. Freedom stood up, his chair tipping over in the process. He walked around the room in circles as if he were a restless animal, contemplating his next move. In the process, he banged on the bar with his fist, then kicked over the podium, then circled some more and knocked over a stack of folding chairs resting against the wall. Othello watched, trembling in fear, but Freedom barely acknowledged him. Finally, Freedom stopped in the middle of the room, near the table, out of breath.

"Fuckin'-A, man, fuckin'-A."

"That's how he said yes," Othello told Jasper and Deon in the Temple later that night. "Then he turned to me, extended his hand and said, 'Show me the way to the promised land.'"

Jasper eyed his partners. The three of them were standing in a loose triangle next to the map of the US. "Now we know the who. All we have to figure out is the how."

THE JIMMY HERMAN MUSEUM of American Decency was alive with anticipation as work crews labored to put the finishing touches on the three-story tribute to the senator and his ideas. Outdoors, a crew of five groundskeepers laid the final patches of rich green sod on the pastoral gardens leading up the front entrance, while other workers busied themselves with parking signs, flower planters and folding chairs for the upcoming opening ceremony. Inside, underneath the filtered sunlight shining through the atrium, Deon stood in the lobby, flanked by Winston Callahan—Big Daddy's oldest son and head of museum operations—and Jacob McCallister, cultural curator.

"Hell," Winston was saying, "you got your Holocaust museums,

your museums of tolerance, neon, television, your ethnic museums—
no disrespect to you, Deon—what more could we do for the man
who's given forty-eight years of his life to this great state than to
honor him while he's still alive?"

Deon smiled a fake smile. "Still you can understand why I would
want a tour of the place before I actually commit to being here for the
opening."

"I'm just sorry the senator had to jaunt up to Capitol Hill this
morning," said McCallister, a pudgy man who was about as masculine
as Charlie. He led them to the first exhibit, the Jimmy Herman Room,
which was an oversized replica of his Washington office. On the walls
were hundreds of old campaign buttons, posters and photos of
Herman through the years.

"This here screen will play all his most famous speeches over and
over," Callahan said as he rubbed his permanent six o'clock shadow
and stood next to a large monitor.

"Once he's gone," McCallister walked behind the solid oak desk,
"we're debating putting a wax figure of him sitting here, contemplating, kinda like the statue of that thinker."

Better make up your minds fast, thought Deon.

For sixty excruciating minutes they led him through the museum. There was the Interactive Room, where kids could play computer games testing their morals on big colorful screens, the History
Room, where families could dress up like their ancestors and have
their picture taken against various American backdrops: Southern
plantation, deck of the Mayflower, protesting at a right-to-life march.
There was also a movie theater which would show, as Callahan put it,
"the few great family films the cesspool called Hollywood has put
out." And there was something called the Hall of Greats, a large two-
story corridor lined with wax figures of men. "Great Southern politicians," McCallister explained, noticing the confusion in Deon's face.

"Oh," Deon said warily, staring at one that looked suspiciously
like Abe Lincoln. Briefly he imagined the man's great-granddaddy
whipping and shackling Deon's great-granddaddy. Or lynching him.
Or raping his wife. Then suddenly, the figure began to speak:

"The nuclear family is this country's greatest asset," it said, moving its eyes and hands like a robot. Deon leaped back; his tour guides laughed.

"Them's just animatronics," Winston said, standing near a switch on the opposite wall. "You been to DisneyWorld, ain't ya?"

Deon stood there unamused, his attention shifting to the end of the hall and a door marked: RESTROOM, STAFF ONLY.

It was the only room he came to see today.

"Time to tinkle," he informed his hosts with the kind of facetious grin he used in his Hanes underwear ads.

"Don't you go to DisneyWorld after all them championships?" said Winston, but Deon walked away, pretending not to hear.

"Perfect," he said once inside the restroom, surveying the one stall and adjacent urinal. His heart pounding, he entered the stall and locked the door. It was there all right, just above the toilet: a square metal plate on the wall, twelve inches by twelve inches with one screw at the bottom. It led to a water valve of some sort, Jasper had said. He retrieved a pair of black leather gloves from inside his baggy Nike jacket and put them on over his slightly trembling hands. That accomplished, he pulled out a screwdriver and began unscrewing the screw, all while Jasper's words ran like a soundtrack through his mind.

Security will be tight. No way will Freedom or anybody else get a gun through the gates. Unless the gun is already there, waiting.

Once done with the screw and the screwdriver, he set them both on top of the toilet tank. With his left hand, he lifted up the metal plate. With his right, he retrieved the gun, a nine millimeter, which was also inside his jacket, wound tight in plastic bubble wrap. Holding it with one hand, he bobbled it, almost dropping the whole package, he was so nervous.

"Steady, man," he said aloud. "This is for you, J-Boy."

But he was getting ahead of himself, he realized. He set the package on the toilet tank and quietly released the metal plate. Then he took out the duct tape from his jacket, ripped off a piece with his teeth, and once again lifted the metal plate, this time taping it to the wall and exposing a hole at least a foot deep and the small water valve near the bottom of it.

These are the blueprints to the whole mess of insanity. There's an employees' restroom here with the perfect place to stash a gun. All we need is a South Carolina basketball legend with nerves of steel to pay the museum a pre-opening visit.

He ripped off seven strips of duct tape, hanging them on the side of the toilet tank. He started to worry about taking too much time.

How will Freedom get in? Easy. Somewhere underneath all that wild hair and those ear, nose and lip rings is a clean cut, wholesome white boy, probably one who, if he dyed his hair blond, could pass for Bruce Jones, CNC journalist.

Trying to be meticulous but swift, Deon placed the duct tape over the plastic wrap containing the gun, making sure to leave excess tape hanging from the sides. Then he held the gun up to the underside of the metal plate and pressed the excess tape onto the plate. With that completed, he peeled off the tape keeping the plate open and slowly brought it down so that it was parallel to the floor. It worked; the gun held.

I'll get Bruce down there on some kind of premise. But he won't make it to the ceremony. We'll have to put him to sleep like Othello put us to sleep when he kidnapped us, knock him out in the hotel. Freedom then takes his press pass and gets the waiting gun. Goodnight, Jimmy Herman, forever.

The gun securely in place, Deon closed up the hole and screwed it shut. Then he took a much needed deep breath and used a toilet seat cover to wipe the waterfall of sweat cascading off his face. It hadn't been that difficult after all, he decided. Just in case anybody was listening, he flushed the toilet and made damn sure he collected the screwdriver and tape and stowed them inside the compartments in his jacket. He then unlocked the stall door and made his way toward the exit, ready for some more attempted brainwashing from Callahan and McCallister. He was back on auto-pilot now, about to swing open the restroom door and put on that ol' D.A. charm for another twenty minutes max, he figured. Then, as his right hand reached for the knob, he gasped at what he saw.

He was still wearing the black leather gloves.

"Oh my God, oh my God, oh my God."

His knees buckled. He held both hands in front of his face in desperation and began a staggered dance around the room, repeating,

"Oh my God," at least a dozen times. His whole life had been an instant away from being over, done with, kaput. He wanted to let out some kind of shriek, but choked it back. After several moments and pleas to himself for calmness, he gathered his senses, then took off the gloves and stashed them where they belonged, inside his jacket.

"I did it!" he told Jasper and Othello in the Temple a day later, omitting the glove incident. "And I did it good! Smooth as James Bond or Richard Roundtree Shaft." He was too excited to sit, instead circling the conference table, reliving his nervousness.

"Then we're just about set," Jasper said. "You'll get word to Freedom?"

"As good as done," Othello said.

"We should go," said Jasper to Deon. "The less we're in LA now the better. Go back to Chicago, be seen having a good time without a care in the world." He turned to Othello. "I have to admit, Rock Star, you've done good."

Othello smiled a proud smile. "We all have. I consider us friends. My first real gay friends outside my manager, and, well, my boyfriend."

Deon walked over to them, towering over his two partners. "Maybe we should get together after this is all over, have a summer barbecue with our lovers."

Jasper's face turned serious. "After this is over, I think we should lay low, let the Fund run itself and forget about all these other levels for while, maybe not meet for six months to a year, depending on the fallout."

Both Deon and Othello looked at each other, realizing Jasper was right.

"So maybe we celebrate beforehand?" said Deon. "We've never done anything social."

Jasper considered it, then said: "I have a ranch in Virginia, pretty secluded. If I turn the staff loose, we could have our run of the place with no worries."

"Lovers included?" asked Deon.

"Not mine," said Jasper. "We've been having problems. But you two bring yours. I'd like to meet them."

"Did you tell Charlie about this?" Othello asked Deon.

"Not Jimmy Herman, no. I don't know how he would react to...killing."

"You tell Raider?" Jasper asked Othello.

"No, same reason as Deon."

"Bruce will never know about this," said Jasper. "It's better this way, fellas. I know it's damn near impossible not to tell someone, especially the person you're most intimate with, but think about what we're all risking here. Is this a secret your lovers can carry to their graves?"

"I don't want to think about it," said Deon.

"Then don't tell," warned Jasper. "This is not like the Fund or even the counter-bashing. Someday in the future, we'll all be able to be social together and we can talk about it to each other."

"I'm sure we'll need to," said Deon. "For therapy, if nothing else."

Jasper gathered up his suit jacket from the chair. "Until the ranch."

"But we must make the date around something I've been planning for quite some time now." Othello's eyes lit up with anticipation.

"And what might that be?" Jasper asked teasingly.

"Well...." He hadn't asked Raider yet, but Othello was praying to the gods his new boyfriend would agree to attend their first ever gay pride parade together—Othello as the old man Joe and Raider as his blond hunky self. For the last week, Othello had dreamed of nothing but the two of them basking in the annual celebration, holding hands in the light of day, acting romantic and carefree along with hundreds of thousands of their gay brothers and sisters. "Just a special date," he said to his partners, not wanting to hear any objections to what would surely be Joe's last public outing. "With my man."

"Then we'll be in touch," Jasper said, and with that, he and Deon left.

For a while, Othello remained in the Temple, sitting on the table and glancing around the room—at the US map, at the TV monitor, at the revolving fireplace upon which he made his entrance during that first meeting of the Wisemen. The orgies of the past seemed light-years away now, their only remnant the sculpted orgy on the ceiling.

He lay down on the table and studied the angelic figures reaching out for one another with raw unabashed passion. I've come so far, he thought, his vision blurring in the whiteness of the plaster. So why do I feel as if I still have such a long way to go?

FIFTEEN

THIRTY MINUTES AFTER Jasper and Deon were gone, Othello decided to leave the Temple himself. Dressed as the old man, he pulled out of the driveway in the Impala, firmly deciding that once Jimmy Herman was dead and buried, some things would have to change. What he would do in the war and how he would do it, he didn't know, but one thing was for sure: Old Man Joe would have to go on permanent vacation.

He made a right turn out of the driveway, thinking about his options until he was distracted by the sight of a white-haired woman across the street. She had to be in her seventies and was watering her lawn in a pink bathrobe—odd, considering it rained all day yesterday. As he passed, she stared him down, then turned away as if scared, accidentally wetting the lower half of her robe in the process. Writing her off as either eccentric or racist, he kept going but glanced back once in the rear view mirror. She was staring at him again.

He picked up speed. His curiosity getting the best of him, he turned his head around for one last look at her. This time, his eye caught sight of a side view mirror on a plain white van facing the opposite direction. There was a face in the mirror—white, tanned, blond, *Raider.* It was Raider, straining to get a look at him through the mirror. Othello's heart stopped. He stuck his head out the window for a better view. The face in the mirror disappeared. Something from within told Othello to turn around and face the wheel. He did just in time to see the front of the Impala about to ram into a blue Mercedes parked along the street. He braced himself and slammed on the brakes. The Impala stopped an inch shy of the Mercedes. In full panic now, Othello put the Impala in reverse, then backed up, put it in drive and took off, too frantic to look back again.

Ridiculous, he tried telling himself as he drove through the streets of Hollywood, his heart and mind still racing. I'm getting paranoid. That was not Raider in a van. But it was. Had to be. It was.

Visions of a hundred TV detectives conducting a hundred stake-outs in disguised vans ran through his head. That would explain so much about Raider's behavior. He was a cop of some sort. Straight, too. But they were dating, kissing, fondling each other. A straight cop wouldn't do that. Right? And a gay cop wouldn't be trying to bust him. Would he? But would a straight man go through all this? The debate raged on as he drove. He knew there was only one way to confront his worst fears. He gave the pedal a little more gas and headed straight for West Hollywood, determined to settle this once and for all.

By the time he parked the Impala a handful of spaces down from Raider's apartment, all sorts of frightening thoughts had run through his head, some of them making him feel like the most paranoid man on the face of the earth, some of them rendering him angry enough to kill the man who claimed to want to be his boyfriend. His adrenaline was at full speed when he got out of the car. He saw Raider's Jeep farther down the street, but that didn't mean a thing. A young Latino man was opening the door to the apartment complex and dragging his collie by the leash through the entrance. Quickly, Othello ran to catch the door. Better to surprise him if he's there, or wait for him if he isn't and catch him driving up in the stakeout van. Too anxious to wait for the elevator, he took the stairs, his heart in his throat, his knees weak with fear. He reached the apartment, 206, and listened for signs of life within.

Silence. Further incriminating evidence.

Anger supplanting paranoia, he pounded on the door five times.

Nothing. Too busy at some headquarters filing a report on Othello. Then he heard a male's baritone voice from inside:

"Door's open."

Othello turned the knob and opened the door.

"Hundred and four, hundred and five." It was Raider, huffing and puffing on a rowing machine smack dab in the middle of the living room. "Come on in, almost finished," he said between labored breaths, then kept on counting to himself. "Hundred and six, hundred and seven...."

In a daze, Othello stood in the doorway, then slowly but steadily moved inside Raider's apartment for the very first time. There wasn't much there: a sofa on the far wall, VCR and small TV on a plastic crate, wood dining table near the opening to the right that led to the kitchen, and that rowing machine. Raider was only wearing a pair of gray gym shorts. His upper body was drenched with sweat, the kind that came from hours of exercise, not sitting in detective vans in residential neighborhoods.

"You've been working out?" was all Othello could think to ask.

"Almost done. Have to get two hours in every day. Gotta keep up with you."

"How long have you been at it?"

"Like I said." He saw me, Raider thought, cursing himself for looking up too soon after the Impala had passed. At least he had reacted quickly enough to race the hell back here, grease himself up with baby oil and water and hit the rowing machine in anticipation of this little visit. "Give me five minutes."

But I don't understand, Othello wanted to say aloud, circumnavigating the apartment, searching for answers. So it hadn't been Raider in the van? But how could Othello have been so sure in that instant? Chalk it up to Raider on the brain?

"Have a seat," said Raider, thankful he'd had enough time to dump the pornos in the trash chute in the hall. Othello ignored him and stood by the window overlooking the street, his senses confounded, his body restless. Perceiving this, Raider brought the rowing machine to a halt.

"Done." He rose up, went over to Othello and gave him a light peck on the cheek, pretending not to be bothered by the pasty make-up on Othello's old man face. "How you doing, baby?" Raider said. "Sorry I look and smell like a pig." With Othello's eyes still fixed on the street below, Raider stole a glance himself, finding what he expected: the white Honda Civic belonging to Gus parked farther down the street. "Wanna drink? Gatorade's all I got." He went to the kitchen and fetched two large plastic bottles from the fridge. "What brings you here? Not that I'm not glad to see you." Raider returned to the living room, handed a silent Othello a bottle, then fetched the towel draped over an arm of the sofa. "No drinking glasses, sorry."

"I just had to see you." He hadn't thought up a reason for being here save confronting Raider. Now, that didn't seem necessary.

"Something wrong?"

Othello didn't answer.

"Why don't we go somewhere, enjoy the day," said Raider. "There's not much in the way of entertainment here. I say we go to the park or grab some lunch."

Othello turned away from the window and set the bottle on the dining table. For the first time since he entered, he allowed himself a good look at Raider's half-naked body: the light patch of dark blond hair skimming his chest, his arms with their distinctive cuts around the biceps, his legs, thick like a soccer player's. "Look at you." Othello shook his head, his voice full of irony. "I couldn't have ordered it up from the gods any better." He sighed, as if to say: what a shame.

Raider laughed a modest laugh, his hands on his hips, the towel draped over one shoulder. "You know, you clean up pretty good your-self when you're not limping around as some old fag hag's gardener."

"Raider," Othello began, trying to stave off the potential for sex-ual heat. "We've got to talk. You know I'm taking some life-or-death chances."

"Of course." Raider sat sideways on the rowing machine and grabbed at his right shoulder as if in pain. "While we talk, would you mind rubbing my shoulders? My clavicle is killing me."

Flustered, Othello paused, then sat on the sofa above the machine and placed both hands on Raider's shoulders, his mind torn between his wants and his needs.

"But take off those raisin-skinned gloves, if you don't mind."

Othello obeyed, then repositioned his real hands on Raider's back.

"I hope you don't mind the sweat."

"Sweat is a good thing, healthy...natural...primitive."

That's my boy, Raider thought. Get into the spirit; forget all about that van. This is your boyfriend here.

"To say I'm risking everything is the understatement to end all understatements," Othello said. Raider was so wet his hands practically slid over his back.

"Baby," Raider moaned. "You got a way with your hands. It's an old lacrosse injury. Fucking Yalie did it to me. I hate Yalies. Always have."

"Because of the risks, I have to investigate every possible leak or problem."

"Smartest thing to do." Raider took one of Othello's hands and guided it to the area just above his right pec. "Here, get these, too. All of me needs working over."

Othello's hands began to roam Raider's upper body freely, his neck, his shoulder blades, the small of his back, the light hairs dancing on his chest. It was the most they'd ever done. Raider was finally relaxing and letting him in, finally conceding to the fact that there was more heat between them than either could resist. No way could this man be a cop, Othello told himself. As further proof, his hands slid down Raider's torso, over his firm stomach and toward the band in his shorts. No resistance. Raider simply arched upward and moaned, his sweat-soaked blond locks brushing against Othello's mouth. Othello took the wet strands of hair between his lips and savored the moist salty taste while his fingers slipped underneath Raider's shorts and landed on top of the soft but sparse bush that was Raider's pubic hair.

But it was Othello who halted things this time, forcing himself to yank his hands out of Raider's shorts and rise up from the sofa. Don't get confused, he commanded himself. You saw what you saw. This man could make every day for the rest of your life a living hell.

"We're going to play it safe, remember?" Othello walked over to a small sliver of a window located over the far end of the sofa.

"Massaging is safe." Raider also stood up, thankful Othello had stopped while Raider was trying to come up with yet another way out of intimacy.

I can't trust you for crap, Othello wanted to blurt aloud.

"I could use a massage every now and then...." Raider said and went on about things Othello didn't hear for he was lost in his own thoughts as he stared out the window:

You get me here, with you all hot and sweaty, teasing me as if I'm some kind of dog you can wave a piece of meat in front of. And for what? What the hell do you want with me? My money? A free ride? To see my ass in jail and you on the cover of Time *and* Newsweek? *You think I'm just going to roll over and let you hustle me because you're a god? You're dealing with Othello here.*

As he came to his senses, his worst fears were confirmed. In the small sliver of a window, he could see a piece of the alley behind the complex. And in that alley, he could make out the back doors of a plain white van.

"You just came from a house in the foothills, didn't you?" Raider said, his first words to command Othello's attention in minutes. Othello turned around. Raider was to the left of the front window now, his body shielded from the outside by the drab green curtain, his head peeking out at the street.

"You should know that better than anybody," said Othello, inching toward the traitor. "You were there."

"I can explain," said Raider. Down below, Gus was loitering near the Impala, doing a bad job of being inconspicuous. Sorry ol' drinking buddy of mine, Raider thought. Time to sell your sorry butt down the river. "I didn't want to get you all worried, but now you have to know."

"Know *what*, Raider?" Othello asked. "If that—or Brian—is your name."

"Of course, it is," Raider scolded. "Look down below, carefully."

Othello peeked over Raider's shoulder. A man in a black leather jacket was standing idly near the Impala. It was Gus from ACTNOW.

"Get back," Raider ordered Othello.

"What's this all about?" Othello said, feeling that things were about to go from bad to worse.

"Gus. He's not one of us."

"And you are?"

"Listen to me," Raider insisted harshly. "After you told me about that high speed chase, I got worried about you and asked him about it. He told me he saw you near Franklin and Wilton, a long-ass way from Franklin and Vine where he told you."

"What?"

"He was lying."

"Oh, shit." Othello turned toward the room, trying to take it all in.

"I had him checked out." Raider couldn't say via the FBI, so he said: "An old Dartmouth friend is an investigative lawyer. Gus's real name is Crane Malloy. He's an member of Guardians of the Scriptures."

"The ones on the news all the time?"

"The rightest right wingers in the country. I befriended him to find out what he was up to, pretended to get drunk with him at the Spike. I told him I was from some other Christian group and he came clean to me."

He turned back to Raider. "So you're from a Christian group?"

"Not me—Gus—*Crane*. Stay with me on this, O, we don't have much time."

"Time for what?"

"Gus is straight as an arrow. He was sent to infiltrate ACTNOW and get them busted. I told him we should combine forces, put our heads together. He fell for it. He's after you."

"He knows who I am?"

"He told me about trailing you one night after an ACTNOW meeting to some house in the foothills. Did you ever go straight to that house? Is that true?"

Othello racked his brain. "Yes, one time. It was a few weeks before the chase. I went to one of the meetings they had after Simi Valley."

"Must have been that night. But he said he didn't want to stick around and look suspicious. He checked out the home later but couldn't find out who owned it. He even had the nerve to knock on the door once."

"Nobody lives there."

"He went back another time and asked some elderly woman across the street to call him if she ever saw the Impala there again. His plan is to follow you to see where you go next and find out who Joe's boss is. He got a call from the lady a few days ago, but missed it."

The day of the interrogation, Othello thought, pacing the floor. "He's on to me. He knows who I am. Him and you. You're both on to me."

"He doesn't know yet. That's why I've been keeping an eye on him." Some Nazi God Squad geek wasn't going to steal Raider's thunder. "I told him to let me know when the lady calls him again so we could both stake you out. That's why I rented a van and was there today."

"Why didn't you tell me about this?"

"And get you worried when everything's going so right?"

"Then why did you lie just now about working out for two hours?"

"I wanted to protect you, do this on my own, but I think it may be too late." With his head, he indicated the window. Othello peered out in time to see Gus planting something underneath the back of the Impala. "My guess is it's a tracking device," Raider said.

"He won't stop." Othello stepped away from the window. "They won't stop. I'm a dead man."

"Not my O."

"I'm a dead man!"

"Bullshit." Raider grabbed a T-shirt and a set of keys from the dining table and headed for the door.

"Where are you going?" Othello demanded, but when Raider didn't answer, Othello grabbed his old man gloves off the sofa and went after him.

"Stay back." Raider slipped on his T-shirt as he raced down the stairwell. "Let me handle this."

"I will not!" Othello was right on his heels, struggling to get his gloves on. "This is my life. How do I know who to trust?"

"Then just stay with the old man act, whatever you do."

They reached the sidewalk. Gus was way down the block, heading away from the Impala. He heard their clamor and looked back. After seeing who it was, he started running down the nearest driveway.

"Stay here," Raider said and took off after him. Othello followed, faster than an old man, slower than the real him. Raider reached the driveway ahead of Othello and saw Gus climbing over a small chain-link fence into the home's backyard. Raider shot down the driveway and leaped it like a hurdler. Ten seconds ahead, Gus ran across the yard, heading for the tall brick wall bordering the back of the property. He scaled the wall using a trash can, knocking it over with his foot before he disappeared into the alley.

Othello ran down the driveway and saw Raider dashing across the yard and taking a long leap toward the back wall. One foot landed mid-wall, the other near the top. Raider then pulled himself over and out of sight. Othello looked around for an alternative route and saw a narrow passageway between the detached garage and the neighbor's garage. He slithered sideways through it until he too was in the alley. There, he saw Raider catch up to Gus and tackle him with the ferociousness of a linebacker. They both went sliding across the concrete, then wrestled on the ground ever-so-briefly before Raider gained control.

"Who the hell are you?" Othello demanded when he reached the tail end of their skirmish, unsure if he was just asking Gus or both of them.

"A traitor." Raider shook Gus, twisted his arm behind his back and forced him to stand. "It's over, Jesus freak. Joe knows all about your sick plot."

"You're on my side," Gus said, wiping blood from his mouth and grimacing at the pain Raider was causing to his other arm.

Raider laughed a cynical laugh. "Gullible fool. You fucked with the wrong queer when you messed with me." Raider cocked his free arm to punch him, but Othello pleaded for him to stop, which Raider did. Othello then eyed Gus, who was still in Raider's clutches.

"What are you trying to do to me?"

Gus paused, then let loose: "Stop you and your old lady friends and all you sinners. Sinners!" he repeated, yelling at the top of his lungs. "Help me somebody! These sinners have got me; help me, please!"

"Get the picture now?" said Raider.

"The God-fearing of this world will prevail," Gus promised. "We'll bring in the law, go to the police, Pat Robertson and the leaders of the right. Help me, somebody, please! Sinners!"

"Shut up, already," Othello said, his mind going numb at the worst possible time.

"I'm not going to let him ruin our work." With one hand still twisting Gus's arm, Raider fished his keys out of his pocket and tossed them to Othello. "Give me the one to the van."

"What? Which? Why?" Othello fumbled for the right key.

"The big long one," Raider said harshly.

Hands shaking, Othello slipped it off the ring, then handed it to Raider.

"Now go back upstairs," Raider ordered him.

"Help me, somebody!" Gus yelled, struggling to break free.

"What are you going to do?" pleaded Othello.

"Go upstairs." Raider twisted Gus's arm tighter. "We don't have time. I'll be back."

Othello looked around anxiously, and fearing the possibility of someone answering the cry for help, he decided to put his life in Raider's hands and did as he was told.

For close to three hours, Othello waited in the apartment, trying to process what had just happened between Raider and himself, what was possibly happening now between Raider and Gus, and what might happen to all of them in the future once Raider came through that apartment door. He thought about leaving a dozen times, even imagined Raider returning with the police. But he stayed there, inexplicably drawn to Raider's command to wait.

In the meantime, he stripped off the old man getup and borrowed a white Dartmouth T-shirt and a pair of faded blue sweats from Raider's closet. He also had the leftover pasta from an Italian restaurant in Raider's refrigerator and went through all of Raider's things. No need to justify the snooping. Raider was far from being in

the clear in Othello's mind. He didn't find anything that further
incriminated Raider anyway. The place was practically bare. The bedroom was as spare as the living room, simply consisting of the bed and
a closet full of dirty laundry. His whole apartment was that of a bach-
elor who was preoccupied with more manly pursuits than the upkeep
of his new pad. It was almost a romantic notion to Othello, if only he
could be sure Raider was indeed the man he claimed to be. To find out
more about Gus or Crane Malloy or whatever his name was, he used
the phone to call Sweeney and have his manager check up on the right
winger. He was on the sofa, hanging up, just as there was a knock at
the door.

"Who's there?" Othello asked cautiously in the old man's voice.

"Me."

Quickly, Othello unbolted the door. Raider staggered in, looking
worn and vacant. He was wearing Gus's leather jacket. His arms were
clutching a big bundle of something inside the jacket. "Close the
door," he said, then made his way toward the bathroom.

"What happened?"

Raider didn't answer; Othello followed him. In the bathroom,
Raider stood over the pedestal sink and opened the jacket. Blood was
everywhere, on his T-shirt, inside the jacket and especially on the
white shirt and pair of jeans that fell into the sink.

"Gus won't bother you or the uprising anymore," Raider said
matter-of-factly.

"What—I—are you hurt?"

"This is all his, not mine," Raider said of the blood. He washed
his hands and looked in the mirror. Behind him, Othello's eyes were
as wide as saucers. He looked on the verge of hyperventilating.

"Let me explain." Hastily, Raider dried his hands, then took
Othello by the arms and backed him out of the bathroom and into the
bedroom. Once there, he sat Othello down at the foot of the bed and
pulled up his gym bag as a seat for himself. "Gus wouldn't have
stopped till he found out who you are." He talked without looking up,
as if caught up in his own personal justification of his acts. "I wasn't
going to let that happen. I care about you way too much. I'm in love
with you, Othello." He looked up. "There, I said it: I'm in love with

you. I'm not about to see you or us or all our dreams go up in flames because of some gay-hating, conservative traitor."

Othello was stunned. "Did you—what did you do to him?"

"The less you know the better, if...whatever. I will say his body is stripped naked and in the mountains near Malibu. If they ever find it, they won't have much to go on. Othello, I hope you know I had no other choice."

"What about other moles?"

"He told me before today he was the only one. I gotta think that's true."

Othello was on the verge of bursting into tears.

"I had to do it," Raider said, his voice almost breaking up. "I don't care if you do doubt me; I did this for you. You've taught me so much; you're so good to me. I wanted this to work—you and me...." He broke off, going for the hurt little boy look.

Othello remembered his accusations against Raider earlier in the afternoon, so much as calling *him* the traitor. Now, Raider had murdered for him, to protect him, to preserve what they had going.

"I'm sorry a thousand times for ever doubting you," Othello stammered. "Can you ever begin to understand how I could be so paranoid? My whole life—"

"Tell me you don't disapprove of what I did," said a still-wounded Raider. "As long as you can tell me that, we can go on from here."

"But the cops...you're in jeopardy...for me."

"The law never has to know. I did a good job. I didn't leave anything on his body that could pinpoint me."

"But you risked your life for me."

"You're worth it, can't you see?" He reached up and grabbed Othello by the shoulders. "Tell me you're okay with this, O, just tell me."

Othello's face was full of tears now, and Raider had a genuine impulse to kiss them away. Instead, he held Othello's face in his hands, gently running his thumbs down his cheeks, tracing the trail of tears. He hadn't expected the mastermind of an assassination plot to be so emotional. In fact, Raider thought Othello would take Gus's death in stride, re-affirm his trust in Raider and reveal the details needed to close the case.

But Othello was truly affected, Raider realized as the pop star responded to the affection by placing his hands on top of Raider's. Sometimes I forget he's a real person, Raider thought, remembering Othello's comments about all those empty nights in the Big House and never coming close to knowing love. And now somebody just killed for him, somebody Othello wanted to love and spend the rest of his life with, somebody who claimed to want to love Othello back. On top of that, Othello was wrought with guilt for having put that somebody into this situation.

Jesus, Kincaide, what the hell have you done?

He fought the instinct to feel guilty. It's called a job, he told himself, pressing his face into Othello's, his lips tasting Othello's tears in an effort to make them go away. Someday, he'll learn that Gus is still alive, Raider reasoned. He'll find out I just dragged the weirdo to FBI headquarters and scared him off the case.

"We'll get the old lady if she's done anything," Raider had yelled at Gus, who had been stripped to his underwear and forced to sit in the middle of a room under bright interrogation lights. "You and your Christian soldiers cut loose from this or get your asses fried for obstructing an investigation."

And someday Othello would learn the bloody clothes were indeed Gus's—after they stripped him at headquarters—but the blood on them was from twenty pounds of red meat, courtesy of Mayfair Market, or as Freedom called it, *Gay*fair. Someday, Raider promised himself, he'd tell Othello all this, to hopefully ease the pop star's conscience. He'd visit the head of the Three Wisemen in the federal pen and tell the guy the truth. Hopefully, that would ease his own conscience as well.

Raider sat back on the gym bag, not having to pretend to be exhausted. "You still haven't answered my question," he said.

"Which one is that?"

"Whether or not you're okay with this?"

"I don't have a choice." Othello ran his hands over his face. They sat in silence for fifteen minutes, no eye contact. Eventually, Othello said: "Guess I can tell you now: I'm in love with you, too." He shook his head for lack of a better reaction. They were both locked together now,

Othello thought. Their lives and futures were irrevocably intertwined
no matter how far the romance went. To that end, he began to speak:

"I have to tell you a story, Raider, I have to."

"Right now?" Raider sensed what was coming and wished he had
a tape recorder running.

"Yes, now, especially in light of what just transpired. It's a little
story about three very famous and wise men who all met at a place
they call the Temple...."

SIXTEEN

THE EARLY MORNING sun hovered over the three mile stretch of Santa Monica Boulevard that ran through the heart of West Hollywood and was the epicenter of LA's biggest and most famous gay neighborhood. Today, as it was for one Sunday every June, a mile and a half of the boulevard was closed to vehicular traffic, no party boys swerving into the next lane while making their way home from all-night dances, no early morning cruisers circling the blocks around Circus of Books in search of the sex they couldn't find last night, no muscle-bound boys roaring past in their Jeeps, ready to hit the weights at the two main gyms on the strip. Today, the four lane east/west thoroughfare would be spared the usual tens of thousands of cars clogging the street. Instead, in three hours, over 250,000 people would gather on the sidewalks for the gay pride parade.

For now though, the boulevard was relatively quiet. Near the wooden barricades bordering the side streets, the men and women of the LA County Sheriff's Department, West Hollywood Division, loitered peacefully around their cars, sipping Styrofoam cups of coffee and chatting. In the grandstands near the end of the route, a television crew was making final adjustments to its cameras for the cable broadcast. Under the rainbow-colored balloons of the main entrance to the all-day festival in West Hollywood Park, a group of pink-shirted volunteers was getting final instructions from a stout, curly-haired woman with a bullhorn. In the many bars on the street, bartenders shined their countertops, anticipating good business from the crowd.

Closer to the parade's starting point, the neighboring streets were buzzing with the kind of backstage nervousness usually reserved for theater premieres. Three male baton twirlers tossed their batons high in the air. Scantily-clad male and female dancers hiked their g-strings just a little farther up their butts. A black gospel choir practiced an African spiritual. And the West Hollywood Cheerleaders, all male, went over their new routine one last time.

Farther down, on a subdued block of Santa Monica that had yet to feel the electricity of the morning, Othello and Raider sat quietly on the curb. Raider was absently rocking back and forth and Othello was gently feeling his face, wondering if Old Man Joe was going to wither away in the encroaching heat. They sat without saying much—focusing instead on the few other early birds wandering by—until Othello could no longer stand the silence.

"I know what you're thinking. I can see the look on your face."

"What look?"

"The look that says we were fools to get here this early, that the parade doesn't start for hours and I should have listened to you."

"That's not what I'm thinking at all," Raider said, trying to be nice.

"Yes, it is."

"No, it isn't."

"Yes, it is," Othello insisted.

"Okay, it is," Raider admitted.

"Well, I wanted to make sure we got a good seat—"

"We're guaranteed that all right."

"Sweeney told me a gazillion people show up and I figured it's like the Rose Parade or something."

"Or Macy's Thanksgiving in Manhattan," mused Raider.

"Exactly," Othello chimed a second before he caught Raider's sarcasm. "Anyway, it's better this way. We're here; we had a nice leisurely stroll from your apartment; plus we get a good look at the layout in case something goes wrong, like my face melting."

"That's one of the reasons you wanted to come early, isn't it? You're nervous about something going haywire."

"No, it isn't."

"Yes, it is."

"No, it isn't."

"Yes, it is," Raider said, drawing it out with a teasing lilt.

"Okay, it is," Othello admitted.

Raider laughed triumphantly. He's like a kid finally getting to go to DisneyWorld, he thought. Just then, he saw two overweight men passing by across the street. They were both dressed like Marilyn Monroe, complete with blond wigs and the white dress she wore over that subway grate. The day was bound to be a weird one, Raider figured, but it was a small price to pay for meeting the other two Wisemen in person later in the week at Jasper's ranch. There, he'd add to the mountain of evidence, and he'd also be able to tell the boys at the bureau: sure I hung out with Deon Anthony—we were like old girlfriends. Intimidated? Are you kidding? You're talking to Panty-Raider, here.

He also had to admit he didn't mind giving Othello this one last day in the sun, especially at an event the pop star had been dying to be a part of. Guy deserved it maybe, even if he was acting paranoid.

"Well, I promise you this, my old man." He patted Othello's arm. "Nothing's gonna happen to Joe on my watch."

"You do have a way of bailing me out, don't you?" said Othello. Raider cocked his head to one side and shrugged, as if to say: what can I say, I'm da man. "Really, you do," Othello went on, knowing when to stroke his man's ego. "Simi Valley for one."

"The Jesus freak for two."

"Let's not mention Gus." Othello glanced around at the sidewalk behind them, noticing the increasing number of legs busily passing by. He still hadn't reconciled Gus's death at the hands of the man he was dating. Having Jimmy Herman bumped off was one thing; his would-be lover committing murder was an entirely different story. But it had to be done, he kept telling himself, for his life to continue "as is," for them, for the uprising. Still, no justification helped him get to sleep at night. "You know," he began, "after Herman, Joe will disappear off the face of the earth. Some of the members of Level 3 are bound to figure out the old lady was behind Freedom. I'll have to sever all ties. In fact, I think I've spoken my last words to Travis."

"So this will be the end of you in the revolution?"

"The Fund has enough money to run itself for years. We put in over a couple million each. The people in charge will have to decide who gets what. Laying low will be top priority. I didn't think of that when I concocted all this, but maybe this was as much as I was meant to do."

"You sure you're ready to retire?"

"What more can I do?"

For a moment, Raider regarded Othello's profile, trying to look beyond the makeup and glasses and fake beard. "Don't do it, O," he said, his tone dead serious. "Call it off; let it go; stop." It was worth a shot, he figured. He couldn't have cared less about The D.A., Hollinquest or the radicals at ACTNOW, but he didn't want to see Othello waste his whole life on a cracker like Jimmy Herman. Hell, Raider said to himself, if he could get Othello to end this now, he'd consider only turning him in on the counter-bashing charges. "None of this is worth your life."

"When I let you in on everything, you agreed not to try and talk me out of it."

"I know, but," he looked up and saw the dueling Marilyns passing by again. They were going the other way this time, "who you doing this for: these people?"

"I'm doing it for myself," Othello paused, "and these people."

"I really mean this when I say I'm worried about you. If you get caught, what they can get you for so far is nothing compared to what you're on the verge of doing."

"It's no less than what you already did," said Othello. "And you did it for me."

"Doesn't mean I wish it had come to that."

"You think *I* wished for Gus to happen? I'll let you in on a little secret, Raider: the closer you and I get, the more I think about the chances I'm taking and the more I wonder if it's worth it. I mean, if I had to choose, I'd much rather be in love without being in danger. Or best of all, in my dream world of dream worlds, I'd rather be in love and just be out, I mean, loving the man I love and the man who loves me with the both of us out and open to the whole damned world. Maybe then, I don't know, I'd end all this madness. At least I'd consider it."

Raider remained silent, having already decided not to make any more promises designed to further sucker Othello, promises that would only serve to break the guy's heart that much more when it all came out in the wash.

Meanwhile, Othello tapped his feet on the pavement, waiting for Raider to say: let's do it, let's declare our love to the entire world and become the most outspoken, gay couple in the universe. Not that Othello was ready to arrange the press conference and come barreling out of the closet, but Raider by his side would be a damned good reason to consider it. But the man from Nantucket offered nothing, apparently just as scared as Othello at the prospect of going public.

"Besides," said Othello, "talk of the Wisemen not following through now is pointless. We couldn't stop things now if we wanted to, and we don't. It's all set. You-know-who already has all his instructions." He drew a short breath and looked toward the haze clearing in the sky.

The final meeting with Freedom had taken place a few days ago and every detail of the plan had been settled. Freedom would fly to Atlanta, where a car would be waiting for him at the airport. From there, he would drive to Columbia, South Carolina, and register in a motel under an assumed name. The morning of the museum opening, he was to show up at Bruce Jones's hotel suite pretending to be a courier with a delivery from CNC. Once inside, he would inject the fledging journalist with the same drug Othello had used to kidnap Jasper and Deon, then make himself over in the image of a respectable blond reporter with the clothes and makeup kit Othello had given him. Next, he would use Bruce's press pass to gain entrance to the opening ceremonies and locate the gun in the staff bathroom near the Hall of Greats. Then it was up to him—and him alone—to get close enough to Senator Evil and aim for immortality.

"Harrison Ford won't be able to do it any better," Freedom had promised, seemingly enthralled with the covert nature of the operation. Right before they parted, Othello had felt the urge to strip off Old Man Joe and reveal himself to his triggerman right there in the boarded-up bar.

"Why you standing there like that?" Freedom had asked when Othello hesitated to leave.

"I just wish we could have gotten to know each other better."

"I'm an open book. Can you say the same?"

Do you know who I am? Othello had wanted to ask. *Do you want to know?*

Instead, he said, "Good-bye and good luck," and turned around and left.

"I just wish you would reconsider this," Raider said now, but his plea was interrupted by a ruckus in the distance.

Fifteen yards away, eight men were carrying signs through an intersection, garnering lots of attention from the dozen or so people crossing the street in the opposite direction. The placards bore warnings. SINNERS REPENT. READ THE BIBLE, IT SPEAKS THE TRUTH. SODOMIZERS SHALL NOT INHERIT THE KINGDOM OF GOD. LEVITICUS 18:22. One man was already making use of his bullhorn. He had long brown hair and a sizable beer belly and wore a black T-shirt that read FEAR GOD. "The Lord will punish you for this day," he said, to which the passersby yelled "shame" over and over.

"And you want to know why I do what I do?" asked Othello, rendering Raider speechless.

As the morning wore on, the sidewalk and wide, grassy median strip that separated east- and westbound traffic began to swell with gays and lesbians—from dozens to hundreds to thousands to hundreds of thousands. Eventually, Othello and Raider had to stand lest they be swallowed by the tide of the masses surrounding them.

"I think I see the first groups," Othello said shortly after 11:00 a.m. The color guard was heading their way, followed by a man and woman carrying a banner that read: CHRISTOPHER STREET WEST PRESENTS THE LOS ANGELES GAY AND LESBIAN PRIDE CELEBRATION. Next came a simmering roar that mutated into a deafening rumble as dozens upon dozens of motorcycles rolled into view.

"This is it." Othello turned to Raider, his big strong man in a white tank top and khaki shorts. "Hold my hand."

Raider cooperated. A small price to pay.

"This must be the dykes on bikes Sweeney talked about," Othello said, wishing his manager would have consented to being here instead of purposely hightailing it out of town with his lover.

The procession seemed endless. Row after row of Harleys and Yamahas came thundering past, topped by women in leather, lace, flannel and denim, some in couples, some alone, all of them revving their machines and the crowd in the process.

My kind of girls, Raider thought, nostalgic for his own Harleys back in DC.

Next came twenty of the parade's organizers. They were dressed in white shorts and official pink T-shirts and received an appreciative round of applause as they walked. They were followed by several convertibles full of city officials and the Republican mayor of Los Angeles.

Then came the Big-Ass Bus, a psychedelically colored bus promoting one of the local radio stations. Madonna's "Holiday" was blasting from its speakers and a heavyset Latino deejay was throwing T-shirts to the crowd from an opening in the roof. "Is gay LA ready to part-tay?" he shouted over his microphone. The crowd gave him the wild response he wanted. This was followed by the Gay Men's Chorus. They marched past wearing white shirts and carrying colorful bouquets of balloons while singing "Everything's Coming Up Roses."

"I had no idea," Othello said. He was brimming with a feeling of pride he didn't know he possessed. Everything he saw he regarded with amazement and wonder, using the time between groups to study the thousands of people around him in all colors, shapes, sizes and ages. There were men with perfect bodies wearing practically nothing, showing off the muscles they worked so hard to obtain, couples in every configuration holding hands, walking arm in arm, kissing, fondling, so much in love. There were cliques of friends laughing and circulating, saying hello to other friends, then moving on down the sidewalk in search of more adventure. There were butch boys, queeny boys, boys in drag, lesbians that looked like pinup girls and still others that looked like they could kick some serious butt. "I've been living a couple of miles away from this for how many years now?" he said to Raider, shaking his head with regret.

Raider looked at the two elderly men coming down the route atop a red convertible. The sign on the door said they'd been together for forty-five years. He was astonished. No straight person in the world would ever believe this scene unless they saw it with their own two eyes, he decided, and all afternoon the running commentary in his mind was incessant: Wouldn't mind taking her home tonight. The mayor? They let the fucking mayor participate in this? Topless women with stickers over their breasts. Why can't *we* have a parade like this?

What are all these bodybuilders doing here in support of gay rights? he wondered at one point, suspiciously eyeing a cluster of ten men directly across from him on the median strip. All of them were over two hundred pounds of solid beef and wearing nothing but spandex shorts hiked up their crotches and asses. He noticed two of them—one black, one white—locked in a long, extended kiss, their tongues sucking each other up heartily. Another one, a short Latino with pecs as big as tits, was cupping the ass of a guy who could have passed for Raider's younger brother Patrick. They're all fags, Raider's brain shouted. All those muscle-bound studs are fucking fags. Didn't even seem right, calling them fags anymore. No wonder Othello was dying to come here.

Morning turned to afternoon and the groups kept coming. There were leather masters in dark sunglasses, swatting the bare butts of their slaves wearing chaps, an equestrian group proudly galloping by on horseback, a diving club hoisting a giant purple octopus high above their heads. There was the Great American Yankee Freedom Band, marching tall and proud while playing "Strike Up the Band."

ACTNOW was also there. They walked in silence and carried miniature coffins and black placards that read: ACT NOW: DEMAND A CURE NOW. Travis was there, along with Trudy, Darnell, Gary the Asian and countless others Othello recognized from the meetings. He clapped especially hard when they passed, catching Travis's attention and receiving a knowing nod and wink. I'm gonna miss him, Othello thought, momentarily saddened by the fact they hadn't had a chance to say good-bye.

The temperature climbed into the 80s. The cloudy condition known as June Gloom usually associated with LA this time of year took the day off. Trying to savor every moment he could, Othello stood and applauded every group as if it were his duty. If they could be here, out and marching, he could honor and support them. Not to mention envy them.

Eventually, both Othello and Raider had to succumb to the laws of nature. On the wide, grassy median strip, they made use of the portable toilets.

"You sure I'm not coming apart in the sun?" Othello asked after Raider emerged from the booth, the fiberglass door slamming loudly behind him.

"As beautiful as ever," said Raider. Near the end of the line, Othello noticed two overweight Asian men kissing up a storm and pulling at each other's bare nipples.

"Must be newlyweds like us," said Othello, his eyes radiant through his horn-rimmed glasses. He grabbed Raider's hand and playfully swung it between them. Knowing what was next, Raider pulled Othello closer and planted one on his nose. Then, to avoid more lip locking, he pulled Othello into his chest and they hugged, something Othello seemed to enjoy just as much.

His chin resting on the Dodgers cap on Othello's head, Raider glanced around to gauge the other parade-goers' reaction to the big blond stud and the old black geezer. There were plenty of stares, but no looks of condemnation, a pattern that repeated itself all afternoon. The lack of judgment was something Raider appreciated and it forced him to loosen up a little more, even try to regard those around him with a little less judgment.

"Should we walk around a bit?" Othello asked. "Get a different view?"

Raider agreed, but just then, something in the nearby intersection caught his eye.

"Take a look up there," he told Othello.

The first thing Othello noticed was the flaming red hair of

Freedom. He was naked except for some tall, black army boots, black leather shorts and a sky blue feather boa wrapped around his neck. He was two feet away from the cluster of religious protesters Othello and Raider had seen earlier. The protesters were now confined to a small roped-off corral set up by police next to the parade route. But that didn't stop Freedom from yelling obscenities at them at the top of his lungs.

"We'd better talk to him," said Othello. "The last thing we need is for him to get himself arrested."

"You're the one who'll burn in hell," Freedom was shouting when they reached him.

"Freedom, enough of that," Raider said. Othello had asked him to do the talking so as to not bring too much attention to Joe.

Freedom swung around and was momentarily stunned by the sight of Raider, then further shocked to see Joe in his arms. "What the...."

"We're dating," explained Othello.

"Well, bend me over and fuck me now." Freedom looked sicker than ever, his eyes sunken in, his skin colorless except for the blue veins on his face. "And score one for the Social Security set." He nudged Othello and winked.

"We both think you should calm down, Freedom," Othello said. "You're not looking too well."

"You wouldn't be either if you just found out you had a fucking lesion on your fucking brain." He turned back to the religious contingent. "Fuck you and Leviticus!"

"How much longer do you have to repent?" came through a bullhorn. It was the man with the beer belly and the black FEAR GOD T-shirt.

"Long enough to show you a thing or two about life and death!" yelled Freedom.

"Freedom come on," Raider said. Othello stood there, temporarily stunned by news of the lesion.

"Come on, nothing. These people come to our part of town on our day. Like anybody here is gonna suddenly say, 'Oh, you're right. I don't enjoy sucking dick. Convert me, save me, baptize me.'" He threw up his hands and yelled the last part, receiving curious looks from some of the gays around the intersection. "You should be over here, too, assholes!" he yelled to them.

"Raider's right, Freedom," said Othello. "You don't need this, especially with this news. Is this how you wanna spend gay pride?" He refrained from saying "your last" gay pride, but judging by the look on Freedom's face, the point was understood.

"Oh, fuck everybody today," Freedom said and walked away, leaving Othello and Raider next to the crusader, who was still crusading through the bullhorn:

"Accept Jesus Christ and he shall cleanse your soul of perversion."

To escape the wrath of the religious, Raider and Othello went farther down the street and found themselves on the median strip as a succession of bar floats went by, each one filled with scores of male and female bodies covered with sweat and very little else. The first one featured women *and* men in hula skirts. They were grinding against gold lamé palm trees and dancing to a remixed version of "We Are Family."

"I'm having such a good time, I don't want it to end," Raider shouted over the music. "How much longer does this go on?"

"We've still got the festival in the park," Othello yelled back, shuffling his feet to the beat booming off the large speakers on the flatbed truck.

"The what?" asked a dismayed Raider.

"The festival. With all the booths and food and exhibits. And there's a humongous dance floor, Sweeney said. Baby, we're dancing till we drop!"

"You can't dance too much, *Joe*."

"Oh, yes I can. What—senior citizens can't jam? I'm not missing out on anything. I'll stay here forever if I have to." Just then, another bar float came by. This one resembled a white clipper ship and featured several boys who were naked except for the US flags around their waists and white sailor hats on their heads. They were dancing to "Go For Love," the fast syncopated dance hit from Othello's *One Nation* album. Immediately, Othello and Raider eyed each other. Then Othello yelled "woo!" and started dancing like someone with arthritis and a funky sense of rhythm. Raider had to laugh, thinking: if only they knew.

The boys on the float noticed the old man grooving and waved and danced in his direction. Some of them grabbed their crotches; others turned to show their asses. As if he didn't need any of that, Othello grabbed Raider by the waist and danced sideways with him, as if to say, I got my man. The sailor boys gave him a thumbs up in appreciation, their eyes sizing up Raider quite approvingly. Flattered, Raider, broke into a wide grin, then waved at the dancers and shouted "woo!" just as Othello had. Then, his hips began moving, then his legs, and before he knew it, he was dancing right along with Othello. What the hell, he figured. When in Boystown....

All too quickly the float passed, but one just as festive took its place. This one was a pick-up truck covered with silver sequins and glitter and packed with dancers in drag, advertising a weekly show at a bar in the Valley. "It's Raining Men" by the Weather Girls was pumping out of their speakers while the drag queens worked the crowd.

"Get it, girls!" shouted a balding, middle aged man who was next to Raider. Othello glanced at the man, then back to the float.

"You go, girl!" Othello yelled, still dancing in place.

"Work it, baby!" Raider suddenly shouted. Othello turned to him, pleasantly stunned. Raider had surprised himself, but he wasn't finished. "Come on, girl," he added. "You better work!"

Othello raised a fist in the air and let out another "woo!" then put his arm around Raider's waist and the two of them began dancing again, keeping it up for the remainder of the bar floats.

As the temperature soared toward the 90s, Othello began to wilt underneath the old man getup, but swore nothing could keep him from enjoying the rest of the day. To combat the heat, they bought ice cream from one of the many street vendors and took a momentary break on a bus bench under a shady tree on the eastbound side of the street—the relatively quieter side of the street a median strip away from the main action. "I want to go on record here and now," Othello said between bites of his Häagen Dazs bar. "Nothing in my life has ever been this much fun, not performing, not touring, not shopping sprees on the *Champs-Elysées*, nothing Raider Kincaide, you hear me? Nothing."

"I'm glad," Raider said. The truth. "Me, too." A lie, but it also wasn't the worst experience of his life.

They were devouring ice cream and recounting the things they'd seen so far when Othello noticed his preppie Irish manager with his equally preppie lover Chandler. They were heading toward Othello and Raider from twenty yards away, a bombshell of a surprise considering the fact Sweeney—a weary veteran of the parade in the '80s—had vowed years ago to never again grace Santa Monica Boulevard on this day. It was also a sentiment shared by Chandler, whom Othello had only met on a handful of occasions.

"What happened to Santa Barbara?" Othello stood and asked when they reached him. "Just couldn't miss all this, eh?"

"Something like that," Sweeney mumbled, sheepishly eyeing his lover. Chandler was six-foot-two with a doll-like face even though he was well into his forties.

"We were up there, antiquing," Chandler began, his voice was full of disdain, "when all of a sudden *he* had this urge to be gay and proud today."

"And check up on his only client, I'm sure." Othello flashed a smile of approval toward his manager, who rolled his eyes as an admission of guilt.

"Well, it is your first gay pride," Sweeney said. "I didn't want you to be overwhelmed." He glanced at Raider.

"Raider," Othello began hastily, "this is Sweeney's better half, Chandler."

Raider stood and shook hands with Chandler, and for the first time, Othello acknowledged to himself the fact that his manager had probably told his lover about Othello being gay years ago, even though Othello had sworn Sweeney to secrecy when they teamed up in the early '80s. But Othello was okay with it, even glad as they stood there, two couples facing each other.

"Overwhelmed?" he said, picking up on Sweeney's comment. "We're having the time of our lives." He put his arm around Raider.

"You see," Chandler chided Sweeney. "No need to baby-sit. Now, can we go?"

"Oh, can't you stay?" asked Othello.

"We've been here two hours already, looking for you," said Sweeney. "That's probably enough for this year."

"And the next," said Chandler.

Othello didn't protest. He preferred to have the man from Nantucket to himself anyway. Chandler and Raider said their "nice meeting you's" and Othello stepped away for a moment alone with Sweeney.

"Thanks for caring," said Othello.

"I happen to love you, you know," said Sweeney.

"Yes, I do know." They shared an easy smile, something they hadn't shared since the night Othello tested positive.

"And because you're having such a good time," Sweeney said, "I won't even begin to bring up the four thousand and one things you need to do for 'our' music career."

"One of these millennia," promised Othello.

"Yeah, yeah, sure," said Sweeney, leaning toward Chandler, who had walked ahead. "Careful today, okay?"

"Sweeney," Othello said, nodding to Chandler. "He knows, doesn't he?"

"Only that you are and that Joe is a one time deal for today," Sweeney said, much to Othello's relief.

"I love you, too, you know," Othello said. Sweeney smiled, blew a kiss and joined his lover. At that moment, Othello wished his manager knew about his getting tested and the bullet meant for Herman, but Othello knew better than to get too carried away. He watched contentedly as Sweeney and Chandler walked away arm in arm.

"Hey, Joe," Sweeney turned back and yelled. "Don't miss this." He pointed toward the parade, then waved good-bye one last time.

Othello grabbed Raider's hand and led him to the edge of the route. Coming down Santa Monica were hundreds of people carrying hand-written signs. I LOVE MY GAY SON AND HIS LOVER. ALL MY DAUGHTERS ARE SPECIAL. MY MOM'S STRAIGHT AND THAT'S OKAY BY ME. I LOVE MY GAY TWINS. MY LESBIAN SISTER IS MY BEST FRIEND.

"Sweeney told me about this," Othello said, edging closer to the curb for a front row view.

No music was needed for this portion of the parade, when the

members of PFLAG—Parents, Friends and Family of Lesbians and
Gays—proclaimed their love for their gay relatives and friends. They
marched side by side, parents and children, straight siblings with gay
siblings, some with babies in strollers, some with their pets, all with
the proudest smiles on their faces and all receiving the most heartfelt
applause of the day.

They have ten times the courage I have, Othello thought with
tears in his eyes, imagining his own family back in Riverside and wondering if they'd accept him for being gay, not because he was worth
millions to them but because they loved him.

"This is something else," Raider said. He was truly moved, but
not so much so that he didn't notice Freedom thirty yards down the
road. He was near the religious corral again, this time merely standing near the protesters with his arms folded. He appeared to be
focused on the crusader with the long brown hair and the black FEAR
GOD T-shirt, watching the man stuffing his bullhorn into an orange
backpack.

"Joe," Raider said, nudging Othello, "take a look at Freedom."

"One sec." Othello was unable to look away from the scores of
families marching.

Raider kept his eye on the crusader, who left the corral, darted
across the parade route, then went down a side street, presumably for
a lunch break—or perhaps he was done for the day. Freedom waited
until the man was out of sight, then he himself darted across the route
in front of a flatbed truck full of men and women line-dancing to
"Boot Scootin' Boogie."

"Joe," Raider said again, his voice more insistent this time.

"Raider, can't it wait?" Othello pleaded. Raider watched Freedom
disappear down the same side street as the crusader.

"Then don't move an inch," Raider said. "I'll be right back."

Othello glanced at Raider long enough to see him walking away,
then went back to applauding the families. Raider walked along the
median strip toward the protesters' corral, then he too crossed the
parade route, running through a performance by the West Hollywood
Cheerleaders, the all-male squad with white T-shirts, red skirts, huge
oversized red-and-white pompoms and bouffant hair for days. The

crowd booed him as he interrupted their formation, but he didn't care. He reached the other side and headed down the side street in question.

The street was small and residential except for the parking lots behind the businesses fronting Santa Monica. Not spotting either man down the block, he decided to investigate the lots. The one on the right was full of cars but lifeless The lot to the left was shielded by a cluster of short palm trees running along the sidewalk. He hurried past them and landed in a small enclosed area surrounded by a white brick wall on three sides.

In the far corner was a long trailer cab on stilts. Next to that was a black pickup truck with its driver's side door open. On the ground beside it was the crusader's sign and backpack. As Raider moved closer, he saw Freedom standing on the other side of the truck's hood, partially hidden behind the large trailer. Freedom was consumed in some act with his back to Raider, who quietly approached. When Raider was fifteen feet away, he saw what Freedom was doing. He had the crusader by his long brown hair and was bashing his head repeatedly into a waist-high stack of cinder blocks. The man's arms were flailing helplessly, his legs about to give out on him. Blood was splattering everywhere, on the white brick wall, on the trailer cab, on Freedom who didn't seem to care.

"Hold it right there, Freedom," Raider said. "Knock it off."

Freedom glanced at Raider, then continued beating the man's head to a pulp. "Can't you see? That's what I'm trying to do."

"Freedom," Raider commanded.

"Go back to your Geritol lover and forget you were ever here."

"Goddamnit, Freedom, you wanna go to jail?" Raider wasn't sure what the fuck he should do with this. This didn't fit into anyone's plans—his or Othello's.

"You try to report me and your head is next," Freedom warned. "I may not have the strength to take you on, but I'll give it my best shot."

"Cease right now, Freedom. I said enough!"

"Fuck off."

The man was about to die if he wasn't there already. To save a life—

"You're under arrest," Raider said.

Freedom stopped, held the limp crusader by the hair and regarded Raider strangely.

"For attempted murder. I'm FBI."

Freedom let go of the crusader, who dropped facedown to the ground, his skull looking like bloodied hamburger.

"Step back," Raider said.

Wordlessly, Freedom backed up to the white brick wall. Raider knelt down and felt the front side of the man's neck.

"Make that murder." Raider stood up.

Unfazed, Freedom made a "tsk tsk" sound and folded his arms. "I knew something was wrong with your uptight ass from day one."

"Why, 'cause I didn't want your sick little hands all over me?" Raider lunged for the man's sign and broke the stick over his thigh, keeping a long jagged piece for a weapon. "Yeah, there's something wrong with me." He couldn't hold back anymore; he was pissed. *"I'm not a fucking fag like you!"* he yelled at the top of his lungs, months of frustration coming out all at once. His words echoed off the brick wall surrounding them, mixing with the sound of disco music coming from the parade one street over. Then he calmed himself. "Don't make this any harder than it has to be. It's over for you. Now turn around."

Slowly Freedom turned.

"And get on the ground facedown."

Freedom hesitated.

"The ground!"

Freedom complied.

Raider backed out of the lot until he was on the side street, then yelled to a black woman selling beads on the boulevard, telling her to summon a cop. That way the LA County Sheriffs could take Freedom into custody and Raider could get back to Othello and figure out what to do next. A few seconds later, two officers, a Latino man and a white woman, rounded the corner. Raider started to wave them over, but felt a pair of hands shoving his chest and some kind of liquid hitting him in the face. Spit, he realized, from Freedom, who bolted out of the lot and ran toward Santa Monica Boulevard.

"Shit!" Raider cried in horror, dropping the stick and trying to wipe Freedom's venom from his face.

"What's the matter, sir?" the Latino officer asked upon reaching him.

"I'm with the FBI. *That* man just killed that man."

Freedom was slipping onto the other side of the parade route where he began running parallel to the median strip, westbound.

"Collar him," Raider said. The female cop ran to the crusader's body.

"I need to see some ID," said the Latino cop.

"I'm on UC, I got squat on me."

"Then I need to—"

"Look, you can shoot me or you can help me catch a murderer." Raider took off, half expecting to feel bullets in his back.

Freedom Clark used every ounce of strength left in his body to run down the median strip, huffing and puffing and clutching the boa to his throat with both hands. He was so caught up in his getaway, he didn't realize he raced right by Old Man Joe, who saw Freedom and tried unsuccessfully to get his attention.

Half a block down, Raider raced after Freedom, assuming at least one of the cops was right behind him. To get on the same side of the street as Freedom, he darted across the parade route again. But this time he was met by a maze of hundreds of bicycles creeping along at a snail's pace. He stumbled and staggered his way through their broken formations, bumping into wheels and pedals and knocking over a whole row of bikes like dominos. When he finally reached the median strip, he'd lost time and saw that he was about to lose even more, for up ahead was Othello.

"Raider, what's happening?" he pleaded when they came upon one another. "What's Freedom running from?"

"I'm not sure, but I just heard some cops say something about him trying to kill a man. Apparently he couldn't wait for Herman. Stay here. I'll try to help him as best I can." Raider took off again. Freedom had a full block lead on him now, but Raider could see that frail body and wild red hair slowing down and losing stamina.

Freedom knew he couldn't outrun Raider on a good day and

decided to duck into the parade route and lose himself in a large group of marchers from an AIDS service organization. The group consisted of several columns of men and women carrying a long rainbow-colored tarp on poles over their heads while singing "We Shall Overcome." He tried his best to blend in, hiding his thin frame amongst the marchers, moving from body to body and looking back for signs of Raider.

Raider saw the red hair disappear underneath the flag and slipped into the tail end of the long tarp. From there, he began dodging through the group, working his way forward. Twice he grabbed redheads thinking they might be Freedom, causing confusion and distress among the marchers, confusion and distress that only multiplied when three cops also joined the hunt under the flag, searching for signs of Raider *and* Freedom. Most of the group kept singing; some yelled, "Watch it!" and "Get out of here!" Ignoring the angry voices, Raider kept making his way to the front.

On the sidewalk, the parade-goers noticed the clamor underneath the flag and pointed toward the commotion, which wasn't lost on Othello as he ran alongside the group, staying on the median strip, desperate to find both his boyfriend and his assassin.

Raider reached the very front of the flag and saw no sign of Freedom. He turned back, ready to search again, and saw the sky blue boa slipping from the middle of marchers back into the crowd on the sidewalk. Freedom then ran down another side street. Raider sprinted after him.

"He's a lousy traitor!" Freedom yelled when he saw that he was still being chased. The boa was now wrapped around his shoulders like a shawl. Raider was gaining on him by the second. Seeing this, Freedom stopped in the middle of the street and turned around. "Lousy traitor, lousy traitor, lousy traitor!" he shouted at the top of his lungs. His eyes were filled with rage, his voice hoarse. He must have not heard the horn suddenly blaring out, nor did he see the large white service truck backing out of the driveway he was planted in front of. Raider saw it and stopped in his tracks twenty feet away. The corner of the truck knocked Freedom over like a rag doll, then halted abruptly. The driver was a heavyset white man. He jumped out and was hysterical. Raider ran up to Freedom's lifeless body lying face-up in the middle of the street. Blood gushed from Freedom's backside, flowing like a river into the street. The right side of his head was caved in, his eyes shut tight as if still feeling the impact.

The cops had seen Raider running down the street and now descended upon the scene along with several dozen witnesses to the chase. The driver was beside himself. "I don't understand it," he repeated over and over to one of the cops while the other officers tried to keep the swelling crowd at bay.

"Is he dead?" said a female child's voice.

"That man was chasing him," said an older woman's voice.

"Somebody call a doctor," said a man's feminine voice.

"I'm a doctor." It was Othello, stepping forward as if it were the most natural thing in the world. The cops let him through.

"He didn't make it," said Raider, who along with the truck driver was still in the clearing secured by the cops. Feeling helpless, Othello knelt down to Freedom anyway.

"Doctor," Raider said with urgency, "there's nothing you can do now."

Othello knew Raider was trying to warn him to get out of there, but the only thing that mattered now was Freedom.

"In a minute," Othello said, taking his eyes off Freedom to survey the growing crowd.

Still wary of Freedom's spit on his face, Raider spotted a street vendor with an ice chest on the sidewalk and rushed over to buy a bottled water. He poured it on his face, then tried to wash his hands with what was left.

Meanwhile, Othello looked at Freedom one last time, as if to say good-bye, but was caught off guard when Freedom opened his eyes.

"You hold on," Othello said. "You've still got a job to do."

Freedom tried to answer, but blood came pouring out of the side of his mouth.

"Don't talk," begged Othello. He wanted to hold him but wasn't sure if Freedom's body could survive movement. Freedom swallowed hard, then made a laborious attempt to wet his lips, unintentionally coating them with blood.

"Get the bastard," he said with a struggle.

"Herman will get his," promised Othello.

"Not Herman," Freedom said. "Your boyfriend." He coughed up a combination of blood and phlegm, caught his breath, then continued: "Your boyfriend's not your boyfriend." He paused, summoned up one last ounce of energy and uttered: "Get him."

Othello's whole body went numb. Freedom closed his eyes one last time and the life drained away from his face.

Sirens closed in. An ambulance parted the crowd. The driver of the truck was still telling his side of the story to anyone who would listen. A half dozen cops were trying to keep the crowd back. The paramedics moved in on Freedom. And over by the sidewalk, for some reason, Raider was trying to rinse himself off.

Freedom was hallucinating, Othello told himself as he slowly rose up. Freedom was delirious, jealous, dementia-ridden.

Or am I the delirious one? Am I the one hallucinating?

He wandered toward the crowd. Raider approached him and began talking, his words streaming by Othello in a blur:

"I'm sure I'm going to have to stay and make a statement since I saw the accident, but you'd better go now, especially after that doctor business. Can you walk back to my place? Here's the keys. I'll be there later to make sure you get home okay."

And Raider went back into the middle of it all, leaving Othello wandering helplessly away from the accident scene, unable to forget Freedom's last words.

SEVENTEEN

THE LONG VERANDAH was as quiet as it was somber. The most dominant sound was that of the wind blowing through the tall oak trees dotting the yellowish-green hills of Summerhill, Jasper's Virginia Beach ranch. Othello and Deon sat at the same table, their heads bowed, their shoulders slumped in defeat. Jasper stood with one leg on the verandah's white wooden railing, elbow resting on his knee, chin resting on his fist as he stared out over the horizon, gaze unfocused.

Their dates for the occasion were equally reserved. Charlie was sitting in a wicker chair behind Deon, gently massaging Deon's shoulders and humming something that sounded like an old Negro spiritual. Raider was swaying back and forth unassumingly in a rocking chair facing the hills. And Sasha, Jasper's date, sat idly on the railing a few feet down from Jasper, twirling a leaf he had found. Sasha Willaman was twenty and a sophomore at Georgetown. He had striking cheekbones that were higher than high, giving his features a hint of Asian even though he possessed stark blue eyes and straight blond hair that was parted in the middle and fell to either side of his hairless face. Bruce had been stripped of his most-favored-boy status, Jasper had explained to Othello and Deon upon their arrival.

The entire Summerhill staff had been dismissed; the six men had total privacy. Still, the afternoon was far from festive.

"I don't know about Blondie and Blondie," Charlie rose up to attend to the huge brick barbecue pit behind him, "but if I'd only known you all were going to be this much fun, I would have suggested hooking up ages ago." His sarcasm was met with silence. He grabbed a skewer and started poking at the coals in an effort to get the fire going. "I mean, the world's best basketball player, one of my top five, all-time favorite musicians and cable man. Now your average Louisa Maes would have said: Whoa, there's a blowout—oh, shit!"

A towering flame shot up over the grill. Charlie reached for the closest bottle on the ledge of the pit and tried to douse the eruption. It was lighter fluid, which sent the flames even higher. "Ricky," he cried in a voice mimicking Lucy Ricardo. "I got some *splainin'* to do."

"Boy!" Deon rushed over, swiped the skewer from Charlie and eventually quelled the fire, after which Charlie said:

"Well, somebody had to get this party started."

"Sit," said Deon.

"I'm not your dog now," Charlie said, then went over to the table and took Deon's seat. "Why is everyone being such a stick in the mud anyway?"

Raider laughed to himself. He was entertained by the queeny boy's antics.

Othello eyed Charlie across the table and thought: you'd be in a bad mood too if you didn't know whom you could trust, your now-dead, possibly-delirious assassin or your alleged boyfriend from Nantucket.

"Well, I'm with Charlie." Sasha joined Deon at the barbecue pit. "I'm still wiped out from finals and I did not come here to mope all day."

"In that case," Deon handed him the skewer, "knock yourself out."

"I'm with Cheekbones here." Charlie popped up to join Sasha. "Let's salvage something out of this day."

"Don't let him touch that grill," Deon ordered Sasha, then crossed the verandah and headed for the bar. On the way, his eyes met

Othello's. The two of them shared an awkward but brief stare, then Deon looked to Jasper and they too eyed each other apprehensively.

Othello shifted restlessly in his chair. The tension was about to drive him crazy. The Three Wisemen hadn't communicated since Freedom's death a few days ago, nor had they been able to speak here at Summerhill save a small exchange at the front door to the Victorian-style mansion.

"You heard?" Othello had said when Jasper greeted him. Othello had purposely hurried ahead of Raider, who was still getting their bags out of the car.

"I don't own a slew of cable networks for nothing," Jasper had said. "But I did have to tell Deon. He's as mortified as I am, if not more."

That was all they had time for. Raider came bounding up the steps and Sasha joined Jasper in greeting his guests. So here they were, their plan shot to hell and the three of them unable to talk about it so far.

From his rocking chair, Raider studied Deon, who was grabbing a beer at the bar bordering the house. Now's as good a time as any to pal around with The D.A., he told himself. But what do I say to the guy?

Any other gay shooting guards besides yourself in the league? Why, Deon, why? You of all people. No offense, man: I know you think you're a homo and all, but, gee, Deon, are you absolutely sure?

He joined Anthony at the bar. Even though Raider was six-two, he felt like a shrimp next to the six-six Chicago Bull. Another megastar Brian, Jr., would kill to meet, he thought. Just like Othello. Then it suddenly occurred to Raider: his eight-year-old kid hero-worshipped two black men who happened to be gay. Maybe it was time to put in more hours in the father department, he decided. He made a vow to do so starting the day he returned to Washington, which wouldn't be long now.

"How's the Molson?" Raider asked, a lame opener, but what the hey.

"Cool," muttered Deon.

"Guess you'd rather be celebrating another championship right now than being down here."

"Don't matter, right now anyway."

Raider reclined against the bar, but slouching made him feel even shorter, so he quickly stood again, his posture stretching upwards. "You know," he began in a hushed tone, as if he were about to break a confidence, "I would've figured you to be the last person to be gay. Even more so than Othello."

Deon mumbled something and walked to the edge of the verandah. There he stared at the white gazebo in a small plain in the distance.

Raider hastily joined him. "I mean that as a compliment."

Deon looked at him for the first time in their conversation. "You and Othello pretty cool, huh?"

"Like this." Raider wrapped his index and middle finger around each other.

"Who's the top? Or are you both?"

"Excuse me?"

"You know," Deon said. "I don't mean to get personal, but—well, I guess I do—who's top and who's bottom? Or do you guys trade off?"

Raider shrugged and stammered. "We trade off. Sometimes we're both tops, sometimes both bottoms."

Deon eyed him strangely. He figured Raider was an airhead, but didn't get a chance to probe any further because Jasper approached, scotch and soda in hand.

"Raider Kincaide, is it?" he asked.

"Yes, sir—I mean, Jasper—Mr. Hollinquest."

"*Sir* will be just fine," Jasper said, then paused for a laugh, which was only forthcoming from Deon until Raider realized it was a joke and also laughed. "Othello said you were an unparalleled lacrosse superstar at Dartmouth."

"Well, not to toot my own horn, but I still am their all-time leading scorer."

"Ever play with a fellow by the name of Beckwith? Dane Beckwith?"

Raider searched his memory. The name sounded awfully familiar, but not as a teammate. He remembered them better than he remembered the women he slept with. "No, can't say I played with anyone by that name. Why, was he one of your—did you know him?"

Jasper laughed. "Personally no. Just a friend of a friend kind of thing."

"Anyway, Othello," Charlie was saying at the table, "can I call you that? I guess I have to. What else am I going to call you? Anyway, I never did believe those rumors about you and Spinderella. Not that I thought you might be queer, but I knew you'd have better taste than her—oh, please...."

Paying little attention to Charlie, Othello regarded the two Wisemen talking to his boyfriend. Raider seemed to be caught up in the glow of celebrity. He was never like that with me, Othello brooded. Maybe because he was too busy being the cool undercover agent. In the next instant, Othello banished the thought. Freedom didn't know what he was talking about. And if he did have some information on Raider, why didn't he come forward sooner? And if the man from Nantucket was some sort of cop, why weren't they all busted long ago?

He *is* my boyfriend, Othello said to himself, as if he were directly answering Freedom fading out of consciousness on that street in West Hollywood. And any day now he's gonna be my lover. I'll tell him about the virus, show him every pamphlet and book ever written that says we can still have a long life together, complete with glorious safe sex, and we'll go onward and upward from there.

"These coals aren't gonna be ready for a while," Sasha said from the barbecue pit. "Anybody up for a swim?"

"Count me in," said Charlie.

"I think that's an excellent idea for the three of you." With his drink, Jasper motioned toward Charlie, Sasha and Raider.

Charlie hopped up and followed Sasha toward the entrance to the house, waddling like a geisha girl in a tight kimono. "Ooo, this is just like *Gone With the Wind*," he said. "We'll go play while the menfolk discuss business and other thangs boring to us Southern girls. Coming, Raider Kincaide?"

Raider looked to Othello, whose eyes were pleading with him to say yes. "Lead the way, Charlie..." Raider began, and since he didn't know his Charlie's name, added: "Anthony."

"It's Dubois, boy!" Charlie could be heard saying as the three of them disappeared through the sliding glass doors.

"Now." Jasper eyed his two partners. "Down to business."

After retrieving their swim suits from their bedrooms, Sasha led Charlie and Raider to the pool house, which was adjacent to the verandah, then showed them to their separate changing rooms.

"Down to business is right, Hollinquest," Raider said once he was alone with the door closed. The changing room was like a small bedroom with a hammock and sofa chair. He set his gym bag on top of the hammock and stripped off his shorts and tank top. From the bag, he pulled out a pair of baggy old swim trunks—no way he was gonna show his package to this crowd. He slipped them on, then brought out a peach terricloth pool jacket. It was a short little number that stopped at the waist and was bound to fit right in. He held it up and inspected the three black buttons on it. He pressed the middle button between his thumb and index finger.

"Smile."

Soundlessly, the third button blinked as if it were an eye. It was ready. Photos of the Three Wisemen would be a solid addition to the evidence hidden away in the safe deposit box in Los Angeles, a nice complement to the audio tapes of the Temple meetings and the videotape of the Silverlake counter-bashing, quite possibly the last piece of evidence needed, depending on the Wisemen's plans post-Freedom.

There was a pounding at the door, followed by the husky voice of Charlie. "You coming, Raider-man?"

"In a minute, Miss Dubois?" He turned his back to the door in case Charlie barged in.

"In that case—Sasha and me—we plunging."

Raider clicked the camera one last time to make sure it was working properly. On the Martelli job, the shutter in his three-piece suit gave him fits, only taking half the roll. Busted them anyway; that's Raider Kincaide for ya. He was so consumed in examining the buttons, he didn't notice anyone else was in the room until he felt a pair of hands clutching his sides and slithering toward his stomach, causing him to jump out of his skin.

"It's just me," Othello said, sounding a bit offended.

"Sorry." Raider grabbed him by the hands. "I was afraid you were Sasha or Charlie. Aren't you and the menfolk supposed to be talking?"

"I just came to tell you we're going out to the gazebo in case you missed me." He tried for a smile but fell short.

"That was nice of you." Raider stroked Othello's face with the palm of his right hand and gazed into his eyes. "I know you all must be upset about Freedom. You gonna be okay?"

"That's what I'm about to find out." Othello placed his hands on Raider's pecs, gently massaging them, carefully gauging Raider's reaction. His hands then moved to Raider's sides, tracing the V in his torso until he landed on Raider's ass. He then kissed the man from Nantucket, noting with relief Raider's comfortableness. Encouraged, he nibbled on Raider's ear while his hands roamed the firm mounds of Raider's butt for the very first time. "We're gonna have to have that conversation about safe sex real soon," Othello whispered.

"Soon as you recover from the Freedom fiasco and figure out your next move."

Why, so you can arrest me or fuck me?

The mood for romance evaporated. Othello drew back from his man's clutches.

"What's wrong?" asked Raider.

"Nothing. Go enjoy your time with the girls." With that Othello left.

Sasha and Charlie were already in the Olympic-sized pool when Raider emerged from the dressing room, peach jacket cradled in his arm.

"Ooo, I'm scared of you," Charlie said looking at Raider's body. Raider set the jacket on one of the padded lounge chairs, then took a good look at the pool. The FBI doctor he saw after the parade had assured him he couldn't catch the virus from things like saliva or bathrooms or pools, so he did what he always did when he went swimming: took a running leap toward the water and cannonballed in.

The scene on the gazebo was tense and divided, all three Wisemen pacing back and forth, unable to come to any kind of consensus.

"I should have known a high-wire act like Freedom would blow it," said Jasper. "Bad judgment to ever, *ever* trust him."

"I thought a high-wire act was exactly what you wanted," said Othello, "especially one knocking on death's door."

"I'm glad the jig is up anyway," said Deon. "We were fools to think we could pull this off. I've had second, third, fourth and *fifth* thoughts even before this mess."

"What do you mean the jig is up?" said Othello. "What about Darnell?"

"The Rasta boogieman?" said Jasper. "Forget it."

"But the gun is already there," pleaded Othello.

"Precisely," said Jasper, "and in the not too distant future, some plumber type is going to need to go into that hole in the wall and discover it."

"You're starting to scare the shit out of me right about now," said Deon.

"It'll never come back to us," said Othello.

"Think about it." Jasper tapped his forehead with his index finger. "Travis, Darnell and who knows who else will hear about the gun on the news and put two and two together. The old lady so much as asked all of them if they wanted to blow Jimmy Herman's brains out. At least one of them—*at least*—is bound to realize Freedom was the grand prize winner, only he was too stupid to stay alive and finish the job. From there, it's only a matter of time before somebody tells somebody else and we're at risk of being caught just the same as if Freedom had fired the shot and Herman were six feet under. Only now, Freedom isn't alive to divert and distract the investigation as planned. It's over, Othello. We have to disperse and lay low as planned. Only difference is, the Three Wisemen flunked their final exam, end of story."

"Nonsense," said Othello. "Since the gun is there and we're at risk, why not get Darnell?"

"You got a way to make him look like a white blond reporter in forty-eight hours?" asked Jasper. "There's not a damn thing we can do that wouldn't be utterly foolish and full of risks."

"Someday they're gonna find that gun and they'll know I was in that bathroom," said Deon.

"You didn't leave any fingerprints, did you?" asked Jasper.

"Of course not, I'm not a fool."

"Then what the hell are you worried for? Tons of people had access to that hole in the wall. They won't link it to you. Worst case scenario: the gun gets traced to Freedom 'cause he bragged about it and they'll be trying to find a black gardener and some old ladies. As long as we disperse, say good-bye to Old Joe forever and remain anonymous, we're in the clear. Use your head and try not to panic for Christ's sake. You think they'll come looking for 'the great Deon Anthony' just because he took a piss in the museum?"

"I am using my head and I also know an insult when I hear one."

Deon and Jasper went at each other, but a sight in the second floor window of the mansion caught Othello's eye. Raider was there, still wearing his swim shorts with that strange-looking peach jacket. Spying on us, huh? Othello said to himself. Where's the rest of your team, about to come charging over the hills like the cavalry?

Just then, Othello saw Sasha and Charlie join Raider in the window. All three of them started waving to their boyfriends, only Deon and Jasper were too embroiled in debate to notice. Another accusation shot to hell, Othello thought. Raider wouldn't be up there spying with the two queens beside him. Guess they all went upstairs for some other reason. He felt ashamed for trying to sow one more seed of doubt into their relationship, which only served to make him realize how troubled their relationship was at the moment. But life was nothing but troubled at the moment. He turned back to the other two Wisemen, glad he hadn't told them he had been at the parade and had actually witnessed Freedom's demise.

"Jasper, Deon, please!" he cried.

"Oh, don't they look so manly down there?" Charlie sighed. He stood to the right of Raider in the window frame. "Our men. Boy, if the world had a whiff of this."

"Jasper would just use his power to just squash the truth anyway," said Sasha. He was to Raider's left.

"He is one powerful mother." Raider said, his fists holding onto his jacket where the lapels would be, his left hand pressing away at the middle button, capturing the gazebo and the Three Wisemen.

"Let's go make our men some big juicy burgers," said Charlie.

"The coals should be nice and white by now," said Sasha. "How 'bout it, Raider?"

"I'm working up quite an appetite myself," Raider said with a confident smile as he took the last of the roll of thirty-six exposures.

"This is not the time to come apart at the seams," Othello was saying to Jasper and Deon. "It's time to figure out where we go from here."

All three men stood apart, anchoring themselves on different sides of the gazebo.

"We dissolve," Jasper said, "for now, perhaps forever. In fact, the more I think about it, forever seems like a pretty damned good time frame."

"Dissolve?" asked Othello.

"We have no other choice."

"What about the Fund?" asked Deon.

"You gonna put any more dough in it?" Jasper asked, to which Deon remained silent. "We've all put in enough to keep it going for years. Besides, they're getting donations now from other rich anonymous sources."

"Just what I always wanted." Othello stared at the worn wooden planks of the gazebo's floor. "There's so much more that needs to be done."

"I don't want nobody linking that gun with me," said Deon.

"We don't have the luxuries we had before," said Jasper. "Old Man Joe *must* disappear. Besides, once they find the gun, getting another shot at Herman will be next to impossible."

"So we quit?" asked Othello. "Just because it gets complicated?"

"It was easy up until now," said Jasper. "Now people are on our trail."

"What people?" said both Othello and Deon.

"Do not worry," Jasper said emphatically, then paused. "It's Bruce and his investigative brain. He's against the counter-bashers and wants to expose them. But pay it no mind. I'll throw him off the trail. You think I can't handle an amateur kid?"

"What if he links the gun to Freedom?" said Deon. "And me to the gun?"

"Enough already with you and the goddamn gun!" said Jasper. "If you're so worried about it, why don't you just *sneak* back in and *remove* the motherfucker?"

"Guys, please!" Othello pleaded, getting the silence he hoped for. "All I know is: we don't have to fight like this and it doesn't have to be over. There must be something we can do for ourselves and the uprising."

"Like what, Othello?" said Jasper.

Othello circled the gazebo. "Okay, maybe not violence right now, or ever again. Maybe there's something else. Perhaps not even illegal. Something legit like the Fund. We could sink a ton of money into a campaign for someone running against Herman."

"Been there, done that," said Jasper. "The fools down there love him too much."

Othello circled the gazebo some more. "Okay, then. We could counter-bash in another city with another radical group, say New York, and find a less volatile version of Freedom there."

"No!" said Deon.

"Forget it," said Jasper.

"Then," he was down to his last resort: "we could come out, the three of us, together in a press conference, announce to the world we're gay and proud and behind the Fund and ready to do more."

Deon scoffed. "You're in fantasy land now."

"Or on hallucinogens," said Jasper.

"We could do it," Othello insisted. "Together."

"Are you ready to come out?" asked Jasper.

Othello paused. "If the two of you—together the three of...." He turned to the house. Charlie, Raider and Sasha were back on the verandah now, around the barbecue pit. Raider seemed to be truly enjoying himself with those two. I could do it, Othello thought. If I knew for sure I had the love of a man like Raider, I could do it in a heartbeat. I think. Maybe. Maybe not. But why do I need to depend on unreliable Raider to be there? He allowed himself to envision a press conference, alone, without Jasper, Deon or the man from Nantucket. The room would be packed, flashbulbs flickering incessantly. He sits down at the microphone, opens his mouth....

Hell no.

He was shaking. He folded his arms and tried to steady his breath. "This just can't be over. I won't let it."

"We all agreed to unanimously assassinate or not assassinate Herman," said Jasper. "If one of us doesn't want to do it, end of story."

"Then maybe the Wisemen should be over," Othello blurted in frustration.

"Finally you're catching on," Jasper said. "I'll deal with Herman my own way, get my Belize hotels one way or another."

"That's the only reason you were ever in it anyway, wasn't it?"

"That and some Puerto Rican punks from my past. Don't get me wrong, I enjoyed it while it lasted."

"Deon, why were you in it? How did I manage to twist your arm?"

Deon looked toward the verandah and Charlie. "I got my own reasons."

"So we're over, just like that?" Othello asked.

"It was a helluva run." Jasper came up and patted him on the back. "Give yourself a hand. Go back to making music and music videos. You said your manager's on you to pay some attention to your career anyway."

"Are we going to remain friends?"

Silence from the other two Wisemen until Jasper finally spoke:

"We need to keep a low profile. That's not a good idea."

Othello then turned to Deon. "D.A.?"

Deon hesitated, then Charlie called to him from the verandah, his words lost in the wind. "Maybe in the future," said Deon, "some day way off." He stepped off the gazebo and jogged toward Charlie, who ran to meet him halfway.

"It's easier for you two because you have things in your life," Othello said, watching Deon running away, "lovers, boys, healthy immune systems."

"You've got your blond jock now," Jasper said, trying to sound comforting.

If I could only bank on that, Othello thought.

"I guess I can admit to you now I had him checked out," said

Jasper. "When you said he knew about Joe, I couldn't take any chances."

"I told you I already did that," Othello said. In the plain between the gazebo and the verandah, Deon and Charlie reached one another and they hugged and kissed. Then Deon picked Charlie up and began spinning him around, causing Charlie to laugh and scream.

"Then you know he was once involved in gay bashing in college," Jasper went on.

"He told me about it himself," Othello said vacantly, still focused on Deon and Charlie.

"Earlier I asked him about the other guy who was involved," said Jasper. "The Beckwith name. Said he didn't remember."

"Why would he want to?" Othello mumbled, a bit confused. The other guy who was involved? Raider had said more than one guy beat the crap out of him that night at a college near Dartmouth. It didn't matter though; what did Jasper know?

"I've heard about guys like him," said Jasper, "so phobic and full of self-hate they take it out on the very guys they want to fuck them up the ass. He must have really done a number on that Dane Beckwith. The guy was too frightened to talk to my P.I. even after all these years, said Raider's Dartmouth buddies scared him into not pressing charges while he was in the hospital and he still saw a couple of them in passing around Concord where he lives now."

"Jasper, what are you talking about?" Othello asked, still distracted by the sight of Deon and Charlie.

"What I found on your jockboy, if you would listen for a second. I guess he gay-bashed this Beckwith guy back at Dartmouth because he wasn't ready to own up to his sexuality. But I take it, for your sake, he's been cured of that and now only goes around counter-bashing the bashers. Quite a one-eighty, I must say."

"The Dartmouth bashing," Othello said flatly, regarding Raider, who was laughing and having a good time with Sasha on the verandah. "That was the only incident your P.I. dug up?"

"You mean there were others?"

"I guess not," Othello mumbled so low he was sure Jasper hadn't heard him.

It was all starting to make too much sense. Freedom's words. The

Nantucket lie. The uneasiness when it came to touching and being touched by the man he claimed to be in love with. And now, the news that the only gay bashing incident in his youth hadn't been *against* Raider at some neighboring college, rather, it had been perpetrated *by* Raider *at* Dartmouth. Sure, he could ask Raider about it, and sure as hell he'd receive some perfectly logical explanation for this latest discrepancy in the life of the man from Nantucket.

But it was the time for the denial to end. No more pretending. No more rationalizing. No more not seeing what had been obvious for, oh, so long.

Your boyfriend's not your boyfriend.

I'm alone in the war, Othello thought, watching Raider pretend to have the time of his life. Alone with two deserters and one traitor.

OTHELLO'S JET IDLED on the runway of the private airport twenty miles outside Virginia Beach, a few minutes away from a clearance to taxi. In the main compartment, which resembled a living room with plush sofas, big screen television and a wet bar, Othello and Raider sat at opposite ends of the same leather sofa. Using fatigue as an excuse, Othello sat stoically silent while Raider played some kind of Sega game on the television.

If only I'd hired Jasper's investigator instead of mine, Othello thought, regarding Raider's profile.

The co-pilot—a Pakistani in his early forties—entered through the curtain. As instructed.

"Mr. Hardaway, sir," he said in an English accent, "there's an urgent phone call from your manager Sweeney. He said something about a record meeting."

"Thank you, Eli." Othello unfurled himself from the couch as his co-pilot disappeared. "I'd better get this up front," he told Raider. "The phone in here has been acting up."

Raider played on. Ten minutes later Othello re-emerged.

"Raider, you'll forgive me. There's some sort of snafu with a contract in LA. I need to go into the airport and use their teleconferencing setup to straighten it out."

"Fine," said Raider. "Let's go."

"You stay," Othello said abruptly. "It's been a long day and I might get a little nasty with these execs. No need for you to see me being ugly."

Raider paused, not sure if he bought it, then said: "If that's the way you want it."

"That's the way I want it. Help yourself to whatever: keep playing, take a nap, have some food. I'll be back as soon as I've set some soon-to-be fired lackeys straight."

With that, Othello disappeared through the curtain again, this time heading for the plane's exit.

For an hour, Raider waited patiently, wondering if Othello's departure had anything to do with the breakup of the Three Wisemen. But an hour turned into two, then three, and the suspicion that started as a small nagging tick in the back of Raider's mind exploded into a full-fledged monster called reality.

He's not coming back.

And if he's not coming back that means one thing: that short black man with the ripped-up body and devious mind knows exactly who I am. Somehow, some way, he knows.

He racked his brain, trying to think about what had happened at Jasper's ranch, then realized:

It was Jasper, asking me about Dane Beckwith. Who is Dane Beckwith?

His thoughts on rapid-fire now, he searched his past. Then it hit him: the fucking fag from Dartmouth.

At that instant, Raider half expected the plane to explode, or take off with him in tow and plunge into the Atlantic. Then, he calmed himself and thought: I know this guy. Okay, so he's on to me. What would he do next? What else does he know?

A few minutes later, it came to him. With newfound determination, he grabbed his bag off the sofa, and just as Othello had done hours earlier, he disappeared through the curtain and headed for the plane's exit.

EIGHTEEN

A SMALL BANKER'S lamp resting on the wooden table next to the door was the only light illuminating the condo's living room. No need to draw the neighbors' attention, Othello had decided. Even though it was past midnight now, maybe some old biddy on estrogen overdrive would think Raider had returned home to DC and come traipsing over with starry eyes and a freshly baked apple pie.

Having gone through both bedrooms twice already, he made his way to the kitchen and opened the refrigerator, cringing at the sight of a blackened, half-eaten sandwich and a green loaf of bread. He surveyed the room. Kitchen items were in short supply, as was any evidence Raider Kincaide had ever cooked a meal in his life save the pasta dish at the Big House. He closed the refrigerator door, killing another source of light, and walked back into the living room. The furniture was modern and modest, dark wood and green leather, better than Raider's place in West Hollywood, but then again, this was his real home, not far from the J. Edgar Hoover Building and FBI headquarters. Briefly, he wondered if the man from Nantucket knew that Hoover was one of the biggest queens this side of Richard Simmons.

Across from the sofa was a fireplace. In a straw basket on the hearth was a pile of CD's. He sat on the coffee table and started rum-

maging through the pile. The CD's were mostly rock bands: Aero-
smith, Bon Jovi, Van Halen. There were no more Othello albums to go
along with the copy of *One Nation* that was stashed among some
straight porno tapes in the dresser drawer in the bedroom. Must have
bought mine for research, Othello figured. He was still going through
the CD's when he realized there was another presence in the room,
behind him in the vicinity of the doorway.

"I guess Hollinquest hired a better P.I. than you." It was Raider's
voice, calm and collected. Othello looked up from the CD's but didn't
turn around.

"Not really," he said. "Your office did a good job covering your
tracks. He still has no idea you're.... I just decided to stop being a complete fool and take you for what you really are. He did know you came
to LA from here, not Nantucket."

"And based on Jasper's tip, you found my condo."

Othello heard the front door close and took it to mean they were
alone. No arresting officers just yet.

"How'd you get in?" Raider asked.

"When you're as rich as I am, you learn very quickly how to buy
the little people, locksmiths included."

"I'll remember that next time I'm rich."

"I wanted a glimpse of the real man behind the man I fell in love
with." He played with the CD's in his hand, still unable to look at
Raider. "To see if he was anything like the Raider I knew. I figured this
was the only way to find out."

"And am I? Like the man who lives here?"

"Not too different, I supposed. With some very glaring and
heartbreaking exceptions." His voice cracked. He tossed the CD's back
into the basket, then stood up and flung an arm in the direction of the
row of bronzed lacrosse statuettes on the fireplace mantle. "You
should have brought your trophies out. They would have been a nice
addition, made me fall even more, if that's even possible."

"I care about you, Othello," Raider said, his voice drawing closer.
Another light came on, the lamp on the end table beside the sofa,
Othello guessed.

'You don't love me."

"I never said I did."

"You said you were *in* love with me." Othello turned and faced the real Raider for the very first time. They were five feet apart, their eyes locked together. "Was it all just one big one-hundred-percent lie? I know I'm a fool for even asking but I have to."

Raider looked toward the ceiling, then back to Othello. "I'm just not that way, Othello."

Othello made a half turn away from him. "Well, you did an Oscar-worthy job pretending. And the nominees for this year's Best Straight Man Posing As A Cocksucker are...."

"Not really," said Raider. "I let you down an awful lot. I freaked out whenever anyone came near me. I about clubbed Freedom at least twice for trying to feel me up."

"Freedom," Othello said wistfully. "He was a thousand times smarter than me. He had you figured out."

"Not necessarily. It was me who saw him crush that man's skull at the parade. I came clean and told him he was under arrest. He ran."

"That's why he tried to warn me," Othello realized. "But I didn't want to listen. Guess I wanted my man even more than I wanted my uprising. And I sent me, Jasper, Deon, Travis, Trudy and everybody else straight up the river for it." He paused, thinking about how they'd soon find out how he'd let them all down. "So what happens now?"

"Some of that depends on you."

"Me? You hold all the cards."

"Othello, we can make this as painless as possible."

"For this to be painless is impossible."

"I mean in terms of a big scene with the media or you and the Wisemen on the run like fugitives. This can be a lot more civilized than O.J.'s slow speed chase down the 405."

The very comparison rendered Othello nauseous. He walked toward the fireplace and hung onto the mantle for stability as Raider went on:

"We've gotta talk, O."

"Talk about what, for God's sake?"

Raider rubbed his head as if trying to clear it. His thoughts were jagged and jumbled. His stomach was even trying to get into the act.

Normally, the routine was simple: cuff 'em, file the report, pick out a sharp suit to wear on the witness stand. Move on.

But this wasn't "normally."

He sighed. "Part of what happens may also be influenced by whether or not you told me the truth when you said the assassination attempt was called off."

"You saw the awkward way we all parted. They chickened out." Othello swung around to Raider. "But not me." He checked himself, fearing further incrimination. "The Wisemen and Joe are as dead as Freedom. Even if I were to be a free man, I'm alone, just like I was the day I started this whole odyssey."

"What began it anyway? I mean, you have so much, wealth, career, fame."

"People grow older, mature, they confront their own mortality." They confront the prospect of a slow, agonizing death in their mid-thirties, he said to himself, walking along the length of the mantle, farther away from Raider. "I decided that, before I died, I wanted to make a difference in the thing that mattered most to me, the thing that was at the core of my soul. I wanted the power to change the face of gay rights. Almost as much as I wanted love."

"I'm sorry I had to play with your emotions. Really I am."

"You don't give a damn about me, Raider." He turned and faced him again. "You're not capable. It was a job for you, a nothing job."

"You're wrong there and I think you know that."

"Then why is my next destination the nearest jail cell?"

Raider paused, then insisted: "I'm not a robot without feelings. You're a good person underneath all that anger. I was flattered that you were in love with me. You could have anybody in the world, male or female, and you wanted me."

"You don't know how much."

"Unfortunately sometimes that's what UC—undercover—work is all about, becoming the avenue to what the person wants so much, a goal, dream, a drug, becoming their drug. Only most of the time, it's guys who don't deserve to take up space on the planet, child pornographers, drug runners, Mafia types."

"And, what, I'm not as bad as your usual suspects?"

"Not even in the same ballpark, Othello."

Othello stood in silence, wondering if it were ever going to be possible to digest and fully understand what had taken place between them. "Weren't you ever curious though?" he asked. "Didn't you ever think about it? Me?"

"There were times I thought about it, sure. Hell, I'm surrounded by gay guys for three months; how am I not supposed to wonder? But I know it's only natural now—to wonder. Everybody wonders. And some gay guys are pretty cool. And buff, like you. And normal, like me. Sure there's the guys—Freedom or that sissy Asian Gary—that I'll never understand, but then there's guys like you who I have no problem with. Now at least."

"So the kissing," Othello said, still trying to decipher what was and wasn't real about his once and never-again boyfriend, "the kissing wasn't enjoyable?"

Raider laughed. "The kissing was pretty crazy. I will tell you this: I know some girls who could use a few lessons from you. A lot of them."

"So I'm a good kisser?"

Raider hesitated, feeling forced into a corner. "I guess you could say that. For a guy."

"And all that making out? Was that so bad?"

Raider stared at the walls. Momentarily, he was lost in his own world. Othello sauntered over to him, not stopping until they were a foot apart.

"I'm also a good sucker," Othello said, "and fucker and butt-licker, too, especially with an Adonis like you."

Raider moved his head to one side for some breathing room. "This is not going to work, Othello. You and I are not going to have sex."

"How long has it been for you, you poor stud, stuck with all those men for so long, seeing those women at the parade and knowing you couldn't have them even if you wanted to. You must be dying to whip out that piece of meat."

Raider laughed the laugh of disbelief, arching his head toward the ceiling but not moving away. "You still want me? After all that I've done. After everything?"

"I'm through with denial. I'm gonna be in a federal prison somewhere hating you with every fiber of my being for the rest of my life, but I'll still want you. I'll still remember what it was like running my hands through your hair and caressing these big, strong shoulders. I'll still think about how I truly believed this was going to be my first love despite all the obstacles, that God or the gods or fate or whomever was finally granting me the one thing I wanted most in life. I'll hate you, Raider Kincaide. I'll hope you'll come to regret not loving me, and sometimes I'm sure I'll wish the worst kinds of human tragedies befall you. But I'll still be in love with you. I'll still think about holding you. And you holding me."

"Even though I'm straight and you know it's women I want?"

"Maybe especially because you're straight and it's women you want."

"I don't get it."

"I don't either fully, but I do know that I would give anything to be the only man you ever loved, ever cared for, ever gave yourself to."

"Knowing that I could never return your affection the way I could a woman?"

"Never say never."

"You got that right." He took a few steps away. "That night on the cliff in Malibu, I almost talked myself into letting you give me a blowjob."

"What stopped you?"

"I wasn't going to prostitute myself for this case."

"What's stopping you now? You've won. Case closed."

"You would still want to give me a blowjob?"

"The best one you ever had. Think of it as a small souvenir to take with you from your biggest case ever. And you'd be giving me a keepsake, the taste of your cum which I can savor as I rot the years away in prison."

"Othello, this is crazy to even think about."

"So is what we've been through these last few months. So is what's about to happen to both of us."

"If we...if this...if you." Raider let out a tight breath. "I could never do anything more than that."

"Deal. You won't be sorry."

Raider scoffed. "You're Othello, man. Why me?"

"Because you're a man's man, this body, this manly physique. You're more of a man than anybody I've ever met."

"Yeah, right."

"I mean it. Your sexy voice, your beautiful eyes, your wonderful face, your great body, your ass, your whole persona."

"Othello, man, you're crazy."

"Tell me something I don't know," Othello said and Raider laughed. Their eyes rested on one another's. "We'll never have this chance ever again."

"Man, if you told anybody...."

"Who would believe me? They'd chalk it up to the ravings of the wronged lunatic." He felt Raider's crotch. "Just let me—"

"Wait, hold on." Raider stepped back. For a moment the condo fell silent. Then Raider spoke. "Into the bedroom."

Othello fought like hell not to explode as he headed toward the hallway, ahead of Raider to keep up the momentum, which didn't seem necessary because Raider was right on his heels. Once inside the bedroom, Raider messed with the dimmer switch until the room was half-lit. Then they stood at the foot of the bed, for a moment unsure of what should happen next. Othello quickly came to the rescue, reaching for Raider's belt buckle.

"Whoa," Raider said, grabbing Othello's hands. "I'll do this." He proceeded to unbuckle his own belt, then lowered his underwear and jeans just enough to expose his crotch.

"It's beautiful," Othello said of his dick, soft and thick and rounded, the head plump and getting plumper. Raider didn't say a word. Instead, he swallowed hard and waited. Disappointed by the lack of romance in the air, Othello nevertheless knelt down on his knees, and not wanting to give Raider enough time to change his mind, scooped up three quarters of Raider's limp cock in his mouth.

Immediately, Raider inhaled a very audible breath. Encouraged, Othello grabbed Raider's hips and took in more of his dick, dousing it with his saliva and slowly twisting and turning his mouth. His lips then traveled backwards until they tasted a plump fat head, at which point he made the journey back down toward the base of Raider's cock. He did this several times, slowly and steadily as Raider's hips begin to sway and his cock stretched and hardened and widened all at the same time. Enraptured with the salty taste of his man, Othello opened his mouth even wider and swallowed Raider whole until his nose was pressed against the spare patch of blond pubic hair above Raider's dick.

"Whoa," was all Raider could say.

Othello stayed there for as long as he could hold his breath, inhaling the funky scent of Raider's skin and pubic hair, which possessed an almost overpowering dose of sweat and musk, something Othello decided to relish, as if his man had just come from a workout or the lacrosse fields. When he had to come up for air, he slowly pulled back, never leaving Raider's cock, and found a big reward waiting for him. In the span of a few seconds, Raider's manhood had expanded to its full roaring size, as big and thick as any Othello had ever tasted in golden days of the Temple.

"You've got a cock to match everything else about you," he said.

Raider laughed immodestly, then stepped back a bit and began kicking off his sneakers. "If I'm only going to do this once in my life, I may as well do it right." After the shoes came the pants, which he threw on the sofa chair next to the dresser. "You can get comfortable, too."

Othello took that as a cue to undress, and as he did, Raider, reclined back on the bed, his legs hanging off at the knees, his dick not losing a millimeter of steeliness.

With their clothes out of the way, Othello took a moment to savor the sight of Raider lying on the bed, then knelt down on the floor between his legs and began caressing his thighs as his tongue dove for Raider's balls. First, he licked them, then took them in his mouth, his right hand playing with Raider's cock and rubbing it against his face. Soon, he was sucking again, full long strokes with his eyes glued to Raider's. Raider alternated between watching and arching his head backwards, his face only showing signs of pleasure, no guilt. Taking this as a good sign, Othello began licking Raider's stomach and chest, cupping his pecs and tasting his nipples.

"Othello, no," Raider moaned.

"You don't like that?" Othello asked between swipes with his tongue.

"I just want you to suck my dick, just a blowjob."

"Then tell me. Tell me what you want."

"Suck my dick."

"I can't hear you."

"Suck my dick."

Othello worked his way back down to Raider's cock, and once again, with his knees on the floor, he sucked away, using his hands to do what his tongue had been ordered not to: explore Raider's chest and thighs. Finally, much to Othello's delight, Raider began to verbalize, moaning "Oh yeah," and "Fuck yeah," and "My dick feels great." With Raider getting into it more, Othello decided it was time to play with his own dick and began jerking himself off. Twice he came close to coming, then couldn't hold back on the third close call, shooting a substantial load on the carpet.

But that wasn't going to stop him or turn down the heat. He'd been waiting for this for months. Leaving his own dick alone, he began concentrating on Raider's again, careful that—when Raider seemed on the verge of coming—Othello would back off and lick around his balls and crotch and as he brandished Raider's cock toward the ceiling.

"This is the best I ever had," Raider said, his voice high and full of amazement and wonder, resembling the voice of a teenage boy.

"Scoot up," Othello said, then climbed on the bed and turned so that they faced the opposite direction. He then lay on his side and once again buried his face in Raider's crotch. Raider moaned and groaned even louder now. After a few moments, Othello rolled their bodies over so that Raider was on top of him, pumping his dick into Othello's mouth in a push-up position. "I'm close," Raider said, sitting up on his knees and trying to grab the base of his dick. Quickly, Othello popped Raider's dick out of his mouth and grabbed onto it, refusing to let Raider stroke himself to orgasm.

"Hold on, baby," Othello ordered him. After a brief struggle, Raider's hand gave up. Guarding Raider's cock with one hand, Othello then burrowed underneath his balls until he came to Raider's ass, which was smooth and without the slightest trace of hair. With his nose leading the way, he parted the cheeks and dove in until he found the warm moist valley that was Raider's anus. He then proceeded to lick, slurp and devour his Nantucket man's butt, squeezing the cheeks with his free hand and making a valiant effort to permanently lodge his face into Raider's ass.

Raider promptly let out a sound that was somewhere between a yelp and a wail, then began grinding his buns into the head below him. He was clearly enjoying this as much if not more than the blowjob, so much so that he rearranged his legs so that he was squatting over Othello's face. "Oh man!" he said over and over and over.

Having no time for words, Othello ate Raider's ass as if it were his last meal on earth, trying to forever ingrain the sight, smell and taste in his mind. After a while, Raider repositioned himself so that once again he was resting on his knees. It was then that Othello suddenly felt something on his own dick: a hand, he realized with no small amount of shock. Raider had grabbed his dick, which had been rock hard since Othello planted his face in Raider's buttocks. Raider was just holding it, not jerking, not playing, just holding. A minute later, Othello's dick felt the wetness of a tongue, then a pair of lips, then the fiery heat of a whole mouth. Raider was sucking his dick, lapping it up, too, as if it were the most natural thing in the world: no harshness, no teeth, no reservations. His mouth was moving up and down *and* side to side, an instant expert. He showed no signs of stopping either. He kept on sucking and sucking while Othello licked away at his ass for several heavenly minutes.

"Raider, you're going to make me come again," Othello was forced to say eventually.

"You came already?" The revelation prompted Raider to get off of him and sit on the bed.

"The minute I touched you practically. But as you can see," he grabbed the side of Raider's ass, "just put this in front of my face and I'm a goner."

Raider paused, eyes cast on the bed. "I want you to fuck me." His voice sounded like that of a kid, no remorse, no hint of guilt. It was simply what the boy wanted without so much as one thought to anything else.

At first, Othello was sure he hadn't heard correctly. "You do?"

"Yeah." There it was again, that voice without contrition, that face registering nothing but contentment. Without further ado, Raider positioned himself on all fours, head away from Othello, whose mind went into overdrive.

Stop! Hold on! Do you realize what you're asking?

But he wasn't about to say no to anything this man desired, unless—

"Do you have any rubbers?" asked Othello.

"In the nightstand," said Raider.

"Which one?"

"Both," he said with a little laugh. "But you're cool though, right?"

In other words: you don't have AIDS like Freedom, do you?

"Raider." Without pausing, Othello opened the nightstand on the left and found over a dozen loose packages of condoms. "We use protection no matter what. That way you and I will always be cool, now and forever."

"Yeah," he said agreeably.

"One sec," Othello said. "I've got some lube in my bag in the living room." Not wanting to give Raider enough time to change his mind, Othello hustled to the living room and retrieved a tube of KY jelly from his rolling carrier next to the sofa. He'd brought the lubricant to Summerhill with faint hope that the trip would produce the magic moment where Raider wanted to fuck him.

Talk about your ironies, he thought, rushing back into the bedroom.

Raider was still on all fours, waiting patiently for the first dick up his ass. Othello stood behind Raider and stroked his dick to get hard. When that was accomplished, he placed a condom over his hard-on, firmly resolved that what he was about to do was acceptable and safe. To make it even more so, he tore open another package and placed a second condom over the first.

"Let me try a finger to begin with," he said, worried that Raider would freak out at the first sign of pain. He knelt on the bed, his cock bouncing up and down. Wanting to be as safe as possible when it came to ass-play, he stuck yet another condom on his index finger, thinking of his own semen from earlier. He was that determined not to give Raider anything but a good time. He lubed up his finger with the KY, then tried to tunnel his way into Raider, not getting half an inch before Raider protested.

"Take it out."

Gently, Othello removed his finger.

"Just let me take a break."

He still wanted it, Othello was shocked to realize. The boy still wanted it.

"Okay." Raider slumped his shoulders toward the bed in an effort to hike his butt higher in the air.

Going slower, Othello tried again. This time, he got his finger all the way in, but Raider didn't seem any happier or more at ease, his moaning a far cry from the ecstatic sounds he made getting his dick sucked.

"Okay, take it out," he commanded after less than a minute. "I think I have to go to the can now."

After Othello removed his finger, Raider made a beeline for the bathroom and Othello lay back on the bed, assuming the quest for anal sex was over. A few moments later, Raider was back in the room, sheepishly declaring: "Nothing came out. Just felt like it, I guess."

"Happens that way sometimes," Othello said, trying to sound reassuring. "Sometimes it's better when you sit on the dick."

"Okay." Raider stood up on the bed, ready to squat down.

"You still want to try it?" Othello asked incredulously. "I was talking about for future reference."

"I wanna feel it tonight."

"Raider," Othello said worriedly, his fist around his half limp dick, "you could barely stand my finger. How we gonna get this in?"

"I still wanna try."

The boy wanted it all tonight and was going to stop at nothing.

In disbelief, Othello started stroking his dick through the two rubbers. "Then turn around and let me get a look at that ass so I can get hard again."

Standing on the bed above Othello, Raider turned and showed his smooth white cheeks to Othello, the sight of which sent Othello reeling.

"Shit, man, that's an ass."

"You like that?" Raider asked, his tone cocky.

"Like I like breathing," Othello said. "Baby, you got a beautiful ass. Perfectly round, great tan lines, smoother than a baby's."

"Yeah, chicks love my ass," Raider said. He started feeling his own butt with both hands, moving his cheeks by shifting his legs side to side.

"That's it, baby," Othello said, stroking his cock. "Put on a show for me."

"Like this?" Raider bent over, pretending to massage his ankles.

"Oh, fuck yeah, I'll do anything for that butt."

Raider stood erect again, and keeping his back to Othello, began dancing as if he were suddenly on stage with Chippendales. But all too quickly, he stopped, following it with a shy, embarrassed laugh. "Just kidding," he said, covering his tracks.

"Fuck no, baby, that's perfect, keep it up," Othello pleaded. "Show me that body; show me that ass."

Raider grabbed the back of his thighs and bent over as if he were a baseball catcher about to settle in behind home plate, giving Othello a perfect shot of his pink supple hole.

"Man, that's incredible. I've never seen a more beautiful butt."

Raider's ego was doing just fine. He kept rubbing his thighs and straightening and bending his legs to show off his buttocks. Othello could have stayed there and watched this for a month, but he was stroking his rubber-coated dick and it was all set for Raider's virgin hole.

"You ready to have a seat?"

Without hesitation Raider turned around, faced Othello and squatted down as Othello lubed up his dick.

"Go as slow as you need now, Raider. You control it."

The opening of Raider's hole found the tip of Othello's head. Cautiously, Raider lowered his massive body down, his face staring at Othello and anticipating discomfort. Othello felt his head drive up inside as Raider's eyes popped open and rolled toward the ceiling. He stayed that way for a few seconds, then looked down toward Othello and began lowering himself some more.

"I don't know if I can do this," he said.

"Go at your own pace."

With one hand, Raider reached around and grabbed Othello's dick, guiding it up and through his canal and lowering himself even more—too soon, Othello thought as he suddenly felt the ecstasy of passing the opening of Raider's anus.

"Oh, God," Raider screamed in a hushed tone, his breathing short and full of panic.

"*Breathe*," Othello commanded him, holding Raider's knees. "Slow, deep breaths."

Raider did as he was told, his breathing becoming calmer and calmer as the seconds passed.

"Oh, God," he started to say. "This is...."

He sat the rest of the way down on Othello's dick, taking in a gigantic breath, his back arching toward the ceiling.

"That's it, baby," Othello said calmly. "Relax now, deep breaths."

Raider looked on the verge of bolting off, but like a trooper, he remained seated, his eyes wide and full of fear and wonder, his whole being trying to take this all in. "Man, oh, man," he said with a smile. As the minutes passed, he relaxed more and more and began to move his ass over Othello's hips. "It gets better, huh?" He inadvertently squeezed Othello's cock with his sphincter muscles. "Oh, God," he cried, ever-so-slightly lifting his ass up and down. "Shit!" Next, he lifted himself up several inches, then back down again. "Oh, fuck!" Then, after several more times, Raider was riding Othello and feeling only ecstasy. "Fuck yeah! Oh, man! Oh, fuck! Oh, yeah! So this is what it's like getting fucked, huh?"

"No." Othello grabbed Raider by the back of his thighs, and—keeping his dick inside—rolled Raider onto his back and rotated their bodies so that now Othello was the one on top. "*This* is what it's like getting fucked," Othello said, then grabbed Raider's legs, which were high in the air, and started plowing his ass.

Raider seemed to love this position even more. His moaning and groaning returned to the familiar pleasurable sounds of earlier, accompanied by grunts with each thrust of Othello's cock. To Othello's surprise, Raider kept eye contact, his face still devoid of any sign of regret. Othello stared back and their eyes remained fixed on each other as he pounded away at Raider's ass. He tried all different kinds of rhythms, slow and steady, fast and furious, all the way out save the last half inch, then all the way back in until his curly black pubes slammed against the pale white skin between Raider's balls and ass. Raider seemed to love those thrusts the most, grunting so loud Othello wondered about the neighbors. But he wasn't about to stop for a condo association or anybody else in the District of Columbia. He had his man. His man had him. They had each other. Finally, they had each other.

Othello even decided that he wasn't going to come. Instead, he would fuck Raider all night long until the man from Nantucket would be forever hooked on the pleasures of taking it up the ass. To that end, the fact that Othello had already come once helped. The double coating of rubbers helped even more. He also decided to stroke Raider periodically, but not to the point of bringing him to climax. The plan failed, however, when after a while, Raider's hips began bucking wildly and his rock-hard dick began to shoot long powerful jets of cum without a hand being near it. The load was thick and plentiful, dousing Raider's chest, neck, stomach and pubes, making it seem as though he hadn't ejaculated in weeks. As he did, his grunts were powerful and unrelenting, his whole body shaking violently with each shot.

Eventually, his noises were reduced to whimpers and all of him collapsed—except for his ass, which suddenly grew tense. Trying to be as gentle as possible, Othello pulled out. Still, Raider flinched and grimaced in agony as the first dick ever inside him left him.

After Othello dismounted, Raider sank into the bed, his being drained of all energy, the rivers of cum starting to sprout tributaries that ran down his body and toward the bed. Nowhere near exhausted, Othello sat on his knees above his lacrosse legend and took in the sight of the only man he ever loved, after the loving, drenched with semen and sweat. It was art, he decided, but interactive art. He bent over and devoured every ounce of cum he could find, in Raider's pubic hair, on the tip of Raider's dick, on his stomach and chest and even the splattering on his neck. The taste wasn't as sweet as Othello had hoped, but he gulped it down anyway. It was nectar from the gods. It was his man's. It was now Othello's, forever a part of him.

"I never thought it would be like this," Raider moaned when Othello ran his tongue over his neck, mopping up the last bits of jism.

"Is that a thumbs up or down?" Othello asked, removing the two condoms and lying on top of Raider so that their faces were inches apart. The only answer Raider gave was a breath somewhere between a scoff and a laugh.

"Thumbs up or down?" Othello repeated, resting his head on Raider's chest.

Raider grabbed Othello by the shoulders, lifted him up and placed him at Raider's side. "It's been a loooooong day, Othello."

"Been a long three months."

Raider let out a small groan in agreement. "What do you say we get some sleep?" He placed his arm around Othello's shoulder and snuggled deeper into the bed.

"Mmm," Othello murmured, keeping one arm draped across Raider's chest. "Sleep is good." And with that, he didn't utter another word. For with Raider's arm around him, their naked bodies falling asleep as one, this was paradise. And, as Raider had said, it was late. No need to disturb paradise any time soon.

AS RAIDER FOUGHT to keep the early morning sunlight from invading the darkness underneath his eyes, he heard an unmistakably familiar sound that jolted him wide awake and reminded him: yes, he was back in DC and last night hadn't been a dream. The sound was coming from the driveway. It was his ex-wife Adele's loud and obnoxious old Blazer. She was probably with the kid, too, and the last thing his ex or his boy needed to see was a naked black man in his bed. He removed Othello's arm from his chest, darted out of bed and grabbed the pair of jeans from the sofa chair next to the dresser, moving swiftly enough to answer the door before they had a chance to ring the bell.

"Well, well," Adele said. "Mr. Dixon wasn't lying. You're back."

"Daddy!" Brian cried from down below. He leaped at his father and hugged him around the waist, causing Raider to stagger back from the door, which gave Adele a chance to step inside. Even though it was the crack of dawn, she was already dressed to draw attention, her petite body bursting out of her black and gold aerobics leotard, her slender face in full makeup, her long brunette hair bouncing off her shoulders as if she'd just taken the curling iron to it.

"It's been a long three months," she said, her voice full of disdain. "When Mr. Dixon called me this morning and said he saw you coming in last night, I said: This kid needs to see his father and vice versa. Even if Daddy wasn't back all alone."

The first of many digs, Raider knew. His boy was still holding onto his waist. He carried Brian, Jr., into the living room. "Hey, son, look at you—it's not what you think, Adele—I think you've grown a whole foot taller. You sure you're only eight and not fifteen or sixteen?"

"Yes." Brian, Jr., threw his head back and laughed, his long whitish blond locks falling toward the floor.

"Mr. Dixon said *two* shadowy figures came in." Adele cocked her head toward the hallway leading to the bedrooms. "At separate times, too."

"Adele." Raider nodded his head toward the kid and made a mental note to never again have the old widower Dixon look after his place when he was out of town.

"So he was right," she said. "Tell me: is *it* still here or did you send *it* on its way in the wee hours of the morning?" She started toward the hallway. "Maybe I should peek in and—"

"Don't, Adele." He sat Brian, Jr., down on the sofa. "Glad to see you son, and your mom."

She stopped and eyed him with that superior look she always used. "You don't mind if I check and see if Brian left the Blue Ranger in your bedroom." She started toward the hallway again.

"Adele!" Raider warned in a voice he hoped was threatening to her but not his son.

"We can't find it anywhere," she said. "I bet it's in your bed—" Just as she was about to step into hallway, Othello emerged. He was wearing Raider's oversized white terricloth robe and mumbling as if he'd just woken up and was unaware there was company.

"Raider, I couldn't find an extra toothbrush in the guest bedroom so I was—oh, I'm sorry, I didn't realize—I'm sorry."

"Not a problem," said Raider.

For the first time in Raider's memory, Adele shut up. Brian was just as speechless, only he stood up and moved toward Othello with his mouth wide open in awe.

"I was trying to find a toothbrush in the guest bedroom, a bit cold in there last night." Othello wrapped his arms around himself as if remembering the shivers. Raider flashed him a knowing, appreciative smile.

"Mom," Brian said when he was two feet away from Othello. "This is—"

"I know who it is, honey. Don't crowd the Othello, I mean, the man."

"It's okay," Othello said, then bent down to Brian, remembering how Raider had once mentioned that his kid was a big fan. "You must be Brian, Jr. You're daddy's been my personal trainer for the last few months and he's told me so much about you."

"You know my dad?"

"Well, of course," said Othello. "He invited me here last night and I stayed in your bedroom. I hope you don't mind."

"No," Brian, Jr., said emphatically.

Othello rose up again. "And you must be Brian's mother. Hello." He stepped toward her and they shook hands.

"Raider didn't tell me he was going to be meeting celebrities out there," she stammered.

Othello looked at Raider. "The man from Nantucket has a way of being full of surprises."

Raider cleared his throat, his eyes growing a tad nervous. "Othello had to be in town yesterday. He got in late and I suggested the extra bedroom instead of a hotel."

"Dad, can I have my *One Nation* CD now?" asked Brian. Suddenly Raider remembered the promise made right before he left for LA, the promise that he'd listen to Othello's album and give it to his son if the lyrics were straight-friendly. Seemed like a lifetime ago.

"Is that your CD of my album I saw in your dad's room?" Othello asked Brian.

"Yes, Dad said I had to wait before he gave it to me."

"Wait?" Othello glanced at Raider with a knowing smile. "Wait for what?"

Brian shrugged. "To make sure it's okay for kids."

"Well, if it's all right with your daddy, now," said Othello, "if he thinks it's not objectionable, I'll autograph it for you."

Full of hope, Brian pulled a thick green neon pen from his pants pocket.

Raider hesitated, then said: "It's in the bedroom. I'll get it."

"No, you stay here," Othello said, then indicated himself and Brian. "We'll get it. I'm sure Mommy and Daddy need a second to talk." When both parents remained silent, Othello took it for a yes, and he and Brian headed toward the bedroom and the CD.

"Why didn't you tell me about this?" Adele said when she was alone with Raider.

"As always, you were too busy assuming the worst."

"I always assume you've got your pants around your ankles for some bimbo, yes."

"Just trying to keep up with you and the Redskins, darling."

"Oh, that's nothing compared to you and those two waitresses, Panty-Raider, dear. What were their names? Slut and Double-Slut?"

There wasn't time for more because Othello and Brian emerged from the bedroom. "And that's why I call it *One Nation*," Othello was saying, "because the whole world should be one big nation that cares for each other."

"This is so cool," Brian said, holding the CD as if it were now his most prized possession.

"Brian," Raider said, "we don't want to bother Othello too much. He's a very busy man and your mom has to go."

"He was hoping to spend some time with his dad while I teach my early morning fat-burner class."

"I'm not really back yet," Raider said. "I just popped in and I'm popping right back out."

"Raider," she said in disbelief.

"A few more days, I promise." He held out his arms to his son. "So come here, give me a kiss." Disappointed, Brian gave his father a lifeless peck on the cheek.

So there is another male whom he loves and kisses, Othello thought.

"And tell Othello good-bye and nice meeting you."

"Good-bye and nice meeting you," Brian said obediently.

"And I'll see you and Mommy real soon, Scout's honor."

After they said their good-byes and the door was shut behind him, Raider breathed the biggest sigh of relief of his life and collapsed on the sofa.

"Thank you," he said to Othello. "Talk about disasters. That could have been my very own personal *Titanic*."

"I've got no interest in hurting your family, especially your son. He seems as wonderful as his dad."

"Thanks just the same."

Othello went over to the sofa and began massaging Raider's bare shoulders. "But if you'd like to show me your gratitude, I'll allow you to do that right here and now." He bent over to nibble on Raider's neck. "Or in the bedroom, I'm easy." He slid his hand down Raider's chest toward his crotch.

"Othello." Promptly, Raider removed the hand. "Last night...last night was last night."

"And?" Othello said, tasting a few strands of Raider's hair.

"Well, it was a one-time thing." Raider shifted uneasily, moving farther down the sofa. "I'm still who I am."

Othello extended his reach and combed Raider's hair with his fingers. "And I still want to taste this incredible body of yours."

"We can't. Ever again." Once again, Raider removed Othello's hand. "I'm not saying I regret it. It's just that...last night was last night."

Othello stood and walked toward the fireplace. "And now?"

Silence.

"I don't have to have all of you all of the time, Raider. Couldn't we just share what we shared some of the time, when you're in the mood for some serious male bonding?"

Raider shook his head, then threw his hands in the air, emphasizing the futility of it all. "Othello, how are we gonna do that?"

Othello turned to him. "You mean with me in jail and you moved on to the next case? And the next case and the next? Not to mention the next piece of pussy."

Raider let his head drop behind him. "Othello, don't do this. You've opened my eyes in so many ways."

"But apparently not wide enough." Othello moved toward his rolling carrier next to the sofa and dug his hand into one of the interior compartments. "Not wide enough to mean a damned thing."

"What am I supposed to do?" Raider said somewhat harshly. "I am who I am and what I am."

A straight FBI man whose mission was and is to bust the celebrity, Othello thought. It hadn't been love for Raider; it was sex, lust, curiosity, maybe a tinge of sentiment, but nothing resembling the watershed of emotions Othello had felt, so much emotion he had actually convinced himself they could be lovers, forget this whole FBI thing and start anew together, somewhere, somehow, some way.

When are you going to stop dreaming, Othello? When are you going to stand up and face the truth about yourself and your life?

"Things are a little complicated now," Raider said, leaning forward and burying his head in his hands.

"Then perhaps we ought to un-complicate them."

Othello found what he was searching for in the rolling carrier: a syringe, just like the ones used on Jasper and Deon and what would have been used on Bruce had he been at the South Carolina hotel waiting for Freedom. Othello had brought it along on this trip just in case Freedom had been right about his boyfriend not being his boyfriend and he needed time to escape. As if, in the back of his mind, he had always known.

He's going to arrest me and send me away forever, Othello thought. All I have left is one last goal.

Without hesitating and allowing for time to change his mind, he plunged the syringe into Raider's arm.

Raider got one quick look at Othello before he went under, his eyes ripe with shock and betrayal. *Now you know how I feel, Othello*

thought. Raider's eyelids narrowed, then shut entirely as he slumped
back on the sofa and slipped into unconsciousness. Othello nudged
Raider's shoulder a couple of times, then opened his right eyelid,
exposing a bloodshot cornea. Out cold.

Working quickly, he retrieved what he was going to wear from
his rolling carrier and went to the bathroom to change. It took a
while, but with that accomplished, he closed up the carrier and
searched for a pen and paper. He found them in the desk in Brian, Jr.'s
bedroom, then wrote a note, which he placed on the coffee table in
front of the man from Nantucket:

> Sorry, Raider, but I have to go out my way.
> In Los Angeles, where I can arrange my affairs
> before you send me away and become a hero to
> your kid, replacing me and Deon Anthony, the
> fags. Come and get me at the Big House when
> you wake up. I'll go peacefully. I promise. No O.J.
> circus.

That should buy me enough time, he thought. He looked at
Raider one last time, so serene yet obviously so troubled by what he
allowed himself to do last night.

Good-bye, my sweet heartbreaker.

He headed for the door, dressed as Old Man Joe for one final performance. Once outside, he inhaled the fresh DC morning, put his
faded green fisherman's hat over his gray-tinted, nappy-haired wig,
then got in the black Ford Taurus he had used to drive here from the
private airport in Virginia. Without the slightest bit of hesitation, he
took off, not for National or Dulles airport, but for the long drive to
Columbia, South Carolina, home of the Jimmy Herman Museum of
American Decency.

NINETEEN

THE SILVER SOUTH CAROLINA Highway Patrol car pulled into the rest stop and crept toward the only other vehicle in the parking lot, a black Ford Taurus parked next to the restrooms. The officer was a gray-haired man with a pockmarked face, most of which was hidden behind a pair of dark sunglasses. When he reached the Taurus, he put the car in park and killed the headlights, the sun having come up half an hour ago. He got out and circled the Taurus, his black boots stepping heavy against the concrete, mixing strangely with the early morning sounds of birds chirping.

An elderly black man was sleeping against the driver's side window. Using his nightstick, the officer tapped on the glass. The man jolted awake, then, seeing it was the law, collected himself and rolled down the window.

"Sorry to scare you, sir," the officer said with a thick Southern drawl, "but you might not want to be sleeping in these parts. Things aren't as safe as they used to be. Black man your age was robbed and murdered not long ago around here. I'm advising you to move on."

"Yes, officer, sorry."

"Think you're alert enough to keep going?"

"I am now."

"Well, get along then, sir."

"Thanks for the warning."

Othello waited until the officer had driven away before getting out and heading for the restroom. So Raider wasn't on to him yet, he thought. Or at least he hadn't issued an APB in Dixieland. He looked at his watch. 6:30 a.m. The knockout injection was almost twenty-four hours ago, meaning Raider must have awakened sometime late last night. Too late for a flight to LA in all probability. Perhaps that was what the man from Nantucket was preparing to do now. Taking a leak, Othello imagined Raider at the J. Edgar Hoover Building in DC, mobilizing the troops for the siege of the Big House.

Not before I complete my mission, he promised, heading back to the car.

Traffic was sparse along the highway. To avoid anymore cops, he kept his speed below the limit, thinking about what was in store less than twenty-five miles up the road. Shortly, he would be caught, that much was certain. And no matter how it happened, the papers were going to have a field day and his ass was going to fry. There was no reason now not to put a bullet in Jimmy Herman's head and really give them something to cream in their pants over. But he'd decided not to implicate anyone else, not Jasper, nor Deon, nor anyone from ACT-NOW. There was no point. He didn't know what all Raider had on them, but he'd take the fall himself. It was his battle plan, his vision. The others were just foils, people he used because he didn't have the guts to come out of the closet or kill another man. Now, he was on the verge of being outed whether he liked it or not. What else was left but to finish the job?

The signs on the highway began to announce the exit for the museum. Much to his surprise, his heart was steady, his breathing calm, his mind focused. The hysterics could come later, he figured, when they dove on him the way they did John Hinckley after he shot President Reagan.

He was still centered when he made the long circular turn off the highway and headed east on the two lane road, which, according to the map sprawled over the passenger seat, led straight to the museum. Even though Columbia was only a few miles away, the area seemed

very rural. Wavy fields of grass dotted the landscape, interrupted
every now and then by billboards promoting cheap family motels and
cheesy ALL-U-CAN-EAT restaurants. There were also a few gas stations
and coffee shops, havens for truckers no doubt. And signs for the
museum.

WHERE HAVE ALL THE DECENT PEOPLE GONE? TO THE JIMMY HERMAN
MUSEUM. FOUR MILES AHEAD.

FAMILY VALUES HAVE A NEW HOME: THE JIMMY HERMAN MUSEUM. TWO
MILES AHEAD.

AMERICA THE WAY OUR FOREFATHERS INTENDED IT: THE JIMMY HER-
MAN MUSEUM. NEXT LEFT.

The white stone edifice was set back off the road, surrounded by
lush gardens and woods. Barricades were everywhere, funneling traffic through two gates leading to the parking lots on either side of the
museum. At both entrances there were orange cones blocking the way
and security guards in red blazers and black pants. Minor obstacle,
Othello thought, passing the museum and making note of the one
pedestrian entrance.

He kept driving until he reached the Sunny Side Up Eatery, a
pancake house a quarter of a mile down. Once there, he ditched the
Taurus in the back of the building and set out for the museum on
foot, walking slowly and deliberately like an old man.

At the pedestrian entrance was a guard's booth. A young white
man in a red blazer was inside.

"Morning, sir," Othello said in his scratchy geriatric voice. He
ambled through the entrance without hesitation, noting the metal
detectors on either side.

"I need to see your pass, mister." The guard hurried out of his
booth and caught up with Othello, who was already past the gate.

"Pass? Never needed no pass before. I works here."

"All employees were issued passes seven days ago. No one is
allowed on the grounds without a pass. I can't let you in."

"Can't let me in to do my job? Son, I gots toilets to clean and
sinks to scrub. You think all the folks here today want dirty
restrooms?"

"Look, Mr...."

"Kincaide. Brian Kincaide." It was the only name to come to mind. "Been working here for a while now. What's the problem?"

"We issued passes to make sure the opening wouldn't be ruined by those opposed to the senator. If you don't have a pass—"

"When did you say they were issued?"

"Seven days ago."

"That last Monday?"

"Yes, sir."

"The day I buried my wife." Othello bowed his head. "That's why I haven't been around. The boss brought over some flowers and some kind of badge, but I didn't pay it no mind."

"That was probably your pass."

"You bury your wife and then try to remember some pass. I just wanted to be here today for Mr. Herman, do my job, take my mind off—oh, Lord have mercy, even forgot my uniform, I was so caught up in grieving."

"Let me just call—"

"Who you gonna call this early? Everybody who's in charge needs their sleep to do their job today. By the time I get back on the bus to get my pass and my uniform, I'll be all tuckered out, the ceremony half over." He turned toward the museum in the distance, his voice growing more and more woeful. "I'm sorry, Mr. Herman, just wanted to do my job. Never knew that pass were so important. Just wanted to do right by you. You been such a good man for this state."

"Okay, look, sir: just go ahead. But don't tell anybody, you hear me now?"

"You're a good boy, boy." Othello patted him on the cheek, taking pleasure from the sight of the guard wincing at the touch of the old man's wrinkled hand. "Now let me go do my job and make those toilets sparkling clean."

He turned and walked away, muttering to himself as an old man might until he was out of earshot of the gate. Then his attention slowly segued to the three-story white building that stood before him.

"Welcome to the Hall of Hate."

Once inside, he stood underneath the atrium and couldn't help marveling at the grandiose nature of the place, its marble floors, its long graceful white columns. Everything seemed so new and pristine. Oh, course it is, he chided, what did you expect?

He tried to imagine where the custodial equipment might be, hoping to find a place to hide for a few hours. To the left, a sign indicated The Jimmy Herman Room.

This he had to see.

He found himself inside what must have been a replica of the senator's office, surrounded by Jimmy Herman memorabilia, and had an impulse to want to set the room on fire, forever destroying all that was Herman. He walked over to the far wall, surveying the many photos of Senator Evil with various historical figures: Nixon, Eisenhower, Billy Graham. Where's the shot of him pulling the lever to the gas chamber? Othello wondered. Then a man's voice bellowed from behind:

"You must be Mr. Kincaide."

Slowly, he turned around, only remembering at the last second that *he* was Mr. Kincaide. Standing there was a tall thin man with a six o'clock shadow and Jimmy Herman himself, shorter in person, but still fat with those chipmunk cheeks and Coke-bottle glasses.

"Yes, sir, Mr. Herman," Othello said without so much as a pause. "Pleased to finally meet you and thank you personally for this job and the job you've done upholding the morals of this state and the whole country."

"Why, thank you much, kind sir." Herman marched forward and extended his hand. They shook; their eyes locked.

"The guard told us of your wife's passing," said the six o'clock shadow. "We're so sorry, but very touched you would want to be here today."

Othello and Herman stopped shaking hands, but Herman held onto Othello's out of sympathy. "Isabella would want me to be here," Othello said, "to serve you any way I can." His brain was on overdrive: this is the demon of hate? He looks so useless. I could stomp him to the ground in ten seconds. "We both have always been big supporters of yours, voting-wise if not in money."

"Well, voting is damn near as important as giving money," Herman said with a laugh as he finally released Othello's hand.

"Uh, Jimmy," said the six o'clock shadow, tapping at his watch.

"Before you go, Mr. Herman," began Othello, "I got a question. My son—he's got a teenage kid who tried to commit suicide earlier this year on the count of being homosexual."

"Oh, dear Lord in heaven."

"Yes." Othello clasped his hands together and looked toward the ceiling. "Well, they did save him—from suicide—and since then they've tried everything, gay-to-straight programs, baptism, church counseling, hypnosis. But the boy insists he cannot give up the desire to be loved by another man—in that way, if you know what I mean. His mother wants to accept him as gay now to keep him from another suicide try, but the rest of us are unsure what to do. Any ideas, Senator, sir?"

Herman and the six o'clock shadow eyed one another, then both bowed their heads. "You may not like my views on this," said Herman, "seeing as how he's your grandson and all."

"Oh, I respect whatever advice a man of your stature has to offer."

"Well, Mr. Kincaide, I'm sorry, but I'm afraid God can't save every sinner."

"You mean, maybe he's better off...you know what?"

"Would you rather him live a few more years only to disgrace the family with an agonizing, financially draining death by AIDS? That is, after all, God's punishment for perversion."

"I hate to admit it, but I wonder that myself, Senator, sir."

"You're a good African American, Mr. Kincaide." Herman reached out and they shook again.

"If only my wife were alive to hear you say that."

The six o'clock shadow approached Othello. "Take this pass to replace the one you forgot. And enjoy the day. I'll tell Willie Jefferson to go easy on you today."

"No, no." Othello took hold of the pass. ALL ACCESS, it read. "Don't want to make no fuss. No special treatment, please. If I need to rest, I'll tell Mr. Jefferson myself. I'm here to do a job."

"God Bless you," Herman said. Satisfied that he had a good dark-ie in his corner, he left the replica of his office with his disciple.

When he was alone again, Othello stood in the middle of the room and studied the images of the senator through the years.

Any man filled with enough hate to believe a young boy deserved to die for being gay needed to die himself. If there still existed a shred of doubt, it had just been snuffed out. Yes, Othello could kill a man. With his bare hands if necessary. He could stomach the bloodshed, the gore, the ripping apart of flesh. He could even live with the knowledge of his actions for the rest of his life. It was simple: Jimmy Herman and those like him were wasted space on the planet. End of story, as Jasper would say.

He exited the room, went through the atrium and made his way down the Hall of Greats. As he passed the animatronic politicians lining the walls, he imagined them spouting more rhetoric like, "God can't save every sinner."

At the end of the hall, he came to the restroom marked: STAFF ONLY. He checked the door. Unlocked. He went inside. Empty. Thank God, Herman's or whoever's, it didn't matter.

He paused and thought of Deon in this very same room a couple of weeks ago, then went into the lone stall and locked himself in. From the inner pocket of his golf jacket, he removed a small brown bag—his lunch, if anybody asked. He reached inside for the miniature screwdriver. His hand started to shake and a layer of sweat invaded his forehead. Okay, so he was still nervous. Who wouldn't be? Just finish the job, he told himself. Live at least one of your visions as a gay man before the Nantucket brigade comes calling.

He used a toilet seat cover to pat-dry his forehead. Then, back to work, he unscrewed the one screw on the square metal plate on the wall over the toilet and lifted it up, exposing the foot-deep hole. The gun was still there in its plastic package, duct-taped to the underside. Full of anticipation, he ripped the package free—just as the bathroom door swung open with a loud creak. In the next second, he let go of the metal plate, plopped down on the toilet seat and dropped the gun into his supposed lunch bag, all in one continuous, not to mention loud, motion.

"Oh, sorry!" pleaded a young female's voice. "Didn't know it was occupied."

"All right!" he stammered, cursing himself for only locking the stall door.

There was no response to his "all right." Maybe the girl was gone. He peered through the small vertical slits on the stall door. Nothing.

"I'm coming out now," he said. Still no response. Deciding he was alone, he stood up and screwed the metal plate shut.

When he exited the restroom, a teenage girl was standing next to the door. She was a petite blonde wearing a khaki skirt and a blue polo shirt with the museum logo on it. "Sorry," she reiterated, her cheeks still flush.

"Forget it," Othello said, barely making eye contact before hurrying down the Hall of Greats in search of a breath of fresh air.

The grounds surrounding the museum were starting to buzz with television crews and a few early arrivals to the ceremonies. To calm his nerves, Othello decided to move to one of the small clearings in the gardens forty yards away. Once there, he sat on a stone bench facing the museum and made a mental note of everything he saw. A long stage was set up in front of the steps to the main entrance and the sea of folding chairs lay between the stage and the gardens. Below the stage, a small cluster of VIP-looking visitors in their Sunday best chatted and sipped on drinks. On stage, a man in an orange workman's jumpsuit began testing the microphone on the podium. "Can y'all hear me out there in Hermanland?" he joked, his voice reverberating over the grounds.

To pass the time, Othello pictured himself on the podium, surrounded by hordes of reporters fighting to record his every utterance.

Yes, I killed him. A queer's gotta do what a queer's gotta do.

He imagined the frenzy and wondered if this would be bigger than O.J., especially when they found out Othello was gay. He made a vow not to hire any Johnny Cochrans or F. Lee Baileys and try to worm his way out of this. Impossible anyway, considering what Raider probably had on him.

Raider, he thought wistfully, glancing down at the pavement. He imagined another press conference and another fantasy, one without arrests and criminal investigations.

"Yes, for the first time in my life Othello is in love and this—" plant a kiss on Raider's cheek *"—is the lucky man."*

What better way for the world to find out he was gay? And after that would come albums full of songs about what he really had the hots for and videos featuring the two of them living out their love for the world to see. And they'd do Barbara Walters, Oprah and everybody else, blowing the hinges off the closet door together.

The microphone made an earsplitting sound, vaulting him back to reality.

"What I would have given," he said aloud. He spent the rest of the morning contemplating a world where he was out and in love.

The next time he paid attention to the sound of the microphone, it was noon. The man who had been with Herman earlier—the tall thin man with a six o'clock shadow—was speaking to a packed audience.

"Afternoon, ladies and gentlemen. My name is Winston Callahan. As president of operations, I'd like to welcome you to the opening ceremonies for the Jimmy Herman Museum of American Decency."

Applause filled the grounds. The stage was lined with white men in mostly white suits, including Herman who was four seats to the left of the podium. The audience was made up of men, women and children, a hundred percent of them white. Even the television crews were white. Jasper had been right: Rasta would have never made it through. The realization that he was the only black person in sight unnerved Othello. He decided to get it over with right then and there less anybody get suspicious and interrupt his plans.

He rose up and made his way toward the television cameras directly behind the audience.

Kill him now; you can do this. Raider cannot have the last laugh. You'll go to jail, but he will have failed. You'll still win; do it, don't think, don't pause, don't stop.

He reached the media island and stepped up onto their shallow platform. A red-coated guard put out an arm and tried to stop him, but Othello flashed the ALL ACCESS pass hanging from his neck and the man let him go.

Winston Callahan was still speaking. "I'm not one for talking much anyway, despite what my friends and family say, so at this point, I am more than happy to turn it over to our cultural curator, Mr. Jacob McCallister. Jacob."

McCallister was a pudgy, queeny-looking man. He rose up from his seat next to Herman and approached the podium, receiving his obligatory round of applause.

Don't think, just act. Fifteen yards. Rapid-fire the whole lot of them. That way you're sure to get Herman. Last chance to back out. Fuck backing out.

He reached inside the brown bag in his golf jacket and his heart and chest caved in.

The gun was still inside the plastic wrapper.

He'd never taken it out after that girl scared him in the restroom. He almost had a heart attack at the thought of bringing out a gun in a tightly-wound bag, then foolishly trying to untangle it while security jumped all over him. The most inept assassination attempt in history. He removed his hand from his jacket and glanced around. The law was everywhere. Uniformed South Carolina State Police officers were on each end of the stage, throughout the audience, and in the parking lots. The red blazers were also out in force, especially around the media island. None of them seemed to pay attention to him, except the one who'd stopped him before. He was down below, a few feet away, eyeing Othello something fierce. To cover himself, Othello coughed a few times and pounded his chest, then humbly retreated from the stand.

"Need water," he said, still coughing as he passed the man.

He made his way toward the museum. He was calm on the outside, but frantic on the inside. His head was riddled with shameful thoughts at his amateurishness as the words from the stage swirled in his head.

"...no one has done more for the state of South Carolina than this man...."

To be as inconspicuous as possible, he went the long way, circumnavigating the ceremony, then finding a side entrance. Once inside the museum, he made a beeline for the staff restroom at the end

of the Hall of Greats, vowing this time to lock the door behind him.
When he reached it, a pack of teenage girls wearing khaki skirts and
blue polo shirts were hovering outside the door. His eyes panned the
Hall of Greats for another restroom. There was none.

He hurried back down the corridor and toward the atrium,
relieved when a sign and an arrow indicated another restroom down
a hallway to the right. He reached it just in time to see a father escort-
ing his two young and boisterous sons through the door. No good.

His panic rising, he panned the hallways around him. His feet
and mind moved in unison but in a blur. He simply followed their
lead.

His hectic journey took him to the third floor. His prayers were
answered. Just off the elevator was a restroom. He seized it. It was
large—six stalls and twice as many urinals—but it was empty. He
double checked the stalls for feet, found none, then locked himself in
the last stall and proceeded to free the gun. When he was finished, he
held it to the light and examined it, then hastily removed the safety
catch and stuffed it back into the brown bag and put the brown bag
back into his jacket. On the way out, he discarded the plastic wrap in
the restroom's trash bin.

To get outside, he used the side entrance again, stepping back
into the cool afternoon air and bracing himself for another attempt.
Before take two, however, he headed back to the cement clearing in
the gardens. Better to wait until Herman was standing and on his way
to the podium. A bigger target for the amateur. He made it to the gardens unharassed and sat on the stone bench, tuning in to yet another
speech.

"...most dearest friend for over fifty years...." a rather large man
was saying. Must be Deon's buddy, Big Daddy Callahan, probably the
one to introduce Herman.

Othello took one last breath for courage and savored the last
moments of freedom he'd ever know. He rose up. To his surprise, he
felt calm and at peace with what he was about to do. Life had led him
down this road and he simply had to accept the fate dealt him. He
took a step toward the stage forty yards away, then heard a demand-
ing baritone voice inches away from his right ear:

"Don't try it."

He recognized the voice right away, yet didn't turn around immediately. Instead, he took a moment to catch his breath and make sure he wasn't hallucinating. Then his eyes shifted to the right, search-ing his periphery.

"Give me one good reason why I shouldn't."

"He's not worth it. I'm not worth it."

He took two small steps away from the body next to him, then gradually turned to Raider. The first thing he noticed was the blond aura, still golden, and those blue eyes, still a deep penetrating blue but deadly serious. It shocked Othello that Raider's beauty was the first thing he thought of, but in the next instant, the man from Nantucket became nothing more than the enemy.

"Why am I not surprised you're here?" said Othello.

"Because we know each other pretty damned well. And I know you well enough to know you're doing this because you're pissed at me."

"Then you don't know squat." Othello moved another step away and lodged his hand inside his jacket, a move not lost on Raider. "I'm carrying out my plan because there's nothing left for me after you cart me off to prison."

"And you don't want me to win and have the total satisfaction of stopping you and your crazy friends."

"I have no friends, except my manager. And by the way, he knows nothing about this. If you try to implicate him, I'll deny it, I swear."

"Othello, I don't want to implicate anybody. I don't want any-body to die or pull out a gun or be arrested or humiliated or any god-damn thing."

"Except me—"

"Not even you," Raider said harshly.

Othello eyed him mistrustfully, his hand reaching deeper inside his jacket. "The safety catch is off this thing. It's good to go."

"Listen to me, Othello."

"For what? More lies?"

"Don't try doing away with Herman and I'll close this case right here and now. Unsolved. You heard me right: I'll let you go."

"Let me go?"

"Let you go," Raider repeated emphatically in a low drone. "I'm not going to ever love you or make love—have sex with you—ever again. We can't even be friends, but if you drop this madness, if you stick to Triangle Funds and stay clean, you're a free man."

"What the hell are you talking about?"

"I'm talking about you and me, walking out of here, together, peacefully, and nobody gets hurt. You go live your life and I'll keep living mine. It's the only and last deal I'll ever offer you. Take it or leave it."

"And now ladies and gentlemen," came from Big Daddy Callahan at the podium, "I give you the distinguished senator from South Carolina, Jimmy Herman."

The audience rose up for a standing ovation; Herman waddled toward the podium. Othello and Raider stood frozen for a moment, locked on one another.

"Thank you, thank you, thank you, good God-fearing citizens of this country," Herman said over the applause.

"What's it gonna be, Othello?" Raider asked.

"You would offer me this? After what I did to you yesterday morning?"

Raider paused and looked away to the stage. Herman had just gotten the audience to sit and was saying: "My heart is just bursting seeing you all here today."

"Why, Raider, if you don't love me? Why this offer?"

"I don't love you. I never will. But I do care about you."

"Why? I'm an evil person who's thisclose to killing a man, a public servant just because he's for God, America and apple pie."

Raider wasn't sure if the public servant was Herman or himself.

"And what about the counter-bashing?" Othello added. "You can't let that go. This is your job."

"Underneath that anger," Raider began, "I see a man who just wants to love and be accepted. I can't give you that, but I'm sure you can meet a gay guy who can. And the counter-bash victims, as far as I'm concerned, they deserved it."

"What about busting Jasper and Deon and ACTNOW?"

"Without you, there's not much of a case against anybody. Can't you just take a good deal when you see one?"

"A good deal? The only thing I see is a man who lied to me from the moment he first met me and was willing to tell me anything to bust my ass."

"Take the deal, Othello. I'm not going to stand here all day, waiting."

"America needs more citizens like you all," said Herman, "dedicated to what is right about our country."

"Why, Raider?"

Raider looked away again, his lips tight, his face hardened.

"It gives me great joy to give you this building," said Herman, "this sanctuary, really...."

Then it dawned on Othello.

"You don't want the world to find out that Panty-Raider Kincaide—all-American, all-time leading scoring lacrosse legend, all-time FBI super agent stud—took it up the ass. From that black fag Othello, of all people. Not 'cause you wanted to bust the case, but 'cause you really wanted to take it up the ass. *After* you had the case solved. That's the *only* reason you want to strike a deal."

"That's horseshit and you know it."

"Well, well. I guess the nasty little details of our night of fucking and sucking probably would come out in a trial, wouldn't they? My mind hadn't even played it out that far. Of course, you could deny it, but then again, thank goodness for polygraph. And your ex-wife and little boy spotting me in *your bathrobe* the morning after you sucked my dick and I fucked you in the ass."

Raider shoved his hands in his pockets and eyed Herman. "It's either win-win or lose-lose for both of us. And believe it or not, I do care about you, although right now I could probably kick your little cocky ass for your smug little attitude."

"Whoa, tough words."

"Shut up. I was formulating this proposition back in DC, before you knocked me out with your wonder drug. Before we even had...." Raider looked away to woods in the distance. "We could have avoided all this had you given me time to figure things out."

"You really don't want the world to know you had sex with another man."

"I could live with it if I had to."

"Could you now?"

Silence from Raider.

"Let me get this straight, so to speak: I walk out of here without shooting anybody, and you'll let me go, live my life normally, as Othello, unarrested?"

"If I ever hear of you connected with anything nefarious, I'm coming after you."

"I can still be me? Free as a bird?"

"As long as you let me and my private life and what we did remain a secret to your grave."

"...only tried to live my life by the word of God," the senator was saying.

"That bastard needs to die." Othello turned halfway towards Herman, making sure he still had a tight grip on the gun. "I met him earlier today. He thinks I'm one of his lackey custodians, so much as said it was fine by him if gay kids committed suicide. When I pretended to agree, he called me a good African-American. Translation: good nigger."

Raider inched closer to Othello. "Being in ACTNOW made me more aware there's bastards like him all over the place. And I was one of them when I beat the shit out of that kid in college. But is he worth your life, Othello? Is he worth spending the rest of your days in prison? Being controlled by others?"

"I didn't think I had a choice before this so-called deal."

"I'm giving you the choice, not just for me, but for you, too. You've got to know that deep down. I've said this he's-not-worth-it stuff before, haven't I? At gay pride, remember? What do you think I was doing back then, if not trying to get you to not waste your life on that old fool?"

Othello looked at Raider. This much was true. On the curb before the parade, Raider had admonished him to stop the assassination attempt. But Raider was to be trusted as much as Jimmy Herman. Othello took a few steps away and said to himself as much as Raider:

"All I could think about these last few months was how my life has been a sham and how people like Herman are partly responsible."

"Even if you somehow got away with this," said Raider, "then or now, you'd still be prisoner for the rest of your life, trapped by your fears that the other two Wisemen or someone from ACTNOW would slip up or turn on you. Is that how you want to live?"

"I wanted to live a long life loving a man like you and influencing the struggle for gay rights with all the power and resources I possess."

"If we had been lovers, truly, you think we would have been happy? Always looking over our shoulders for the law? You thinking I murdered Gus for you?"

Othello eyed Raider with shock and confusion.

"I never killed him." Raider scoffed. "I just roughed him up at headquarters and told him to take a hike. He really was some God-squader and I didn't want him fucking up my case."

Othello lowered his head and breathed a sigh of relief.

"But think if I really had killed Gus for you, Othello. What would that have done to us as lovers?"

"But it was all a pack of lies. We were anything but lovers."

"Don't be a idiot and miss my point, Othello."

"I see your point." Othello shifted restlessly, trying to block out Herman's words echoing throughout the grounds:

"...we are the keepers of the American dream...."

"Three people dead is enough," said Raider.

"What do you mean, *three?*" asked Othello. "You just said Gus is alive. That means just Freedom and the man he killed—who else? Someone from the counter-bashings has died?"

"You don't know," Raider said flatly. "You really weren't a part of it?"

"Part of what? What are you talking about? Who else is dead besides Freedom and the Bible-thumper from the parade?"

Raider sighed. "Bruce Jones, Jasper's reporter slash lover. Had a fatal car accident in Long Island yesterday morning, about the time you were drugging me."

"No."

"Yes. Convenient, considering he was in the process of investigating the counter-bashings, at least that's what they said he was doing on one of Jasper's rival news networks."

"He was," Othello said in a daze, "according to what Jasper said at Summerhill. Bruce didn't agree with our tactics, but Jasper said not to worry, he'd take care of him."

Raider blew a sarcastic breath. "He did a thorough job. My guess is Hollinquest was also trying to send a message to you and Deon."

"Don't fuck with him."

"You learn quick."

"Can you stop him?" Othello asked. "Get him for murder?"

"Realistically? No. But can't you see, O, this has all gotten way out of hand. What's next? Who's next? It's like a snake feeding on itself."

Othello circled the clearing, digesting this latest news and trying to sort out the chaos in his head. "I had nothing to do with Bruce Jones's death."

"I believe you."

"And you give me your word—whatever that's worth—that you're on the up and up with this deal thing?"

"You say you know me; you figure it out."

Othello stopped pacing and stared at the stage.

"When I came face to face with Herman this morning, all I could think about was how pathetic and ugly he looked, not just aesthetically ugly but hideous in the soul. His fat bulges were just physical manifestations of his inner evil. And for a second, I thought to myself: this man is worthless to me and who I am. But I was too caught up to dwell on the thought. I've been too caught up since the night I got my—I shot up his image on the television." He took a long, drawn-out breath and shook his head. "I can't go back to the life I've known, but I don't want this either. I don't want to waste my life putting a hole in his head." He turned to the FBI agent from Nantucket. "Or yours either, Raider Kincaide."

The relief in Raider's face was visible. "I always said to myself you had brains."

They both shared the slightest hint of a smile, then looked down to the ground out of shyness, as if they were in the early stages of dating all over again.

"Raider, do me a favor." Othello's whole body began to tremble—a delayed reaction to the day's build-up. "Let's get out of here. You said we're going to walk out of here together. Can we do it now?"

"You betcha. Only it may not be as easy as all that. We have to get to the parking lot by walking through that pedestrian gate."

"Oh, God, the metal detector."

"Exactly. You'll never get away with packing that piece in there."

"I'll dump it."

"Right. But we also can't just leave it here to be found. Tell you what: is it just out in the open? In your hand?"

"It's inside a brown bag. My lunch bag."

Raider nodded to the trash can at the far end of the stone bench. "Discreetly dump it in there. Then we walk away. Once we're at the gate, I'll say I forgot something and you go on out. I'll come back for it and use my federal agent ID to get it out, say it's mine."

"Perfect." Othello took a few steps toward the trash can, then halted abruptly, three months of clever lies washing over him like an ominous shadow.

He turned back to Raider. You almost had me, Othello's face read.

"What?" protested Raider. "This is legit."

"You just want the gun away from me, then pounce—game, set, match, Kincaide."

"I thought you knew me better than that."

"All I know is the fantasy you trumped up for me." To distance himself and stall for time, he walked to the opposite end of the clearing.

"There are those who oppose decency," Herman was saying, "but they shall not have their day in the great state of South Carolina."

"Othello, I'm being honest here."

For a long, still moment, Othello regarded the man from Nantucket—mind, body and soul.

"I'm not going to be arrested for pulling a gun on Senator Evil or you," he then said. "Uncle Sam can get me on the other charges, but not attempted murder." He removed the brown bag from his jacket and walked over to the trash barrel. Raider leaned forward, but he held his ground. Othello took one good look at him, then bent over and carefully placed the bag at the bottom of the trash can. "Your move, 007," he then said, but before either of them could react, they caught sight of Winston Callahan, the six o'clock shadow, hurrying toward them.

"There you are, Mr. Kincaide."

Both Othello and Raider started to react—Raider because he'd just heard his name and Othello because he wasn't sure if Callahan meant Mr. Kincaide, the custodian, or Mr. Kincaide, the FBI agent who'd just gotten the suspect to relinquish the gun.

"We've been looking all over for you." Callahan made a beeline to Othello and grabbed his hand for a good hearty handshake. "The senator has a great idea—oh, hello," he said when he saw the real Mr. Kincaide, who was standing there looking quite confused.

"This is Mr. Baumgartner," Othello said, quickly indicating Raider. "One of our fellow upstanding citizens."

Callahan and Raider shook, then Callahan explained to Raider: "The senator was so touched by Mr. Kincaide's coming to work even though he just buried his wife, we would like him to speak up on the podium."

"*Say what?*" came from Othello.

"That's right," said Callahan. "We don't have a single representative of the ethnic communities up there and the world would just love to hear your story."

"That's not possible," Othello uttered hastily just as Raider said: "He can't do that."

"You see," Othello continued, "I'm shy. I could never get up and perform in front of an audience. I'd probably have a heart attack and join my Eliza—Isabella."

"Besides," Raider began, "Mr. Kincaide was just telling me how he was starting to feel ill in all this sun and I was about to offer him a ride home."

"And I was about to accept."

"So come on," Raider check himself for a split second to make sure he called the old black man by the right name, "sir, uh, Mr. Kincaide. I'll get you home." He grabbed Othello by the elbow and began to escort him off the clearing.

"No," Callahan insisted and grabbed Raider's arm. "The senator

needs Mr. Kincaide." He then smiled at Othello "Won't you give us a
few minutes? He'd be greatly appreciative."

"I can't," Othello said, and he and Raider continued walking.

"I think you can if you try. Your supervisor, Mr. Jefferson, would
be rightly impressed, I do know that."

"Mr. Kincaide said he's tired," Raider said forcefully.

"I think Mr. Kincaide ought to decide for himself," said Callahan.

Othello turned to him. "Do you want a heat-exhausted, black
heart attack victim on your hands today?"

Callahan fell silent. Not wasting any time, Raider began leading
Othello toward the front gate once again.

"Get me out of here, stat," Othello pleaded under his breath.

"Take 'er slow, old man. Don't look back."

Frustrated, Callahan put his hands on his hips and stomped his
foot to the ground. Then he decided to see what the old man had just
put in the trash can moments earlier. The barrel was empty save a
brown bag. He lifted it, surprised by its heaviness. He opened it, saw
the shiny black firearm and gasped and dropped the bag. The gun
clanked back into the barrel, causing a shot to be fired. It was a muffled shot, contained inside the barrel, but loud enough to garner the
attention of the entire grounds.

"A gun!" Callahan shouted. Half the crowd began screaming and running, the other half ducking for cover between the rows of folding chairs.

"Come on," Raider said and took off for the gate. The crowd's
frenzy multiplied by the second. The other men on the stage dove on
Herman. At least eight state policemen and red blazers ran toward
Callahan, who began spinning around and grabbing at the sides of his
head. The men reached him and tackled him to the ground. As he was
going down, Callahan tried to point to the real culprits running
toward the exit, but his words and motions were lost in the confusion
and Raider and Othello made it to the gate.

"Nobody gets out of here!" the guard yelled to them. "This is a
security alert!" It was the same young man who had let Othello on the
grounds without a pass.

"This man is ill," Raider said, holding Othello by the waist. "It's
his heart."

RANDY BOYD

"Emergency teams are on their way. We have strict rules for secu-rity alerts."

"He's an old man, he needs help now!" Raider yelled.

"You trying to tell me about security?" the guard yelled back.

Raider let go of Othello and stood toe-to-toe with the guard. "Do you want a heat-exhausted, black heart attack victim on your hands today?"

"The paramedics will be here faster than anything you—"

The guard's words were interrupted by a blow to the back of his head. He fell to the ground, revealing Othello standing behind him, holding a large rock in his hand. As a way of explaining, he nodded behind Raider at the two state cops running toward them from the Callahan fracas. And they weren't the only ones after them. Two other red blazers to the left of the gate were forty yards away and gaining.

"This way," Raider said, and they took off to the right, toward the parking lot. "Run ahead of me."

"What? Why?"

"Just do it. Like I'm chasing you. Run. Fast. Faster. To hell with Joe—run!"

Othello did his best imitation of an Olympic sprinter, churning his legs until they were burning. When he glanced back, Raider was far behind. Even farther back were the two cops and two red blazers. All four of them were now running past the pedestrian gate, taking out their guns.

"Behind the vans!" Raider yelled to Othello when they reached the parking lot. Up ahead were two long columns of media vehicles—television vans and 4x4s. Othello ducked between them and kept run-ning. Seconds later, Raider followed. The uniforms saw this and cut across the gardens, hurdling hedges and benches and making a bee-line for the parking lot. Closer to the lot, they split up—two breaking right to pursue from behind and two breaking left, hoping to head off the suspects at the end of the column of vehicles.

The two who broke left were fifteen yards away from the end of the column when Raider came running out from the vehicles with-out Othello. When he saw his fellow officers of the law, he threw his hands helplessly in the air and shouted: "Where the hell is he?"

The two cops, a mulatto man and white woman, rushed him, guns pointed. "Freeze right there!" ordered the woman.

"Did you see him?" Raider kept his hands in the air for two reasons: to drive home the helpless act and to keep these local yokels from getting trigger-happy.

"Hold it and keep those hands up!" yelled the mulatto cop.

"I'm FBI, you idiots." Having anticipated this, Raider kept his hands up, but with his right one, carefully brandished his badge in the direction of both cops. When he felt the momentum begin to swing his way, he threw the badge to the lady cop.

The two red blazers who had pursued from behind caught up with them. "That's one of the two the suspect Callahan ID'd," said the shorter of the two.

"I'm here on a tip in a federal investigation," Raider said.

"Looks legit," said the lady cop, flashing the badge to the red blazers.

Raider snatched it back and hurriedly retraced his steps until he was once again in the parking lot, searching the area he had just exited. "Where the hell did he go? Anybody see him?"

The others—still somewhat suspicious—followed him, staying on his heels and also scouring the parking lot for the other suspect. As they did, the mulatto cop said, "Mr. Callahan—the man in custody, the head of the museum—claims he saw a black man putting the gun in the trash can,"

"I saw you helping that black man club one of the members of our private security force," said the taller red blazer.

"I didn't know who it was." Raider moved up and down the row of vehicles, his mind more on the search than the information they were bombarding him with. "He said he was having a heart attack. I was helping him. Next thing I knew, he knocked your man out. I lost him between the trucks."

"Is this the guy you got the tip about?" asked the lady cop.

"The guy I'm after is white."

"What about the gun?"

"I don't know about that. We're wasting time. He's not here."

"We need to spread out," said the shorter red blazer, "call more officers to this area."

"Let's check under the vehicles," said the ever-efficient lady cop, standing next to a blue news van.

Raider shook his head, then pointed to a white semi at the far end of the lot. "I saw somebody dodge under there right before I saw you guys. He probably went out the other side and into the woods."

Underneath the blue news van, Othello lay as still as humanly possible, his eyes locked on the pair of black women's boots less than a foot away. Another pair of men's dress shoes walked toward her.

"I'll radio for help," the man's voice said.

"The woods are our best bet." It was Raider's voice. His white, worn-out sneakers joined the duo a sneeze away from Othello.

"He couldn't have gone far," the lady cop said. "I say we search under the vehicles."

"There he is!" Raider pointed to the forest on the other side of the parking lot. "Just came out from behind that tree."

"Let's go," said the mulatto cop and the five of them took off toward the woods.

Othello took his first full breath in minutes when he heard the legs of the law scampering off. Raider had been on the up and up, or so it seemed. Still, it was impossible to fully trust the man, especially as several minutes passed without one sign of Raider returning as he promised he would when he convinced Othello to hide like this.

A few minutes turned into several. Several turned into an eternity. In the distance, he could hear the cacophony of sirens and bullhorns and people moving chaotically as if Jimmy Herman had actually been shot and was now bleeding to death up on the stage. Twenty minutes must have passed, or so it felt, and he had all but given up on Raider and began trying to come up with an escape plan on his own. He was about to move out from under the van and do just that when he heard the sound of a motorcycle engine growing closer and closer. Staying under cover, he saw a motorcycle tire rolling into view, then stopping right at his face. Next to the tire, he saw a pair of white, worn-out sneakers.

He couldn't help smiling as he crawled out from under the van.

"I was beginning to wonder if you abandoned me."

"Took longer than I expected to throw everybody off." Raider glanced around. "We're still not out of this yet. Stay down."

Cautiously, Raider rolled the bike along the row of vans and 4x4s while Othello crept along him in a crouched position. The chaos was still plentiful. Between each vehicle, they could see a virtual army of cops and security guards surrounding the grounds while the media scrambled to get the story and museum-goers huddled together as if just surviving a natural disaster.

"Wait," Raider said, sizing up the last van in the row. "I've got an idea."

THE RED LOCAL NEWS van rolled toward the entrance only to be stopped by a young highway patrol officer. From the driver's seat, Raider sighed, as if tired of the routine, and flashed his badge once again.

"FBI, going home," he said wearily.

"Then move it," the cop said, waving him through. The van pulled away. In the back, lying flat on the floor face up, Othello actually contemplated the possibility of the tension releasing its stranglehold on his entire being.

Thirty miles away from the Jimmy Herman Museum, the cheap motels and ALL-U-CAN-EAT restaurants began to give way to endless green fields and Raider pulled the van over behind an abandoned barn. Out of the back came the motorcycle, the two of them hoisting it to the ground. Afterwards, Raider hopped on and started it up.

"You coming or not?" he said putting on his green half-helmet.

"This yours?"

"One of two. How do you think I got down here so fast after your ass? What, you thought I took the airlines? This, my friend, is the only way to fly."

"You rode this?"

"How else was I gonna look for you at rest stops along the way?"

Othello looked at the Harley-Davidson logo on the gas tank. "I've never ridden on the back of a bike before."

"Well, we can't stick around here all day being shy."

Othello climbed on awkwardly, not knowing where to put his hands. "You don't have another helmet?"

Pretending to be perturbed, Raider took the half-helmet off his head and placed it on Othello's. "Happy now?"

"I will be when we're out of South Carolina." Othello removed the helmet long enough to take off his fisherman's cap and stuff it into one of Raider's saddlebags.

"It's okay to put your arms around me. You don't want to fall off, do you?"

Othello did as told, tentatively at first so as not to give Raider the wrong impression. "Raider, I have a confession," he then said.

"Oh, no."

"I've never ridden on the front of a bike before either."

Raider turned around, shocked and bewildered.

"I've never been on a motorcycle period," Othello said, trying not to sound too defensive.

"Well, sure as shit, there's a first time for everything, ain't there?"

Raider didn't wait for a response. Instead he slammed the door to the van shut with his foot and revved up the engine. They took off, heading west, getting up to fifty in a matter of seconds, then sixty, then seventy where Raider kept it for the next 200 miles. Othello was part terrified, part relieved and part thrilled to be clinging to Raider. And cling he did, more out of fear than anything. For most of the way, his arms were wound tight around Raider's torso, his head buried securely in Raider's back.

They drove without stopping except for gas, junk food and urinals. They drove past stretches of green pastures, past more cheesy highway stops, and finally, past the South Carolina state line and into Georgia. At one gas station, Raider bought a map and they avoided the main highways in favor of the back roads. The afternoon wore on and the sun began its early summer descent. Then, a little over three hours into their journey, Othello saw a sign that announced Atlanta thirty miles away and yelled in Raider's ear, asking him to stop. Raider turned down a dirt road and drove another half mile until they were out of view from the highway.

"Again?" he asked, pulling over next to a tall oak tree in a lazy patch of grass, assuming Othello needed to take another leak.

"No." Othello got off and stretched. "Quitting time. For you and me." He set the helmet on the ground and began removing the geriatric getup, starting with the raisin-skinned gloves and latex beer belly.

"Don't be ridiculous," said Raider. "I'm going to live up to my end and take you to Atlanta."

"I think we both survived this ordeal now, as long as the fallout doesn't bite us in the ass. Speaking of which: you think that Callahan character can nail me?"

"Nah. He'll be too busy clearing himself. And after they figure out a black man *was* involved, they've got no prints on the gun."

Othello took off his wig and facial hair and wiped the makeup on his sleeve. "Wait a minute: what about my car back at that pancake house?"

"Was it rented in your name?"

"A fake name. Under one of my dummy corporations. The idea was for us all to get to Summerhill as incognito as possible. That's why it was waiting for us right as we stepped off the plane, on the tarmac."

"I can finagle my way into having it confiscated and shipped back up to Virginia before anyone can find out anything about it. I can also have whatever was in it sent to you."

"There's nothing in it," Othello said. "I dumped everything but my wallet in a dumpster back in DC. When they caught me after I shot Herman, I didn't want to have anything on me, anything traceable but my ID."

Raider unstraddled the bike and sat sideways, contemplating the thoroughness of Othello's actions. Then he glanced up at the sun setting through the tree and said: "So what does Othello do now?"

"You mean in the future?"

"I mean, when you walk away from here? Atlanta isn't exactly around the corner."

"I could use a long walk. To clear my head from the three-month-long fog I've been in. I've got funds. I can arrange a car when I get tired and a plane after that. Back to LA and the big empty Big House." There was a long pause, then Othello asked: "What about you?"

"Me? Guess I'll ride back to DC. Got some head clearing to do myself. Plus, I need to figure out how I'm gonna turn in the case unsolved. Not right away, after what happened today. In about a week or two." Suddenly he had a troubled look on his face. "Or more."

"Is all this going to put you in a heap of trouble?"

"Maybe." He thought about it. "Definitely. But if nothing panned out, nothing panned out."

"What about all the evidence? Don't they already know things?"

"Not enough to do anything. I kept all the big shockers to myself." He laughed at himself, shaking his head. "I was gonna spring it all on 'em like some goddamn movie. Now, there's not much to tell. Some gardener was giving money on behalf of some rich old fag hag. She had no idea what ACTNOW really did with it and we can't even say for sure ACTNOW ever committed a felony. That's where it ends. They—we—knew about your $20,000 check cashed by Travis."

"That night," Othello said regretfully.

"That's why they sent me out in the first place, but that...that was just a lone contribution by a rich gay singer from what I gathered."

"What about the old black man from Simi Valley?" Othello asked. "What about the old black man from today? Can't they connect the two?"

"To what?" Raider scoffed. "Panty-Raider fucked it up, lost the lead. Who was the guy? Where the hell did he go? Where the hell is he now? If he never surfaces again, how can they find him?"

"Raider, I don't know what to say."

"Here. Take this." From his pocket, he pulled out a key and tossed it to Othello. "It's to a safe deposit box at Unity Federal Bank in West Hollywood. It's got all the evidence I collected."

"How am I supposed to get access to a safe deposit in your name?"

"I'll authorize you—oh, and there's this...." He retrieved a miniature roll of film from one of the saddlebags attached to the Harley. "Pictures from Summerhill. You didn't think I'd wear that peach jacket for real, did you?"

"Not my man," Othello said, taking possession of the roll. They both laughed quietly. "Raider, God I'll never forget you."

"I've given you all the evidence, O, if that's any indication of how serious I am about letting you go as long as you stay legal and never breathe a word—"

"I could never hurt you," Othello promised. "Not in this lifetime." He then stuffed Joe's hair, belly and gloves into the saddlebag. "Here's my collateral."

"We're not done," Raider said, then reached into the saddlebag on the other side and pulled out a change of clothes for Othello. "You don't need to be wearing anything remotely resembling an old man right now." He handed Othello a gray polo shirt and the smallest pair of jeans he could find in his closet. He also gave him a canteen full of water and a towel so Othello could completely remove the makeup on his face. After Othello got over his astonishment, Raider watched the pop star transform himself back into his real self. The clothes were way too big, of course, but Othello didn't seem to mind. He did use Joe's belt to keep the pants from falling down, but other than that, he was Othello once again.

"You brought all this down from Washington?" Othello asked in disbelief as he finished cuffing the jeans a good six inches. "For me. You were that sure you could get me to go along with your deal?"

"Like I said, I know you got brains."

"So why didn't you give me this earlier, like anytime in the last few hours when I was riding through South Carolina on the back of a bike, dressed as Joe?"

Raider shook his head and smiled the smile of someone whose experience in these matters was second nature. "Which do you think would have been easier to explain if we had been stopped by the cops: Raider Kincaide with an old black man who just might be my partner who doesn't have his ID with him, or Raider Kincaide with *the one and only Othello?*"

They both laughed.

"You really are a good agent, Raider," Othello said. "And a good man, Agent Kincaide."

Raider bowed his head, surveying the grass beneath his feet. "You know there's a good possibility I might lose my job for this. I'm sure I'm going to come off like one pretty incompetent dipshit—all kinds of questions, more excuses than answers. They may even think all I did was string the investigation out just to party in Hollywood on the government for three months."

"Is this what you really want to do?"

Raider thought about it, then shrugged. "Why should I work for a bunch of homophobes?"

Othello smiled, remembering the good times, the tenderness. "Raider. Isn't there *any* way—"

"Othello," Raider said, knowing what was coming next. "You know the answer to that."

"Life isn't fair," Othello said, looking at the key in his hands.

"Tell me something I don't know." For a moment there was silence as they both contemplated life without each other.

"Who you doing this for?" Othello asked.

"What do you mean?"

"Are you just doing this so the world won't find out that Panty-Raider Kincaide took it up the—so that people, the people that matter in your life, your son, your buddies, your fellow agents, your family, your mom and dad—so they won't all find out you had homosexual sex? Or are you doing this because you really care about me? In your own Raider Kincaide, all-American way?"

Raider laughed and threw his head back. "Othello, come on. Does it matter?"

"To me it does. I wanna know."

"You're something else, you know that?"

"Yes, I do. Now tell me. Please."

Raider looked away and stared at an empty field in the distance. "Is it possible the reason could be *both* reasons? Ever hear of something called 50/50?"

"Yeah," Othello said softly, then came up with another angle. "Would you say *exactly* 50/50 or one reason more than the other? I mean, like there's 60/40, 70/30, 90/10, 99/1."

Raider let out an all out guffaw.

"Well, I just wanna know," Othello said.

"Tell you what," Raider said with a big old grin. "Three months we've been under each other's microscopes, right? I'll let you decide for yourself."

Othello opened his mouth to protest but closed it and smiled. That was all Raider was going to offer, plain and simple. Maybe it didn't matter anymore anyway.

"We'd better get going," Raider said before long. "You sure I can't give you a ride all the way to Atlanta?"

"Head clearing, remember? For both of us. Besides, I got some serious plans to make."

"Othello," warned Raider.

"*Legal* plans," Othello promised, "aboveboard in every sense, without Jasper or Deon or any other coward who won't join me. There's more than one way to start an uprising, you know."

Raider regarded him curiously. "Be careful. I'd hate to see you get hurt."

Suddenly, Othello had a desire to reveal his HIV status, not only because they'd had sex, but also to provide their relationship with that much more intimacy. But he checked the impulse. The moment didn't seem right for any more intimacy than what they'd already shared. Besides, as far as transmission was concerned, they had been doubly safe with two condoms for anal sex, and the chances Raider might have been otherwise exposed that night were slim to none. It'll keep, Othello thought.

Raider started the engine. Othello handed him the helmet. As Raider took it, Othello placed his hands on top of Raider's, feeling them one last time. Raider didn't jerk away. He just held them there and they shared what felt like the last smile they'd ever share.

"Good-bye, my man from Nantucket."

"Take care of yourself, Othello Hardaway of Riverside, California."

With that, Raider put on the helmet and took off, retracing their path down the dirt road until he was on the highway again, only this time heading east.

Othello fought the urge to cry and stood there until Raider was completely out of sight. Then, he started walking along the dirt road toward the main highway. Upon reaching it, he headed west toward Atlanta.

Two miles later, he was feeling a bit parched and stopped at a dilapidated old gas station for a soda. The lone man at the station was

a toothless, raisin-skinned, elderly black man who didn't seem to recognize Othello.

I wonder who he is underneath his old man getup, Othello asked
himself as he paid for the drink.

With his thirst quenched, he made his way to the outdoor pay
phone on the side of the station. Using his calling card, he dialed Los
Angeles.

"Sweeney, my oldest and dearest and most-trusted friend." The
very words almost brought him to tears, but he didn't want his manager to think anything was wrong.

"Othello, my only and most elusive client, where the hell are
you?"

"Down South. Had a vision about a career move, but it didn't
pan out."

"Career? Does that mean you actually still care about that thing
called your music?"

"More than you know, my preppie Irish friend. Sweeney, we got
work to do: picking the next single, shooting the next video and making sure One Nation stays at the top of the charts. I see the single as
'Succulent' and the video will be me and a hot blond man on a
romantic date, ending with us making sweet, passionate love."

"You're drunk."

"Yes, I'm drunk, Sweeney, with life and me being me, a hell of a
man who can go through just about anything and still come out on
the other side. I found a new way to fight the hatemongers, Sweeney.
It's called coming out to the world, being who I am, hip, hot, ripped,
funky, sexy and queer. That's right, my man—my one and only
man—it's time to make history, you and me, the right way."

"You want to come out?" Sweeney said flatly.

"I could crap in these jeans I got on just thinking about it, but I
can't go back to where I was. I've seen the light outside the closet door,
Sweeney. I've seen gay pride and ACTNOW and even got a glimpse of
what it must be like to be in love. Time to step all the way out into that
light and bask in it for the rest of my life, as long as I live."

"Othello, slow down. It's times like this when I feel like your parent."

"No need. Got two fine parents out in Riverside. Listen, why don't we talk about all this when I get back. I need you to arrange a car and a plane right now."

He gave Sweeney the location of the gas station, then thought of one last thing.

"Oh, and Sweeney. Never mind. It can wait."

No need to go into testing positive on the phone. That was a conversation that could take place in person as soon as possible. The world would also learn about his HIV status someday, on his terms, before an illness involuntarily outed him.

Leap one hurdle at a time, he told himself, hanging up the phone and heading toward the road. First, he'd tell Sweeney about being positive and together they'd find the best AIDS doctor in LA. Then, he'd map out a strategy to come out as a gay man to the world. And he'd do it his way, first through his music and videos, then interviews but only *after* he'd whipped the public into a frenzy of speculation and curiosity. Perhaps Barbara Walters would get the first interview. Yes, definitely Barbara Walters. A whole hour with Barbara. Or maybe Oprah.

From there he'd fight, for laws, for rights, for the teenage kids Jimmy Herman wanted to see commit suicide. He'd fight harder than Madonna or Ellen or any other celebrity. And this time, it would all be aboveboard and legal, not because he promised straightboy Raider Kincaide, but because the Jimmy Hermans of the world weren't worth being held prisoner to, in jail or out. Just as Travis Little Horse had said.

Staring down the long dusty road to Atlanta, he was too giddy to wait at the gas station and decided to walk toward town and keep an eye out for the limo, all the while thinking of all the hot young men he would soon be crooning over—and who would be salivating over him—in his videos.

RANDY BOYD is a native of Indianapolis and a 1985 graduate of UCLA. His fiction has appeared in *Blackfire* magazine, as well as the following anthologies: *Certain Voices, Flesh and the Word 2, Sojourner: Black Gay Voices in the Age of AIDS, Flashpoint* and *MA-KA: Diasporic Juks.* In addition, his nonfiction has been featured in the following publications: *Frontiers, Au Courant, The Washington Blade, The James White Review* and the anthology *Friends and Lovers: Gay Men Write About the Families They Create.*